DANCE OF STEEL

STEEL AND FIRE BOOK THREE

JORDAN RIVET

Copyright © 2016 by Jordan Rivet

All rights reserved. No part of this publication may be reproduced, distributed or transmitted in any form or by any means without the prior written permission of the author.

Contact the author at Jordan@JordanRivet.com

To receive an exclusive short story and discounts on new releases, please join Jordan Rivet's mailing list.

Cover art by Deranged Doctor Design

Editing suggestions provided by Red Adept Editing

Audiobook narrated by Caitlin Kelly

Maps by Jordan Rivet

Dance of Steel, Steel and Fire Book 3/ Jordan Rivet – First Edition: September 2016, Updated: March 2021

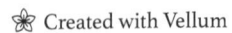

❀ Created with Vellum

For my parents.
Thank you for your advice, support, and cheerleading.
I literally could not do this without you.

CONTENTS

Map of the Continent	vii
Map of Trure	ix
1. The Fissure	1
2. The Road	12
3. The Final Stair	22
4. Soraline	32
5. The Plains of Trure	38
6. Rallion City	51
7. The King	62
8. The Fountain	71
9. The Guard	81
10. The Rooftop	88
11. The Races	93
12. Gone	102
13. The Visitor	109
14. Captivity	119
15. Air Sensors	129
16. The Soolens	137
17. Council	144
18. The Wild	156
19. Storm Clouds	164
20. The Fighters	178
21. Roan Town	187
22. Training	196
23. Winter Market	201
24. Ridge Road	214
25. Shadow	221
26. The Vintner's Rest	233
27. The Library	242
28. Tollan	249
29. The Cellar	259
30. The Peace	270
31. Fork Town	281
32. Chase	294

33. The Fork	306
34. The Plan	313
35. Steel Pentagon	320
36. The Waterworker	329
37. Fire	338
38. The Blue House	351
39. Pendark	360
40. Dance of Steel	369
41. The Queen	379
42. Sunset	386
Epilogue	391
Acknowledgments	395
City of Wind Excerpt	397
About the Author	403
Also by Jordan Rivet	405

MAP OF THE CONTINENT

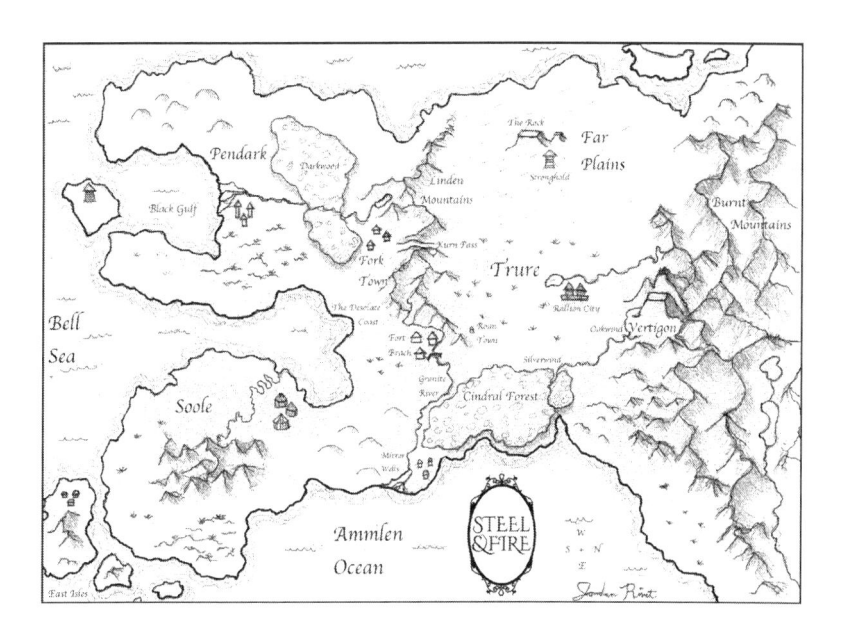

MAP OF TRURE

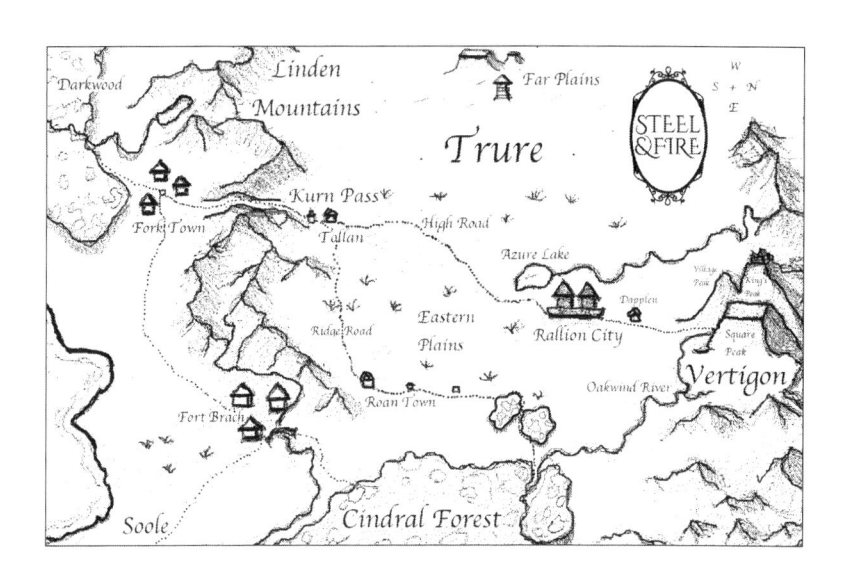

1
THE FISSURE

THE wind howled through the Fissure, tearing at Dara's hair and blasting ice across her cheeks. Her muscles, already sore from her encounter with the Fire, throbbed with the effort of staying upright. And she was cold! Ever since molten Fire rushed through her body in an intoxicating torrent, she'd found it almost impossible to retain any heat. She only hoped the effect was temporary.

Siv trudged beside her, one hand on his cur-dragon's arching neck. Ostensibly, he was keeping Rumy from flying around and giving away their position, but Dara noticed he relied a little too much on the creature as he picked his way down the cliffside path. He had lost a lot of blood during the fight in the Great Hall yesterday. He needed time to recover as much as she did.

But time was a luxury they didn't have.

Snow flurries whirled across their path. Dara listened for any hint of pursuit. The shrieks and sighs filling the air could be the calls of the wind just as easily as the menacing shouts of her father's men coming after them.

Siv stopped at a bend in the path and eased down onto an outcropping of rock. Rumy rested his head on Siv's knees, one of the few places on his body that hadn't been stitched back together recently.

"We have to keep going," Dara said.

"Give me a minute." Siv pulled his cloak closer and studied the path behind them. Their footprints marked the way they had come, snaking down the pathway that clung to the side of the Fissure. It was a treacherous journey in the best of circumstances. Most people never traveled in or out of Vertigon in the winter—for good reason.

"Siv."

"I know. I need a breather. Turns out hiking with stab wounds is even more painful than doing squat lunges." He attempted a smile, which ended up more like a grimace. The nasty slash across his temple must hurt a lot. The bandage wrapped over the stitches didn't make his features any less handsome, though. His dark hair was messy, and the early traces of a beard shaded his high cheekbones. His eyes, normally bright with good humor, looked pained and dull as he gazed at the ridge at the top of the Fissure. Dara knew his injuries weren't the only cause.

"Don't look back," she said.

"We shouldn't just walk away," Siv said. "It seemed like a good idea last night, but—"

"You saw how powerful he is," Dara said. "We can't fight him."

"I am—I was—the king. It's my duty to protect Vertigon no matter what."

"You can barely stand up."

"You're not exactly your usual spry self either," Siv said.

Dara ignored the way her body ached with every shiver, the way she wanted nothing more than to lie down and sleep for a year.

"He knows we're still alive," she said.

"I doubt he'll look for us here yet," Siv said. "He'll search the peaks first, and the snow is already covering our tracks."

"We can't take any chances." Dara glanced back at the road climbing King's Peak, expecting pursuit any minute. "We have to keep moving."

Siv sighed heavily, his breath fogging the air.

"I know, Dara. I saw what he can do."

He lurched to his feet and continued gingerly down the winding trail. Dara followed, resisting the urge to sit on the outcropping herself for a moment.

The path was wide enough for two people to walk side by side, but they'd been trudging single file for most of the day, trapped in their thoughts. Dara could still hardly believe what had happened. Once again, she had underestimated her father. She thought he would work from the shadows and send the Rollendars and their swordsmen to do his dirty work. She thought he would stay safe in the Fire Guild or far away on Square Peak behind that impenetrable wall of Fire. She had been wrong.

She shuddered at the image of her father standing triumphant in the middle of the Great Hall, the surviving Castle Guards held by shackles of Fire, a cage of molten Fire and metal closing in on Siv. Worse was the look of shock and betrayal on her father's face when she revealed she could Work the Fire. He would never forgive her for keeping it from him—not that she could ever face him again after what he'd done. With each step, Dara became more certain she could never return to Vertigon.

The wind shifted, whipping Dara's braid across her face like a slap. Rumy picked up his head and sniffed, then he shuffled his dark wings and whacked Siv's thigh with his tail.

"What's wrong, boy?" Siv said.

The creature gave an agitated whine and snorted smoke from his nostrils.

"Someone's coming," Dara said.

"He could have just smelled a burrlin—"

"We need to get off the path."

Dara grabbed Siv's hand and tugged him toward the side of the slope. The road switched back and continued far beneath them. If they could get down the rocky slope, it would cut time off their descent. They'd risk being exposed down on the lower part of the road, though.

"Tracks, Dara," Siv said as he eased over the edge beside her.

"If we go fast enough—"

"It won't matter. Neither one of us could outrun a pullturtle right now."

Despite his words, Siv kept pace with Dara as she slid down the slope on her backside. The rocks beneath the snowdrifts scraped her legs, and a clump of snow found its way inside her gloves as she scooted down the mountain. Fear clutched at her. They were going to be caught. They were going to be taken back to her father. She still had her Savven blade, and Vine had given Siv a rapier before they left her greathouse that morning, but it wouldn't be enough.

Dara looked back. The swirling snow obscured her view. Their pursuers could be right on top of them. She fought to control her racing heartbeat. They had to find somewhere to hide. The wind-blasted slope was bare of trees and didn't offer much cover.

"Wait," Siv said. "I have an idea. Rumy, come here." Siv reached out to his cur-dragon, who had been scooting down the incline alongside them. The creature put his nose in Siv's hand and sniffed at his glove. Siv stroked his scaly head and spoke to him in a low voice.

"I need you to go up and wipe out our tracks, Rumy," he said. "Blast a few false trails along the path. And find whoever's chasing us. Got it?"

Rumy huffed and snapped his jaws.

"Uhh, are you sure he understands all that?" Dara said.

Rumy fixed her with an affronted stare and ruffled his wings. Then he scrambled back up to the path, swinging his tail back and forth as he went. As soon as he reached the top, he let out a jet of fire and began melting the snow along the path to disguise their tracks.

"Now you've offended him," Siv said. "Quick, let's find cover. He'll only be able to distract them for so long."

Siv scrambled sideways along the slope, checking rocky outcroppings for cover. He moved erratically, so the patterns he left in the snow looked more like they belonged to a strange creature than a fleeing king. Dara did her best to imitate him. It was wearying work, and her bones ached as she descended.

"Do cur-dragons understand everything we say?" Dara asked to distract herself from the pain.

"Not quite," Siv said. "They're very intelligent, though. Smarter than povvercats and most thunderbirds. They can acquire a limited understanding of language. I think Rumy's smarter than most."

A roaring sound above them indicated Rumy was still blasting the snow with his fire. Wisps of smoke drifted out over the Fissure. They were still nearly two days from the bottom of the steep canyon through Vertigon Mountain that divided Square Peak from King's and the Village. If someone was already following them, they'd never make it all the way down the mountainside.

Dance of Steel

Dara's breath came in gasps. At least thirty feet separated them from the lower stretch of the road. The icy gale felt like a physical force holding them atop the mountain.

Then they heard the unmistakable sound of a man's voice. A different voice answered him a second later.

"Someone's definitely up there," Dara said.

"This is as good a place as any." Siv stopped at a dip in the rocky slope. Calling it a cave would be a stretch, but the lip of snow-covered stone might shield them from sight.

"Maybe we should keep moving," Dara said urgently. A hint of flame flickered on the road they had left behind. Rumy was taking his false trail duty very seriously.

"We'll never outrun them, Dara," Siv said. "I'm about to drop, and even though you won't admit it, so are you. We have to hide."

There was no time to argue. The voice reached them from the road above again, its tone crisp and military. Dara slid into the hollow beside Siv, pressing back against the stone. There were at least three voices up there, though she couldn't make out what they were saying. Her father had wasted no time in sending a search party after them—and Dara and Siv were outnumbered. In their current condition, they wouldn't stand a chance in a fight.

Dara prayed the snow was falling fast enough to hide the trail leading to their position. Siv breathed heavily beside her, waiting. Had the group above them stopped? Did that mean they'd found their trail? Dara gathered her strength for one last fight.

Then there was a squawk, and sounds of a commotion echoed over the Fissure.

"Damn cur-dragons!"

"Get away! I don't have any food for you."

The men's voices were more annoyed than angry as Rumy pestered them. Siv grinned at the sound. Dara barely dared to breathe. He might trust the creature, but that didn't mean they were safe yet. They didn't know who was up there. What if someone recognized the king's favorite pet?

"Stop wasting time with that thing," said the crisp, military voice. "They have a head start. We must keep moving."

"I'm sorry, sir! He's grabbing my . . ."

The wind howled, drowning out the voices again. Dara and Siv remained frozen, listening for any hint that the men were still out there. A large rock dug into Dara's thigh, but she didn't dare move. Would those men hurt Rumy? Where was he now?

All they could do was wait. Their hiding place offered some shelter, but it wasn't much warmer than up on the windswept path. Long shadows stretched across the Fissure before them. The snow swirled, not disguising the fact that the sun had started its descent. They only had a few hours before nightfall.

"Think it's safe?" Dara whispered after a while.

"Let's wait until dark to keep moving."

"We can't travel the Fissure in the dark," Dara said.

"Can't you do some sort of Fire thing to light our way?" Siv asked.

"It doesn't work like that. I have to draw the Fire from somewhere, an access point in the mountain or a Work with enough Fire inside it." Dara wasn't sure she could draw on the Fire right now even if some were available to her. The very idea made her quake. Unlike Siv, she wasn't outwardly injured, but her extreme exhaustion suggested the Fire had done more damage than she thought.

"We should have borrowed a Heatstone from Vine," Siv said, hunching against the cold.

Dara shifted uncomfortably on the rocks. She reached out tentatively in case there was some trace Fire in the mountainside. The effort made her senses recoil. It was like bumping against something when you were achy from a fever, or trying to eat after scalding your tongue with hot cider. She stopped trying to pull Fire from the stones and resigned herself to shivering.

"I'd offer to share body heat," Siv said, nudging her arm, "but I might rip open at the seams and get blood all over everything."

"It's okay," Dara said, clenching her teeth to keep them from chattering. Why was she so cold?

"Sheesh. You sound like a chattering krellfish," Siv said with a chuckle. Despite his injuries, he raised his arm, inviting Dara to scoot closer. Slashes scored his ribs and chest, so she leaned her head carefully against his shoulder. His left arm settled around her. His right arm had taken the worst of the damage during the fight. Dara would be surprised if he could lift it at all.

She shifted nearer. Siv's body was warm against hers. She would never have snuggled up against him like this a few days ago, intimate enough to feel his breath on her cheek. But things were different now in ways she couldn't fully grasp yet. And she needed his heat. Needed to be close to him, to know that he was still with her. Weariness slipped around her like a blanket. She should be alert to the men hunting them, but with Siv lending her his warmth, she could hardly keep her eyes open.

Murmurs and sighs sounded outside their hollow. Was it the blustery weather, shrieks of pain, blasts of dragon fire, voices? There was no way to tell who was out there. Dara was all too sure she knew who had sent them, though. She fought against the exhaustion. Siv's arm remained tense beneath her head. They couldn't let their guards down yet.

Dusk fell slowly. The snow outside thickened, and the temperature dropped as the hours passed. Dara remained snug against Siv, sharing his warmth. The cold in her bones retreated gradually.

They hadn't heard anyone for a while. The snow should have covered their tracks by now. Still, Rumy did not return. What if something had happened to him? Would the men out there kill him if he got in their way? Siv loved the little guy, and he had endured enough loss for one day.

Dara glanced up at Siv's face as the last light faded away. He stared at the opening, waiting, ready. He was in no danger of dropping to sleep, even after hours in the hollow. He must believe their position was more precarious than he let on.

"Did you hear that?" he whispered suddenly, his arm tightening around her.

"All I hear is the wind."

"Wait . . . there it is again!"

Dara held her breath, straining to distinguish any noise other than the rush of the gale. Then she heard it: a scraping, tumbling sound, like a rock rolling down a slope. A crunch of footsteps in the snow. Someone was approaching their hollow.

Dara reached for her Savven blade, aware of the strange new warmth in the hilt. It was no longer scorching, but it had a heat all its own. She fumbled the blade as she tried to draw it. Her fingers didn't seem to be working properly.

"Give me your sword," Siv said.

"I can—"

"You can barely hold your head up," Siv said. He nudged Dara's cloak open and drew the weapon from her belt with a soft rasp. He couldn't hide the wince as he moved his sword arm. Then he drew Vine's blade from his own belt and sat forward, a weapon in each hand.

Dara wanted to protest. She should be the one defending their position. She had to protect her king, but her hands still trembled, and her bones creaked. She had never felt so helpless—and she hated it. She wouldn't be much use in combat in this condition. Grudgingly, she let Siv move forward to defend them both. His two blades glinted in the dying light.

The scraping sound came again, closer now.

Dara and Siv waited, the bare rock of the mountain at their backs. Closer. Siv tensed. The hollow was too low for him to stand, so he crouched, weapons at the ready.

Another scrape. Dara reached for a rock to throw to distract their attackers. She may be weakened, but she wouldn't let Siv fight alone.

The sound of heavy, guttural breathing joined the crunching footfalls. Dara tightened her grip on the rock.

Then a dark shape loomed in the mouth of the cave, strange and grotesque. It wasn't a man. It wasn't a cur-dragon either.

"What in all the Firelord's realm?" Siv muttered.

Some huge animal was prowling in front of the hollow. Hot breath huffed into the cave, and a peculiar stench reached them, like rotting fruit and leather. Then a vicious roar exploded in the darkness, and the shadowy creature lunged toward them.

Siv met the attack, both blades stabbing. The creature had inky fur and a bald, leathery head with wicked yellow teeth. It moved quickly, lurching to avoid one of Siv's first hits, claws scraping the dirt. Yellow teeth snapped a few inches from Dara's face. Siv stabbed again, and the night-black Savven blade sank into the creature's muscular shoulder. It roared in agony and convulsed backward, yanking the Savven straight out of Siv's hand. His injured right arm fell to his side, spasms rendering it useless.

Siv slashed with the second blade, and the creature retreated, hackles raised. The stench of rotten fruit was overwhelming now. Dara took in an ugly, hairless head and bulbous eyes as it prowled at the edge of the hollow. Pure animal rage quivered in those eyes. She'd never seen anything like it.

Siv swore steadily under his breath as he waited for the monster's next move. The creature stalked them on all fours, its movements somewhere between those of a cat and a primate. It was bigger than Dara and Siv combined—bigger than a mountain bear—and it wasn't backing down.

Dara hurled her rock at the grotesque bald head, hoping to distract the creature long enough for Siv to finish it off. The rock struck its broad snout with a thunk. Instead of being disoriented, the monster let out a snarl that shook the roots of the mountain and launched itself toward Dara with all the strength in its horrible body.

Siv struck as the creature attacked, his reflexes lightning fast, and sank his blade through its chest all the way to the hilt. The momentum of the savage assault carried the animal forward, bowling Siv over. The creature slammed on top of him with the force of an avalanche and let out a final bone-chilling growl as it died.

"Are you okay?" Dara scrambled forward on her knees. She could barely see Siv beneath the massive, still-quivering corpse.

"This thing stinks," he wheezed. "Get it off me before I pass out!"

Dara let out a relieved breath and edged around the creature, pulling her Savven blade from its meaty shoulder as she passed. She wiped it quickly before the creature's putrid black blood could stain the blade. Then she wrapped her hands around a clawed hind foot and pulled.

The creature didn't budge.

"Anytime, Dara," Siv said, his voice muffled by the inky fur.

"I'm trying." She pulled harder, and the monster slid a few inches. After a decade of daily training, Dara was strong and well built, but even if she'd been at her best, she wasn't sure she'd have been able to lift the thing. Now, with her body still severely weakened by her encounter with the Fire, she felt like a child trying to move a grown man.

She shifted her grip on the animal and braced her feet against the stones at the entrance to their hollow, limbs trembling. Had they accidentally taken the creature's living space, or was it looking for a meal? They probably would have noticed the smell if the hollow had been its nest. She pulled harder, the effort making spots float before her eyes, and Siv groaned. His stitches couldn't possibly all be intact at this point. The carcass slid a few inches. This was going to take a while.

Suddenly, a shuffling sound came from behind Dara. Her hand flew to her Savven blade, her body tensing painfully. But it was Rumy who appeared at her elbow. Snow and ice coated the cur-dragon's scaly back. He looked unharmed, even a little smug. Rumy immediately took hold of the strange animal's other hind leg and helped Dara haul it off of Siv. Rumy was big for a cur-dragon, but he looked small beside the fallen monster.

"It's about time you showed up," Siv said as he sat up, scrubbing at the black blood and fur covering his cloak.

Rumy dropped the creature's leg and gave him an injured look.

"I'm sorry. You're right," Siv said. "You were doing very important work. You sure took your time about it, though."

"We should move this thing farther away," Dara said. The creature didn't smell any better dead than it had alive.

"How about it, boy?" Siv said. Rumy fixed him with a flat stare and didn't budge.

"I think *you* offended him this time," Dara said.

Rumy huffed and shook the snow off his back. Then he curled up on the floor of the hollow and put his head under his wing.

"Fine." Siv pulled himself to his feet and helped Dara drag the dead creature a few paces farther away from the entrance to the hollow. It left a trail of black blood in the snow.

"What is this thing?" Dara said, dropping it heavily as soon as it was far enough away from their hiding place. She scanned the darkness for any sign of their pursuers. The mountain was empty except for them and the dead monster.

"That's a cullmoran if I've ever seen one," Siv said, yanking his rapier from its chest.

"*Have* you seen one before?" Dara asked.

"Nope. First time for everything."

They limped back to the hollow, leaving the putrid creature behind. They kicked snow over the blood trail as they went. More snow fell steadily from the sky. With luck it would cover their tracks—and the dead animal—before long.

Rumy was still curled up on the rocky floor of the hollow. He lifted his wing and sniffed at them and then turned his face away.

"We'd better keep moving," Dara said.

"Come on, boy," Siv said. "It's time to go."

Rumy ignored him, ruffling his wings and letting out what sounded suspiciously like a feigned snore.

"He might have a point," Siv said. "We should sleep for a few hours."

Dara sighed, lacking the energy to argue. She'd never wanted anything more than she wanted sleep at that moment. She couldn't stand feeling weak. If she was going to resume her protector role, she needed rest. "All right. Let's hope nothing comes near that carcass in the meantime."

"The smell should keep unwanted visitors away," Siv said. "And we'll definitely feel more stealthy after a nap."

"Agreed."

They crammed in on either side of Rumy. He gave them an annoyed grunt but shifted around so they'd have some room. His body was hot and reassuring, and Dara soon drifted to sleep with the steady beat of the cur-dragon's heart keeping her warm.

2

THE ROAD

SIV slept fitfully. He hadn't told Dara just how bad his injuries felt after his scuffle with the cullmoran. Two of his wounds had reopened, and he had to apply pressure for a while to stop the bleeding. He kept quiet, not wanting Dara to worry. Although she didn't have any stab wounds, she needed time to recover from her ordeal with the Fire too. She had given up *far* too easily when he suggested they rest. He had never known her to tire before him in practice, and if she felt worn out now, she must be in bad shape.

Siv managed a few hours of rest, listening to Dara and Rumy breathe in the darkness. Night had fallen, and precious little moonlight reached them through the thick veil of snow.

It was hard to believe it had only been one day since a wall of Fire had shot up around Square Peak and changed everything. Only a day since an army of swordsmen had burst into the Great Hall, followed closely by the towering figure of Lantern Maker Ruminor.

Siv could just make out the faint shine of Dara's golden hair in the darkness. Something large stirred in his chest. She had saved him from her father, risking his wrath—and her life—but it hadn't been enough. The Lantern Maker had won.

Siv shifted on the rocks, welcoming the pain in an effort to distract himself from completing his recollection of the night before.

Dance of Steel

But the images came to him anyway: swordsmen leaving his sister's tower, blades dripping red. Pool's body sprawled on the ground. The destruction of everything he held dear.

He had failed. It was his duty as a king to rule well and protect his realm. It was his duty as a brother to take care of his sister. Now they were both gone. He couldn't do anything to help by staying in Vertigon, but he was wracked by guilt for fleeing. It didn't matter that his body had been slashed to shreds and his allies had been defeated. He was still running away.

Poor Sora. Even though they teased each other mercilessly, they had grown closer since their father died. Sora had helped him navigate his first days as king. She had a good head for politics, she was observant, and she gave surprisingly good advice. Siv's insides twisted as though he were being stabbed again. It had all gone so wrong.

His only hope now was to find his mother and other sister safe in Trure, the kingdom of his grandfather. He needed to regroup and decide what to do. He doubted he could retake his crown without throwing the mountain into turmoil. Besides, Vertigon was virtually unassailable. Getting down the mountain was hard enough. They could never bring an army up it—even if that was what Siv wanted.

No, he faced a future in exile, unless the Lantern Maker sent assassins after him to finish the job. He may try to eliminate the Amintelle line entirely, which kept Siv moving toward Trure. He had failed Sora, but he could still protect Selivia.

Dara moved beside him, mumbling in her sleep. She had to be struggling with what had happened last night too. Confronting her father must have been agonizing. Siv and Dara had barely spoken in the days leading up to the feast, but they had patched things up beforehand. He still felt hurt that she had kept the truth about his father's murderer from him. But now Dara was all he had in the world. His trust in her had been fractured, but it hadn't been destroyed.

He thought of their encounter with the creature now stinking up their hiding place. As he had stared into the cullmoran's ugly maw, for one wild moment Siv had wondered if everyone would be better off if it won. It would be a gruesome death, but quick. He almost felt he deserved to fall for failing his kingdom. But a visceral need to survive and protect kept him fighting. He wouldn't allow that revolting bastard to beat him, not with Dara behind him. If he didn't defeat the monster, it would kill her next. Siv couldn't let that happen. Not to his Dara.

He reached beneath Rumy's wing and took Dara's hand in his. Sword calluses textured her palm and index finger, reminders of her strength and dedication. She shifted sleepily, but her breathing remained steady. Siv didn't move for a moment, holding Dara's hand, thinking about what would happen next. He was no longer the king. He was no longer betrothed to the treacherous Lady Tull. What did that mean for him and Dara? That large something shifted in his chest again.

He eased back against the rough stones, ignoring the throbbing of his wounds and the sting of his memories. He held on to the thought of a future with Dara, one shimmery gold thread against the darkness, as he dropped to sleep.

WHEN SIV AWOKE, the world was quiet. Dara and Rumy were still asleep, and the wind had stopped. Fingers of silver stretched through the opening to the hollow, a trace of moonlight piercing the darkness. Siv released Dara's hand and crawled out from beneath Rumy's warm belly.

The mountain glowed white. The moon was sliding down, almost at the crest of the nearby peak, but the air was crystal clear. Siv estimated he had slept for nearly five hours as the blizzard retreated. He felt refreshed, though his wounds ached worse than ever. And he was hungry! He'd probably be even hungrier if the stench of the dead cullmoran weren't still filling the air around their hollow.

The snowfall had wiped away their tracks from the night before. Unfortunately, it also hid any sign of their pursuers. They had no way of knowing if the men had turned back or if they might encounter them somewhere farther down the road. Each switchback presented new opportunities to be captured, but they had to take the chance.

Siv turned back to the hollow. "Dara," he whispered. "Are you awake? It stopped snowing."

Dara jolted upright, and Rumy scrambled off her, flapping his wings irritably.

"How long was I asleep?" she said urgently. She looked disoriented but as ready for a duel as ever.

"Not long enough, probably. What do you say we make some progress before it starts snowing again?"

Dara agreed and joined him at the entrance to the hollow. They shared some of the jerky and flatbread Vine had packed for them, then scrambled down the slope to the road. Dara seemed sprightlier than the day before. Hopefully with a bit more sleep she'd be as good as new soon. She'd probably make him run laps or something as soon as she was healthy, but it would be worth it to see her back to her usual self.

"Think we should travel off the path?" Dara asked.

Siv scanned the mountainside. There was no sign of lights or movement anywhere. It felt as if they were the only people in the world.

"I think speed should be our priority right now," he said. "The Lantern Maker won't give up."

"No," Dara said, her expression grim. "He won't."

They resumed their journey, walking side by side down the switchbacks, the deep snow crunching under their boots. The path narrowed at times, and they drew closer together, not speaking much. The moonlight faded, replaced by a predawn gray.

They continued deeper into the Fissure, only sometimes able to see the bottom where the canyon wound down toward the Lands Below. Siv had made this journey many times before, but never in the depths of winter. Normally when he traveled to Trure with his family, they passed through blooming, verdant orchards and meandered back and forth down the side of King's Peak at a leisurely pace. Tough mountain ponies would carry their luggage, and Siv's grandfather would send horses to meet them at the bottom of the Final Stair. This was where the switchbacks of the trail ended and a weathered stretch of Fireworked stone steps descended the rest of the way to the bottom of the Fissure. It was nerve-wracking enough to walk the Final Stair in the spring. Siv was not excited about taking those steps covered in ice. Rumy could melt them clear, but there was no sense in announcing their position with such fanfare. The tracks they left in the deep snow of the path were bad enough. If only they had thought to bring Heatstones! He'd definitely think of that next time he had to flee for his life in the dead of winter.

The sky grew lighter, and King's and Village Peaks cast sharp shadows on the slopes of Square Peak across the Fissure. Another road led down the side of Square, but there was no movement on it as far as Siv could tell. What had happened over there in the aftermath of the Fireworker attack? Had anyone tried to resist? Rafe had had a full day by now to cow any remaining opposition and establish his reign. Siv hoped the crown gave him a headache.

They had lunch while they walked, passing through an orchard full of leafless trees. It was deserted at this time of year, and the trees cast creepy shadows across their path even in the middle of the day. Sadly, all the fruit had been harvested months ago, and they still had to rely on bland traveling rations.

"How are you holding up?" Siv asked Dara around a tough bite of goat jerky.

"Better. I tried to draw on the Fire again, but I couldn't find any in the stones."

"Think they used it all up in the attack?"

"It doesn't really work like that." Dara rubbed a hand across the hilt of her Savven blade. "The Fire can be solidified into things, so it's finite, but it can also be reused depending on what you do with it. You know how Fire Gates work, right?"

"Don't remind me about Fire Gates," Siv said. "What I wouldn't give for a nice toasty Gate right now."

Dara smiled. "I'm cold too. But the Gates just circulate Fire to warm a room. They don't use up much of the power. Most of it can be recycled. I'd be willing to bet that wall was the same."

"Just how much *do* you know about the Fire?" Siv asked.

"I grew up around it."

"Isn't it different now that you can Work, though?"

Dara was quiet for a moment. She kicked the dark toes of her boots through the ice-white snow.

"Yes, I suppose it is. I learned more from the Fire Warden over the past two months than I did from my parents in years. I guess I paid closer attention when the lectures about the Fire became relevant to me."

"Oh right. You were training with Zage." Siv couldn't quite keep the bitterness out of his voice. It still stung that his closest friend and his oldest advisor had conspired to keep several massive secrets from him.

"Siv, it was necessary to—"

"It doesn't matter," he said quickly. "We shouldn't make too much noise."

Dara didn't press the issue, but the reminder dampened some of the warmth Siv had felt toward her the night before. Even if she and Zage had been honest with him, it might not have changed the outcome in the end, but that didn't lessen the sting. And now Zage was dead too. He had been Siv's teacher and friend for many years. He wished he could remember him without the sour feeling of betrayal.

They trudged on in silence. Rumy ambled along beside them, occasionally flying ahead to explore their path. The trek was slow and tiring. They didn't stop to rest, both well aware they were exposed against the bright-white side of the slope after they left the orchard. At least the blizzard hadn't started up again.

The snow-covered path before them remained smooth and free of footprints. If their pursuers had passed them while they slept, they must be far ahead by now. Hopefully they weren't lying in wait somewhere farther down the road. There had been at least three men after them. Maybe more. Siv didn't think he—or Dara, for that matter—would survive another encounter with the Lantern Maker anytime soon. They couldn't afford to slow down.

By the time they reached the top of the Final Stair, evening had fallen. They hadn't seen another living thing—human or otherwise —all day. They stopped to rest and eat more jerky. Siv scooped snow into a metal canteen and had Rumy melt it for them to drink, hiding the little jet of dragon fire with his cloak.

"Thanks," Dara said when he handed it to her. "How are your wounds?"

"Starting to itch," Siv said. "Think that's a good sign?"

"You'll need to have them cleaned the minute we arrive in Trure."

"A hot bath is at the top of my list," Siv said. "After a strong drink."

Dara gave the canteen back to him, smiling tentatively. Siv was relieved to see the expression. They hadn't spoken in hours. The journey to Trure would feel very long if they couldn't talk. Siv may feel hurt, but he and Dara needed each other more than ever—and the fact that she had been so quiet was starting to worry him. Ordinarily she'd be lecturing him about not being serious or not working hard enough or something.

"Have you ever been to Trure?" he asked as he refilled the canteen with snow.

"I've never left Vertigon before." Dara looked up at the bridges crisscrossing the sky above them. Vertigon was its own little world at the top of the mountain. Siv wasn't surprised to hear she had never left. Most Vertigonians never descended as far as the Final Stair.

"You'll like it," Siv said. "Dueling isn't as popular there, but the food is great. And they have horse races. The Trurens raise the finest horses on the continent. And we can swim in the Azure Lake come spring."

"I thought you hated Trure."

"That's only because of my vapid relations." Siv waved the canteen at Rumy and lifted his cloak again to hide the flame as he melted the batch of snow. "I had to attend too many boring dinners during my childhood. They're always angling for favor in Trure. But I should be off the hook now that I'm a king without a crown."

"You don't think there's any chance of winning it back?"

"I don't know if I should even try." Siv looked up at Dara and asked a question that had been at the back of his mind for hours. No point in putting it off any longer. "Do you . . . do you think your father will treat the people well?"

Dara frowned and drew her Savven blade. She traced the intricate hilt with her fingers, the black metal shining in the light from the setting sun.

"I wish I knew. I never thought he was an evil man, but he's done terrible things over the past few months. I . . . I think he would have killed me if Zage hadn't stepped in. He craves power. Being able to

Wield that much Fire... It's intoxicating. I'd never felt power on that level before yesterday. It was terrifying, but I can also see why he wanted more. He obviously doesn't care who he destroys along the way. And my mother is worse than he is."

"That's not very reassuring." Siv jumped as the canteen in his hand heated to boiling. "Ouch! That's enough, boy." He hadn't been paying attention as Rumy wheezed fire beneath his hands. He set the canteen in the snow and cooled his hands while Rumy gave him an innocent stare. A bit of smoke drifted over his head.

Smoke. Like smoke from a fire.

"Dara?"

"Yeah?"

"Have you ever tried dragon fire?"

"Excuse me?"

"This Working or Wielding thing. It means you can touch the Fire without being burned. You can control it. Do you think it works with dragon fire too?"

"Fire is a name for a specific substance," Dara said. "It's like liquid magic. It's not the same as the flame that burns wood or paper in lands without Fireworks."

"Does the other kind hurt you, though?"

Dara opened her mouth and closed it again, frowning. "I don't actually know," she said. "There's not much need for flame when we have the Fire."

"If you could somehow draw the flames or Fire or whatever from Rumy, do you think you could melt the ice from the stairs? It would make the final stretch of our journey a lot easier without drawing too much attention. Besides, it would be good to have access to your power in a pinch."

"I can try," Dara said. Her eyes had brightened, regaining some of their usual intensity. Siv recognized the determined expression she often wore when she was learning a new dueling move.

"Come here, Rumy," Siv said. "Be good for Dara."

He held up his cloak to hide as much of the flame as possible. Dara reached out and scratched Rumy's head. He snorted into her hand, leathery wings creaking. She breathed deeply.

"What's happening?" Siv asked.

"Don't distract me."

"Are you trying it now? I can't see anything."

"Shh. I'm sensing for Fire."

"Do you feel—?"

"Do you want me to do this or not?" Dara snapped.

"Sorry. I'll be quiet."

Siv waited, eager to see what she could do. Rumy relaxed under Dara's hands, but nothing happened. She closed her eyes and ran her fingers along his neck and down to the underside of his belly.

The warm glow of the sunset colored the snow surrounding the pair. Dara's cloak spread around her, her golden braid falling loose over it, and Rumy's tail lashed back and forth contentedly. Siv wished he could tell what she was feeling. His arms began to grow tired from holding up his cloak, the right one throbbing painfully from his wounds.

Then Dara opened her eyes.

"Now," she said.

Rumy reared up and let loose a jet of flame. Dara stuck her hand directly into the fire.

Siv started forward in surprise, but Dara's hand didn't burn. She held it in the spout of Rumy's flame, turning it back and forth. For an instant her hand shone like it was made of gold. Then Rumy's flame died away and he snapped his jaws, looking rather smug.

"Did it work?" Siv asked.

Dara sat back on her heels, studying her palm.

"I don't know. I feel something inside my skin, but it's different. It doesn't feel like the Fire normally does."

"Can you Work with it?"

"I'm not sure. My senses are still rattled. The heat is kind of jumping around, but I can't tell if that's because dragon fire is different or because I'm still recovering."

Dara laid her hand on the ground. The snow sizzled and melted around it, leaving a perfect Dara-sized imprint on the path.

"Incredible," Siv said. "Does that mean you can Work as long as you have a friendly cur-dragon around?"

"I wouldn't be so sure." Dara frowned and withdrew her hand from the snow. "The heat is already draining away. Besides, Fire-workers and cur-dragons have lived on the mountain together for centuries. I think someone would have noticed if they wielded the same Fire."

"But what if—"

Siv stopped abruptly at the sound of something whistling through the air. He realized what it was at the last instant and dove to the ground, pulling Dara with him. An arrow struck the spot where he had been standing a second earlier.

3

THE FINAL STAIR

ARROWS rained down around Dara and Siv. They must not have hidden the dragon flame well enough. They'd alerted their pursuers to their exact location. Fear spiked through Dara as another arrow zipped into the snow right beside her.

"Never mind about stealth," Siv said. "Rumy, blast us a path down the stairs!"

Rumy screeched and took flight. He streaked away from them, flames already shooting from his throat. Dara and Siv followed, hurling themselves down the treacherous steps of the Final Stair as Rumy melted the ice before them.

Dara clutched at the residual heat as they ran. She had been surprised that she could draw a bit of power from Rumy as he breathed fire over her hand. Trace amounts of true Fire laced his flame. Dara had never heard of something like that before, but she didn't have time to question it as they fled for their lives. She pulled at the hints of Fire and spun them behind her in threads as she had seen Zage do. The threads were tiny, but she managed to burn one arrow out of the air and nudge another off course as they fled the assault.

The arrows ceased after a few minutes, and shouts followed them as their attackers gave chase.

The Final Stair was narrow and steep. Dara had lived in the mountain heights for her entire life, but even she felt a sense of vertigo as they raced down the steps. Cliffs edged the stairs on either side, a final plunge before they reached the bottom of the Fissure. Nowhere to go but down.

Rumy's jets of flame became erratic. He was running out of energy, and they weren't to the bottom yet. The footsteps behind them grew louder. Dara and Siv were both weary from their journey and their injuries. They fought through the exhaustion. They couldn't let their pursuers overtake them.

Dara cast about for a plan. They had to delay the men behind them. Rumy would be too tired to cause another distraction, and they'd been seen with him now anyway.

She gathered more Fire from the vestiges of Rumy's flame, a miniscule amount compared to what she normally Worked with above the Fire Warden's Well. What could she do with a tiny amount of Fire?

Siv's long legs churned. He was beginning to outpace her. He had his blade in hand already. They weren't going to make it to the bottom without a fight.

Dara scrutinized the steep drop beside the Final Stair. It was too far to jump. A fall from this height would be deadly.

She knew what she had to do.

"Canteen!" she gasped.

Siv didn't question. He tossed her the metal canteen. It was cheap, flimsy steel, but it would be good enough for her needs. Dara held it with both hands and forced the Fire she'd gathered into the metal, noticing it had already warped when Siv used it to melt snow. The water evaporated in a flash of steam, and the canteen began to melt. Dara kneaded the metal as she ran. She didn't have time to do it with her mind alone. She stretched the steel of the canteen into a long thin bar, its silvery length nearly invisible against the wet stone steps. The Fire helped it keep its shape, though she didn't have time to solidify it properly.

She glanced back to make sure their pursuers weren't in view yet, then she skidded to a halt and bent the edges of the steel bar, thrusting them into the stone on either side of the stairs with the last of the Fire. It wasn't pretty, but the thin metal rod crossed the path exactly at ankle height. With any luck, it'd catch one of their pursuers unaware and slow the others.

Dara hurtled after Siv as fast as she could. A stitch burned in her side, and her breath came in gasps. This was it. The final point. The championship bout. She would not give up in the final stretch. Dara ran faster.

Moments later, a brutal scream echoed across the Fissure.

Then came the whistle of air and the thud. Dara winced. Her trap had worked. A string of curses thundered from above, farther away now. The others would tread more carefully after what had happened to their comrade.

"Nice one," Siv wheezed. "Almost there."

Rumy had stopped producing flame. He flapped ahead of them, his flight labored. The sun sank below the peak, and darkness closed in around them. They took the final steps at a dead run, heedless of the remaining ice. Feet skidding dangerously, they reached the bottom of the Fissure, where a wide avenue bordered with trees led into the darkness.

"Hide?" Dara gasped as she leapt off the final step.

"Here." Siv led the way into the trees on the opposite side of the cobblestone road. Rumy landed and shuffled along beside them with a dull whine. The grove was sheltered, the branches thick enough to keep the ground free of snow. They'd leave no tracks.

As they pushed through the trees, a rushing sound filled Dara's ears. She couldn't put her finger on what it was. Her exhaustion nearly blinded her. Branches whipped against her face, and brambles tugged at her cloak. She followed Siv's tall shape through the darkness, trusting that he had a plan. Shouts rang out behind them, still too close. They slid down a gentle incline, picking up speed as they scrambled onward. Seconds later, they burst through the trees on the banks of a vast, icy river.

Dara had forgotten about the Oakwind River running through the Fissure. Starlight glittered on the water rushing by. Used to mountain springs and streams, she'd never seen a river this wide and wild up close before. She had no time to stop and admire it, though. Siv hurried along the riverbank to a simple wooden dock. A dozen boats bobbed beside it.

"Get in," he said, rapidly untying one of the boats. Rumy snorted and dug his claws into the dock. Shouts filtered through the trees. They didn't have time for delay. Their remaining pursuers must have reached the bottom of the Final Stair and entered the grove by now. Dara grabbed Rumy around the middle and hauled him into the boat with her. They both toppled to the bottom as Siv pushed away from the dock, paddling fiercely.

"Shouldn't we get rid of the other boats so they can't follow?" Dara said.

"No time," Siv said. "Let's hope they search the woods before they check the river. We'll be long gone by then."

The current buffeted them about as they pulled into the center of the river. Chunks of ice scraped their hull, invisible in the darkness. The boat was too small for the three of them. Dara and Rumy crowded forward in the bow to give Siv room to row. Black water rushed beneath them, and Dara's stomach lurched at the sight. She had never been in a boat before.

She avoided looking at the inky depths and churning, white-tipped peaks. She scanned the shore for any sign of pursuit. Whoever had been sent after them wouldn't give up. But they were moving fast on the water. They had to be getting farther away—unless their pursuers had horses waiting for them in the Fissure.

The Oakwind carried them swiftly through the night. Dara became more certain that they weren't in danger of being overtaken with each passing minute. Gradually, her heart rate returned to normal. Their hunters were no matches for the river. It was a good thing Siv knew about these boats. He'd taken the journey through the Fissure to Trure many times and must have gone by boat or visited the dock on one of his previous trips. If she had been alone, she would have run straight down the road and hoped she was faster than the men her father had sent to retake her.

Retake her or kill her, Dara amended. Those arrows had been flying with impunity. Her father may have ordered his men to kill Siv and take Dara alive, but there were no guarantees. She shied away from thinking of her mother. She feared Lima Ruminor cared even less whether Dara lived or died than her husband did.

Her father may feel differently now that he knew she could Work. But whether the revelation would produce a lethal desire to punish Dara or inspire him to draw her back into the family, she couldn't say. She could never join him, not after what he'd done. She grimaced. The break between them hurt worse than any physical injury.

The moon rose over the river as they sped along the bottom of the Fissure. They passed the shadowy indent where Orchard Gorge sloped down into the deeper canyon. Then Village Peak rose on their right, where Dara had lived for her whole life until she moved into the castle a few months ago. Mists floated above the river, obscuring her view of the peak, but she could picture its uneven edges. She imagined the two levels of Stone Market, which must be directly uphill from where they were now. She pictured the uneven pathways, busy with villagers and mountain goats, and the porch in front of her parents' home lined with Fire Lanterns. She thought of the breeze and the mists in her face as she crossed the Fissure a thousand times on bridges now invisible in the darkness. She was truly leaving her home behind. She had no idea what she'd find in the Lands Below.

The creaking of the oars ceased. Dara turned in time to see Siv hunching over them, breathing heavily.

"Let me do it for a while," she said.

"It's just my stitches," he said. "No worse than a couple of zur-wasp stings." But his face was white, and his limbs shook from pain and fatigue.

"Move over," Dara said. "We'll take turns."

Siv didn't argue. He pushed himself up, and they shuffled awkwardly around each other to change places. Rumy had fallen asleep in the bottom of the boat. He gave an annoyed grunt when Dara accidentally stepped on his tail.

"Sorry," she said, shifting her feet, unable to see much in the darkness. Her foot struck the oarsman's bench, and she lurched sideways. Siv caught her just before she tumbled over the side.

"Easy." He held her still for a moment, both hands on her upper arms. She regained her balance, but he didn't let go.

"I'm okay," Dara said.

"I know." Siv didn't remove his hands.

Dara looked up at him. Moonlight glinted on his dark hair and made his bandage glow. There was weariness and desperation in his eyes. It was as if he'd intended to steady her and then let her go, but he got caught, trapped in a single moment. Dara felt tethered, as if

Siv were a lifeline holding her up, holding her together. Exhaustion had left her raw. She clutched his sleeves, feeling exposed and vulnerable after everything they'd been through. So much loss. So much peril. And he looked at her as if *she* were the only thing holding *him* together, the only thing he'd ever wanted. He tightened his grip, drawing her nearer, and for one silver second she felt a little less lost in his arms.

Then the boat hit a patch of ice, and they both pitched over the side.

The cold shock of the water devastated Dara's senses. It was like being hit with a massive jolt of Fire and a blow to the head at the same time. She was almost too surprised to do anything. Through sheer luck, her head broke the surface, and she gasped in a breath.

"Dara!"

Siv swam swiftly toward her as the river carried them downstream. The boat picked up speed, shooting beyond their reach. Rumy poked his head above the gunwale with a surprised squawk. Dara's sodden cloak dragged at her, but they were moving too quickly for her to sink. The snowy riverbank swept by, and cold and terror hit Dara at the same moment. She swallowed a huge gulp of icy water.

A second later, Siv grabbed her arm.

"Swim," he urged.

"Right," she choked. Now wasn't the time to tell him she couldn't. She kicked hard, her muscles screaming in protest. She wasn't sure what to do with her arms, so she flailed one and held onto Siv with the other. They swept forward, not getting any closer to the riverbank as far as Dara could tell.

"There's a bend coming up," Siv called. "Try to swim crossways out of the current."

Dara was concentrating too hard on keeping her head above water to respond. Then she caught a glimpse of the shore straight ahead. That must be the bend Siv was talking about. She kicked harder, imagining that she was hurling herself into a flying lunge with each stroke. More water rushed down her throat, blade-sharp and freezing.

They inched closer to the river's edge. The bend neared far too rapidly. Dara kicked and flailed, knowing full well that her life depended on it. She wouldn't die now, not when they had made it this far.

Suddenly Siv rose out of the water. Dara gasped, disoriented, before she realized he was standing up. They had reached shallower water where the river rushed around the bend. Siv turned and hauled Dara the rest of the way out of the high-speed current. They trudged through the shallows and crawled out of the water. Siv flopped onto the snowy riverbank, his breathing ragged. Dara wanted nothing more than to lie down beside him, but they weren't out of danger yet.

"Get up," she said urgently. "We have to take our clothes off."

"I've been waiting my whole life for you to say that," Siv said sleepily.

"This isn't a joke."

"Of course not, Dara. You never joke."

"The cold will kill us almost as fast as the water." Dara yanked on Siv's arm until he grudgingly sat up and began undoing his cloak with clumsy fingers.

A dark shape rushed overhead, and Rumy settled onto the snow beside them. He snapped his jaws anxiously. Dara hoped he'd gotten enough rest in the bottom of the boat to make fire again. They were going to need it.

"We should move farther under the trees," Siv said. "Less snow there. I'm burning tired of snow." Despite his joking tone, he was removing his coat and boots as quickly as Dara. He understood the danger they were in.

"Good idea." Dara dumped the water out of her own boots, which were stiff and icy, and picked up the cloak and coat she'd already taken off. They hurried away from the river under the cover of the trees. Each step on the frozen ground was like walking on knives.

Rumy trundled along beside them. He sneezed, releasing a burst of flame as if to show them he was ready to help. Dara was about to remove the rest of her clothes and begin gathering firewood, when she spotted something through the trees.

"What's that?"

"This? Why, this is the makings of a fine pair of scars," Siv said.

Dance of Steel

He had already pulled off his shirt, and he prodded at the bandage across his ribs. It was soaked with blood as well as water.

"No, *that*." Dara pointed through the trees at a structure in the darkness. It had a thatched roof, and Dara never would have noticed it if not for a slight glint of metal that had caught her eye when Rumy sneezed out a burst of light. It must have come from the heavy steel latch holding the door shut.

"Oh. *That*," Siv said, "might be our first dose of luck in a long time."

He strode through the trees, and Dara followed. His broad shoulders looked bluish from the cold, but his steps were sure and straight. They reached the structure, a little cabin set in a clearing no bigger than the Ruminor dwelling back on Village Peak. The shutters were closed, and the place looked abandoned. Siv knocked once, and when no one answered, he lifted the latch and pushed the door open with a rusty squeak. He stepped back and held the door for Dara, teeth chattering.

"Welcome, my lady."

"Are you sure it's empty?"

"Probably doesn't matter now, unless you'd rather freeze to death," Siv said.

"Fair point." Dara entered the cabin, catching a whiff of dust and dry earth. It was almost as cold inside as outside, but at least the cabin appeared to be vacant.

"This used to be a messengers' rest stop," Siv said. "My father showed it to me once. They don't use it much anymore, though. Too far from the road."

"That's good for us."

Dara groped around in the dark for a light. Rumy shuffled in behind her, rubbing against her legs, and Siv let the door fall shut.

"There should be a lantern or something," Siv said. A bang and a clatter echoed through the cabin, and he let out a curse directed at whatever he had stumbled over.

Dara moved more slowly. Her body was beginning to go numb. This was not good. They needed to get warm soon. Her knees collided with something soft. She reached down and felt the quilted top of a bed.

Light burst around her, killing the shadows in an instant.

"Found the Fire Lantern!" Siv said proudly. He held up the Work, wrought in a simple style, which must have been covered with a cloth when it wasn't in use. He had moved to the right of the door while Dara moved to the left, and now he faced her across the cabin. There was a small table beside him, where the Fire Lantern had been sitting, and a chair on its side, which must have been what he had tripped over. The cabin had a cupboard topped with a stone washbasin, and an old boot with a hole in the toe leaned in a corner. A layer of dust coated everything. Rumy pranced across the center of the cabin, snapping at dust motes floating in the Firelight.

An old fireplace waited at the foot of the bed. More importantly, cut wood was stacked beside it in a teetering, moldy pile.

"Good news," Dara said. "We're not going to die after all."

They built a wood fire quickly. Neither of them had ever done it before, having grown up on the Fire Mountain, but it was remarkably easy with a cur-dragon for a companion. They simply tossed a bunch of wood into the fireplace and had Rumy hurl flames at it until the logs dried and caught fire. Satisfied with his work, Rumy curled up in front of the roaring inferno and went to sleep.

In addition to the quilt spread across it, more blankets were folded at the foot of the bed. These smelled musty, and the top one had a light pattern of mildew. Dara and Siv were shivering so hard they barely noticed. They took off the rest of their clothes and spread them over the table, chairs, and the foot of the bed to dry. Dara was too cold to feel embarrassed. She had seen Siv without his shirt before, and as much as she wanted to sneak another look or two, she had to focus on getting warm. They quickly wrapped themselves in dry blankets and crawled under the quilt.

Dara's teeth chattered so hard they hurt, and her muscles had begun to seize up. The room warmed quickly with the crackling fire, but it took longer for the heat to work into her body. She burrowed further into the blankets, scooting closer to Siv to share his warmth. He didn't have as much to spare as usual, but he hugged her to his bare chest and shivered alongside her.

The sudden closeness might have made her shy in other circumstances. She was near enough to hear Siv's heartbeat, to feel the soft hair on his chest against her cheek, to smell the blood seeping through his bandages. Dara had never dared hope they might one day be wrapped up together like this without the barrier of his crown between them. She had spent months fearing that any intimacy would only make things harder in the end. But now? She didn't know what their future held, but he wasn't the king anymore. Her heart thundered in her chest as she considered the possibilities. She very nearly forgot how exhausted she was.

But at last, the ordeal of their flight began to catch up to her. A fog slipped around her senses. She fought to stay awake. She wanted to enjoy having Siv's arms around her for a little while longer. His fingers brushed her skin, tender and warm. For the first time Dara allowed hope full rein in her heart. Could they be together after all? She was afraid to speak, afraid to ask what he thought lest the hope shatter like glass. Without so much as a good night, she pressed her face into his shoulder, pulled the blankets over their heads, and succumbed to sleep.

4

SORALINE

SORALINE Amintelle paced across her antechamber. She had been shut in her room for a day and a half, ever since her world ended. She was not allowed to speak to anyone, and she had no idea what was happening in the rest of the castle. A pair of Soolen guards stood watch outside her door at all hours, vigilant and grim. They responded to every question, plea, and rebuke with the same stony silence.

Sora scrubbed angrily at her red-streaked cheeks. She felt as if she'd been crying nonstop, but she was out of tears now. All she could do was pace and pace and wait for the Lantern Maker to determine her fate.

Rafe Ruminor had told her she would be queen. It was all she had ever wanted. For one terrible moment she had felt happy. Sora cringed at the memory of the uncontrollable burst of joy she'd felt at the idea of herself as the Queen of Vertigon. It was a mini betrayal on a night that had been full of them. But she knew the Lantern Maker wanted a puppet, someone with the Amintelle name who could give the illusion that a coup had not destroyed the Peace of Vertigon. He wanted her to wear the crown of her fathers and rule in their name, all while doing exactly what he said like a good little girl.

We'll see about that.

Sora's pacing took her to the window, where Vertigon sparkled white in the snow. The sun rose in a clear sky. It had snowed all day yesterday, making Sora feel as if she were enclosed in a swirling white cage instead of her tower bedroom. Now every rooftop was coated in a thick blanket, giving the illusion that all was well. The city was quiet, as if her people had decided to hide away until spring.

Sora drummed her fingers on the windowsill, feeling the cold seeping through the heavy glass. She was the last Amintelle left on the mountain. Her mother and sister were far away. Her father was dead. Her brother was dead. She was alone. And she wasn't even the queen yet. Not truly.

But after a day and a night of crying, anger was all she had left—and she'd had enough of waiting. She marched to the door and pounded her fist against it.

"I want to see the Lantern Maker," she shouted.

"He will speak with you later."

"When?"

"When he has time."

Sora scowled at the door, imagining her guards could see her displeasure.

She was under no illusions about what the Lantern Maker expected of her. She would be queen in name only. Her name had always been all that mattered. Noblemen courted her for it. Usurpers spared her for it. It didn't matter that she actually had a good idea of how to run a kingdom. It didn't matter that she'd invested far more time than her brother in getting to know the nobility and understanding the intricacies of the political system, both in Vertigon and the Lands Below. No, she would be made queen for her name and *be* queen in name alone.

She had to admit it was a decent strategy. Vertigon would balk at the idea of a coup. The Amintelles had ruled it well for a hundred years. If the Lantern Maker gave the impression that the attack on the royal family had failed and the Amintelles remained in power, it would assuage the fears of those who could otherwise cause trouble for him. She suspected he would spend a few years strengthening his hold over the kingdom through her—until he no longer needed the façade. Then he'd poison her tea or ship her off to a foreign land. She had a lot of work to do before then if she meant to stop him.

Sora banged on the door again. "I demand to see the Lantern

Maker," she said. "I'll throw myself from the window if you don't bring him to me."

There was silence outside. Sora doubted the guards believed her. She certainly had no intention of resorting to suicide after only a day and a half as a prisoner. But her guards must have decided they couldn't take the risk. She heard the tap of footsteps as one of them left to fetch her captor at last.

Sora settled into her armchair to wait.

Her antechamber was neat and orderly. She had carefully arranged all of her books and maps on a pair of shelves opposite the windows. Her couch had a pair of cushions at each end with embroidered covers imported all the way from Soole. A Soolen tapestry hung on her wall between the two windows, depicting a ship leaving the harbor for a journey across the Ammlen Ocean. Sora scowled at the tapestry. She'd loved the idea of brokering an alliance between Vertigon and Soole by marrying the Crown Prince. It was to be her legacy. Then the Soolen army had invaded Cindral Forest and sent men to join the coup against her brother, perhaps in concert with House Rollendar. She still wasn't sure how all the pieces fit together, but she was much less enthusiastic about the idea of Soole now.

Captain Thrashe, one of the men who guarded her door, was from Soole. Sora saw him whenever her serving woman delivered her meals. They weren't permitted to speak to each other. Captain Thrashe would loom above the poor woman, arms folded over his barrel chest, and watch her with his single eye. A battered leather patch covered the other eye socket, not quite hiding the long scar across it. The serving woman would set down Sora's tray of food with shaking hands, give her a frightened smile, and flee that one-eyed stare. She was never allowed to stay long enough to clean, but Sora always kept her space tidy anyway. Captain Thrashe would depart without a word, ignoring her attempts to talk to him or win him to her side. He remained immovable and silent. Her threat had done the trick, though.

Sora tapped her foot impatiently and adjusted the sleeves of her simple maroon dress. She wished she were wearing Amintelle blue to confront the Lantern Maker, but it was too late to change now. She combed her fingers through her curly dark hair and tied it back with a black ribbon.

At last the door opened, and Rafe Ruminor the Lantern Maker swept in. He was an imposing man, tall and broad, with a strong jaw and golden hair edged with gray. He carried a roll of papers under one arm like a scepter. In his other hand, he held the Amintelle crown. He seemed to fill the space, as proud as if he were a king in his own right—and always had been.

Sora remained seated, lifting her chin like a true queen, and met his eyes despite the nerves sending fireflies through her stomach. "Master Ruminor."

"I understand you wish to speak with me," he said. "I've been rather busy, but I had to give you this anyway. Congratulations, Queen Sora."

He held out the crown as though it were nothing more than a mug of cider. The Firejewels in its band winked cruelly. Sora's fingers twitched, but she did not take it.

"Come now, we needn't stand on ceremony," Rafe said. "The crown is yours, as we discussed."

"Rulers of Vertigon are crowned before the body of their predecessor," Sora said. "It's tradition."

"Traditions change," Rafe said. He smiled indulgently at her. "I expect you and I will change a number of them in the new Vertigon."

Sora's grip tightened on the arms of her chair. The crown still glittered in the Lantern Maker's hand. "I want to see my brother's body."

"I'm afraid it's too late for that. Besides, your brother's body was not . . . presentable. Sword fights are savage business."

Sora swallowed as the urge to cry rose up in her again. She clutched for the anger and held onto it like a kite string.

"How do I know he's really dead?"

"My dear," Rafe said, not unkindly. "You've been through a lot. I am sorry for your loss, but imprinting the image of your brother's corpse on your mind will not make it easier to move on."

"But—"

"I lost my daughter, you know, and I shall never forget the sight of her body."

"Dara's dead?" Sora asked, caught off guard.

"Not Dara. My firstborn. Long ago." Rafe frowned, his eyes

glazing for a moment. Then he straightened and crossed to the table. He set the crown on it with a thunk. "When you are ready."

Sora sat straighter in her chair, resisting the urge to stand.

"I can't remain imprisoned here."

"I quite agree," Rafe said. "You'll make a public appearance soon. The arrangements are already underway."

"If you plan to rule through me," she said, "we'll have to communicate."

"I have not forgotten our bargain. There will be no need to resort to dramatics in the future." Rafe set the roll of papers on the table beside the crown. "You are to be the queen, but I have particular plans for Vertigon. You can start by signing these royal edicts." He smiled as he turned for the door. "Feel free to read them first if you wish."

Sora scowled at his back as he swept out. She caught a glimpse of Captain Thrashe outside before the Lantern Maker closed the door behind him. She leapt from her seat as soon as he was gone and resumed her pacing.

Dramatics? She could read them if she *wished*? She couldn't allow him to dismiss her like that. She forced herself to stop pacing and take a deep breath. She straightened her sleeves and smoothed out her maroon skirts. She'd need to deal with Rafe Ruminor in a way that was both strategic *and* dignified. Anger may make her brave, but she had to be smart too.

She thought back over their conversation. Something he had said stuck with her. His firstborn daughter had died—implying that Dara still lived. And Dara had vowed to give her life for Sora's brother. Sora was pretty sure she had been in love with him too— enough to protect him against her own father. If Dara had survived, maybe she could help Sora escape the Lantern Maker's clutches.

Was Dara still on the mountain? The last time Sora had seen her was when she escorted her from the Great Hall and assigned Denn and Luci to guard her door. Sora had wanted to stay behind. She had helped to calm a frightened crowd of young noblewomen when the Fire first encircled Square Peak. She could have supported her brother as he decided what to do next. But Dara had insisted that she retreat to the safety of her chambers while they dealt with the crisis. Dara hadn't been able to protect Siv in the end, but maybe she could still help Sora.

She filed away the possibility for when she was finally allowed to communicate with the outside world again. In the meantime, she had work to do. She went to the table and unrolled the Lantern Maker's edicts. The crown sat beside her, just out of reach. The Firejewels glowed like watching eyes as she settled in to read about what the Lantern Maker planned to do with her family's kingdom. Her eyebrows rose higher with each word. By the time she finished, she was pretty sure the Lantern Maker didn't just want to create a new Vertigon. He intended to change the world.

5

THE PLAINS OF TRURE

SIV woke with Dara in his arms. He felt disoriented at first and wondered if he was dreaming. It wouldn't be the first time he'd dreamed about holding her. She smelled like snow and smoke, and her warmth was the only thing assuring him they were really here.

The fire had burned low, and the cabin was toasty and dry. He had a feeling they had slept for a long time. He knew his wounds would start hurting again as soon as he moved. He'd also probably pulled a few muscles in their frantic run, row, and swim of the night before. Or two days before. Who knew how much time had passed? If he moved, he'd feel every ache.

Besides, if he moved, he'd have to let go of Dara. She was sound asleep, her breathing steady and peaceful, cheek pressed against his chest. Her golden hair had escaped from its usual braid and cascaded over his arm in a tangled wave. If he moved, he'd have to remember that she had kept secrets from him for months. He'd have to acknowledge that her parents had killed his father and his sister and taken over his kingdom. If he moved, she'd once again be Dara Ruminor, Castle Guard, Fireworker, and Lantern Maker's daughter, and he'd be Sivarrion Amintelle, former King of Vertigon.

He stayed still for a moment longer. This. This was what he wanted. He was just Siv, and she was just Dara, sleeping, warm and perfect, in his arms.

Then with a heavy sigh, he moved. And misery hit him like a charging cullmoran.

He eased out of the bed and staggered to the chair where his trousers hung to dry. He pulled them on, his movements wooden, and began the slow, painful process of loosening his stiff muscles. He focused on simple tasks: stretching, putting on his boots, relieving himself, and filling the washbasin with snow from outside. A clean mantle of pure white surrounded the cabin. The quiet rush of the Oakwind River and the distant trilling of crundlebirds were the only sounds. They were safe for the moment.

Siv returned to the cabin and lowered himself down to sit by the fire. He tossed a few more logs onto it and began to melt the snow in the basin. As he worked, the weight of everything that had happened settled over him. He had been so focused on survival during their journey down the mountain that it hadn't all sunk in yet. But now that his body was rested, it was time for his mind and emotions to take a beating too.

He jabbed at the fire with his rapier. One of the logs broke apart with a soft thump, sending sparks across the floor. Dara sat up, a muffled groan escaping her lips. She must feel as bad as he did right now. She rubbed her eyes blearily as Siv tapped Rumy's scaly hide to wake him too.

"We'd better move soon," he said. "In case anyone sees the smoke."

"What time is it?"

"Late afternoon as far as I can tell. We needed that sleep."

Dara started to stand and then seemed to remember that she had undressed the night before. Her cheeks reddened, and she retreated back under the covers like a morrinvole. Siv tossed her dry clothes over so she could dress and turned his back like a gentleman, only stealing one glimpse at her long legs and the smooth curve of her back. Okay, maybe two glimpses. Before she noticed him looking, he returned his attention to the slowly melting snow.

"Do you know how much farther it is to the Truren capital?" Dara asked. She sat beside him on the floor of the cabin and began to stretch, looking as stiff as he felt.

"When the Fissure Road leaves the mountain, it becomes the

High Road, which cuts all the way through the Truren Horseplains. Rallion City is a two-day ride from there. It'll take us longer on foot."

"We'd better stay off the road as much as possible."

"Agreed."

"Will we need to sneak into the city?" Dara asked. She shifted into a shallow lunge, grimacing at the pain. "Do you have any enemies there who'd stop you from reaching your grandfather?"

"You ought to know that better than me," Siv said sullenly.

"Why?"

"You're better acquainted with my enemies."

Dara looked up, startled. "I told you I've never been privy to my father's plans."

"He's your father." Once he started on the topic, Siv couldn't quite stop himself. He couldn't ignore the heaviness of everything that had happened any longer. He definitely shouldn't have moved. "You must understand him a little bit, Dara. I knew *my* father very well."

Dara's face fell, as if he'd shattered something small and fragile within her.

Siv slumped, avoiding her gaze. "We should get going."

"Clearly you have something you want to say," she said. "You think I'm your enemy now?"

"Forget it."

"It's too late for that." Dara stood and put her hands on her hips. He half expected her to drop into her dueling stance. "We can't keep ignoring what happened. We've gotten some rest. We're out of danger for the moment. Let's talk."

"Your father killed half my family, Dara." Siv's breathing grew rough. He stuck a hand in the washbasin to see if the water had warmed yet, but it was still icy to the touch. "Talking won't change that."

Dara opened her mouth to answer and then closed it again. Her eyes were bright and intense, full of almost as much misery as Siv felt. Her arms dropped to her sides.

"We should clean your wounds. You need fresh bandages," she said.

"Oh yeah, change the subject," Siv muttered. "That will help things."

"You just said you don't want to talk," Dara snapped.
"Fine. Great. Don't talk, then."
"Fine. I don't want to talk either."
"Glad we agree."

Dara glared at him for a minute then stalked to the other side of the cabin and rummaged in the cupboard. She pulled out a loaf of rock-hard, moldy bread and a mismatched selection of tin cups before finding an abandoned tunic and ripping it into strips for bandages. Siv watched her, feeling miserable.

He wished he could turn back time. He wanted it to be this summer, when Dara had snapped at him for nothing worse than his failure to take dueling practice seriously. When they'd moved in sync across the dueling floor. But remembering the summer brought back images of Sora's gentle teasing, of his father's grip on his shoulder after the attack in Thunderbird Square. He couldn't look at Dara without thinking of them. So where did they go from here?

Perhaps sensing the mood, Rumy shuffled outside to explore as Dara brought over the makeshift bandages and one of the tin cups. She leaned in and started unwrapping the bandages Vine Silltine had given him. Had that only been three days ago?

Siv winced as the bloodstained cloths pulled away from his wounds. Dara dipped the cup into the water basin and held it close to the fire for a minute to warm it. She held it much closer than Siv ever could, practically sticking her fingers into the coals. Siv looked away from this reminder of who she was.

Dara wet a cloth in the steaming water and began the delicate task of cleaning his cuts. Her hands moved gently over his skin. They didn't speak, and he gritted his teeth against the pain, his breathing shallow. The coppery smell of blood disguised Dara's smoky, snowy scent. He hated being this close to her. Hated and loved it at the same time.

He had once been sure that he and Dara could never be together regardless of how he felt about her. Now that he might not be king, he had a better chance of being with her than ever before. But could he love her for who she was and how she made him feel and hate what she represented at the same time? Why couldn't she have just told him the truth from the beginning?

"I'm done. You can stop scowling at me," Dara said as she tied the last bandage around his sword arm.

Siv nodded, avoiding her gaze. "Let's go, then."

They ate more jerky and a bit of the now-soggy flatbread as they left the cabin and walked through the woods, listening for any hint of the men who had pursued them down the Final Stair. They heard nothing but the rustle of leaves, the crunch of their own footsteps, and the occasional call of winter birds. The river had carried them beyond the reach of their enemies—for now.

Siv could picture the map of the region in his head, but he wasn't confident he could find the way to Rallion City without the High Road to guide him. He was no woodsman. They agreed it would be wisest to find the road and travel out of sight beside it until they reached the city gates.

They spoke infrequently and only about practical things. Dara slipped back into Castle Guard mode, the formal way of speaking she had adopted after his engagement to the treacherous Lady Tull. She was a guard without a castle, and he was a king without a crown. What a pair they made. A sullen mood settled on Siv like frost.

Rumy was the only one who seemed to be enjoying the journey. The long night's sleep had done him good. He disappeared into the woods to find a meal and returned ten minutes later with a morrin-vole clutched in his teeth and a triumphant expression on his face. His usual snuffing was almost a purr after he filled his belly. Siv scratched his scaly head. At least Rumy was on his side.

Just before dark, they reached the pass where the High Road met the Fissure and descended into the lowlands. They waited in the shadows, scanning the twilight for signs of trouble. Nothing moved on the plains. The road snaking back into the Fissure appeared empty. Siv thought he heard a whisper of voices on the wind, soon silenced. He shivered. It was damn creepy, but at least the road seemed safe.

This was the border between Vertigon and Trure. The Mountain and the Horseplains. The two lands had been allies for years, and there was no need for guards to patrol the border. The emptiness was eerie, but then Siv had never been through here in winter before. Maybe this was normal. Travel between Trure and Vertigon was uncommon at this time of year, and the recent blizzard made it even less likely that many people would be making the journey.

After a few minutes, Siv and Dara exchanged glances and began the slow trek downward through the snow-dusted trees, leaving Vertigon behind.

Eventually it grew too dark to see the trees in front of them. After acquiring an impressive collection of bumps and scratches between them, they agreed to leave the woods and walk on the road. They kept their ears perked, ready to dive for cover at the first hint of footsteps behind them.

Around midnight they passed the last clump of trees and entered the broad expanse of the plains. Trure was a rolling, grassy land, and in the darkness it appeared even flatter than it actually was. All they could see was the fuzzy gray line dividing land and sky.

The air grew warmer as they got farther from the mountain. It was a relief to leave the snow behind. Winter in Trure was a blustery, windswept affair, but at least they didn't need to trudge through snowdrifts. Siv had had enough of that to last him a lifetime. And no snow meant no tracks pointing their enemies straight to them. He still jumped every time he heard a sound, but they hadn't been caught yet.

They stole a few hours of rest, huddling on either side of Rumy in a sheltered dip in the plain, and were on the road again before first light. They walked in silence most of the time. Weariness stayed with them as they got farther into the plains. The rhythm of their boots on the path pounded into Siv's brain. He felt as if he'd been walking for half his life.

Rumy alternated between flying and trotting alongside them like an overgrown dog. He seemed to catch their brooding mood after a while. Siv wanted to say something to break the tension, but the longer he waited, the harder it became. Something had fractured between him and Dara, possibly something irreparable. He missed the easy companionship they'd enjoyed back in the dueling hall. He missed his friend. But he missed his father and sister too.

Scattered farms dotted the landscape, but they didn't encounter another soul until the afternoon of their second day on the road. Rumy heard it first. He raised his head, listening intently, and snorted a warning. A second later, the beat of hooves on the packed earth reached them. Hunters! They'd been found! They hurried off the road, hiding in the brush alongside it seconds before three riders on horseback topped the ridge in front of them.

The riders didn't just cross the ridge. They raced as though all the marrkrats of hell were after them. The earth shuddered with the hoof beats, and dust billowed in the cold afternoon sunlight. The horses neared, their powerful legs eating up the distance. One of the riders whooped as his mount stretched out its neck and took the lead. Horse and rider each wore a flowing yellow crest. Siv cocked his head. There was something familiar about the leader...

At the last second, he charged out from their hiding place, waving his arms over his head. Dara called after him in surprise, but he was too busy jumping up and down by the side of the road to get the racers' attention to explain.

He feared the riders wouldn't see him. He waved frantically, wondering if he should dart into the road. Then the leader pulled up his horse and skidded to a halt in a cloud of dust.

"Ho there!" he called. "You'd best have a good reason for stopping us. I was about to win that race."

"We have a mile to go yet," one of the others shouted indignantly. "It was still any man's game."

"What's your business?" asked the rider with the yellow crest, ignoring his companion. He was a tall rapier of a man with a rich voice and sunburnt cheeks. His hair was longer and grayer than the last time Siv had seen him, but there was no mistaking him, especially sporting that particularly garish shade of yellow.

"You don't recognize your favorite nephew?" Siv said.

The man leaned closer, pale, piercing eyes studying him. Then he burst out laughing.

"Well, if it isn't young Siv! It has been a few years, my boy. You're taller and more bearded than you used to be."

"It's good to see you, Uncle Tem." Siv scratched at the five-day growth on his chin, already feeling some of the tension draining from his shoulders. They were saved.

"My lords," Uncle Tem called to his companions. "May I introduce my sister Tirra's eldest son, Sivarrion Amintelle? Now then, you didn't run away again, did you?" He chuckled richly. "I'll never forget the day I intercepted you trying to sneak out of the palace gates as a boy. You said you aimed to walk all the way back to Vertigon by nightfall."

"Beg pardon, Tem," said one of the riders, a younger, thicker man wearing vibrant green. "Isn't Sivarrion Amintelle now the King of Vertigon?"

"Well, stab me with a pitchfork, I forgot all about that." Uncle Tem turned back to Siv and squinted at him suspiciously. "What are you doing out on the road?"

"There has been trouble on the mountain, I'm afraid," Siv said. Uncle Tem opened his mouth, but Siv raised a hand to forestall him. "I'd rather not discuss it until we reach my mother and grandfather." Siv wasn't looking forward to that conversation at all. He would have to tell his mother that his sister had been killed—and he hadn't stopped it. He didn't feel like repeating the story to Uncle Tem now.

"Can you provide us with a ride?" he asked.

"Of course, my boy," Uncle Tem said, furrowing his brow. "We have spare horses in a village not far from here. We'd planned a racing holiday, but we can return to the city straightaway."

"Thank you, Uncle Tem." Siv inclined his head, trying not to slump in relief. He was burning tired of walking. And they needed this stroke of luck. "Oh, and this is Dara, my . . . bodyguard."

The third man snorted. Dara stared at him levelly until he ducked his head and fiddled with the bronze buttons on his purple coat. She looked rather intimidating, with her tattered Guard uniform, her shadowed eyes, and the black Savven blade at her waist.

"I'm terribly curious to hear your story," Tem said. He looked between Siv and Dara for a moment, lost in speculation. One of his companion's horses huffed impatiently, and he started, his attention returning to the group on the road. "Oh, this is Lord Firnum." He indicated the grumpy-looking man in purple. "And Lord Bale." The younger, heavier man in green bowed low from his saddle. Both had the light eyes characteristic of their countrymen.

"Your lady bodyguard can ride with me to the village, Sire," Lord Bale said. "Old Fence here can carry us both. He was going to beat Tem and his fancy charger if you hadn't happened by."

"You have my gratitude, Lord Bale," Siv said, hiding a snicker. *Fence? Who names their horse Fence?*

He nodded reassuringly at Dara as she approached Lord Bale and his tall stallion. She was wary of the strangers—as well she should be—but she looked downright terrified of the horse.

"Have no fear, my lady," Lord Bale said. "He's never bitten a soul."

Dara froze a few feet from the horse, as if biting hadn't even occurred to her. "Uh . . . how do I . . . ?"

"Let me help." Siv went over to offer a boost with his left hand. His right arm still hurt like hell irons. Before he hoisted Dara onto the horse's back, he leaned in and whispered, "Don't tell him anything. Sounds like the news hasn't made it off the mountain yet."

Dara shot him a look that said she didn't need to be told and scrambled indelicately onto the horse's back. With a muttered apology she wrapped her arms around Lord Bale's thick waist and held on for dear life.

Siv pulled himself up behind Uncle Tem with more grace. His uncle looked back over his shoulder, and Siv noticed a few lines in his face that hadn't been there before. Tem was the youngest of his mother's siblings, and he still had plenty of youthful energy despite his age.

"Comfortable?"

"I'm ready if you are."

Tem's charger danced beneath them, no doubt annoyed at the extra weight. It kept tossing its head, making the yellow crest flutter.

"Horses don't like cur-dragons much," Uncle Tem said. "Make them nervous."

"Oh right. Rumy, why don't you follow us from a distance?" Siv said. The creature cocked his head to the side suspiciously.

"You expect the damned lizard to understand?" Lord Firnum grumbled.

Siv ignored him. Trurens never understood dragons.

"Don't worry about us, boy," he said. "I'm sure you can take down these horses if they try anything."

Rumy snapped his jaws in agreement then took a running start and launched into the air.

"Shall we, Uncle?" Siv said.

"Aye! Race you back to the inn, my lords."

The three men wheeled their horses around and started back the

Dance of Steel

way they came at a swift canter. Rumy flew ahead, occasionally circling back and squawking as if to make sure they were okay. Wind whipped into their faces, carrying the scent of dry grass, cold earth, and a hint of horse manure. Siv relaxed into the rapid movement. He could get used to this. Anything was better than walking.

Uncle Tem and Siv apparently had different ideas of what "not far from here" meant, though. It was dark by the time they reached Dapplen Town, where the lords had left their spare horses. The village was the closest settlement to Vertigon, serving as a way station for merchants and other travelers. Siv breathed a sigh of relief as they rode in amongst the first buildings. The lights burning in the windows promised rest, comfort, and hopefully a decent mug of ale or two. The town looked quite prosperous, with more than one inn and its own racing grounds. Trurens did love their races.

After a brief consultation, they agreed to stay the night at the inn and ride on to the capital city in the morning. Siv's legs buckled beneath him when he slid off Uncle Tem's horse. It had been a long time since he went riding. He felt sore in muscles he'd forgotten all about. Sleeping on the ground so much lately hadn't helped either. He limped toward the inn, trying not to let Dara see his slightly pathetic condition. She positively skipped away from her horse—though that might have had more to do with her desire to get some distance from the creature.

After handing off their horses to the stablemen, the group sat down for a hot meal in the inn's well-appointed common room.

"This is the best inn in town," Uncle Tem said as the innkeeper placed five steaming bowls of stew before them. "We come out to Dapplen in the winter because there aren't many people on the road to Vertigon. We have it all to ourselves. There's nothing like a road race."

"We're fortunate you were here," Siv said in between shoveling bites of stew into his mouth. "It might have taken us a week to walk to the city."

"I'm sure plenty of other riders would have been thrilled to assist the King of Vertigon," Lord Bale said. His green coat hung open, revealing his large belly straining against the ties of his shirt.

"Now, now." Uncle Tem turned to make sure the innkeeper was not within earshot. "Let's not shout about that here."

"Thank you, Uncle," Siv said. "I'd rather go unrecognized for now."

"You've turned into a strapping young man," Uncle Tem said. "I doubt anyone will recognize you from your last visit. You used to be quite a gangly fellow. And you're looking a little, shall we say, rough. Are those bandages a disguise?"

"Afraid not."

"Alas." Uncle Tem took a long swig from his mug of ale. "I was hoping you and your lady were merely eloping."

Siv coughed and glanced over at Dara. She had frozen with her spoon hovering over her bowl.

"Come now," Uncle Tem said with a chuckle. "I recognize a romantic pairing when I see one. You don't expect me to believe she's really a guard, do you?"

Siv cleared his throat elaborately before Dara could start wielding her spoon like a sword.

"We thought it sensible to leave the mountain," he said. "Romance had nothing to do with it."

Uncle Tem frowned. "Can you give me any hints about the trouble you're in?"

"I'd rather wait until we reach the palace." Siv gave a meaningful glance at the nearest table, where a handful of merchants playing a drinking game could easily overhear their conversation.

"All right. Sorry to push," Uncle Tem said. "I'm sad to hear it of Vertigon, though. The world's not the same these days, what with Soole on the move." None of the other guests in the common room wore the distinctive Soolen clothes or had their coloring as far as Siv could tell, but Tem still lowered his voice. "And after your father died like that, well . . . I'm glad my sister came home when she did."

Siv didn't answer. He trusted Uncle Tem. Indeed, of all his mother's relations, he was probably the best person who could have found them, but Siv didn't want to talk about what had happened in an inn full of strangers. He didn't particularly want to talk about it at all. Besides, Lords Bale and Firnum were listening nearby, their ears perking up higher than their horses'. Even Tem still appeared to be struggling against the urge to press Siv for details.

Siv and Dara retired as soon as they finished their meals, partly because they wanted to avoid further questions and partly because they could barely hold their heads up. Uncle Tem paid for their meal and room as neither one had any money. Siv had lost the coin purse Vine Silltine lent them during their unplanned dip in the river. Rumy had been sent to sleep in the yard behind the inn after the stablemen flat out refused to give him a stall near the horses.

Siv had decided it wouldn't be prudent to ask for separate rooms for him and Dara. The less Uncle Tem knew about her the better. Being a Ruminor might make her a target when word got out about what had happened in Vertigon. If Uncle Tem believed she was Siv's mistress, it would be easy to dodge further speculation. Besides, he hoped he and Dara could make up when they were alone again. He didn't like feeling out of step with her.

But as soon as the door closed behind them, Dara strode to the bed and separated the two blankets spread on top of it.

"I'll sleep on the floor," she announced, voice crisp as a summer apple.

Siv blinked. "Huh?"

"I don't care what your uncle thinks of us, but *you* haven't spoken a civil word to me for two days," she said. "I'm not sharing your bed."

"Dara."

"Siv."

"*Dara.*"

She scowled. "I'm serious."

"Maybe I've been a little grumpy lately, but—"

"If we're not friends anymore, then we're not friends," Dara said. She spoke rapidly, as if she'd been holding this in for a while. "I'll try to help you. I owe you after what my parents did, but let's keep things professional."

"Professional?" Siv gaped at her. "You've been giving me the silent treatment too."

"I'll talk when there's something to say," she said. "But I'd rather sleep on the floor than beside someone who considers me an enemy."

"Not an enemy," Siv said. Okay, he'd implied as much the other day. But still, she was the unreasonable party here. "A liar, maybe," he muttered, not quite under his breath.

"Good night," Dara said. She sat straight down on the floorboards and yanked off her boots.

"Oh yeah?" Siv said, kicking off his own boots. One thudded into the wall with a bit too much force, and someone shouted a curse from the room next to theirs. "Well, what if *I* don't want to share a bed with *you*?"

Dara raised an eyebrow. "That's fine. I'll sleep on the floor."

"Look," Siv said, abandoning that tactic. "We both need a decent night's rest, and you won't get it on the floor. Stop being stubborn."

Dara jutted out her jaw and engaged Siv in a staring contest. He'd seen that before. Dara never broke eye contact because she thought losing one of her little staring contests meant she'd lost the argument. But Siv was on to her. He crossed the floor in two swift steps and swept Dara into his arms like a baby.

She squawked in protest, sounding a little like Rumy, but he held her to his chest and stalked to the bed. His plan to tuck her in backfired a little bit when his injured arm gave out, and he dropped her unceremoniously onto the mattress.

"Okay, fine. We'll share," Dara said, clearly trying to salvage a bit of dignity. "Good night, Your Majesty." And she crawled under the covers and turned her back on him.

Siv gave a satisfied nod and climbed in on the other side. If that wasn't progress, he didn't know what was.

6

RALLION CITY

DAYBREAK found Dara and the others on the road once more. The three Truren lords had brought extra horses for their racing jaunt, so now they each had their own mount. Dara rode Old Fence, whom Lord Bale insisted had taken a liking to her. The horse was the biggest living thing she'd ever seen, except maybe the cullmoran that attacked them back on the mountain. Old Fence had a sleek brown coat the color of strong tea, and his mane was black and flowing. Dara would much rather admire him from a distance than sit on his back, though. She kept a death grip on the leather saddle as they trotted out of the village. His powerful muscles rippled beneath her, bouncing her around with every step.

Siv, on the other hand, rode his dappled stallion as if he'd been born to do it, which she supposed he had. His mother was Truren after all. He sat straight, rolling easily with each step, and chatted amicably with his uncle at the head of their group. Every once in a while he looked back to make sure Dara hadn't fallen off Old Fence, but he didn't speak to her.

Dara had been grateful that exhaustion sent her to sleep before she reached out to him across the bed last night. It grew painful to be near him the closer they got to reuniting with his royal family. They were riding out of the wilderness and back to cold reality. She winced at the thought of the hope she had indulged that night in the cabin, the fragile possibility that they could be together. She had been lulled by his heartbeat, his warmth, his arms around her. He had shattered that hope the following morning with a few words. *Your father killed half my family, Dara.* He wouldn't forget it, and neither could she.

But Dara was tied to Siv. They had been through a lot together, saved each other's lives. If anything, she cared more for him now than she ever had. She couldn't leave him, even though it would be better for her heart to keep her distance. So she tried desperately to resume her role as his bodyguard. They had been polite to each other that morning, and she had literally jumped out of bed when she felt tempted to pull him close.

Siv turned back to check on her again. She avoided his gaze, reaching down to give Old Fence a tentative pat. The creature huffed, his huge body expanding beneath her, and she quickly resumed her grip on the saddle.

Lords Bale and Firnum rode on either side of her, proving to be pleasant travel companions. They shared the courtly gossip from Rallion City and the latest rumors about the Soolen army's movements in the mysterious depths of Cindral Forest.

"The forest dwellers are still giving them trouble, I hear," Lord Firnum said gruffly.

"Do you think they'll invade Trure next?" Dara asked.

"If they dare, our cavalry will teach them the error of their ways," Lord Bale said.

"Maybe." Lord Firnum didn't sound entirely convinced. "At any rate, they'll stay put until spring. We don't get much snow, but the plains get mighty soggy in the winter rains."

"I sure hope the rains are better this year than last," Lord Bale said. "My estate had a hard year, and the wife has expensive tastes."

"I reckon your racehorses are more expensive than her fancy dresses, Bale," said Lord Firnum.

"Perhaps." Lord Bale chuckled. "But they're so darn pretty. I can't help myself."

The conversation turned to the races once more, and Dara let their voices wash over her as they rode deeper into the Land of the Horse Keepers. It was a vast country of gently rolling hills and wide, grassy spaces. She found it hard to judge distances without the familiar boundaries of the three peaks. The dark smudge of Vertigon Mountain was smaller every time she looked back.

By noon, farms patterned the entire landscape. The fields were bare and brown, but Dara imagined they must be beautiful in the spring and summer. Villages sprawled beside the road at regular intervals as they got closer to the capital city. The thatched houses were built in wide, flat shapes with lots of space between them. Paddocks and stables accompanied most of the structures.

The people working the farms and strolling through the villages sometimes looked up to admire their fine stallions. Other riders began to appear on the road, crowding them with the smell of their mounts and the creak of leather saddles. Dara was glad her own horse seemed content to follow its companions. She wasn't sure she could stop Old Fence if he decided to trot off and join another party.

She wished Siv would ride with his head down. She had no idea how far her father's tendrils spread. Siv may have a bandage on his head and a simple cloak around his shoulders, but he sat his horse like a king, and someone was bound to notice. They weren't out of danger yet.

He had bribed Rumy to stay out of sight with a large hunk of meat from the inn's kitchen that morning. Rumy had gobbled it up and taken off, flying high into the clouds. He'd meet them at the royal palace in Rallion City. They didn't want him drawing unnecessary attention on the road. Cur-dragons had a good sense of direction, which was why they often carried messages. He should be able to find his own way.

The sun had passed its zenith by the time they rode over a low ridge and the massive expanse of Rallion City sprawled before them. Tan-and-brown buildings scattered far across the plains, blurring into the distance. Dara thought it must take days to walk from one side to the other. No wonder the Trurens needed so many horses! Oval racing grounds were visible throughout the city. Shops and houses crowded around them like beads rolling toward a dip in the floorboards.

A wide lake interrupted the city sprawl in the west. Its shimmering waters caught the sun, making it look like a pool of silver at the city's edge. The thin, irregular line of a river meandered away from it across the plains. Dara paused to admire the elegant body of water. It was the largest she'd ever seen, impressive even at this distance.

"Azure Lake," said Lord Bale, stopping beside her.

"It's beautiful."

"Indeed. Great place for swimming in the summer too."

"I can't swim," Dara said.

"You can't *swim*?" Siv had dropped back to join them without her realizing. "What about the river?"

"I got lucky," Dara said with a shrug.

Siv stared at her, shock painting his face. Perhaps he hadn't realized how close she was to drowning back in the Oakwind. "But you could have—"

"We made it out," Dara said. "No harm done."

"Well, the lake is nice to look at even if you don't swim," Lord Bale said. "My manor house is right on the shore if you fancy a visit."

Dara thanked him politely, hiding a grin as Siv gaped at her.

"Hurry along, my friends," Lord Tem called. "I fancy a bath before dinner."

They spurred their horses forward and rode down the ridge. The outer borders of the city weren't clearly marked. The sprawl of houses and taverns simply thickened alongside the road, the trickle of people slowly becoming a crowd.

Dara couldn't believe she'd fled down the snowy mountain mere days ago and now she was riding a massive horse through the streets of Rallion City. She had never expected to leave Vertigon in all her days.

A mix of Trurens and travelers from the other Lands Below filled the streets. Dara had never seen so many foreigners before. Few people made the trek up to the heights of Vertigon unless they were merchants or visiting dignitaries. Once a year foreign duelists would visit for the Vertigon Cup, but they looked just like Vertigonians in their dueling gear. Here, the people wore a fanciful selection of clothes in strange styles, the fabrics light and ethereal. It was warmer on the Horseplains than on the mountain, though many people still wore coats in the winter chill. Many of the Truren women had colorful scarves around their heads, the ends floating on the breeze like feathers.

The light Truren eyes were everywhere, and many people had

white-blond or dust-light brown hair to match, almost the same color as their tanned skin. The paler Vertigonians tended to have darker hair—black and dark red and bronze—and brown eyes. Dara's golden hair was less common—though not unique—on the mountain. It looked dark as honey against the pale blonds of Trure. She spotted a few dark-complexioned Soolens from the sun-drenched peninsula to the south. They moved warily through empty patches in the crowd, as if they carried the weight of their country's recent aggressions on their shoulders.

The road was broad and dusty, with shops lining it on either side. The wares on display included colorful textiles, unfamiliar foods, and saddles in every style imaginable. Dara spotted a shop advertising Vertigonian Fireworks and metals. Another sold Fire Lanterns. She didn't look closely enough to see if any of them were Ruminor Lanterns.

The clang and hiss of furriers competed with the clop of hundreds of hooves and the murmur of strangely accented voices. None of the people milling alongside the main road paid any heed to the five mounted members of their party. With any luck, they would go unnoticed despite the hundreds of eyes sliding over them as they passed.

It took an hour to ride to the city center. Deep within the sprawl was an inner ring surrounded by high brick walls. The massive gates stood open, allowing people to pass in and out freely. Armed guards patrolled high towers on either side of the entrance, alert and tense despite the open gates. The afternoon sun reflected off their burnished bronze armor.

Dara tightened her grip on Old Fence's reins as they approached the gates. She focused on breathing calmly, her hand on her Savven blade. After the events of the past week, she didn't trust anyone, whether they worked for Siv's grandfather or not. Siv himself didn't even glance at the guards, apparently confident that all was well.

They passed the inner city walls without being challenged. As soon as they were through the gates, Lord Bale bid them farewell.

"You still owe us another race, Lord Tem," he said.

Siv's uncle grinned, showing off a row of perfect white teeth. "Wouldn't miss it."

"I'll send a man to pick up Old Fence later, my lady." Lord Bale bowed in his saddle to Dara. "I hope he has served you well."

"Um, I could walk from here if you—"

"Not at all. One never approaches the royal palace on foot."

Dara inclined her head, wishing he would take the horse back already. "Thank you, my lord."

"A pleasure," Lord Bale said. "If you and His Royal Highness wish, do visit my manor. My wife and I would be honored to host you."

"Thank you, Lord Bale," Siv said, guiding his horse closer to Dara. "We'll have to speak with my grandfather before we accept any social invitations. I must ask you not to mention my presence in the city to anyone."

"Of course not, Sire." Lord Bale studied Siv for a moment, a pensive expression on his face, then he nodded and set off down the street. Lord Firnum grumbled a more-abbreviated farewell and rode in the other direction.

Dara, Siv, and Tem continued through the city proper, climbing a gentle slope toward the palace. The buildings in the inner circle were larger than in the rest of the city, much like the finest greathouses in Vertigon located on King's Peak. Dara assumed this was where the nobility lived.

There were racing grounds here too. They passed a large arena mere blocks from the royal palace. A race had recently ended, and spectators streamed out of the gates and around their horses, chattering and laughing. Siv fell back beside Dara as they rode alongside the racecourse, allowing Lord Tem to ride out of earshot. The babble of the crowds helped to cover his words.

"I'd like you to stay with me when I speak to my grandfather and mother," he said.

"Yes, Your Majesty."

He sighed at the honorific and pressed on. "I don't know how much control I'll have over what happens here, but we need to emphasize that you're on my side, not your father's."

"I thought you weren't sure about that."

Siv fiddled with his reins, and his horse danced closer to her.

"None of this was your fault, Dara," he said. "I'm just . . . it's a lot to get my head around."

"I know." Dara resisted the urge to reach out to him. She was his guard, nothing more. Pain tightened in her chest. "It's hard for me too."

"Truce for now?"

"Always."

Siv hesitated for a moment.

"You really can't swim?"

"Nope."

"I'd better teach you before our next deadly adventure."

He flashed a grin and squeezed his knees to urge his horse forward. Dara started, grabbing Old Fence's saddle lest he spook. The animal tossed his head and ambled after the two lords.

Dara forgot all about horses and swimming lessons as they turned a bend in the road and she got her first good look at the royal palace.

It was a wide building constructed of massive blocks of light-rose stone, with low walls and two identical towers rising on either side of a flat center. Obviously not built for defense, the palace had large windows, many of them standing open to let in the crisp breeze. Beautifully manicured gardens filled the grounds right up to the pink stone of the palace itself. Winter roses bloomed in the gardens, their sweet aromas mingling with the ever-present scent of horses.

A stone balustrade bordered the flat rooftop space between the two towers. Dara caught a glimpse of leaves trailing over the edge high above them. Perhaps a rooftop garden? The overall effect was of a flower box overflowing with life, even in the depths of winter.

The gates swung open for them, and the guards greeted Lord Tem. Still on horseback, they approached the steps leading to the palace doors, which were carved from a white wood Dara had never seen before. She had no time to look at the carvings before the doors burst open and a teenage girl flew out of them at top speed.

Siv dismounted so fast he was almost falling. He only made it to the second step before his youngest sister, Selivia, threw her arms around his neck with a shriek. She had a bright-yellow scarf over her dark, curly hair, and she looked as if she'd grown another inch during the past few weeks.

"What are you doing here?" she demanded, laughing through her tears. "I've been going crazy here all alone. Uncle Tem sent word you were coming. I haven't been able to sit still for hours. What took you so long? Have you set a date for your wedding? Where's Sora?"

Dara stayed on her horse, hands clutched tight around the reins. Siv didn't set his sister down, his head still buried in her shoulder as she fired off more questions. Dara found it hard to breathe as she watched her friends, waiting for Siv to deliver the news. She wished Selivia's babble could continue forever, filling the courtyard with joy and light.

Finally, Siv set her back on the steps.

"What happened to your head?" Selivia said, finally taking in his appearance. "You look terrible."

"Let's go inside," he said. "I need to talk to Mother."

"But . . . where's Sora?" Selivia looked over at Dara and her uncle, still waiting on their horses. "Didn't she come with you?"

"Let's go inside," Siv repeated, voice breaking. "It's good to see you, Sel."

Lord Tem helped Dara dismount, and stablemen appeared to whisk away their horses. They followed the king and his sister inside. Princess Selivia was about to turn fourteen. When she left the mountain to visit Trure with her mother, she'd had red streaks dyed in the edges of her hair. The streaks were gone now, and she wore a Truren-style dress with wide sleeves and light ruffles, which floated over the wide sandstone floor as they entered the palace.

A grand space opened directly through the doors, more like a courtyard in the center of the palace than an entrance hall. Potted plants and marble statues were arranged at tasteful intervals around the space. High ceilings stretched far above them, lit by the late-afternoon sun streaming through the large windows. Grand staircases rose on either side of the hall leading to the two towers at either end of the palace.

Their footsteps echoed in the vast hall, and a breeze swirled through the open windows, carrying the scents of the garden. Dara glanced up and noticed that a massive painting covered the entire expanse of the vaulted ceiling. It depicted a magnificent herd of horses crossing a rolling plain. Some of the horses were rider-less. Others carried godlike figures in flowing robes, with bright flowers woven into their hair. At one edge was an illustration of a flat-topped rock, which Dara knew was located in the Far Plains territory to the west. She turned slowly, unable to see the whole painting at once. On the opposite side of the hall from the rock was the green outline of a forest. To the north and south, mountain ranges stretched out of the boundaries of the painting. One of these represented Vertigon and the Burnt Mountains. Her former home.

She felt a hand in hers. "Isn't it pretty?" Princess Selivia said.

"It's stunning," Dara said.

"You have to lie flat on your back to enjoy it."

"Maybe later." Dara pulled her gaze away from the painting and the vast, foreign land it represented. She felt very small.

"Why is Siv so sad?" Selivia asked quietly. "And you too. What happened?"

"I'm sorry, Princess," Dara said. "I shouldn't—"

"Sivarrion! What has happened?" A new voice echoed across the immense hall, and a woman hurried toward them from the grand staircase to their right. She was tall and bright cheeked, with light Truren eyes. She wore a yellow scarf like Selivia's.

It took Dara a second to realize that this was Tirra, the woman who had been Queen of Vertigon for Dara's entire life—and Siv and Selivia's mother. Here in her home country, Tirra was transformed. Her skin had more color, and her movements had an energy and vitality that had never been there when she drifted through Vertigon like a sad wraith. She wore an elegant gown of sapphire blue and somehow looked more substantial than she ever had before.

She wrapped her son in a hug, and for a moment Dara felt envious. It had been a long time since her own mother had greeted her with such warmth. But she knew the joy on Tirra's face wouldn't last long.

"Mother," Siv said, pulling back and taking her hands gently. "I must speak with you and Grandfather immediately. It's about Sora."

"The king is out riding," Tirra said.

"Then maybe we should—"

"Tell me now."

Princess Selivia continued to hold onto Dara's hand as Siv began his tale, clutching her tighter with every word. Servants and attendants passed by every once in a while, and he spoke quietly so his voice wouldn't carry. This grand hall seemed like a strange place to have this conversation. The sheer size of the room made them look powerless and insignificant—as powerless as they had been against Dara's father.

Tirra didn't move as Siv recounted everything that had happened. Lord Tem listened nearby, the blood draining from his face. When Siv got to the part about the swordsmen leaving Sora's room, their blades tipped in blood, Lord Tem sent for a chair and a cup of hot lemon tea for his sister. He eased her into the chair while Tirra stared at nothing, her eyes glassy.

Siv finished his account with their chance meeting with the three lords on the road. He looked deflated, and Dara wished she were near enough to put her hand on his shoulder.

"But . . . you didn't see Sora?" Selivia said in a small voice.

"No, we were unarmed, and there was no way to get into her chambers," Siv said.

"So she could still be alive?"

"Sel . . ."

"If you didn't see her, she's not dead."

"I don't think she could have made it," Siv said. "I'm so sorry."

"You're not the one who should be sorry." For the second time that day, Dara didn't recognize Tirra's voice. It sounded harsh and empty now, like an icy winter wind. "I warned you about the Ruminors. So tell me what *she* is doing here?"

Dara blinked when she realized the former queen was pointing directly at her.

"She wasn't involved," Siv said. "The Rollendars were behind the swordsmen, and her father—"

"Her father!" Tirra shrieked. "I told you to watch out for her father, and you didn't listen."

"She fought against him," Siv said. "The Lantern Maker would have killed me if not for Dara."

"I want her out of my home this instant," Tirra said raggedly. Then she hurled her delicate celadon teacup across the hall.

Dara ducked the flying cup, which shattered on the floor in a thousand pieces. Some of the boiling liquid spattered over her face, but the heat didn't bother her. She knew Tirra was lashing out, looking for someone to blame. She had picked the appropriate target.

"I'll wait outside, Your Majesty," she said, rubbing tea off her face. The scent of lemon rose around her. Tirra was right. She couldn't stay by Siv's side after what her parents had done. She and Siv had barely exchanged a friendly word in days. He probably didn't want her help anyway. The fragments of the cup crunched under her boot as she turned to go.

"No." Siv's voice cut like a blade. "Dara has been trying to protect me all along."

"Your father, Sivarrion," Tirra said. "Your *sister*."

"I—"

"How dare you bring her here!"

"I trust Dara with my life, Mother," Siv said. "If you have a problem with that, we can take rooms elsewhere. You will not tell me whom I can keep by my side. Dara stays."

Dara felt rooted to the tile floor. Siv faced his mother, bandaged and unshaven, but there was no mistaking the command in his voice. He was vouching for her. Did he mean it? Did he truly trust her after everything that had happened? Despite the pain and uncertainty of the past few days, warmth like dragon fire filled her heart.

Tirra stared at her son for a moment, then her face crumpled into tears. Siv's shoulders relaxed, and he swept his mother and sister into a hug. The sounds of their shared grief were soft and heartbreaking.

Dara stayed back to give them space, shifting her feet awkwardly. She was grateful that Siv had spoken up for her. She should have known not everyone in his household would welcome her. Lord Tem laid a hand on her arm, making her start.

"I'll arrange rooms for you and send word to my father the king," he said.

"Thank you, my lord."

"Aye. He's a good lad. He'll need your help in the days to come."

Dara nodded, and Tem strode across the vast expanse of the hall, summoning servants with a snap of his fingers. They would all need help in the days to come.

7

THE KING

S IV felt a little better after a hot bath, though perhaps not as hale and hearty as he would have liked. Following the emotional reunion with his mother and sister, he and Dara had gone to rest and clean up before their audience with his grandfather. A healer came to replace the dressings on his many wounds. Some were starting to scab over, but at least one gash looked red and infected. The healer coated it with a salve that smelled like a mixture of mint and death itself.

When the healer left, Siv lounged on the grand bed in his room—the same one he'd stayed in during visits as a boy—and tried not to fall asleep. He had dreaded delivering the news to Selivia and his mother during the whole journey. Now that it was over, he felt as if a weight the size of a velgon bear had lifted from his chest. He could finally start thinking about their next steps.

Unfortunately, he had no idea what to do. A cavern of uncertainty yawned before him. His initial inclination was to forget Vertigon ever existed. He could live in Trure as an exile, dueling with Dara and racing horses with his uncle and keeping his surviving family close. It wouldn't be a bad life. On the other hand, he wasn't sure he could live with the knowledge that the Lantern Maker ruled his mountain. Besides, he still hated Trure.

Siv rolled off the bed and went to the window to watch the sun sinking low over Rallion City, still wincing with every step. It was cloudy, and shades of amber and purple sailed across the sky as evening descended. From his tower bedroom, he had a good view of Azure Lake, sparkling like a sheet of ice in the distance. Okay, maybe Trure wasn't so bad. It still smelled like horse manure, though, even with the palace gardeners waging constant war on the odor with their year-round flowers. But the sprawling city had a certain charm, colorful both inside and outside the high brick walls.

On the other hand, Siv hadn't seen any of his simpering cousins yet. That would sour him on Trure soon enough. And it wasn't his mountain.

He pulled on his boots and went to fetch Dara for dinner. She had been given a small room beside his, the same one Pool had used during their visits throughout his childhood. A Truren palace guard was stationed outside his door now, the saber at his side appearing more decorative than functional. Siv found himself missing his bodyguard's comforting presence and dour charm as he knocked on Dara's door. Pool had died at the hands of Bolden Rollendar. The fact that Siv had killed Bolden did little to assuage his grief. He wished he could put everything that had ever happened in Vertigon behind him. Well, everything except for Dara.

She emerged from the room promptly, her face shiny and clean. She wore a midnight-blue dress in a Truren style with wide sleeves that opened at the elbows and fell past her knees. She had buckled her sword belt around her waist even here, and it swayed against her hip as she strode beside him. Siv glanced down to admire the sight as they walked, realizing he'd only seen her wear a dress a handful of times before. It looked great on her.

"Siv," Dara said as they headed toward the king's dining chamber. "I wanted to thank you for speaking up for me in front of your mother."

Right. They had serious things to discuss. He shouldn't be looking at her backside.

He cleared his throat. "I meant what I said. You've always been on my side."

"I won't let you down," Dara said.

"I know." Now that he was clean and patched up again, some of the heaviness of their journey lifted. Whatever else happened in the days to come, he would be fine as long as Dara was with him. "Sorry for being grumpy on the road," he said.

Dara grinned. "I was going to go with petulant. But it was a tiring journey. You know, if you worked out more, you wouldn't—"

"Oh, look! We're here." Siv gave her a nudge and darted ahead to the wide double doors leading into his grandfather's dining chamber. The twinge of pain at his quick movement reminded him it would still be a while before he could exercise without risking bleeding to death. Dara would just have to run laps without him.

Selivia and his mother were already seated in the dining room. Tirra had changed into a black dress made of the same ruffled material she'd worn earlier, and a matching black scarf covered her hair. Selivia's eyes were reddened from crying, but she hadn't changed out of her bright-yellow dress. She stared at Siv as if daring him to tell her Sora was dead again. The sight made his heart shrivel like a winter pear. Sora and Selivia had been very close.

An oversized table filled most of the large dining chamber, and tapestries and sconces for lanterns and vases appeared at regular intervals along the walls. Most of the dozens of high-backed chairs around the table were vacant. The king's many grown children often visited in the summer season, but most did not live in the palace. He had five daughters, and they kept manors and country estates all across Trure with their noble husbands and offspring. Uncle Tem was one of two sons and the only one of the king's children who remained unmarried.

Siv was relieved to find the room empty of other relatives today. He still wasn't feeling all that well, despite the healer's attentions. Even Uncle Tem had stayed away to give them privacy in which to consult the king. Vertigon had long been Trure's closest ally. But would the usurpation of the throne be enough cause for Siv's grandfather to march on the mountain? Siv prayed it wouldn't come to that. On the other hand, without Trure's help there was little chance he would ever regain the throne. He needed an alternative solution.

Siv pulled out a chair for Dara, insisting that she sit beside him. He leveled a steady gaze at his mother when she started to object. He wanted to set a precedent here and now. He would never send Dara away, and it was time he started treating her as his partner and friend, not just his guard. It may be inappropriate, but he was beyond caring about that sort of thing. He was rewarded with a beautiful smile when he dropped into the chair beside her. *Firelord*, she was pretty.

The servants had poured them each a goblet of wine by the time King Atrin made his entrance.

"Sivarrion," he shouted, pushing the double doors back with a bang. "I've heard a tale from Tem. Madness, I say. Vertigon has fallen into madness!"

Siv's grandfather was a tall man, bigger and more muscular than the typical whip-thin riders of Trure. He hadn't lost his muscle in his old age, though he had an extra layer of fat over everything now. He had fierce blue eyes and white hair, still as thick and luxurious as ever.

"We must stop this insanity," the king said as he stomped toward the head of the table. He pounded it with his fist so hard the goblets shook. "I will not have this outrage against my family. We march on the mountain at once!"

Dara's mouth dropped open. Siv gestured for her not to worry. This was just the way his grandfather was: all hyperbole and bluster. And rage. There was plenty of rage in the man.

"Hello, Grandfather. It's good to see you."

"Good? *Good!* This insult will not be tolerated. I will pull down these usurpers and drag them behind my stallion for the length and breadth of the plains!"

"Father," Siv's mother began.

"Don't 'father' me, Tirra," King Atrin boomed. "I should never have sent you to that blasted frozen mountain. These blackguards will feel the wrath of Trure. They dare insult me! I will not tolerate it for an instant. Who are the dung smugglers responsible for this outrage?"

"It was a combined effort by House Rollendar and the Fireworkers, led by Rafe Ruminor the Lantern Maker," Siv said.

"Ruminor?" King Atrin strode back to the door and banged on it with the strength of a terrerack bull. The doorman pulled it open and immediately leapt to attention.

"Your Majesty?"

"I order you to find every Ruminor Lantern in the city and have them destroyed. Send them all straight to the Ammlen Ocean and cast them into the waves. Let them burn for eternity at the bottom of the sea!"

"At once, Your Majesty," the doorman said.

"Now that's done, tell me your plan, Sivarrion." The king stomped back across the dining hall. Before Siv could answer, his grandfather paused at a sconce where a Fire Lantern hung, shuddering from the force of his footsteps. "Is this a Ruminor Lantern?"

"I don't kn—"

But the king had already torn it from the sconce with his bare hands. He carried it to the door, light spilling out around his feet.

"This one too!" he shouted and hurled the lantern through the door.

"Maybe you shouldn't tell him my name," Dara whispered in Siv's ear.

He chuckled. "He'll calm down. The doorman will probably put that lantern right back where it came from, and Grandfather won't even notice it tomorrow. This is just how he is."

King Atrin stalked back across the dining hall to the head of the table. Siv and the others stood respectfully until he sat. Siv's limbs shook a bit as he lowered himself back into his chair. Strange. His sister gave him a curious look.

"Well, what are you waiting for?" King Atrin roared, making Selivia flinch. "Bring out the meat, and start talking."

Siv told his story again as his grandfather attacked a whole roast pig with gusto. It was getting easier to recount what had happened. With each repetition, the events became a little more real in his mind. A little more inescapable. He glossed over the part about Dara in this telling, focusing on Zage Lorrid's final actions to save them from the Lantern Maker. He gave Dara only the briefest mention as a member of his Castle Guard. His grandfather's sharp eyes missed nothing, but he seemed to decide they could go into more detail about the young woman at Siv's side another time.

At the end of the tale, his mother spoke. "I don't want you to go back there. I never want another one of my children to set foot on that mountain again. You are safe here. Let that be the end of it."

"Now just a minute, Tirra," King Atrin said. "My grandson is a king. He can't give up his kingdom without a fight!"

"There was already a fight," Siv said. "We lost. We don't have the resources to move against the Fireworkers yet, not without heavy casualties."

"I'll show those dung-eating firelovers casualties," the king growled.

Dara shifted beside him.

A knock sounded at the door, and a rider rushed in with a harried look on his face.

"Cur-dragon, Your Majesty!" he shouted.

"Oh, that's Rumy," Siv said. "He's with me."

"Beg pardon, Sire. Your pet arrived a few hours ago. We've just now had another one. The horses are quite upset, my king. But the lizard brought an urgent message from Vertigon."

"Stop your blathering, and give it to me," the king said.

The rider crossed the room and handed over a leather tube tied with a Firegold ribbon. The king pulled out the parchment rolled inside and held it up to the light. His eyebrows slowly disappeared into his luxurious white hair as he read. Siv and Dara exchanged glances. The letter didn't appear to be lengthy, but the king stared at it for a very long time.

"Well," he said after what felt like the world's longest pause. "This is an interesting development." He handed the parchment across the table to Siv. "Read it out, son."

Siv took the message, trying to figure out what his grandfather's expression meant. The king fixed him with piercing blue eyes that seemed to look beyond him, calculating the repercussions of whatever news the letter brought. Siv lifted the thick piece of parchment and read aloud.

To His Royal Highness King Atrin of Trure,

I regret to inform Your Majesty that the reign of King Sivarrion Amintelle, the Fourth King of Vertigon, has come to a tragic end at the hand of an assassin. It is believed the perpetrator acted on orders from the Kingdom of Soole. This is an unforgivable act of aggression. As the newly appointed Chief Regent of Vertigon, I call upon our strongest ally, the noble King of Trure, to assist us in answering this outrage lest Soole continue to threaten the sovereignty of Vertigon and its allies.

With regards,

Rafe Ruminor, Fire Warden and Chief Regent

When he finished reading, Dara tugged the paper from Siv's fist and studied her father's signature intently.

"He's trying to blame Soole," she said. "Why would he do that?"

King Atrin rose from his chair and slammed a hand down on the table.

"This damned Lantern Maker thinks he can provoke me into a war."

"He's starting wars now?" Siv said. His head had begun to feel hot and clouded, and his wounds itched worse than zur-wasp stings. But one thing was clear: "We have to get rid of him."

"I won't do this usurper's dirty work for him," King Atrin said. "However, I cannot march on Vertigon."

Siv met his grandfather's eyes, not surprised by the sudden swing from raging about vengeance to refusal. King Atrin knew what would come of assaulting the sheer slopes of the mountain. But without his help, Siv didn't stand a chance of retaking Vertigon. He scratched at the stitches on his ribs.

"I can't return at the head of a foreign army, even one from Trure, anyway," Siv said. "I think our best option is to retake the castle with a small attack force—if you can lend me the men." He had gotten at least one thing from Bolden besides a body full of stab wounds: the idea for an alternative solution.

The king tapped his knife against the meat board, glowering at the pork bones. Siv waited for his grandfather to work through the rest of his rage. His anger burned bright, but underneath was a shrewd ruler who would not make a rash decision. At least not too rash.

"Vertigon is strong," King Atrin said at last. "You're my flesh and blood, and I'm sorry you lost your throne, Sivarrion, but we can't get into a conflict with the mountain. Not with Soole breathing down our necks."

"I have to go back somehow," Siv said. His grandfather may not want to help him, but he realized now that he had no choice. He had failed his sister, but he would not leave Vertigon in the Lantern Maker's clutches. Especially when he was already stirring up trouble. "Again, it needn't be an all-out assault," Siv said. "If you could lend me a handful—"

"My answer is no," King Atrin said.

"But what about Sora?" Selivia asked, sitting forward anxiously. "Dara, do you think maybe your father is keeping her a prisoner?"

"Father?" King Atrin said.

Dara gulped audibly. "I—"

"*Father?*"

"This girl is a Ruminor," Tirra said. "I want her out of the palace."

Siv raised a hand to forestall his mother. He noticed his fingers were vibrating a bit. That was odd. His head somehow felt hot and cold at the same time.

"Dara will come with me," he said. "And we'll be gone soon enough. In fact, we should leave tonight."

"You cannot return, Sivarrion," Tirra said.

"I won't abandon the mountain."

"Siv, maybe it's not such a good idea," Dara said. She was giving him a peculiar look, as if she was worried about *him* rather than the revelation of her identity.

"I have to try," Siv said. He felt as if they were going around in circles. A mist was slowly forming in his brain. Why did his wounds still hurt so much? He tried to stand, his body feeling heavy. "I . . . I need fighting men."

"Stop!" King Atrin said, leaping to his feet.

"Grandfather—"

"Don't 'grandfather' me," the king said. "I received a report from the healer. You have an infected stab wound. You've been on a grueling journey. You are in no condition to launch an assault on Vertigon."

"But—"

"Do not interrupt me." The king stabbed his knife into the meat board with a thunk. "We can talk after we gather more information. I may reconsider your request, but I won't have you running off into the night when you are unwell."

"But—"

"This Lantern Maker is trying to provoke a war!" the king roared, making the tapestries shudder. "He insults the alliance I gave my own daughter to secure! I will rip his head from his shoulders for his audacity, but I will not rush into action."

Siv wanted to argue, but his grandfather uttered an animal growl and stalked from the room. Siv started to stand to go after him, but Dara pressed her knee against his under the table. He wasn't sure if she meant to keep him in place or to steady his shaking limbs.

The mist seemed to thicken in Siv's mind, and he realized he was feverish. *Oh, right. That must be the infection.*

"Siv," his mother began. He raised a hand—or tried to until his muscles seized up.

"I will rest now," he announced regally, avoiding Dara's intense gaze. There was no sense in admitting that his grandfather's healer was right. *Damn*, his wounds hurt. "And then we're going to figure out a way to help Vertigon."

He pulled himself to his feet and lurched to the door. Dara joined him, slinging his arm over her shoulder without a word. Okay, maybe he did need time to recover, but he would make up for leaving his mountain somehow. And he would rescue Vertigon from the clutches of the Lantern Maker, even if it killed him.

8

THE FOUNTAIN

SORA prepared to leave the castle for the first time since her brother died. She put on her thickest winter cloak, wrapping it around her shoulders like armor. It was a deep purple that made her think of royalty, even though she didn't feel particularly regal. She tucked a stray curl out of her eyes and took a deep breath. *You can do this,* she told herself. *You'll do what you have to do.*

She had been out of her room a few times now, always to greet the associates of the Lantern Maker and his wife in one of the castle parlors. This was the first time she would go out among her people, though. She hoped she was ready. At the last possible moment, she set the Amintelle crown on her head, standing a little straighter to hold up its cold weight.

She exited her antechamber and found half a dozen Castle Guards waiting to accompany her. All of them wore the crisp blue uniforms her brother had commissioned for his squad of duelists known as the New Guard. Her hands closed into fists at the sight.

Captain Thrashe, the Soolen guard with the eye patch, delivered instructions to an unfamiliar Vertigonian man with an officer's knot on his shoulder. The Vertigonian saluted and led the way toward the stairs. Captain Thrashe remained behind. Apparently he didn't want to be seen outside the castle. It would be hard to maintain the ruse that the rightful queen held Vertigon if she were guarded by foreign soldiers.

At first Sora didn't even want to look at the guards surrounding her, wearing New Guard blue. These must be the mysterious swordsmen who had been involved in her brother's downfall. She was sure stupid Lord Bolden Rollendar would never have been able to defeat Siv on his own. The traitor who stabbed her brother could be standing right beside her. She forced herself to breathe calmly. She had a job to do today.

But as they marched down the stairwell from her tower and rounded a corner at the bottom, one of the guards caught her eye. He was the tallest man she had ever seen. She stopped short.

"You were on my brother's New Guard," she said. "You're one of Dara's duelists."

"Yes, Your Majesty." The tall man bowed. He had a kind face and sad eyes. "My name is Oatin Wont."

Sora looked more closely at the other guards. Two of them had also been members of Dara's hand-selected team: a man with a red beard, a bandage poking out from beneath his sleeve, and the former soldier Telvin Jale. A sickening feeling of betrayal rose like bile in her stomach.

"You serve the Lantern Maker so easily?" Sora asked, trying not to look at Jale in particular. She had thought him so noble once—not to mention handsome.

"Your Majesty, we are under guard as much as you are," Oat said. He nodded to the lead guard with the knot of rank, a man with deep-bronze hair and a weather-beaten face who was listening to every word. He was definitely Vertigonian, as were the remaining two. There wasn't a Soolen guard in sight now.

"We have been assigned to accompany you on public excursions," Oat explained, "so the people will know you're being cared for by your brother's loyal men."

"I see," Sora said. On closer scrutiny, she realized Oat, Telvin Jale, and the red-bearded man carried empty sheaths instead of weapons. So they were part of the show. This day was going to be one big farce. She sighed. "Carry on."

She and the six guards marched into the castle entryway, striding right past the Great Hall. The doors stood open, but all evidence of the ill-fated engagement feast had been removed. The tables were pushed back against the walls, and the throne stood on the dais as it

Dance of Steel

had for as long as she could remember. Sora looked away as she followed her guards through the front doors and out of the castle.

The courtyard glistened with ice. A warmer day had followed the recent blizzard, and some of the snow had melted and then refrozen, encasing every tree with a thin layer of glass. The sun sparkled on the ice, and it would have been beautiful in other circumstances. Sora pulled her grand purple cloak closer around her and strode along a path that had been melted through the snow.

Halfway across she slipped, feet skidding on a patch of ice. A guard reached out to catch her before she fell. He hadn't been on the New Guard, so he must be one of the Lantern Maker's men.

"All is well, Your Majesty," he said. And he gave her a wink as he steadied her.

Sora frowned. She recognized him after all. Kelad Korran was a duelist sponsored by Lord Bolden Rollendar. Selivia had had a huge crush on him, along with half of the young ladies in the city. He must be one of the swordsmen who had conspired to attack her brother. She pulled her arm roughly out of his grasp.

If Kel noticed her strong reaction to him, he didn't let on. He simply returned to scanning the courtyard, keeping an eye on the three guards who had been loyal to her brother. He was wiry and strong, though only a few inches taller than Sora herself. *He* carried a sword, the Rollendar House sigil glinting on the pommel. She wondered if Oat, Telvin, and the red-bearded guard would have a chance against Kel and his two companions. No, the red-bearded guard moved stiffly and appeared to be injured, and Kel was supposed to be among the best young duelists in Vertigon. Her guard had clearly been selected with care.

The Lantern Maker's wife, Lima Ruminor, met them outside the castle gates. A luxurious fur muff warmed her hands, and she stood tall and regal in the snow. Sora could easily see the resemblance to Dara. They had similar height and handsome features, though there was a cruel sharpness to Lima's thin lips.

"Did she give you any trouble, Lieutenant Benzen?" she asked.

"Not at all, Madame Ruminor," answered the bronze-haired Vertigonian officer. Apparently he didn't consider the fact that Sora had been chatting with her guards-under-guard to be troublesome. Maybe she could use that.

"Good. Are you ready?" Lima said.

Sora inclined her head, the crown slipping forward slightly. "I know what I have to say."

"Keep in mind that we will have Fireworkers on hand should you try anything. Can we expect any trouble from you?"

"No. I will adhere to our agreement," Sora said hollowly.

"See that you do."

Lima turned and led the way down the icy steps into Lower King's Peak. In their few interactions, Lima had never referred to Sora with an honorarium, not even a standard "my lady." If she wasn't mistaken, Lima herself wasn't a Fireworker at all. Sora wondered where she got her confidence. And her bitterness.

Lima was right to be wary, though. Today Sora would come face to face with some of her family's longtime supporters—the very people the Ruminors must have been worried about when they decided to establish her as their figurehead. So far Sora had met with several groups of nobles chosen from among the Ruminors' allies. Her captors had tested whether she would speak out against them before they risked displaying her in front of a wider audience. But today she would prove whether or not she'd be a good little puppet.

Sora hadn't dared ask any of the nobles for help yet. She had a pretty good idea which ones had supported the usurpation plot led by House Rollendar. The Zurrens, the Samanars, and of course the Denmores and Ferringtons were at the top of the list. The Ruminors may not realize how well informed she was, though. Sora had made a habit of paying close attention to the friendships among the nobility for years now. None of the visitors she'd received so far would offer her any assistance. She hadn't even tried, and hoped the Ruminors would take that for cooperation.

Still, the Ruminors had to show the rest of the mountain that Sora was indeed alive and well. So this afternoon, they had arranged for her biggest test yet.

The temperature dropped as they descended the long steps from the castle, and the wind drove ice across Sora's cheeks. She kept her head high, knowing that the people must be watching her from the curtained windows of their dwellings and greathouses as she passed.

She had to show them how Amintelles carried themselves in a crisis. She had to be brave.

The guards were a comfort, even though three of them were prisoners too. They formed a loose box around her, helping to block the wind. Oat's height and Telvin's broad-shouldered form were familiar shapes in her peripheral vision. She could almost imagine that her brother walked beside her, that Lima was Dara, and that they were just out for another stroll on their mountain.

She hadn't seen much of the Lantern Maker over the past few days, but she was starting to get a clearer picture of his plans. He had sent a letter to Sora's grandfather in Trure blaming Soole for her brother's death. It was convenient for him that Soole had so recently made aggressive movements beyond their boundaries. But Rafe had also sent a letter to the royal family in Soole itself, not so subtly blaming the city-state of Pendark for the assassinations and suggesting that a new alliance between Soole and Vertigon would be welcome. There had been swordsmen from Soole amongst her brother's attackers, and until this excursion all her guards had been Soolen too.

Rafe was playing a dangerous game in trying to provoke both Trure and Soole—and in getting Pendark involved—especially while apparently working with Soolen allies. She wasn't sure of his end goal yet, but it went far behind pulling the strings behind the throne of Vertigon. He wanted to extend his influence into the Lands Below, something that no Vertigonian leader had attempted for centuries.

He'd also made her sign edicts granting noble status to the most-powerful Fireworkers and revoking any restrictions on the flow of the Fire through the mountain. Today, they'd be making that change official.

Despite these hints about Rafe's ambitions, he couldn't move too quickly. He still had to show the people that all was well and that Vertigon remained stable. Sora's contingent of Vertigonian guards—most of them recognizable sport duelists—would reassure the people that Soole was not in control. Sora wondered whether anyone would figure out her actions weren't her own. She had no idea if she had any friends left on the mountain at all.

Sora and her entourage processed through Lower King's Peak,

collecting a small following of curious onlookers. They reached a broad, sloping avenue lined on either side with shops. They continued their slow parade all the way to the end, where a stone fountain was situated above a small cliff. A semicircle of stone seats cut into the slope above the fountain, forming a small amphitheater in the hillside where people could sit and enjoy the view when the weather was good.

The fountain had been dry for as long as Sora could remember. Snow piled within its low stone basin, and ice glistened on the statue rising above it. The statue was shaped like a Firewielder of old, her hands raised high over the outlook. She wore a long cloak, and holes in the palm of each hand indicated where water had once flowed into the basin. The statue's face was rubbed smooth with age, leaving only a hint of a strong jaw and a high, proud forehead.

A few people already sat on the stone steps facing the fountain, their hands wrapped around Heatstones to protect against the cold. She recognized old Lord Silltine and Lords Roven and Farrow, among others. Those three houses had long been loyal to the Amintelles. A handful of influential merchants who'd enjoyed great prosperity under her family's rule were here too, skepticism carved in their furrowed brows and thinned lips. The well-connected Lady Atria sat with this group, wearing a scarlet cloak, the edges dusted with snow.

The nobles stood as Sora approached with her guards. Lord Silltine's wrinkled face was placid, and he kept his arms wrapped tight beneath his cloak, as if to steady shaking hands. Lord Roven looked at her with concern and pity. He hadn't brought his wife or young daughter to this event, even though Sora knew they had been invited. He and the others must still be wondering exactly who ruled Vertigon now. How much did they know about what had happened a few days ago? And if she called on them, would they help her?

They may not be effectual even if they wanted to assist her. Carefully placed beside each nobleman or lady was a Fireworker. Raising the status of the Fireworkers had been one of the primary goals behind the coup. The Workers looked incongruous beside the nobles, with their cloaks bearing house sigils. In many cases the Fireworkers' clothing was just as fine as the nobles', but where the nobles were wary, smug triumph painted every Fireworker's face.

Master Corren, a Firegold spinner and known ally of the Ruminors, looked as happy as if it were his birthday.

Rafe Ruminor himself stood beside the snow-covered fountain, wearing a coat of a deep red that was almost black. Firegold embroidery curled around the high collar. He had a regal presence, drawing every eye. The sun caught his golden and white hair, making it glimmer like a crown. Sora resisted the urge to reach up and touch the crown resting on her own head.

Rafe nodded at his wife, and Lima bent down to whisper in Sora's ear.

"Do not deviate from the speech we prepared."

"I know."

"Do you have it memorized?"

"Of course." Sora lifted her chin and strode forward. She didn't have to grasp for anger to combat her fear now. It flooded her like rain in a gully. She was about to betray everything her family had stood for over the past century, and she had no recourse to resist. "Good afternoon, my lords and ladies. Thank you for coming out in the cold for this special ceremony."

A wave of bows swept through the little crowd. More onlookers gathered to see what was going on.

"As you know, I lost my father several months ago, and my brother perished last week in attacks by a company of assassins from Soole." Sora repeated the words she had memorized, her voice sounding small as it disappeared into the mountain air. "I wish to thank each of you for the condolences you have sent to the castle over the past few days." She hadn't seen any of these notes of condolence herself, but Lima had told her to mention them. "It is my deepest wish that I will be able to serve Vertigon as the Amintelle family has for generations. In that spirit, I have asked Lantern Maker Ruminor to advise me in the days to come as my Chief Regent."

Rafe bowed his head, not quite managing to look humble. He would no doubt be perceived as a reliable leader next to a short, round-cheeked teenage girl. Sora wished she could speak without her voice shaking. But whether fear or anger had greater prominence, she couldn't achieve the icy calm she'd hoped for.

"As you all know, Vertigon owes its status as one of the great kingdoms to the presence of the Fire and the noble efforts of the

Fireworkers." She glanced at the Workers in the crowd. Master Corren fingered the Firegold embroidery on the sleeve of his fine coat, grinning widely. Lord Roven met her eyes, his face a flat mask.

"With the help of the Fire," Sora continued, "we can make sure Vertigon remains strong in the face of Soole's attempts to harm us. As one of the first acts of my reign, I have decided to acknowledge the great work of those who tamed our Fire. I have granted nobility to all Fireworkers who can wield the power at a high level—as determined by the Chief Regent—and I look to them to shore up our defenses against the forces of Soole. The greatest amongst the Wielders will henceforth be full members of the royal court."

Mutters broke out amongst the nobles. It may have sounded like a simple statement, but with these words Sora was changing the entire balance of power in Vertigon. The speech glossed over the part about only the strongest Workers attaining nobility. Rafe had already given her a list, and she had little doubt it only contained his closest allies.

"My . . . my father planned to carry out this very edict before he died."

Lima gave her a sharp look, and Sora fought to keep her features neutral. Her father most certainly had *not* planned any such thing. Lying about his wishes felt like an insult to his memory, but she had no choice right now. "As a symbol of our renewed strength, and in memory of my father and brother, I have gathered you here to rededicate the Fountain of Pala."

Sora turned to the worn stone figure. She couldn't bear to make eye contact with any of the Workers or nobles anymore. They must know now that her actions were not her own. The question was whether they would take a stand against the Fireworkers to help her. She didn't know if any of them believed as strongly as her father had that the Workers needed to be controlled. Setting them loose was a dangerous thing. But there was nothing she could do to stop it. Yet.

Rafe drew himself up, and the muttering crowds fell silent. He stretched a hand toward the stone statue in the center of the fountain, not quite touching it. He kept his eyes open and focused on the figure with the intensity of a master craftsman.

At first they heard nothing. Rafe stared at the statue of Pala, his face like iron. Stillness reigned on the mountainside. Then a few of the Workers began to murmur, as if they could sense something happening. Something powerful. Sweat beaded on the Lantern Maker's high forehead. Still, he didn't move.

Then the statue began to vibrate. Sora's heartbeat quickened. The nobles muttered behind her. Feet scraped nervously against stone. The vibrations intensified, and a low rumble built within the mountain. Sora clenched her fists to keep her hands from trembling.

Suddenly, the snow filling the basin around the fountain melted rapidly, turning to water and then to steam. Heat poured over Sora's face, but she didn't step back from the fountain. She had agreed to the Lantern Maker's demands. She could not retreat now.

A groan came from deep within the earth. The ground around the fountain warmed up, sending needles of heat through Sora's legs. More snow melted, spreading outward from the fountain in a ring. Sora glanced at the nobles, who shifted uneasily on the hot stones. Lord Silltine took a few tottering steps away from his seat and bumped into Telvin Jale, who reached out to steady the old man.

Sora looked back at the stone fountain and the Lantern Maker. Sweat bathed Rafe's forehead now, and his eyes burned as bright as Firegold for an instant.

Then the statue of Pala gave a mighty shudder, and Fire burst from its fingertips. The molten magic glowed hot, shimmering in the cold air. It streamed from the holes in the stone hands where water used to flow and splashed down into the basin. Rafe turned over his hands as if he were directing music, and the Fire swirled around and around the basin in a glistening whirlpool. There were gasps from the watching crowd. The Fire gleamed like liquid gold.

Heat blasted Sora like wind, but she still didn't step back. Gradually, the shaking in the earth subsided.

The Fire spewing from the statue slowed to a steady trickle. The basin had filled almost to the brim. Rafe nodded as the flow steadied. He must have solidified the Work somehow, so the Fire could pour from the fountain but not overflow.

He turned to Sora. "It is done."

She nodded, fear slipping through her at the triumph in his eyes. She knew he had done much more than create a fountain. Deep within the mountain, the magical containment system designed by her forefathers had been destroyed. Rafe had unleashed the Fire to roar through the mountain once more, ready to be claimed by those with the strength.

She addressed the onlookers again.

"Let this fountain be a memorial to our departed kings and a symbol of a bright new future in Vertigon. The Fire has been freed from the channels that once restricted it. Those who have the strength can Wield it at will and help to keep our mountain strong."

Applause spread through the crowd, polite from the nobles and joyous from the Fireworkers. A short Worker with wispy white hair and muscular arms wiped a tear from the corner of his eye. Another rubbed her hands together eagerly. Lords Roven and Farrow exchanged worried glances. They knew what had happened here today.

"Long live Queen Soraline," Rafe said. Then he gestured for Lieutenant Benzen to escort her back to the castle. She had played her part. A new era in Vertigon had begun.

9

THE GUARD

SORA glowered at the snow beneath her shoes as she trudged back toward the castle. She had hoped to stay behind after the fountain dedication to speak to some of the nobles. They had to figure out how to work against the Lantern Maker. She couldn't defeat him through sheer strength, but she wouldn't allow him to keep her as his puppet forever. She needed allies.

But Lieutenant Benzen had ushered her away from the newly awakened fountain immediately, leaving the Lantern Maker and his wife to speak to the crowd of onlookers and accept the congratulations of the Workers.

At the very least, Sora had hoped to speak to Lady Vine Silltine, whom she considered a friend. But the noblewoman hadn't accompanied her elderly father to the ceremony. That was unusual. Old Lord Silltine rarely went out without his daughter. He seemed to have left early anyway. The last Sora remembered seeing him was when he bumped into Telvin Jale as he eased away from the spreading ring of heat.

They left the broad avenue and took the road past the old Fire Warden's austere marble greathouse. She wondered which Worker Rafe had assigned to watch over the Well deep beneath it. He and his wife had taken up residence in the castle. Perhaps it didn't matter who lived above the Well now that the Fire had been freed from the containment system invented by her great-grandfather. She wondered if the spectators truly grasped what they had witnessed today. She herself was terrified of the repercussions.

The six guards surrounded Sora in a loose formation as they climbed the ice-slicked streets. After the Fire Warden's dwelling, they passed the smaller Atria greathouse beside it. The sun hadn't set yet, so the parlor at the front of the notorious house was empty. A hint of movement caught Sora's eye. *That's odd.* The front door was open a crack, as if to let in a breeze. Why would Lady Atria want to admit all this biting-cold air?

She glanced at Telvin Jale walking beside her to see whether he had noticed the open door too. That was when she realized the sheath swinging at his hip was no longer empty. Someone had given him a sword.

Hope leapt in Sora's chest. The three actual guards were spread out, with one behind her and Kelad Korran and Lieutenant Benzen in front. Kel rolled his wiry shoulders and coughed.

Then with lightning speed he drew his sword and rammed the Rollendar-marked pommel down on the back of Benzen's head. The lieutenant dropped like a marionette with its strings cut.

Sora stifled a gasp. The other guards were already moving. Telvin drew his newly acquired blade and thrust it through the throat of the guard behind Sora. A faint gurgle passed his lips, and he didn't even have time to shout a warning. The red-bearded guard hurried forward to help Kel with the man he had knocked out.

"Quickly, my queen," Oat said. He took her arm and pulled her through the open door of House Atria.

Telvin followed, dragging the guard he had killed by the feet. Then came Kel and his companion hauling their unconscious superior. The door snapped shut behind them, plunging them into darkness.

It had taken mere seconds.

The men shuffled around in the darkness of the hallway, grunting and tripping over the bodies of their erstwhile jailers. Then light bloomed in a doorway off the darkened corridor.

"In here," came a familiar voice.

Sora hurried forward, Oat close by her side, and ducked into a small sitting room. Lady Atria waited inside, an Everlight clutched in her hand.

"Are you all right, darling?" she asked. She wore a deep-green gown and the same scarlet cloak she'd had on earlier. Snow clung to her hem. She must have had to run full tilt to get here ahead of them. "My dear Sora, you gave such a lovely speech today. Brought a tear to my eye. Oh, gentlemen, do join us."

The others crowded into the small room, pushing back the table to make room. Telvin offered her a crisp bow, and Sora's cheeks warmed. She felt bad for doubting him earlier. He was decent and noble after all!

"This guy's heavier than I thought," Kel said as he and the man with the red beard dragged their captive through the door. "Whew, thanks for your help, Yuri. Lieutenant Benzen needs to lay off the goat pies." Kel straightened and cracked his back. "Forgive me, my queen. Kelad Korran, at your service."

"But . . . but you were with the Rollendars," Sora said. The reality of what had just happened was dawning on her. She had been rescued!

"I was spying on them for Dara," Kel said. "I got caught, but in the confusion surrounding the death of my liege, your surviving enemies failed to realize I wasn't still on their side. The Lantern Maker decided to put me on the Guard, along with the rest of Bolden's men." He nudged Lieutenant Benzen's prone form with his toe.

"So you weren't one of the men who killed my brother?" Sora asked.

Kel blinked. "Killed . . . My lady, I am loyal to the Amintelles. Besides, I'm not convinced your brother is dead."

"What?"

"I saw him and Dara in the Great Hall during the Lantern Maker's attack," Kel said. "I don't want to get your hopes up, but I definitely didn't see their bodies afterwards. They made a run for it."

Sora clutched the high back of a nearby chair. Was it possible Siv had survived? She barely dared to hope. She couldn't keep her lips from quivering.

"Oh, Sora, darling, I am so sorry this has happened to you." Lady Atria dropped the Everlight onto the table and wrapped Sora in a hug. "Your brother was such a sweet boy."

"*Is*, I reckon," Kel said. "Dara is burning—sorry—*very* tenacious. They won't beat her for long."

"We shouldn't delay any longer, my queen," Telvin said. "We can escort you out of the city. Kel has allies who can help us."

"Allies?" Sora asked

"Plenty of people don't want the Fireworkers to have their way with Vertigon." Kel leaned jauntily against the table in front of her, the Everlight illuminating his handsome face. "And Berg Doban nearly ripped the castle door off its hinges trying to save you the second the Fire Wall around Square came down. He's itching to do something to help."

Sora didn't answer for a moment. She was still processing everything. There was a chance Siv was alive! If he was, though, he had left her behind. Hurt twisted through her at the thought. Perhaps he believed she was dead. But she was safe now. The guards could help her flee the mountain. No more crying through the night and waiting around for the Lantern Maker to bring her more dangerous edicts to sign. No more forced speeches betraying her family's legacy. She could flee to her grandfather's palace and rejoin her mother and sister.

If she wanted, she could probably leave Vertigon behind forever.

Sora frowned, looking around at the four men who had risked their lives to rescue her, even though they were near strangers. Lady Atria's eyes were kind and concerned. These were her people. They were loyal. There had to be more like them in Vertigon, like Kel's allies who didn't want to give the mountain over to the Workers.

She was still an Amintelle—and she was their queen. Her brother had been defeated, his title lost. But Sora held the throne of their fathers. However ceremonial her position was at the moment, she would effectively be abdicating if she walked away now. Would the people still want to help her if she left? It was not as if she could conquer Vertigon with her grandfather's Truren army. She couldn't wrest the crown back without doing irreparable damage to Vertigon. If she relinquished her tenuous hold on the castle, there would be no turning back.

"I can't leave," she whispered.

"What was that, dear?" Lady Atria looked at her quizzically.

"My lady, we want to get you to safety as soon as possible," Oat said. "We don't know what Master Ruminor will do now that he can access as much Fire as he wants."

"That's the point," Sora said. "I can't run away and abandon Vertigon to the Lantern Maker. I need to hold the throne." She was sure Siv would come back for her if he was alive. He hadn't truly left her behind, had he? She couldn't let doubt assail her now. She stood a little straighter. She may be shorter and younger than everyone else in the room, but she was the queen, and this was her decision.

"Sora, darling," Lady Atria said. "I thought you'd be happy for our help."

"I am." She squeezed Lady Atria's hand. "Thank you all for what you've done today. But I have a duty to Vertigon. I have a chance to work against the Lantern Maker from the inside and gather support against him. I can't go now."

The others were silent for a moment. Kel and Oat exchanged worried glances. Lady Atria closed her eyes and sighed, clasping her hands over her expansive bosom. But Telvin Jale studied Sora thoughtfully for a moment. Then he placed the point of his sword on the floor before her and knelt.

"I understand duty, my queen," he said. In the cramped room he was close enough to brush against the folds of her dress. He craned his neck to meet her eyes, one hand placed firmly on the hilt of his sword. "I served Vertigon as a soldier, and I served your family as a Castle Guard. Today, I pledge my life to your service in whatever capacity you need me. If you remain behind, I will do everything in my power to protect you."

"Thank you." A blush rose in Sora's cheeks. No one had ever pledged themselves to her before. But she knew what to do. She placed her small hand over his strong, calloused one and said, "I accept your service. I pledge to carry out my duties as queen and try to be worthy of your honorable vow."

"Thank you, my queen," Telvin said, his voice deep and solemn. Then he climbed to his feet, moving awkwardly around her in the tiny space. Sora's blush deepened.

"You're so noble, Jale," Kel said with a chuckle. "Truly, isn't he a charmer? All right, then. I'll help too."

Sora inclined her head. She didn't know much about Kelad

Korran, and she didn't know why he was doing so much to help her and her family. She was grateful, though.

"What do you think, Lady Atria?" asked Yuri, the red-bearded guard. He turned toward her, looking a bit like an overgrown puppy.

"I think it's magnificent and brave," Lady Atria said. "I was so enjoying hosting this rescue in my home, but I'd be happy to know there's a resistance effort too."

"I still think you should flee, my queen," Oat said quietly. "Your enemies have already shown they're willing to hurt young women. My Luci—one of the guardswomen—was killed during the attack."

"I'm so sorry for your loss." Sora reached up to lay a hand on Oat's shoulder. "You don't have to join me if you're not comfortable with it."

Oat sniffed and straightened. "No, I'll help too. Luci would want me to."

"Glad that's settled," Kel said briskly. "Now, we have to figure out a way to talk ourselves out of this rather compromising position." He nodded to the two guards they had overcome—one dead and one still unconscious.

"How about the partial truth?" Sora suggested. "We can say this man betrayed you and tried to overwhelm the others. He had time to knock out Lieutenant Benzen, but you killed him before he could spirit me away."

"That could work," Kel said. "It would be a shame to blow my cover."

"We'd better hurry," Telvin said. "They'll wonder why we're not back yet."

"I agree," Sora said. "And we'll have to figure out a way to get a message to my grandfather. I'd rather not involve Trure, but I might need his help eventually."

"The Fireworkers have been inspecting all the messages leaving the mountain, but I'll try to arrange something," Lady Atria said. "I have friends in Trure, and it won't be so unusual for them to hear from me."

"Good. That's settled, then." Sora looked around at her little knot of allies. She'd wanted to make a list of people who might help her today. It looked as if she had more friends than she realized. It was a start. "We need to figure out the Lantern Maker's weaknesses. I'll see what I can do from the castle."

Rafe Ruminor had her in his clutches now, but Soraline Amintelle was no puppet. She would figure out some way to work against him from the inside. She couldn't leave the city and allow him to solidify his hold on her kingdom. She was a queen now, and she would not abandon her throne.

10

THE ROOFTOP

DARA'S boots shuffled on the paving stones. Advance. Retreat. Advance, advance. Lunge. She felt limber, and though her muscles still protested the exertion, she grew stronger every day. All she had needed after her encounter with the Fire was lots of rest and food. She'd be as good as new soon.

It was early morning, and the rooftop garden was deserted. She had chosen a spot on a paved pathway between two rows of magnificent rosebushes, some taller than her. It had quickly become her favorite place in the royal palace to do footwork. Her room was too small, and the Grand Hall, though spacious, was usually too busy. She had quickly tired of the servants and guards whispering about her as she worked on regaining her dueling form. Plus, she did everything she could to avoid the attention of Tirra and King Atrin. Their other relatives visited the palace often as well, and they weren't supposed to know she and Siv were there. The rooftop garden suited her nicely.

She hadn't been out into the city at all since they arrived. She worried her parents would send men to bring her back to the mountain. She couldn't risk being seen. She would have liked to explore Rallion City, but at least the rooftop offered a decent view of the sprawl. From here she could see that many of the other buildings had rooftop gardens as well, filling the skyline with greenery. Even the humbler houses had decorative plants growing from their thatched roofs. It must have been magnificent when the flowers bloomed in the spring. Dara wondered if she'd still be here then. She didn't know where else she'd go.

Her Savven blade sliced the air, unnaturally swift. The power in the blade worked with the Firespark in her blood, lending her speed and strength. She leapt back from an imaginary opponent, parried, and lunged again, delivering a series of rapid jabs to the hand, head, heart. Her blood warmed, and her senses felt heightened, her actions empowered.

Suddenly, a hint of color caught her eye, and she whirled, cutting the buds off a few winter roses.

"Easy there. That could have been my eye!"

Siv strode around the rosebush, hands raised in surrender.

"What are you doing out of bed?"

"I'm sure my bed is as tired of me as I am of it," Siv said.

"You're a terrible patient," Dara said, brushing a few strands of sweaty hair out of her eyes. "Didn't the healer say you need at least another week of bed rest?"

"Did she? I was too distracted by the deafening boredom to hear that."

"You need your strength."

"I'm as strong as ever," Siv said. But he eased down to sit on a stone bench beside the pathway that had become Dara's practice strip. He did have more color in his face. The fever he'd undergone after their arrival had been alarming, but he was on the mend. "The infection is gone at least."

"Good." Dara had sat beside him while he was at his most feverish, holding his hand and wishing she could pull away some of the heat. But the Firespark didn't work like that. She wondered if he had known she was there. Tirra had sent her away whenever she caught her by his bedside. At least she hadn't kicked her out of the palace. Yet.

"I figure in another week I'll be ready to ride back to the mountain."

"Siv—"

"I know you think we should give it up, but I can't abandon Vertigon."

Dara sighed. They had been around and around this topic. He wouldn't let it go.

"Do you even have a plan?"

"Yes," Siv said. "You can do a Fire thing."

"A Fire thing?"

"Yeah. I still like my small-attack-force idea, but I know that doesn't solve the whole scary, powerful Fireworker variable. But I have a Fireworker on my side too. You can be damn scary."

Dara snorted. "You have *a* Fireworker. My father has *all* the Fireworkers. And I hardly count. I only started learning a few months ago."

"I didn't say it was a fully formed plan," Siv said. "What do you think?"

"I—"

"Shh. Someone's coming. Hide!"

Siv dove behind a nearby rosebush, gesturing frantically for Dara to join him.

"What does it matter? No one cares if I practice up here."

"It's not you," Siv said, and he disappeared behind the bush.

Footsteps sounded near the entrance to the garden. Dara spotted the palace healer's frizzy white hair through a veil of greenery. She stalked along a row of shrubs with her hands on her hips, occasionally pausing to peer beneath them.

"Let me guess." Dara fought a smile as she joined Siv behind the rosebush, which was large enough to conceal both of them. The scent of roses and dirt drifted around them. "You've been ordered to stay in bed, and you snuck out under your healer's nose."

"You know me well."

"Maybe she's right," Dara said. "You're still weak."

"Am not. See." Suddenly Siv snaked his arms around her waist from behind and lifted her straight off her feet. Dara stifled a squeak, clutching at his wrists. She didn't have time to struggle before he grunted and set her back down again. "Okay, maybe I could use another day or two of rest."

Dara rolled her eyes and peeked around the rosebush to see if the healer was still there. Siv didn't remove his arms from around her. They stood in the shadows, his chest pressed against her back, breath soft in her ear.

The healer paused nearby, her eyes sliding over the roses.

Siv's hands drifted lower on Dara's waist to rest on her hips. Her breath caught in her throat. She leaned back against him slightly, the closeness making her dizzy.

The healer frowned, eyes narrowing.

Siv's scruffy stubble tickled Dara's cheek. She stifled a gasp as his lips brushed her jaw then skimmed down the side of her neck, his touch moth-light on her skin. She didn't dare move.

"How about it?" he whispered against her ear as the healer walked away to continue her search of the garden. Dara barely noticed her departure.

"What?" she said hazily.

"The Fire thing? Do you think you can come up with some sort of move that would work against your father?"

Dara stiffened and pulled Siv's hands from her hips, perhaps a little too brusquely. The moment skittered away from them like a cut bridge line. Surprise flitted through his eyes as she turned to face him.

"I can't go back there," she said.

"But—"

"He's too strong." The image of her father Wielding Fire in the Great Hall flashed before her—a memory drenched in terror and pain. A fierce torrent of panic swept through her. "I can't do it."

"So practice," Siv said. "You're the one who's always telling me you have to work harder to get better at things. Isn't it the same with the Fire?"

"No," Dara said. "Can't you drop it?"

"I've never known you to give up before. I thought we were in this together. You think staying here and practicing footwork will solve anything?" Siv glared at the roses as if this was all their fault. He looked back at her suddenly, pinning her with his gaze. "What are we even doing, Dara?"

Her eyes dropped to his lips before she could help it. His eyes were intent on her face, his body too close. She took a step back.

"You're recovering from your infection," she said. "You should get back to bed before I call the healer." She drew her blade and resumed her dueling stance, all too aware that it would prevent him from drawing her into his arms again. "If you'll excuse me, I have to resume my training."

"What for?" Siv scrubbed a hand through his hair, looking frustrated. "You're not even a duelist anymore."

Dara ignored him, cutting the air with her blade once more. Siv's words hit much too close to the mark. She didn't look at him as he trudged back through the garden.

She couldn't face her father. The idea sent icy panic through her veins. She wasn't sure she ever wanted to touch the Fire again for as long as she lived. But if she wasn't a Fireworker and she wasn't a duelist, what was she?

11

THE RACES

SIV sat in the royal box at the racing grounds and fumed. It had been over two weeks since he arrived in Rallion City, and his grandfather was still no closer to lending him the men he needed to return to Vertigon and remove the Lantern Maker from power. The king could be more stubborn than a bullshell in a salt mine.

It was a relief to get out into the fresh winter air, surrounded by the sounds of the crowd and the smells of Truren sweetmeats and sweating horses. He had hated being bedridden with fever in the royal palace. He'd been restless, grumpy, and far sicker than he wanted to admit. But after enduring the overbearing attentions of his grandfather's healer, he felt almost back to normal now.

The stands around the racing grounds were only half full today. It had rained earlier that morning, keeping many people indoors. The horses raced so often that the stands rarely filled up anyway. The liveliest cheers came from the betting arena sheltered beneath a vast green tent beside the racetrack. The races could be a full-time job for those with high risk tolerance. Siv was tempted to meander over and place a bet, but he hadn't felt particularly lucky lately.

While he'd been confined to his bed, he'd had plenty of time to mull over the options for returning to Vertigon. His best plan was still to sneak into the city with a small group of swordsmen—not unlike the one Bolden had engaged—to conduct the operation. He hoped that would be enough to overcome the guards in the castle. Siv wasn't sure how they'd deal with the Fireworkers themselves, but he felt confident that Dara would come up with something—as soon as she admitted he was right, of course. He had never known her to back down from a challenge.

But King Atrin still resisted the idea of moving against the throne of Vertigon, no matter who held it. He may be offended by the Lantern Maker's efforts to provoke further conflict, but with Soole threatening his eastern border, the king didn't want to risk his alliance with the northern mountain.

Dara didn't think they should go back either. She insisted mere men couldn't defeat the Fireworkers, and the effort would be futile. She may be right that swords were no match for a Fireworker like Rafe Ruminor, but there had to be some way to counter his power.

Siv frowned and picked at a splinter in the railing around the royal box. He had shouted at Dara that morning, truly shouted. They had both been on edge lately, but he had never done something like that before. He'd felt horrible about it immediately. He didn't want to become the kind of man to fly into rages, like his grandfather. But fury had been bubbling within him since he left Vertigon behind. He was angry with the Lantern Maker, with the Rollendar traitors, with his grandfather for refusing to help. More than anything, he was angry with himself for losing in the first place. He couldn't seem to keep from lashing out. He had cursed at the tapestries and tossed cushions across the room a few times in private after his grandfather continued to refuse his petitions, but that morning he had yelled at Dara herself.

She had been trying to convince him not to return to Vertigon. To give it up and start anew.

"I can't believe you want to leave the mountain to him," Siv had said. "You're supposed to be brave."

"He's too powerful," Dara said.

"There has to be a way."

"Look what happened last time." Dara brushed a finger over one of his new scars. He tried to ignore the jolt of heat that went through him at her touch. Being near her spun his brain in the worst way.

"You won't last a day if you go back," she said.

"I have to try."

Siv had pulled away from her to pace in front of the window. The glittering expanse of Azure Lake mocked him in the distance. It would be all too easy to abandon his responsibility to the mountain and stay there forever. Stay there with Dara. He realized a huge part of him wanted to do it too. That was when he'd slammed his fist against the wall.

"You are just going to let him win!" Siv wasn't even sure if by "you" he meant Dara or himself. Maybe both.

Dara had folded her arms, skewered him with one of those level stares of hers, and let him rage. When he ran out of energy, she poured him a goblet of wine and left the room. It was worse than if she had smacked him upside the head.

Siv shifted uncomfortably in his seat, watching the next round of horses trot to the starting line. Dara's respect was important to him. She probably understood that he was struggling to come to terms with what had happened—most of all the death of his sister—but that didn't make it acceptable for him to lose his composure like that. He grimaced. His father would have been disappointed. Sevren had treated people with unfailing patience and kindness, no matter how frustrated he became.

The fact that Siv was supposed to be dead had only aggravated his frustration. He'd been restricted to the royal palace ever since he got to Rallion City. He disliked the place in the best of times, and the confinement was driving him crazy. Today, he'd reached his breaking point.

When Uncle Tem had dropped by for a visit on the way to the races, Siv had decided to assemble a disguise and accompany him. He'd only be out for a few hours. He looked enough like some of his cousins that—with the help of some Truren clothes and a strategically positioned hat—he didn't think anyone would recognize him.

Now he slouched beside Uncle Tem as the man droned on about the merits and weaknesses of each horse lining up for the race in exhaustive detail. Siv nodded politely, wondering what would happen if he accidentally spilled a goblet of wine on the man. He would probably go right on talking. Siv was a decent rider, but hearing about horses in literally every conversation got tiring fast. *Firelord take the Trurens and their races.* They were nowhere near as exciting as a good duel.

A horn sounded, and the horses took off around the track, their hooves thundering, dust blooming around their feet. Siv wished he could run like that, faster than any man. He'd race straight back to Vertigon and find a way to make up for fleeing. Even if the Lantern Maker burned him to a crisp, at least he'd have tried.

"Go, go, go, go, go!" shouted Uncle Tem, far too close to Siv's ear. "Go Princess Suki! You can do it!"

Tem leaned forward, as if he could urge his horse to run faster through sheer will. His gray hair was combed back from his temples in a handsome sweep. All he seemed to do was race and watch the races. Siv wondered if he ever even bothered to visit his manor house on the Eastern Plains.

He supposed that if he stayed in Trure, his life could be like Uncle Tem's: free of responsibility and expectation. Siv frowned, stealing another glance at his uncle out of the corner of his eye. That used to be all he ever wanted.

The crowds roared as the racehorses streaked around the track. Princess Suki was in the middle of the pack. Uncle Tem hollered her name, urging her onward. She eased past two more horses, a yellow crest flying from her rider's helmet. Tem whooped. Princess Suki stretched out her long neck as the pack rounded the bend.

Despite himself, Siv leaned forward in his seat.

Suddenly, the lead horse slipped in the mud. The rider pitched off, barely managing to roll out of the way as the rest of the horses thundered past. He lay still. The crowd gasped and murmured, more excited than worried. Then the rider scrambled to his feet, apparently unharmed, and the spectators shouted louder than a blizzard in the Burnt Mountains.

The rest of the pack charged around the track. Their muscles churned, and sweat lathered their sides like soap. The ground rumbled as they rounded the final bend. Siv clutched the wooden railing.

Princess Suki was in second now. Uncle Tem rose to his feet, abandoning lordly decorum to jump up and down. Princess Suki barreled down the final stretch. The leader sped up, putting more distance between them. She wasn't going to make it.

"Go Princess Suki!" Siv hollered, leaping to his feet.

With a final surge of effort, she pulled ahead seconds before crossing the finish line.

"Yes!" Uncle Tem thrust his fist into the air.

"Woohoo!" Siv thumped his uncle on the back. "Wow, she almost didn't make it. Great finish!" *Okay, maybe the races are a little exciting.*

"That's how it's done," Uncle Tem said, dropping back into his seat with a satisfied smile. He poured himself another goblet of wine. "I'll make a racing fan of you yet. You ought to get yourself a horse or two if you're going to stay in Trure."

"I don't think I'll be here much longer," Siv said. "I just need some men and—"

Uncle Tem raised a hand to silence him. "Siv, my boy. I don't believe my father will change his mind. Don't let your hopes get too high."

"I have to help my people."

"I doubt they're being tortured." Uncle Tem tipped his head back, emptying his goblet. He reached for the pitcher again. "This Lantern Maker may have control over Vertigon, but that doesn't mean the people will suffer. They may hardly notice."

Siv narrowed his eyes. "What are you saying?"

"I'm saying you should let it go," Uncle Tem said. "Vertigon will survive without you."

"But—"

"You can talk about rescuing your people, but the only reason to go back is if you want to retake the throne for yourself."

"That's not what this is about," Siv said slowly. "I don't even like being king."

"Then don't be king." Tem gripped his shoulder. "You're off free. Enjoy yourself. Race, drink, and marry that pretty guard of yours."

Siv stared at his uncle, not sure what to say. As Uncle Tem released his shoulder and refilled his wine goblet, Siv was reminded suddenly and forcibly of his father. It was as if they were having a weird, flipped version of all those conversations with his father about duty and responsibility. As King Atrin's youngest son, Tem had been spared such lectures, and he lived a life that was freewheeling, even indolent. Siv had long thought that was all he wanted too: to be free of the responsibilities of kingship. To be able to marry whomever he wanted. What if his uncle was right, and Vertigon really was going to be fine? The Lantern Maker couldn't be such a monster that he'd endanger the people, could he? His men had killed a seventeen-year-old girl, it was true, but now that he had control, what more could he do?

The thought of Sora made his gut twist as if he'd been stabbed. He'd failed her as a brother in addition to failing as a king. Maybe Vertigon wouldn't even want him back.

Siv frowned into his wine, pondering the glint of light on the burgundy liquid. His wounds were almost healed. He should be well enough to resume his dueling training soon. Maybe he could teach Dara how to ride, and they could take a manor out on the Horseplains somewhere—if she'd have him. Maybe he could walk away and start a new life.

Siv wished he hadn't yelled at Dara that morning. He should go back to the palace at once and apologize. Maybe he could buy her a gift along the way. He'd have to explain that he'd gone out without her, of course. Dara didn't know Uncle Tem had turned up with an invitation to the races. She thought he was spending the afternoon moping in his room and had gone to visit Selivia, who was preparing for her birthday party the following day.

Yes, he would go straight to Dara and explain before she had a chance to get mad. He owed her an apology. And if he smiled wide enough, maybe she wouldn't lecture him about the dangers of venturing out without her. He'd need to finish off the last of his wine first, though. For courage.

And while he was at it maybe he'd finally get the courage to tell Dara exactly how he felt about her. He assumed she knew how she ensnared his thoughts and drove him crazy with her smile. She had to know he wanted her by his side no matter where they ended up in the future—and not just as his guard. But he had never explicitly told her he loved her. Maybe it was time.

Attendants ran out onto the track, smoothing out the mud to prepare for the next race. Riders were already moving fresh horses toward the start line. The animals pranced and snorted, eager to get moving.

"Hello, my lords!" A familiar man with a wide girth and a green coat approached their box. It was Lord Bale, his uncle's racing companion. "Great race. So close at the end! She was one of yours, wasn't she, Tem?"

"Indeed! She's having a mighty strong season."

"Aye." Lord Bale leaned against the box. He wore tall black boots spattered to the calves in mud. "How are you enjoying the races, Sire?"

"They're great," Siv said. "This isn't my first visit to Trure, my lord."

"Of course not. Nice to see you out and about."

"I'm technically in disguise," Siv said. "I guess the hat wasn't enough."

"Well, I knew to expect you," Lord Bale said with a chuckle. "I don't imagine anyone else realizes the deceased King of Vertigon is sitting there beside old Tem."

Siv cleared his throat, wishing the man had a quieter voice.

"Did you have a horse in the race, Lord Bale?"

"I know better than to run against Princess Suki. My Justina is in the next one. She's a long shot, but I think she'll surprise us."

"In that case, I'll put some coins on her," Siv said.

"Thank you, Sire. It is a pleasure to see you again. Where is that fine-looking bodyguard of yours?"

"Dara's back at the palace," Siv said.

"Is she now?" Lord Bale's eyes swept over the royal box with a sudden sharpness that was at odds with his genial demeanor. "It's a shame for her to miss the races."

"She's not a horse person," Siv said. "I'm going to go place that wager. Excuse me, my lords."

Lord Bale inclined his head and walked off in the opposite direction. Uncle Tem was busy scribbling calculations on parchment after Princess Suki's race. He didn't even notice when Siv left the royal box, tugging the brim of his hat lower over his eyes.

Instead of placing a bet, Siv made his way out of the racing stadium and meandered through the shops outside the entrance. Something about Lord Bale didn't sit right with him. He figured it would be wise to depart before he brought on any unwanted attention. Besides, Dara might have realized he'd gone out by now. He really should buy her a gift to apologize.

The racing grounds were the primary hubs for commerce throughout Trure. Merchants liked to catch the spectators the moment they left the arena, flush with their winnings. The only places where people were more eager to spend their gold were the horse markets. Somehow Siv didn't think Dara would appreciate it if he bought her a horse. He ambled slowly through the shops, keeping his head down and his hat pulled low. It started to rain again, and the crowds thinned as people retreated indoors to escape the drizzle.

Which shop to choose? He'd already given Dara the finest sword he'd ever owned, and he wasn't sure what else she would like. She was such a practical person most of the time. She never wore jewelry, and she didn't seem to have much patience for books. He'd convinced her to read a little bit while they'd been confined to his grandfather's palace, but she still approached books cautiously, suspicious of anything that required zero physical exertion to enjoy. The other day he'd caught her doing footwork with a book in one hand, advancing and retreating while she turned the pages.

Selivia's birthday was the following day, and she was much easier to buy gifts for. She loved pretty things: dresses and scarves and jewels. She also loved pets, but Siv's grandfather probably wouldn't be too happy if he bought her a crundlebird or something. Those were damn noisy. Still, he might get her one anyway. After losing Sora, he found himself wanting to spoil his remaining sister rotten.

A glint caught Siv's eye. A gem shop sat at the corner where the road turned back toward the palace. That was as good a place to start as any. He ducked into the little shop, nodded at the voluptuous shopkeeper, and shook the rain from his hat. The door flew shut behind him in a gust of wind.

Jewels glimmered in the light from a single Vertigonian Fire Lantern hanging from the ceiling. Siv perused the cases of jewelry, brushing his fingers over the glass as he admired the stones. Refractions of color and light swept the walls as the lantern swayed from the slamming of the door.

Selivia's gift was easy. He spotted a bright-yellow brooch that would go with one of the headscarves she'd taken to wearing in Trure. Dara was more difficult. He wasn't even sure if she liked jewels. His mother would say he shouldn't be buying gifts for his guardswoman anyway, but he cared less about that with each passing day. He wanted to see her smile, to see her intense eyes soften when she looked at him. That was worth any price.

He circled all the way around the shop and started on another pass when the shine of a necklace caught his attention. He bent over the glass case beneath the window. Fuzzy shapes moved through the rain outside it.

The necklace in the case featured a simple stone pendant. Vines of dull gold curled around the stone, looking a little like a pair of dragons rearing back to back. That was the one. It wasn't too fancy, but it reminded him of Dara.

Siv gave the shopkeeper his most-charming smile and complimented her wide, pale-green eyes. She knocked a few marks off the prices for the two pieces of jewelry. *Works every time.* She wrapped the two gifts in cloth and handed them back to him.

It was raining harder than ever outside the shop, but Siv didn't care. He was excited to deliver the gift to Dara. She would be so surprised! And she would definitely smile at him. He did love to see Dara smile.

Siv wore a little grin of his own as he left the shop and strode into the rain. Or at least, he tried to stride. That was made more difficult when a dark shape emerged from the shadows beside the shop door and clobbered him over the head. Siv dropped into the mud as the world went black.

12

GONE

DARA sat on the wide, corn-yellow rug and stretched as Selivia chattered about her birthday party the following day. The princess danced around the room, unable to sit still in her excitement. She was turning fourteen, and her cousins were traveling from all across the Truren countryside for a luncheon on the rooftop garden. The royal palace had been caught up in a frenzy of activity, not helped by the fact that Selivia darted around asking questions about every last detail, making it impossible for the workers to get anything done.

"Do you think the rain will stop, Dara? Oh, I hope it does. It would be so sad to move the party indoors."

"The Grand Hall almost feels like it's outside," Dara said.

"That's true. But it's so lovely to have sunshine! That's the problem with having a birthday in the wintertime." She paused to peer out at the rain for half a second then continued prancing around the room. "I'm excited for you to meet my cousins. They'll be so impressed to hear about your dueling! We mustn't tell them your name, naturally, but do you think you could do a demonstration? There's plenty of room on the rooftop."

"I don't have anyone to duel against," Dara said. She wasn't excited about the prospect of meeting all of Selivia's relations after the cold reception she'd gotten from Tirra and the thinly veiled suspicion from King Atrin. She continued to avoid them whenever possible.

"Why not duel Siv?" Selivia said. "He can pretend to be your training partner. He'll have to keep his face hidden beneath a dueling mask. Or we could make him wear face paint, like you did for your Nightfall duel! He'd definitely do it. It's my birthday after all."

"I don't know, Princess. He's still recovering from his injuries." He had mostly healed by now, but there was no point in pushing it. Dara herself was almost back to peak dueling condition. On the other hand, it *would* be fun to see Siv wearing face paint.

"He was doing lunges in his rooms just the other day," Selivia said. "He's really restless, isn't he? He needs something to do." Selivia skipped back to the window, looking pretty restless herself. Rain fell in a quiet rush over the city.

"Maybe."

Dara stretched her legs out and reached for her toes. She didn't feel like talking about Siv. They'd argued that morning, and it was all she could do to keep from telling Selivia how frustrating he was sometimes. He had gotten petulant and grouchy as he waited for his body to heal. She'd told him again that she didn't think they should return to Vertigon, and he'd shouted at her about giving up. She knew he felt stressed over his next steps, grief-stricken over his sister's death, and ashamed of himself for leaving Vertigon, but that didn't mean he had any right to yell. She grimaced and shifted into another stretch.

"What are you going to wear to the party?" Selivia asked.

"Probably this." Dara brushed her fingers over the deep-blue Truren gown she wore now. The skirts were wide and flowing, giving her plenty of room for her stretches, though the wide-hemmed sleeves sometimes got in the way.

"That's pretty," Selivia said, "but how about something brighter? Purple would look great against your hair."

"I don't know..."

"I'll find something for you." Selivia clapped her hands. "It's going to be a wonderful party. Now, let's go visit Siv and ask him what he thinks about the dueling demonstration!"

"I don't want to talk to him," Dara said before she could stop herself.

Selivia stopped waltzing around the room. "Why not?"

"We... sort of argued this morning."

Selivia sat on the floor beside Dara, leaning forward curiously. "About what?"

"The usual. We disagree about whether to go back to Vertigon."

Selivia chewed on her lip for a moment. "You don't think you can save Sora?"

Dara frowned, brushing a strand of hair out of her eyes. The princess still refused to believe that her older sister had been killed. Her party distracted her right now, but she'd need to come to terms with it eventually. Even though Dara hadn't seen Sora's body, she had seen the blood on the swords of the assassins leaving her tower clearly enough. There was no point in trying to convince Selivia now, though. She deserved to enjoy her birthday.

"I don't think we can fight my father, Princess," Dara said instead. "At least not yet. I told you about how I was learning to Work, but I'm not skilled enough. And I can't practice here because there's no Fire."

Dara had worked up the courage to try Working with Rumy's help again, but the feeling of the Fire in her veins had conjured vivid, searing memories of that night in the Great Hall. The night her father had nearly killed her. All because of the power.

The true Fire within Rumy's dragon flame only came in small spurts anyway. Like dueling, Fireworking was best done in Vertigon. She had no place, no purpose in the Lands Below. Despite the pain it caused, she had noticed that she felt antsy the longer she went without touching the Fire. She would get as irritable as Siv soon if she wasn't careful. Something needed to change.

"Would you hurt your father, Dara?" Selivia asked quietly.

"I don't know," Dara said. "I tried to learn how to stop him without hurting him, but that didn't work. I may have no choice if it comes down to it. That's the other reason I don't want to go back."

"But Siv thinks he has to?"

"Yes."

"And you pledged to protect him."

"Yes."

"Aw, I see why you're so solemn," Selivia said, reaching out to squeeze her hand. "I wish I could give you some advice."

Dara smiled at the young princess and resumed her stretches. "Thank you. I think Siv and I just need to work it out."

"Have you tried kissing him?" Selivia said brightly.

Dara nearly pulled a muscle in her thigh. "What?"

"That's what happens in the storybooks," Selivia said. "The couple finally kisses, and then all their problems are solved."

"I don't think it's that simple," Dara said. "And we're not a couple."

To her surprise, Selivia laughed. "But Dara, don't you love my brother?"

"I..."

Selivia continued to smile guilelessly at her. Dara sighed.

"Yes. I do love him."

"And he loves you too. It's obvious you're a couple." Selivia leapt to her feet and went back to dancing around the room. "Just kiss each other. It will make everything better."

Dara abandoned her stretches and stood. "I'll think about it, Selivia. Thank you for the advice."

"Anytime! And make sure you wear a pretty dress to the party. And let me do your hair! Boys pretend not to notice that sort of thing, but he'll be impressed."

"Maybe I will."

Dara decided not to tell the young princess that she and Siv had kissed once before. It hadn't solved their problems. If anything, it had made it impossible to continue pretending there was nothing between them. She thought about that kiss in the stairwell all the time. Every moment in each other's company was a little harder because they couldn't do it again. But in others ways it had made everything better, every light brighter, every taste sweeter. Ever since their exile began, their different stations had mattered less. They had stepped closer and closer to an invisible line. Sometimes it was all she could do to keep from kissing him again.

Maybe it was time to stop fighting it.

Dara started for the door. "I'd better go see if Siv'll stop sulking long enough to join us for dinner."

"Have fun," Selivia sang. "And don't forget about the dress!"

Dara strode out into the corridor, nodding at Princess Selivia's bodyguard, Fenn Hurling, on her way out. The woman had grown more sullen and silent than ever after learning of the attack on the castle in her absence. Her brother had been on the mountain—and if Sora was dead, he had most likely been killed too.

Dara frowned, straightening her dress over her hips. Their lives had been in peril too often of late. She and Siv had faced down death together again and again. She had almost lost him. They shouldn't be wasting their time snapping at each other.

Without another moment's hesitation, Dara marched to Siv's room. Maybe it wouldn't make everything better, but she ought to listen to Princess Selivia. It was her birthday after all. The least she could do was follow her advice.

Anticipation flooded Dara like Fire. She was going to give Siv the best kiss of his life.

But the palace guard was missing from the corridor outside Siv's door, and his room was empty. Dara searched the palace for him, checking the nooks and crannies he'd shown her over the past two weeks where he liked to hide out and read. There was no sign of him.

She climbed up to the rooftop. It was empty too. Though the rain was turning the grounds to mud, she went down and searched the gardens surrounding the palace and the shelter near the stables where Rumy slept. The cur-dragon was napping contentedly, but Siv was nowhere in sight. Worry started to pull at her, biting and irrational. Where was he?

She tramped back to the palace through the rain. None of the gardeners and stablemen she encountered along the way had seen him in hours. She squeezed a bucketful of water out of her skirt before entering the Grand Hall. She glanced up at the magnificent painting of horses churning across the plains and shivered. She wouldn't want to be out riding on a day like today.

She was steeling herself to check for Siv in the one place she'd avoided so far—his mother's chambers—when a soft voice called out to her.

"Can I help you, my lady?"

"I was just looking for—oh, hello, Zala." Dara recognized the young woman crossing the vast tile floor toward her. Zala Toven was a handmaid from the Far Plains who had been brought to Vertigon to help Princess Selivia learn the language of the Plainsfolk (though she spent more time helping Selivia dream up new outfits). She had returned to Trure along with the princess and her mother before the attack on the castle.

"I'm looking for King Siv," Dara said. "Have you seen him lately?"

"I believe he went out with Lord Tem."

"Out?"

"He asked me to find him a hat," Zala said.

Dara blinked. "A hat?"

"Yes. He intended to disguise himself before accompanying his uncle outside the palace."

Outside the palace? Of all the foolish things Siv had done…

"Do you know where they went?" she demanded.

"No, my lady."

"What did this hat look like?"

"It was light brown, with a wide brim." Zala put her hands about two feet apart to demonstrate. "It's a common style on the Far Plains."

"Thank you. That's very helpful."

Zala inclined her head and continued toward the other side of the Grand Hall. Dara turned in a slow circle, scanning the vast space and wondering what she should do. Worry made her stomach muscles tighten. She had no reason to think Siv's uncle meant him ill, but it was irresponsible of him to invite Siv to leave the palace. He'd been going a bit stir-crazy, but she didn't think he'd be stupid enough to go out into the city with nothing more than a hat for a disguise.

On second thought, Siv had snuck out of the castle in Vertigon several times in the relatively brief span of time she'd known him. Maybe he was that stupid after all. She dropped into a lunge and did a bit of footwork across the sleek tile floor, her boots skidding, as she contemplated what to do. She'd have no idea where to look for him out there.

Maybe Rumy could help her. His sense of smell was as good as that of a dog. Plus he could fly. She was just heading back out to the gardens when the doors burst open, and Lord Tem strode into the palace. Alone.

"Has he returned?" he demanded as soon as he saw her.

"What?" Dread grasped Dara's heart like a fist of iron.

"Siv and I were at the races," Lord Tem explained. "He went to place a bet and never came back. I thought he'd be here by—where are you going?"

Dara didn't answer. She was already sprinting for her room to retrieve her sword.

13

THE VISITOR

DARA ran through Rallion City, grateful for the time she'd spent building her endurance back up over the past few weeks. She hunted for any sign of Siv in the unfamiliar streets. Every second she slowed, every second she didn't spend searching, he could be getting farther away. Or he could be nearing death, stabbed in an alleyway by a common footpad or by an assassin sent by her father to finish what he'd started. She couldn't think about that. *Focus, Dara.*

She hadn't even taken the time to change out of her dress before leaving the palace. She'd buckled on her Savven blade and demanded that Lord Tem take her to the last place he'd seen Siv. Then she jogged in ever widening circles around the racing grounds, combing the streets for hints of his passing.

Zala's description of Siv's Far Plains hat was all she had to go on. She couldn't exactly ask people if they'd seen the King of Vertigon. He wasn't supposed to be alive, much less in the city. She asked passersby if they had seen the hat on a tall, handsome man with a scruffy beard. Heads shook one after another, and fear wrapped around her like a cloak. She wanted to shake the truth from someone. He couldn't have just vanished.

She kept her head, though, and systematically worked her way outward from where Siv had disappeared. Lord Tem and the soldiers of the city guard helped her search, but she didn't trust them. For all she knew, Tem had betrayed Siv and his supposed worry was a façade. Dara had to find him herself.

The rain worsened as night fell, soaking Dara to the bone. Mud caked the hem of her dress. She wanted to cry, but she had to keep running, keep searching. Hope threatened to abandon her, but she wouldn't let it. She *would* find him.

When it grew almost too dark to see, Dara circled around to the racing-ground entrance again. She found Lord Tem speaking to a voluptuous woman wearing a fine green cloak. A young soldier with ears like the handles on a cider mug stood beside him, shifting from foot to foot as if waiting to deliver a report. Tem forestalled him with a raised hand and leaned in closer to the woman. Dara scowled, annoyed that Tem would flirt at a time like this. *She* wouldn't wait.

As she stomped toward the pair, Tem looked up and waved her over.

"I may have a lead," he said. "This kind lady saw a man who matches our friend's description in her shop not long after I lost track of him."

Hope sparked like Fire in Dara's chest. "What kind of shop?"

"I sell jewelry," the woman said. "Your friend came in wearing a hat like the one you described. Handsome fellow. He bought a brooch and a necklace. Paid too much for both, I'm afraid."

"Was he alone?" Dara asked.

"Aye."

"Where?"

"At the end of the road there. The shop on the corner." The woman laid a hand on Lord Tem's shoulder, and her voice became sultry. "If you need anything else, my lord, that's where you can find me."

Dara didn't wait to hear his answer. She hurried toward the shop. The door was closed and locked up tight. Dara scanned the street around it. Enough traffic had passed by throughout the day that it was impossible to tell whether any of the hundreds of footprints belonged to Siv.

The spatter of the rain hitting the mud puddles was the only sound. A lone figure trudged by, cloak pulled close against the blustery weather. Where would Siv have gone after visiting the gem shop if not back to the palace? And why was he buying jewelry at all?

That didn't matter. She had to figure out where he was likely to go next. She stood on the step and surveyed the street until she spotted a tavern. Light and laughter spilled out of the windows. That was as good a place to look as any. It *was* Siv after all. If it turned out he'd merely gone drinking without telling anyone, she'd make him pay for the hours she'd spent searching in the rain. After she kissed his stupid face, of course.

Dara started toward the tavern. Before she'd gone three steps her boots crunched on something in the soft mud. A fabric-wrapped package was squashed into the muck not far from the door of the gem shop. Dara picked it up and unwrapped the damp cloth, revealing a sparkling yellow brooch and a pendant necklace. Dara didn't know much about jewelry, but the pieces looked expensive. She would expect someone to take care not to drop them—if they had a choice.

She ran back up the street, relieved to find that the shopkeeper was still talking with Lord Tem. Her hand rested on his lapel, and he was whispering in her ear, making her giggle. The mug-eared soldier was still waiting patiently, his face red.

"Are these the jewels the man with the hat bought?" she demanded as she skidded to a stop beside them.

The shopkeeper looked at the muddy packet in Dara's hands.

"Yes. Where did you get that?"

"It was on the ground right outside your shop. Are you sure you didn't see anything suspicious?"

The woman shrugged. "I was inside the whole time."

"You say this was on the ground?" Lord Tem said, his face grave.

"Yes." Dara met his eyes. He must have come to the same conclusion she had. "Siv has been captured."

An hour later, Dara stood before King Atrin in the royal dining chamber as he shouted loud enough to shake the tapestries on the walls.

"How dare they kidnap my own grandson in my own city! When I find out who did this, I'll have them drawn and quartered. I'll feed their bloody pieces to my horses. My own city!"

"Father, your heart—" Tirra began.

"Don't lecture me about my heart, Tirra! It's as strong as ever. And you, Tem. Of all the spineless, foolish things you could do. Letting your nephew get kidnapped out from under your nose. I ought to exile you to the Soolen salt mines."

Lord Tem grimaced, and his boots squeaked on the tile floor. "He was right beside me when—"

"I don't see him here now!" the king bellowed. "Don't you dare make excuses! I want my grandson found." He pointed at the mug-eared soldier who'd been helping them search. "Call in every soldier posted across the plains, and have them scour the city this very instant. I want every barrel overturned and every shifty reprobate questioned within an inch of his miserable life."

The soldier ducked his head. "Of course, Sire. I already have men searching the—"

"And you!" King Atrin rounded on Dara next. "Aren't you supposed to be looking out for him? Where were you when my grandson was being kidnapped?"

"I didn't know he'd left the palace."

"This is why women shouldn't be bodyguards," the king growled.

Dara's face burned, but she stood as still as a statue. King Atrin couldn't possibly make her feel worse than she already did. She should never have let Siv out of her sight—even if it *was* his fault for leaving without telling her. He'd better be alive, or she'd kill him herself.

A knock sounded, and a doorman poked his head in.

"My king, your daughter Lady Vila and her noble husband have arrived for the princess's birth—"

"Can't you see I'm busy?" King Atrin shouted. "Vila knows where her room is. I will see her later."

"Yes, my king." The doorman disappeared as if he was afraid the king would throw something at him.

"Do you have any clues for where Siv went?" Selivia asked. She sat at the huge table, looking small and subdued as her grandfather raged.

"He went into a gem shop," Dara said. "He bought this but then dropped it right outside. That's where I think he was taken." Dara laid the muddy cloth containing the brooch and the necklace on the table.

"He bought these?" Selivia asked.

"The shopkeeper saw him," Tem said. "Or at least she saw a young man who matched his description."

"I don't know why he would have been buying jewelry, though," Dara said.

Selivia opened the packet and gave a little squeal as she took out the yellow brooch. "Oh! For my birthday, of course. This is my favorite color."

The gem sparkled in the Firelight. Tears stood out in Selivia's eyes. "He's a good brother." She reached back into the muddy packet. "This one must be for you, Dara."

"What?"

"Look, it's not my style at all. He must have bought you a present too." She held out the necklace, the pendant swinging from a simple chain.

Dara took it, suddenly unable to speak. Siv had bought her a gift? She examined the metal twining around the stone. It looked like two dragons back to back, sharing a single filigree spine. A team united against all odds.

Dara clutched the pendant in her fist. She would find him.

Another knock came at the door, and a different doorman poked his head into the dining chamber.

"My king, your royal heir Lord Valon has arrived with his children and his lady—"

"Not right now!" King Atrin snapped. "Unless those useless children of his intend to join the search, they can wait until I'm not busy."

"Of course, Your Highness. I'm sorry." The doorman disappeared.

"Father, perhaps we should ask for help from Valon's retainers," Tirra said, drumming her fingers anxiously on the table. "If more men help search for Siv, we may find him faster."

"I don't want word to get out that the exiled King of Vertigon was here and we lost him," the king said. "He's still supposed to be dead. We'll lose our advantage if we decide to move on the mountain."

"But he's in danger."

"We'll sweep the city for him, but I won't have my careless offspring revealing any hint of weakness. Valon and Vila are the worst gossips I've ever met."

"We ought to be looking at who has the most to gain by taking him," Lord Tem said.

"The Lantern Maker is the obvious choice," Tirra said. She rose and turned to Dara, not looking remotely fragile now. "You will tell me where my son is, or I will have you flogged."

"Mother!" Selivia gasped.

"Now, Tirra, don't talk like that," Tem said.

"You may be on to something," King Atrin said. He glared at Dara. "You're a Ruminor, eh? Thought you'd wait until no one suspected you before you acted against my grandson, did you? You treacherous little—"

"Come now, Father," Tem interrupted. "Miss Ruminor has been distraught ever since Siv disappeared."

"A likely story. It's an act!"

"Why would she be here if she had arranged Siv's kidnapping?" Tem said. "Wouldn't she be dragging him back to Vertigon by now? Be reasonable."

But the king didn't listen. He nodded to two of his guards waiting in the shadowy corners of the room. They strode forward and grabbed Dara's arms before she could do more than place a hand on her blade.

"Take her to the dungeon," the king ordered.

"Grandfather!" Selivia cried. "Dara is on our side. She would never hurt Siv. Tell him, Dara."

"I pledged to give my life for him," Dara said. The guards tightened their grips on her arms, as if they sensed her desire to rip away from them and run out in search of her missing friend. She didn't feel afraid for herself, but they were wasting time. "I had nothing to do with it."

"You failed," Tirra said. Tears filled her eyes, and the anger drained out of her. "I thought it would be good for Siv to keep you by his side, but you failed to protect him. And now he's gone, just like my daughter."

"I know," Dara said. "But I'll get him back somehow. I swear it. You have to let me go."

Dance of Steel

Tirra met her eyes, looking like she might relent, but she wasn't in charge here.

"I won't have you interfering with the search," King Atrin said. "I want my grandson found, and then we'll discuss your loyalties, young Ruminor."

A knock sounded on the door for the third time.

"My king—"

"How many times do I have to tell you to leave me alone?" This time the king picked up a goblet and hurled it against the door. Wine spattered the wood like blood. "Tell whichever of my dung-eating children has arrived to show themselves and their progeny to their rooms. I will receive them when I'm not busy dealing with a blasted life-or-death crisis!"

"I'm sorry, King Atrin," the doorman squeaked. "It's not one of your children. A messenger has arrived from Vertigon. It is most urgent."

"Why didn't you say so? Quit sniveling, and bring me the messenger!"

"She's right here, Your Majesty." The fellow clutched the door, tentatively as if he expected the king to throw something else at him. Then he pushed it open the rest of the way.

And Vine Silltine swept into the room.

"Well, isn't this cozy? I do so love Truren architecture."

Dara gaped as Vine glided around the dining room, admiring the decorative sconces along the walls. She wore a dress of vibrant green, the fabric fine but practical. Embroidery twisted around the sleeves and simple collar. Her gorgeous black hair hung loose over her shoulders as usual. What was Vine Silltine of all people doing in Rallion City?

Vine paused to clasp Siv's mother's hands. "Hello, my dear Queen Tirra. It has been too long. King Atrin! It is a great honor to make your acquaintance. I am Lady Vine Silltine of Vertigon."

Vine dropped into a majestic curtsy, flinging back her lustrous dark hair. The king stared, mouth slightly ajar. For once he seemed at a loss for words. It was as if Vine had waltzed out of a storybook. She gazed around the room with a beatific expression. Her eyes slid over Dara, arms still firmly in the grasp of the palace guards, but she didn't let on that they knew each other. She turned her attention to the young princess.

"Princess Selivia, I noticed preparations for what is sure to be a delightful party on my way up. I hope you have a lovely birthday."

Selivia gawked at her, as surprised as everyone else.

"Uh, thank you," she said.

"Well, what's the message?" King Atrin said gruffly, apparently wrong-footed by Vine's breezy demeanor.

"Your Majesty, I bring news of Vertigon and our good Queen Sora," Vine said. "I've been looked at with some suspicion since the disappearance of King Siv, and I decided it was time I took a holiday in Trure. I wish to inquire about your plans to assist our queen."

Utter silence filled the room for a moment. Then Selivia leapt from her chair, knocking over her goblet.

"Queen Sora! See! I told you she isn't dead!"

"Goodness no," Vine said. "I admit that the skies have been watched closely of late, and she may not have been able to get a message to you, but Sora lives and reigns as the Good Queen of Vertigon."

"I knew it!" Selivia said.

"My girl," Tirra whispered.

Dara felt only shock. They'd been wrong. They'd left the poor girl behind.

"We have to go back for her!" Selivia said, crying and laughing at the same time.

"I forbid it," Tirra said, looking shaky and ethereal once more. "You will never set foot in Vertigon again."

Selivia didn't listen. She danced over to Vine and gave her a hug, then she did the same with Dara. The soldiers holding her captive grumbled disapprovingly.

"This changes things," King Atrin said. "I cannot march against my own granddaughter."

"No, I doubt Vertigon would like being invaded either." Vine looked around the dining room, enjoying the effect her news had had. "If you didn't know Sora was even alive, what *do* you know?"

"We got a letter from the Lantern Maker saying my grandson was assassinated by men from Soole," King Atrin said. Incredibly, he sounded eager to please Vine. Dara didn't know how she did it.

"That's inaccurate unless a good deal has changed during my journey," Vine said. "House Rollendar worked with the Fireworkers to arrange a coup. The Rollendars didn't make it through the night, though. I wonder why the Lantern Maker blamed Soole for everything?"

"He wants to provoke a war," King Atrin growled. "If I ever meet the man, I'll rip him apart with my bare hands."

"We must avoid a war," Vine said. "I'm sure King Siv would agree with that." She glanced around the dining room, her eyes sliding over Dara again. "I'm surprised he's not here now."

"He was kidnapped," Selivia said breathlessly. "Just this afternoon."

"Oh dear! That is poor timing. I'd hoped to entreat him to return to the city. Sora is very brave, but she needs her family."

"We'll get him back," Dara said fiercely. "What is my father doing now?"

"Silence," the king barked at her. "You're not a part of this discussion."

"I have no doubt you will find the good king," Vine said. Something like amusement touched her voice as she eyed Dara's guards. "Do let me know if I can be of any assistance."

"Do you have any of those spies of yours in Rallion City?" Dara asked, remembering how Vine always seemed so well informed. King Atrin glared at her for speaking again, but he didn't scare her. Siv was too important.

Vine gave a tinkling chuckle that sounded nothing like her usual laugh. "Why on earth would I have spies in Trure, my dear Dara? I'd better go freshen up from my journey."

She offered the king another deep curtsy and glided toward the door.

"Lock this one up until I decide what to do with her," the king said to Dara's guards. He gestured to the mug-eared soldier. "And send me the captain of the city guard. I want my grandson found."

"At once, Your Highness."

The palace guards ushered Dara toward the door. She tried to catch Lord Tem's eye, but he simply shrugged. As the king's youngest son, there was nothing he could do against his father. Selivia was powerless too. Dara looked desperately to Tirra, but she avoided her gaze. She couldn't be thrown in the dungeon. She had to find Siv, and they were wasting time!

Tirra joined Vine outside the dining chamber and accompanied her down the corridor, asking for more details about Sora's health. The last thing Dara saw before the guards dragged her away in the opposite direction was Vine looking back at her and winking.

14

CAPTIVITY

SIV shifted on the floor of the cellar, trying to ease the pressure on his bound wrists. Was it morning yet? He had no idea how long he'd been unconscious, but the hours since he'd woken had been among the more miserable of his life.

As far as he could tell, he was in the cellar of a tavern. Footsteps danced and pounded overhead, and the smell of ale and stale wine assaulted his nose. Once a pair of feet had marched through the cellar, but their owner hadn't spoken to him. The person had disappeared before he could roll over and see their face.

A foul gag was stuffed in his mouth, and he was so thirsty he might not have been able to shout for help even if his mouth were free. That was probably the worst part of all. The thirst. Or the rope cutting into his wrists. Hadn't his captors ever heard of tying people up with silk cords? They'd hold him just as effectively.

The good news—as far as he could tell—was that he most likely hadn't been taken out of Rallion City. He'd caught a whiff of the unmistakable horse manure scent that pervaded the capital when the door had opened briefly. The better news was that if his captors had taken the trouble to tie him up and hide him in a cellar, they probably didn't plan to kill him. Someone would find him eventually, or he would escape. His grandfather's men were probably scouring the streets for him already, with Dara driving them on like a sheepdog.

He was glad she hadn't been with him when he was attacked. She'd have fought to protect him, and she might have been killed. Whoever wanted *him* alive may not feel the same about her. Unless he'd been captured by the Lantern Maker. He'd rather not entertain that possibility.

Footsteps creaked overhead. It had been a raucous night in the tavern, but it sounded as if the patrons were slowly returning to their homes. He'd held out some hope that a drunken tavern-goer would discover him accidentally and set him free, but he was out of luck for one night.

Siv shifted around, trying to find a more-comfortable position. All he needed was a sharp object, and he'd be able to saw through his bonds. That or a nice soft pillow where he could lay his head for the rest of the night. Being tied up was exhausting work.

Steps thudded on the stairs. Someone was coming. Siv rolled over to more or less face the cellar entrance, banging his head against a barrel in the process. He shook the stars from his eyes as a wide shape darkened the doorway.

"Here he is. Just like I promised."

"Can you prove it is him?"

Two more figures followed the wide man into the cellar. One crouched down, grabbed Siv by the hair, and shone an Everlight directly in his eyes. Siv blinked, unable to see past the glare.

"Sure as my own name," said a familiar voice. "And he was sitting with his uncle in the royal box at the racing grounds."

"If you are cheating us—"

"Look at him. He's an Amintelle through and through."

"We're wasting time, Charn," said the third man. "Master Choven has met him before. He'll know if we're being deceived."

"Very well," said the man with the Everlight—Charn. He released his grip on Siv's hair and turned back to the wide man. Siv caught a glimpse of a green coat. "You will have half your payment now and the rest when we confirm his identity."

"I told you I don't want to see any of you again after this," said the man in green. Siv definitely recognized his voice now. Lord Bale. *That bastard!*

"Your decision," Charn said. "Half the gold until we know it's him."

"They are already searching the city," Lord Bale said. "Just give it to me. I can't be seen with you."

Charn snorted. "We'd rather not be seen at all."

There was a sudden rasping sound and a glint of steel above Siv's head. Then came a wet thrust and a wheezing grunt. Lord Bale dropped to the ground beside Siv, eyes already glazing over in death.

Siv bit back a curse. He tried to scramble backward, but the two strangers hurried forward and hauled him up between them. He struggled against his captors, noting that one was swift, with dark hair in a sleek ponytail, and the other carried a sword dripping red. Siv was a little too preoccupied by the blade to notice what that man looked like.

He caught a glimpse of movement in his peripheral vision. An instant later the world went dark again.

Dara paced across her cell like a cat in a cage. This was ridiculous! She wasn't afraid for her life. King Atrin would no doubt get over his latest rage and let her out eventually. But he was wasting precious time. Siv needed her. She should be out with the city guard, searching the streets.

Instead, she was locked behind bars in a dungeon cell. A palace guard rested on a low stool on the other side of the bars. The only way out was through a wooden door blocking access to the flight of steps she'd been dragged down a few hours ago.

Dara dropped into a lunge, forcing herself to breathe steadily and remain calm. She still wore her mud-spattered blue dress, and she felt chilled from the rain. They had to come to their senses and let her out soon. She could be helping!

She ran her thumb over the pendant necklace Siv had apparently bought for her. The guards hadn't taken it from her—unlike her sword—when they tossed her into the cell. It comforted her to hold the object, slowly growing warm in her palm. It was natural human warmth. The pattern twining the stone was not made of Firegold—unfortunate in these circumstances. If she could get even a tiny bit of Fire from it, she might be able to do something about the lock on her door. Although then she'd have to deal with the jailer sitting on a stool outside her cell. He was wider than Berg Doban, and she wasn't sure she could get past him without a weapon.

She shouldn't have returned to the palace at all. She should have kept searching through the night. But some news might have arrived, a ransom note or a threat or a clue. She'd taken a risk going into that room with Tirra and King Atrin, and now she was trapped. She scowled, picking up the pace of her footwork.

"Will you stop that?" her jailer grunted. "I'm trying to nap here."

"Aren't you on duty?" Dara said.

"This isn't the dung-eating army." The guard shifted on his stool and folded his huge arms over his chest.

Dara continued with her footwork. She should really be resting up for when she was released, but she couldn't sit still. Siv was out there somewhere, injured or dead or captured. She tightened her grip on the pendant.

It may not be Firegold, but it gave her an idea. What if she could draw Fire from elsewhere in the palace? There was none at all in the rock around her cell. It was strange to feel no heat in the earth. It reminded her just how far away from Vertigon she truly was. But she'd spotted a few Fire Lanterns here and there, and there had to be other Works in the palace. Could she reach far enough to pull the Fire all the way through the stones to her cell?

Dara abandoned her footwork and sat on the floor. The guard grumbled his approval. She ignored him. She had to focus.

She breathed, calming her mind and reaching for the Fireworks that she knew had to be there somewhere. Tiny pinpricks of power emerged at the very edge of her senses.

There! The nearest Fire was above her and to the left, possibly in the ground-floor library. She wasn't sure what kind of Work it was, but she pictured a Fire Lantern. She held the image of a burning core in her mind and drew on it, willing the Fire to pass through the Work and into the wall, then the floor.

She was out of practice. She should have been exercising her Fire ability as much as her footwork over the past weeks. A few attempts with Rumy's flame did not amount to real training. She had shied away from her power, hoping to leave it behind just as she'd left her parents. But she needed it now. She concentrated harder on that burning core and pulled.

It was working! The Fire flowed excruciatingly slowly, but it was drawing nearer. Dara concentrated, not allowing her grip on the power to falter.

Her guard began to snore. She had no idea how much time was passing. Pulling the Fire from such a distance was a strenuous task, but she couldn't ease up. She breathed steadily, sweat breaking out on her forehead.

At last a glowing teardrop of Fire dripped through the ceiling of her cell.

Dara caught the Fire and pulled it into her veins before her guard noticed anything. His snores continued, and his eyes remained closed.

It was less Fire than Dara had expected. She'd lost some as it made the slow journey through the palace. She needed more. She reached out with her senses, located another Work, and called on the Fire once more.

The hum of the power in her blood made it easier the second time. She focused on the slow journey of Fire through stone. It inched toward her, finding its path through the vast palace. This was going to take a while.

WHEN SIV WOKE UP AGAIN, it was pitch dark. He was still gagged, still bound, and now he had a sack over his head. *Great.*

He was also in motion. He had apparently been stuffed in the back of a wagon. They moved with a slow, steady gait, but he felt every rumble of the wheels over the uneven ground. Above the creak of the wood, the occasional whinny and snort indicated more horses were traveling alongside the wagon. But the sounds of the city were notably absent. Had they left it behind already, or was it simply the middle of the night?

Siv tried to change his position and banged his already-aching head against something. He cursed into his gag and tried to feel his way around instead. Escaping was going to be a real challenge if he couldn't see. He tried scooting toward the back of the wagon and banged his head again.

Siv gave up on moving and attempted to collect his scrambled thoughts. He had been kidnapped. Lord Bale had sold him out, and he'd been murdered for his troubles. Even if Uncle Tem suspected him, they'd get no word out of him about where Siv was being taken.

Where *was* he being taken? His captors had used the names Charn and Master Choven. Soolen names if ever he'd heard them. If Siv had to bet his life on it—and he probably did—he'd say he'd been sold off to Soole as leverage of some kind. Well, this was just grand.

The wagon lurched to a halt. Siv's captors murmured to each other, too quietly for him to make out the words. He twisted his head and tried to find the edge of the sack with his chin. It'd be easier to use his teeth, but then if he weren't gagged he'd be shouting himself hoarse right about now. He was in deep trouble if they had left the city.

Suddenly the sack was ripped off with enough force to make his ears sting. The back of his head thudded against the bottom of the wagon. It wasn't quite as dark as he'd thought. Was that a hint of dawn in the sky above him?

"Is it him?" said a voice that Siv was pretty sure belonged to Charn.

A familiar face blotted out his view of the sky.

"It's him. Commander Brach is going to be pleased."

Siv mumbled a curse through his gag. It was burning Chala Choven, a Soolen trade alliance representative who used to drink and play mijen with him. He'd seen this same Chala Choven with the secret duelists training in the cavern on Square Peak a few months ago.

"Hello, Siv," Chala said. "No hard feelings, I hope. This is just business."

Siv growled at him.

"We're far enough away from the city," Chala said, pulling back out of Siv's sight. "Remove his gag, and give the poor man a drink."

"Yes, Master Choven." Charn climbed onto the wagon with Siv, his movements quick and catlike, and yanked off the gag.

Siv thought of an even more-creative curse and hurled it at Chala Choven as he walked away. The Soolen man chuckled.

"Good to see you still have a little fight in you," he said over his shoulder.

Charn dumped some water in Siv's mouth, preventing him from responding. He sputtered and choked, trying to swallow as much as possible. He was still lying in the wagon, unable to see anything but the lightening sky and Charn's humorless face. So they had left Rallion City. He sure hoped someone came after him soon. Otherwise, it would be a long journey to Soole in the back of this wagon.

Dara quivered with Fire and fatigue. She had pulled as much power as she could reach from the Works scattered around the royal palace. The task required unrelenting focus. She hoped it would be enough.

Her jailer hadn't said anything in a while. Pretending she wasn't up to anything took concentration too. She leaned back against the wall of her cell, hoping he wouldn't notice the heat that had begun to radiate from her as she collected more and more power. She didn't want to hurt him, but she would do what it took to get Siv back.

When she held as much power as she could possibly retrieve, Dara crawled forward and clutched the metal bars of her cell. Her jailer slept on. Dara sent the Fire into the bars, the steel warming and melting in her hands. The scent of hot metal filled the cell. The guard shifted, grumbling in his sleep. Dara concentrated, willing the steel to melt faster.

The bars in each hand softened at last, and she pulled them loose from their anchoring with faint scraping sounds. She molded and solidified them into two rough spears, barely more than sticks. She didn't have time for anything else, and she hadn't gotten far enough in her training to do much with metal anyway.

She hefted the spears and climbed out of her cell, keeping her attention on her snoozing jailer. She was close enough to smell his sweat and his rank breath. She crept to the door, her still-wet boots squelching with each step.

The guard shifted in his sleep.

Dara held her breath. Almost there.

Suddenly the door crashed open, and Vine Silltine swept into the dungeon.

"Dara! I've come to visit—"

"Shh!" Dara waved frantically, but it was too late.

"What's going on?" The guard lurched to his feet.

Dara spun around, the cooling metal swinging in her hands. She cracked the guard in the head before he could take two steps, and he fell with a thud.

"Oh! I'm so sorry to interrupt your escape attempt, Dara," Vine said. "That was a lovely move. I'm so pleased I was here to see it. I came to say hello and talk to you about—"

"I have to get out of here," Dara said quickly. "Is there anyone in the corridor?"

"No. I've already given a sleeping potion to the guard at the top of the stairs."

"You what?"

"I came to free you, Dara, not only to catch up." Vine wore fitted trousers instead of her usual flowing gown, and she had a pair of saddlebags over her arm. "I'm happy to see we were of a similar mind about your need to escape."

"Let's go, then," Dara said.

"I brought you some clothes," Vine said. "And your sword was leaning against the wall beside the other guard. That's really no way to treat a Savven blade."

Dara dropped her makeshift spears and took the Savven from Vine's outstretched hand, relieved to feel the unnatural warmth in the hilt. She slung the sword belt around her hips, glancing back to make sure her jailer was still unconscious.

"Do you have a way out?"

"I doubt we'll be seen if we walk quietly out the door," Vine said. "Most of the inhabitants of the palace are at Princess Selivia's birthday luncheon. Our dear king has the loveliest relations. And the sky cleared beautifully. It's a perfect day for a picnic on the rooftop."

"Luncheon?" Dara asked. "Already?"

"Why yes. You've been imprisoned since late last night. I do hope you got some rest."

"Not really." Had she been trying to draw on the Fire all night? She didn't realize it had taken that long. She was surprised there hadn't been a guard change, but maybe it had been later than she thought when she was first imprisoned. Unless Vine had something to do with that too. As promised, the palace guard at the top of the steps was snoozing peacefully. The rest of the corridor was deserted.

"I have a friend who keeps a manor nearby," Vine said. "We can plan our next steps there."

Dara followed Vine through the palace. They moved stealthily, keeping to the shadows, but they didn't encounter anyone after passing the guard Vine had put to sleep. They crept out a back door not far from the stables. The gates in the outer wall near the stables were closed. Dara prayed they could be unlocked from the inside. Normally palace gates were designed to keep people out, not in.

Dara and Vine hurried across the grounds, hiding behind rose bushes whenever they could. A babble of voices drifted on the air, no doubt from the rooftop garden. The entire palace must be at Selivia's birthday party. They couldn't take any chances, though.

They drew nearer to the walls. The sound of horses and carriages passing by outside reached them. Almost there.

Then a familiar squawk cut through the air. Rumy soared over their heads, chattering angrily.

"Rumy!" Dara said. "Please be quiet!"

The creature squawked louder, his tone reproachful.

"We have to help Siv," Dara hissed. "Don't give us away."

"He does draw the eye, doesn't he?" Vine said, sounding anxious for the first time.

The cur-dragon landed beside them, continuing to grumble and scold. Voices rose nearby, far closer than the rooftop garden. A pair of stablemen was coming toward them.

"Rumy!"

"I rather suspect he'd like to join us," Vine said.

"We can't sneak with—"

Rumy gave an almighty squawk and fixed Dara with an intelligent stare.

"Okay, fine," Dara said. "But only if you don't get us caught."

Rumy snorted and took off. He soared straight for the approaching stablemen and stole the hat off one's head. The man shouted angrily and lunged after him. Rumy tossed the hat in the air and flapped his wings, staying just out of reach. The stableman leapt up and down, his face going purple. His companion doubled over laughing.

"Now's our chance. Go!"

Dara and Vine sprinted for the sally port beside the main gates. They shoved it open and hurried away from the palace, dodging the horse traffic on the road outside. Shouts came from behind them. Had they been seen, or were the men still distracted by Rumy?

They made it to the nearest side street, and Vine darted down it, weaving amongst the people strolling along. Dara looked back as Rumy soared over the low palace wall. Someone hurled a rock at him as he retreated, just missing his wings. Rumy chirped indignantly and dropped the hat in the dirt outside the gates.

He circled once more around the palace gardens, scolding and squalling, and then flew over the street toward Dara. Once she was sure he was following, she turned and sprinted after Vine.

She caught up as Vine rounded a corner into a smaller, less-crowded street. They slowed to a fast walk to avoid attracting further attention, keeping their heads down.

"Where are we going?" Dara asked.

"To see my friends," Vine said.

"Are you sure they won't give us away?"

"Nothing is ever sure, Dara. Isn't it wonderful?"

Vine stopped before an unassuming manor house halfway down the quiet street. Dara took in pale mud walls and a red-tiled roof as Vine tapped out a signal on the door. Before Dara could ask about these mysterious friends, the door opened and quick hands pulled them inside.

15

AIR SENSORS

THEY found themselves in an open-air courtyard. Rumy soared over the high mud walls and landed next to them. The house on the other side of the courtyard was low and wide, with a breezy colonnade in front of large windows. A shallow pool filled most of the courtyard, its surface rippling gently. Dara stopped to catch her breath and stared in wonder.

At regular intervals around the pool, people sat cross-legged on the ground, gazing calmly at the water. Their clothes indicated that they came from a mixture of social stations: some noblemen, some traders, some servants. None of them even glanced up as the door slammed shut behind Dara and Vine. In fact, though they stared at the water, they didn't look as if they really saw it. They merely sat, light Truren eyes open and placid. Dara almost wondered if they were statues, but the shoulders of the man nearest to them rose and fell gently. He was breathing at least.

"Welcome, Vine," said the woman who had pulled them into the courtyard, her voice a low musical hum. She wore a scarf embroidered with roses over her hair and a white gown with the characteristic Truren ruffles. "You give us a gift through your return."

"Thank you," Vine said. "You give me a gift through your welcome."

"Will you entrust me with the name of your friend?"

"I will. This is Dara and Rumy. Dara, I entrust you with the name of Meza, who has spent the last several years gifting me with her wisdom."

"Thank you for the gift of your name, Dara." Meza placed her hands on Dara's shoulders and kissed her on each cheek. Meza was a head shorter than Dara and had to stand on her tiptoes to reach. She wasn't wearing shoes despite the winter chill.

"Uh... hi."

"Come. You must be weary. Allow me to give you the gift of hospitality."

Meza turned and glided around the pool toward a door on the far side of the courtyard. She moved like a dancer, but Dara got the sense that she was older than she looked. Vine followed, her calm smile giving no indication that they'd been running for their lives moments ago.

As Dara stomped after them, her boots still squelching, a glimmer of movement caught her eye. She froze. The cross-legged people sitting around the pool hadn't stirred, but water was rising from the center of the pool like a fountain. Dara watched, transfixed, as the water began to morph and curl through the air. Its movement was rhythmic, pulsing. The seated people swayed in time with the water. The noonday sun flashed on the droplets, making it look as if the fountain were full of sparks. A sound like gentle rain pattered through the courtyard.

"Is that Watermight?" Dara whispered. "I didn't think that was possible this far from Pendark."

"Not Watermight," Vine said. "Air."

"What?"

"They are coaxing the Air, sensing its movement, guiding it."

Dara gestured to the fountain. "But the water—"

"When enough Air Sensors collaborate," Meza said over her shoulder, "they can move mountains."

She pushed open the door to the manor house and beckoned Dara and Vine into its shadowed depths.

"You'd better wait outside, Rumy," Dara said, resting a hand on the cur-dragon's scaly head.

"Nonsense," Meza said. "We always welcome our animal friends."

Rumy snorted happily and pushed past Dara to follow Meza

Dance of Steel

inside. The front room was large, bare, and lit only by sunlight. The floor was paved with a multitude of painted tiles forming an intricate pattern of rose, cream, and robin-egg blue. It was wide enough to hold two dueling strips. A sense of serene cool filled the space.

"Come. Sit," Meza said. They crossed the painted tile floor to a nook with low couches beneath another wide window. Trurens did love their windows. The hair stood up on the back of Dara's neck as a breeze drifted around her.

"I will give you the gift of food and refreshment," Meza said. She disappeared through an arched doorway across from the nook.

Dara turned to Vine. "What is this place?"

Vine was already settling on one of the couches. She spread her dark hair out over her shoulders and arranged her saddlebags at her feet. She looked fresh-faced and placid, not at all as though she had just helped Dara escape from the palace dungeon. Dara herself still wore muddy boots, and her dress was stiff and itchy after drying overnight. She hoped she wouldn't get dirt on the pale-rose fabric of the seat.

"This is the Sensors Manor where I take my Air retreats," Vine said.

"Your what?"

"I've told you about my meditations and my training with Air energy before. Weren't you listening?"

"Uhh..."

"It has helped my dueling immensely," Vine said. "You really ought to pay more attention to new strategies, Dara. I thought you wanted to be a contender."

Dara dropped onto the couch—forgetting about the dirt on her clothes—and tried to cover her surprise. *She* wasn't a contender? She had never taken Vine's meditations seriously. The idea had always seemed so insubstantial. But she had seen the way the water moved above that pool. That was all done with Air?

"I come here at least once a year to renew my mind and reconnect with the energy of the Air," Vine explained. "Meza has been my energy coach on each of my visits."

"Wait a minute, you actually use the Air in your duels?"

"It's not cheating," Vine said primly. "I don't directly coax the Air.

I simply sense the vibrations around my opponent and use it to guide my steps. It's as legitimate as using my eyes."

Dara wondered if Vine had confirmed the legitimacy of such a tactic in the dueling regulations, but she didn't have a chance to ask before Meza returned. She glided over to their nook and set a tray on the table before them. Steam rose from three teacups arranged around a plate of flatbread with honey and delicate slices of sweetmeat. Dara reached for the food first. She was very hungry after her night in the palace dungeons.

"Thank you for giving us a place to hide," Dara said, dropping a piece of sweetmeat on the floor for Rumy. "I hope it's not too much trouble."

Meza smiled vaguely over her teacup. "You only need hide if you run," she said.

Vine sighed. "You are so wise."

"Right." Dara cleared her throat. "Well, we shouldn't stay long."

"Take a moment to relax and breathe, Dara," Vine said. "Your distress is preventing you from thinking clearly. The city guard has been searching all night, and they haven't turned up a single clue about our friend's whereabouts. We must approach the problem with more grace."

"What if he's been taken out of the city?" Dara said, panic seizing her despite their serene surroundings.

"Then it is all the more important that we don't run about like you have been so far." Vine patted Dara on the arm and turned to her friend or energy coach or whatever Meza was.

"Meza, we are most grateful for the gift of your hospitality," Vine said. "I must also ask you for the gift of help. We need to find a missing friend."

"You know what you must do," Meza said.

"Yes, but I fear I've been less tranquil than I ought to be of late," Vine said. She glanced at Dara with a look that could almost be interpreted as accusatory. "I hoped you might guide me in the meditations."

Meza smiled gently. "Of course. You always bring the gift of joy when you visit us, Vine. I feel blessed to sit with you and guide where I am permitted."

Dara was still confused. "Uh, what meditations? How will sitting and thinking help us find him?"

"Sitting and thinking are more powerful than you may yet understand." Meza set her teacup back on the platter and adjusted her rose-embroidered headscarf. The ends seemed to flutter of their own accord. "What is the one thing that touches you and me and your lost friend at the same moment?"

"I assume we're talking about air?"

"Not just air," Meza said. "We are touching *Air*. Its presence fills the plains of Trure and reaches its warm embrace across the hills and all the way to the distant waves."

Dara shivered, feeling the hair stand up on her neck again. Meza's eerie voice and pale gown did little to dispel the ghostly sensation. Vine watched her raptly. Rumy had fallen asleep on the painted tile floor. Apparently this strange, ethereal woman didn't disturb him.

"The Air speaks to us if we listen," Meza said, "and gives us the gift of help if we ask."

"You're saying you can reach out with the Air and find out where Si—our friend is?"

"I am saying we can ask," Meza said.

Dara didn't really understand all this stuff about asking—as if the Air were a conscious being. She was used to the magic of the Fire, but it was a tangible substance. Yes, she could control it with her mind, but it was still a physical thing that flowed through the mountain. It had an identifiable source—the Well beneath King's Peak—and concrete limits. Air was just . . . air. Her father had never paid much heed to the Truren Air Sensors. Dara had thought they all lived out on the Far Plains anyway. She was surprised to find them right here within running distance of the palace. But if there was a chance to find Siv, she wasn't going to argue.

"How long will it take?" she asked.

"We cannot hurry the Air," Meza said. "The men and women you saw out in the courtyard have been coaxing the Air to move the pool since sunup. You happened to arrive at the moment when it granted their request, but you must give patience if you wish to receive help in return."

"How much patience?" Dara said.

Vine chuckled. "Don't worry, Dara. I want to help our friend too." She poured herself another cup of tea. "You should get some rest. You've had a long night. Worry is clouding your judgment and driving you to haste. Take some time to calm yourself. I will find out where he is."

Dara wished they could hurry up and get started if it took that much time to get the Air to cooperate. They could coax the Air if they thought it would help, but they needed answers soon. She didn't want to contemplate the possibility that it might already be too late.

Vine and Meza took their time finishing their lunch, chatting amicably about prior Air retreats while Dara restrained herself from leaping up and searching the streets again. When they were finally done, Meza insisted that Dara wait in a guest room at the back of the house while she and Vine worked.

"You have an anxious energy," Meza said. "I must ask you to give us the gift of space and not disrupt our meditations."

Dara bit back the urge to ask her for the gift of speed. She may not understand this power, but right now it was their only hope of finding Siv before he was beyond help. She didn't want to get in their way. *Rumy* apparently didn't have a distracting energy, because he was allowed to continue snoozing in the nook while Dara was directed to her room.

She used the washbasin and a pitcher of steaming-hot water in the austere guest room to freshen up and changed into the clothes Vine had brought for her (blue Castle Guard jacket, gray trousers, and black blouse). She tucked the necklace Siv had bought for her underneath her blouse for safekeeping, the metal-wrapped stone warm against her skin.

Now that she was clean and fed, fatigue hit her like a sword thrust to the chest. She stretched out on the bed, resolving to close her eyes for a few minutes and gather her strength. She needed to be ready to move the second Vine came up with a location.

The manor house was quiet. Calm. No sound came from the city outside the walls. A gentle breeze whispered around her bed. That was odd. Dara didn't think the guest room had any windows. She drifted to sleep.

DARA SAT BOLT UPRIGHT, reaching for her sword. A single candle burned on the table beside her bed. The room was empty. She had been so sure she sensed a presence a moment ago. She shook her head to clear it. It had been a dream. A dream where her mother stood over her while she slept, twirling a ball of Fire between her hands.

Dara got up and went to the washbasin. The last of the water in the pitcher was ice cold. How long had she slept? She felt remarkably well rested.

She put on her boots, buckled on her sword belt, and crept out of the guest room. The hall was quiet, except for that strange whispering breeze. She walked toward the front of the house, feeling uneasy. Shadows cloaked the walls. It must be the middle of the night. Had she truly slept through the entire afternoon?

She stopped at the sight of two familiar figures. Vine and Meza sat on cushions on the painted tile floor, each facing one of the wide, darkened windows at the front of the house. Their eyes were open, but they didn't acknowledge Dara as she approached them from the side.

Both women were breathing deeply, sitting utterly still. They wore the same clothes as when Dara had last seen them what must have been hours ago. She waited beside them for a few minutes, wanting to ask how it was going, but they didn't turn toward her.

She scanned the rest of the shadowy room and noticed the tray on the table had been replaced with a plate of fresh fruit and flatbread. When the two women still didn't move, Dara went over and helped herself. She felt impatient as she waited for them to complete their work. Rumy had moved from the floor to one of the couches. Somehow Dara didn't think Meza would mind. He opened one eye when she sat beside him, then went right back to sleep.

After her breakfast, Dara stretched on the tile floor, watching for any signs that Vine and Meza were almost finished. Still nothing. It must be so frustrating to sit still like that for so long. The first hints of dawn had begun to peek through the windows.

She did footwork to pass the time, advancing, retreating, breathing. She lost herself in the rhythm, quieting her mind, focusing on her steps. She thought of the many hours she had spent training with Siv. She wanted to go back to when nothing mattered but staying in shape and winning duels. She breathed steadily, thinking of Siv, praying he was all right, hoping they'd find him soon.

The breeze moved around her again, reassuring rather than eerie this time.

Suddenly Vine rose to her feet.

"I've found him!" she said. "Come, Dara. He's been taken out of the city. The time for patience has ended. We must follow at once before he is beyond our reach!"

16

THE SOOLENS

SIV wished he could see where he was being taken. Riding in a wagon with his eyes covered was even less fun than it sounded. For a while he tried to guess his position based on the noises around him, but all he heard was the creak of the wagon, the sigh of the breeze, and the *clop-clop* of the horses.

He slept a bit, figuring he'd need his strength if he had any chance of escaping. His grandfather was sure to send men after him, and he intended to assist in his own rescue. It was slightly embarrassing that he had been captured so easily.

He gradually became aware of darkness descending, despite the sack over his head. That meant he'd been a prisoner for more than a full day. He was afraid they were going to travel through another night, but Chala called a halt at last. The sounds of men setting up camp replaced the clop of the horses. In short order, Siv was dragged from the wagon and deposited on the cold ground. Crackling sounded nearby, and the warmth of a campfire touched him a second later. It reminded him of Dara. And Rumy. He shouldn't leave Rumy out.

He hoped Dara wasn't too worried about him. She was the type of person to blame herself when things went wrong. He was quite certain that this little kidnapping escapade was entirely his own fault. He should have known better than to go walking through the city alone. His two weeks confined to the palace had made him reckless. He was certainly paying the price for it now.

He managed to pull himself into a sitting position without accidentally pitching into the campfire. He shifted around until only a handful of rocks dug into his backside.

"Any chance I could get something to drink?" he called.

His captors exchanged quiet words. They had been careful not to talk around him so far. Wherever they were taking him, they intended to keep it a secret.

"Here."

Someone pulled up the sack on his head enough to uncover his mouth and knocked a canteen against his lips. Siv tipped back his head to drink, trying to get a good look at his surroundings under the edge of the sack while he had the chance.

There wasn't much to see, just a flickering fire with a few dark shapes lounging around it. He was pretty sure Charn was the one holding the water, blocking most of the view. He tugged the sack down over Siv's eyes again as soon as he pulled the canteen away.

"Thank you kindly," Siv said. "Got any wine?"

Charn snorted and didn't answer. So he wasn't the friendly type.

Charn shuffled away from him. He returned a moment later and tapped Siv on the shoulder.

"Food," he said, pulling up the sack again. This time he made sure Siv couldn't see anything at all.

"Wouldn't it be easier to bind my hands in front so I can feed myself?" Siv said.

"Shut up." Charn pressed something against Siv's face. He opened his mouth, and his captor stuck an enormous chunk of jerky between his teeth and yanked the sack back over his face. It was all Siv could do to chew without choking. At least that distracted from the slightly rancid taste of the meat. He missed the cooks in Vertigon very much indeed.

"Chala," Siv said after he managed to choke down the jerky. "You there?"

"Don't talk to him," Charn said.

"It's all right. I'm here."

Chala's voice came from Siv's right. He turned toward it.

"Got any wine, Chala? You may be kidnapping me, but we can at least be civilized about it."

"He's your prisoner, not your friend," Charn snapped.

"Oh, what can it hurt?" Chala said.

Siv recognized the blessed music of a cork being popped. Then another bottle was put to his lips. He tipped his head back for a long swig, and this time he managed to see a bit more from underneath the sack. There were two men apart from Chala and Charn around the campfire. One was big and burly, and the other had the lean, muscular look of a hardened criminal. Charn he recognized by his swift movements and sour expression before Chala repositioned the sack over his head.

The heat from the wine rushed through Siv faster than usual. He must be more worn down and dehydrated than he realized. Could he take four men in this state? Chala was a soft man who preferred parlors and dining rooms to dueling halls. Siv didn't rate him as a fighter. But Charn's swift movements suggested he knew how to handle himself, and the other two looked just as dangerous from what Siv could tell.

There was also still the problem of Siv's bound wrists and ankles. And the fact that he had no weapon. Escape wasn't going to be easy.

"Do you plan to keep me tied up all the way to Soole, Chala?" Siv asked. "My arms will fall off if you don't let me get the blood flowing."

"Who said anything about Soole?" Chala said.

Siv frowned. Where else would a party of Soolen men be taking him if not Soole? He remembered a name he'd heard earlier that day. Or was it yesterday? He was beginning to lose track.

"So Commander Brach isn't in Soole? My spies suggest otherwise."

"Spies?" came a gruff voice from across the campfire. "What spies?"

"Quiet, Tech," snapped Charn.

"Oh, Vertigon has spies all over the place," Siv said. "I know a lot more about what's going on than you realize. You boys are making a big mistake."

"Why?"

"Shut up, Tech."

"It's a mistake because you think Commander Brach is loyal to the crown. Ha!" Siv tried to lean nonchalantly—difficult with his wrists and ankles still bound. "What if I told you you're betraying Soole and your own countrymen by trying to deliver me to Brach?"

To his surprise, the men chuckled.

"Obviously," Tech muttered.

"Siv, you're smarter than this," Chala said. "I'm disappointed."

Siv shifted uncomfortably, thinking fast. They were actually betraying their countrymen? On purpose? He tried to remember what he'd heard about Commander Brach but didn't come up with much. Wasn't Brach a wealthy house? Sora would have known. She always kept track of important figures in every country.

So he'd been taken by a bunch of Soolens who weren't loyal to Soole. But they planned to deliver him to a Commander Brach. Would he be with the force that had invaded Cindral Forest? That was much closer to Trure than Soole. Maybe his arms wouldn't fall off after all.

"So how much longer until we get to Cindral Forest?" Siv asked.

"How did you—?"

"Shut *up*, Tech."

Siv heard a smack from across the campfire. Point to Siv! Not that the prospect of being delivered to Cindral Forest was much better than Soole. He still had the hostile Soolen army to worry about. The only good news was that he might not have to ride in the wagon for quite as many weeks if they were truly heading for the mysterious forest.

A low mumble indicated that the men were discussing something they didn't want Siv to overhear. Even though Cindral Forest was closer than Soole, this trip was going to get boring fast if no one would talk to him.

"If you're not going to include me in your chat," Siv called, "you could at least give me another sip of that wine."

Dara, Vine, and Rumy left the Sensors Manor before the sun rose. Unfortunately for Dara, they had decided to ride. Meza gifted them

Dance of Steel

a pair of horses: a palomino mare for Vine and a gray gelding with a black mane for Dara.

"This is the lovely Goldenflower, and this is Storm," Meza had said, introducing them like old friends. "May they aid you in your travels and give pleasant companionship on the road."

Storm wasn't quite as large and strong as Old Fence, but Dara didn't feel any more comfortable on horseback than she had before. They needed the speed, though. Siv had gotten a head start, and even with Vine's assurances that he was still alive, Dara wanted to get to him as soon as possible. He didn't even know Sora was alive!

Vine spent a few minutes whispering in Goldenflower's soft ear before bidding Meza a final farewell and leading the way into the city. The streets filled with a quiet rustle as people ambled to their jobs, bread rolls clutched in hands and sleep clinging to eyes. As ever, the soft whinny of horses permeated the air. The sunlight of the day before had dried the mud, and the city took on a shiny, new feeling as fingers of light spread from the rising sun.

Dara felt surprisingly well rested after their stay with the Air Sensors. She brushed a hand over her Savven blade, that mysterious warmth giving her strength. She'd picked out the stitches on her Castle Guard coat to obscure the sigil. She wrapped Storm's reins tightly around her hands and tried not to fall off as they bounced along the street. Siv's pendant swung around her neck, tapping steadily against her chest like an extra heartbeat—not that she needed any reminders of her mission.

They traveled south, skirting around the royal palace to reach the city boundaries. The silver expanse of Azure Lake appeared in flashes between the buildings. Vine followed an invisible trail in the Air, insisting it would lead her directly to Siv and his captors. She was certain he had already been taken beyond the outer borders of the city. Dara was skeptical, but they had no other clues. Besides, if they stayed in Rallion, the city guard would eventually spot her and throw her back into the palace dungeon. She'd already instructed Rumy to trail them by a hundred feet or so to avoid drawing unwanted eyes.

Dara wished she could have left a note for Selivia, but the princess would trust her. Tirra and King Atrin would have to forgive her for escaping if she brought Siv back safely. The city guard was searching for him too, but Dara didn't know if they had any Air Sensors in their employ. If Siv had truly been taken out of the city, she and Vine might be his only hope.

The sun climbed farther into the sky. They exited the wide-open city gates and eventually left the outer sprawl of Rallion City behind. They followed the High Road south into the vast expanse of the Horseplains. The well-maintained road ran through the rolling, grassy center of the country in the opposite direction of Vertigon, leading all the way to the other side of Trure, where Kurn Pass and the Linden Mountains marked its southern border.

Dara was surprised Vine wanted to go south instead of north toward Vertigon.

"I'm surprised too," Vine said when Dara questioned her. "Isn't it interesting that your father may not have been the one to capture him? I do love a good mystery."

Dara was less enthusiastic about the prospect, but this was Vine's realm of expertise. She had to believe her friend knew what she was doing.

Rumy caught up when they were a safe distance from the bustle of the city. He trotted along beside them, occasionally veering off to explore a curious dip in the road or chase invisible creatures through the brush. He wisely made himself scarce whenever other riders approached in the distance. They didn't want to draw attention in case King Atrin decided to send soldiers after them.

The road was rough and pockmarked after all the rain, giving Dara some hope that she and Vine could overtake Siv. His captors likely couldn't travel fast if they had to haul him along. He wouldn't make it easy on them.

But after they'd been riding confidently onward for a few hours, Vine stopped Goldenflower in the middle of the road. Dara tugged on her reins until Storm halted too. He snorted irritably at her.

"What's wrong?" she asked.

"Give me a moment," Vine said. She patted her horse's neck and breathed deeply.

A party of riders passed, babbling and kicking up dust all around them. Vine didn't seem to notice. She sat with her eyes partially closed and listened to the Air. Dara shifted in her saddle uneasily, but none of the riders asked why the two women were sitting motionless in the road. They rode on toward the city without a backward glance.

Vine still didn't move. Storm huffed and meandered to the edge of the road to chomp on some dead grass. Rumy swooped low overhead and squawked a question. Dara shrugged.

"Vine?"

"I believe we are on the wrong road," she said at last.

"What? I thought you said—"

"The Air does not give explicit instructions," Vine said. "I have a general sense of where we need to go. The High Road took us in the right direction for a time, but I believe our quarry is actually traveling overland now. This way."

Vine squeezed her knees into her horse's side, and they trotted into the brush beside the road.

"Are you sure?" Dara called, hesitant to set off into the vast expanse of the plains.

"Nothing is ever sure," Vine said. "But I have a good feeling about this direction."

Dara gritted her teeth, indecision warring within her. If they left the High Road, there was no telling where they'd end up. She didn't know much about the Truren countryside, but she didn't like the idea of getting lost in the middle of nowhere. Vine's vague statements didn't inspire confidence.

A wind rippled across the plains, making the winter grasses shimmer like silver. The smell of dirt and rain swirled through the air. A few farms dotted the landscape here and there, but most of the plains were vacant and wild.

Rumy released a brief burst of flame near Dara's shoulder, as if to prompt her to hurry up. Vine was already shrinking in the distance, her long hair floating on the breeze.

Dara had no choice. Vine's method may be imprecise, but it was all they had. Siv could be getting farther beyond her reach by the second. She clutched her reins tighter and followed Vine into the wilderness.

17

COUNCIL

SORA sat at the head of the polished wooden table in the royal council chambers, with Rafe Ruminor on her right and Daz Stoneburner the Firesmith on her left. A mixture of noblemen and Fireworkers filled the rest of the table, trying to crowd each other out with elbows and strategically angled chair backs. Rafe had selected the Workers for the royal council, but he hadn't stopped the noblemen from assuming their usual positions.

Extra chairs had been brought in, and the council chamber felt stuffy and hot with so many people. Sora had always wanted to be allowed to attend these meetings, though this wasn't quite what she had in mind. This room definitely needed a window to let in the sharp mountain air.

She shifted in her chair, wishing she could truly lead the meeting. She'd prepared a neat list of items to address, but every time she tried to speak, Rafe would jump in to carry on the topic. He made it look as if he'd coached her to begin conversations only so he could take over and guide the discussion as her Chief Regent. She had stopped trying lest she give the impression they were truly working together. Unfazed, Rafe had carried on without her. The council members didn't even look at her now.

"The Square Workers wish to revisit the matter of establishing our own guild," Daz Stoneburner was saying. He was a short man with thick, muscular arms and white hair. Sora noted that he addressed the full assembly whenever he spoke. Most of the others directed their comments to the Lantern Maker. "We've agreed it is more beneficial for us to draw on the Fire together after our success with the Wall."

"We only need one Fire Guild," Lima Ruminor said.

"Our interests have diverged from those of the King's Peak Guild," Daz said. "We've made great strides, and we want to focus on our collaborative Works now that the Fire is free."

Lima looked down her long, proud nose at the man across the table from her. "I don't see how setting up a new guild will help you."

"Forgive me, Madame Ruminor," Daz said. "You wouldn't understand."

"Excuse me?"

"You cannot Wield," Daz said. "With all due respect to your husband, I don't know why you're even at this council meeting."

Lima's lips thinned dangerously.

"Come now, Daz," Corren the Firespinner said. "You know what an important role Lima has played in our work over the years."

"The changes we've brought about have gone a long way toward restoring the Workers to their former power," Daz said. "We wish to keep the distinction between Firewielders and cold-fingered men and women clear."

"Who is 'we' exactly?" Lima demanded. Daz's face remained placid, despite the daggers Lima was sending in his direction with her eyes. Sora would be running the other way if Lima looked at her like that.

"'We' Square Workers agreed to help you so the Fireworkers could regain our rightful place," said a woman with bony features and thick, dark eyebrows giving her face a skeletal look. Madame Pandan was a Metalworker from Square Peak, though Sora had never spoken with her before. She knew many of the Workers, but she still had some catching up to do now that they were taking on more-prominent roles.

"Are you not aware you're at a royal council meeting in the presence of the queen?" Lima said, not even bothering to glance at Sora.

"Yes. Along with the same old nobles." The Metalworker made no effort to hide her disdain as she waved a bony hand at the men and women crowding around the table. "Are we to have our efforts sullied by nepotism too?"

"Madame Pandan is correct," Daz said. "There has been an imbalance against the Workers for a long time. We have done well in banding together of late. If we're to start anew, the Firewielders ought to carry more weight—in the council and elsewhere."

"No one is disputing that," Lima said. "But Square can't just form their own guild."

Madame Pandan raised a thick eyebrow. "Can't?"

"My friends, let us not argue." Rafe stood, looming over the table. Sora felt like a doll sitting beside him. His presence oozed command, perhaps even more than her father's had. She sometimes found herself wishing she were a large man instead of a small, round girl.

"The Square Workers have been doing impressive work since they began pooling their Fire shares," Rafe said. "In fact, I have a few ideas I wish to discuss with you in that regard. Would you be willing to stay after the meeting, Daz? I'd appreciate your expertise." He looked directly over Sora's head to meet the Firesmith's eyes.

"Very well." Daz folded his hands and rested his muscular arms on the table, looking unconvinced. "I'm sure the topic wouldn't interest the non-Workers among us anyway."

"Excellent." Rafe turned to the others, perhaps choosing to ignore the blatant skepticism on Daz's face. "Shall we discuss the status of the winter food stores?"

Lima and Madame Pandan were busy staring each other down and didn't object as Rafe steered the conversation away from the issue of a Square Peak guild. For her part, Sora had nearly forgotten that Lima couldn't Work. At times, the woman seemed more dedicated to the Fireworkers' cause than the Lantern Maker himself. She showed little interest in winter storage, bridge repair management, and even hobnobbing with the nobility. Sora had gotten the impression that Lima was one of the main driving forces behind the coup. What kind of work was left for her now that it had succeeded?

"Does anyone have other business they wish to discuss before we adjourn?" Rafe asked. A warning glance suggested he didn't include Sora in this invitation.

"Soole," said Lord Roven. A broad-shouldered, jovial man who had a daughter not much younger than Sora, he was the first among all the non-Fireworkers to speak during that day's meeting—apart from Lima—and he didn't look so jovial now. He met the Lantern Maker's eyes levelly. "Soole invaded Cindral Forest without provocation. After what the Soolen assassins did to our king, we want to know how you plan to deal with them."

Lord Roven didn't mention the Soolen swordsmen that still lurked in the castle itself. Sora wondered how many people knew about them. But the implication was not lost. Lord Roven wanted to know whether the Chief Regent had officially allied with Soole to attain his position.

"I am mindful of Soole's aggressions," Rafe said, "but you needn't fear, Lord Roven."

"Forgive me if I don't take you at your word, *Master* Ruminor," Lord Roven said. The other nobles shifted uncomfortably. Lord Roven's gaze didn't waver. "What do you intend to do if Soole attacks?"

Rafe smiled. "Our kingdom has restricted experimentation with Fire Weapons for many years. Thanks to the edicts of Queen Soraline, we have been released from that limitation." He reached into his coat and pulled out a piece of parchment—one of the many Sora had signed that first day. "The mountain will protect itself from Soole—and anyone else who crosses us—with Fire."

Lord Farrow muttered a foul curse, not quite under his breath, and even Lord Roven looked shocked. The nobles did *not* like the idea of Fire Weapons. The prospect made Sora nervous too. Unlike Fire-forged steel and blades imbued with a Fire core to make them faster, Fire Weapons used the molten substance itself to burn and maim. Outlawing them had been one of the First Good King's most-important acts—one that she had reversed. She glanced at the parchment on the polished wooden table. That was the most-troubling edict she had been forced to sign. No wonder Rafe had waited until now to reveal it to the others.

Using Fire Weapons to defend the mountain was one thing, but she doubted it would end there. If the Fireworkers started making the Works, what would happen if they disagreed with one another?

The nobles murmured amongst themselves. Some scooted their chairs farther away from the nearest Workers. Even Lord Samanar and Lady Tull, who had supported the Rollendars in their part of the coup, didn't like the turn the conversation had taken. They had been notably subdued since Lord Von—their choice to ascend the throne in Siv's place—had been killed. The Lantern Maker had used the Rollendars for their men and conspired to put Bolden on the throne instead of his father because they deemed him easier to control. The Rollendar supporters had thrown themselves behind the Lantern Maker after Bolden's death, but Sora wondered if they would be uncomfortable enough with this new turn of events to take action. They couldn't want the Workers to produce Fire Weapons.

On her left, Daz Stoneburner and Madame Pandan whispered to each other, blocking their words with their hands. Daz at least looked troubled by this development. Another Worker from Square leaned in to join the discussion. If the Lantern Maker noticed their rapid chatter, it didn't disturb him. On the whole, they seemed less enamored of Rafe's control than the others. Sora had already seen what the Square Workers could do with the Fire Wall the night of the coup. What would they be capable of if they turned their attention to creating Weapons? The idea of a fight of Fire between Worker factions filled her with dread.

The nobles left quickly when the meeting ended, not waiting to chat with their new peers. Sora leapt up and eased around the Lantern Maker to intercept Lord Roven before he got to the door.

"Do you have a moment, my lord?"

"My queen," Lord Roven said gravely. "I am glad to see you. Are you well?"

Sora glanced at the open door, catching sight of her guards hovering outside the council chamber. Kelad Korran and Telvin Jale were on duty—both her allies, though the Ruminors still believed Kel was their loyal swordsman. The men guarding her were always Vertigonian when the nobles came to visit. Captain Thrashe and the other Soolen guards would be waiting somewhere out of sight. Still, the presence of her friends outside the door reassured her.

"I'm okay," Sora said. "I wanted to ask if you've heard any news—news you might not want to share with the general council?" She glanced back at the Lantern Maker, who was speaking to Daz Stoneburner. Lima watched her suspiciously but didn't stop her from talking to Lord Roven.

"We aren't receiving any messengers right now, my queen," Lord

Roven said. He too looked over at the Fireworkers. "The Chief Regent is still restricting the flow of information to and from the mountain."

"If you hear anything of Trure and my grandfather, would you let me know?" Even though the Soolen army hadn't yet moved beyond the boundaries of Cindral Forest, she worried about her mother and sister. And Siv, if he still lived.

"Of course, my queen," Lord Roven said.

Sora studied the broad nobleman, with his reassuring bulk and his height that almost matched the Lantern Maker's. He had long been her father's ally. Would he be hers?

"Do you know if any of the nobles are unhappy with recent events? And the Chief Regent's rule?" Sora kept a neutral expression plastered on her face, nothing more than a queen making small talk with a subject.

Lord Roven frowned. "Forgive me for saying so, my queen, but I don't think you should be asking such questions."

"I'm just gathering information."

"For what purpose?"

"You heard him talking about Fire Weapons." Sora knotted her skirt in her hands. "He's destroying the Peace of Vertigon, everything my father worked for. We have to stop him."

"You can't stand against him." Lord Roven abandoned his formal demeanor and rested a heavy hand on her shoulder. "You're barely older than my Jully, Sora. Don't put yourself at risk."

"You don't think I should even try?"

Lord Roven shook his head firmly. "The Lantern Maker has won. He will find you a foreign prince to marry, and then you can be rid of this place. All you have to do is hold on until then."

"But—"

"I'd better take my leave," Lord Roven said, raising a hand to stop her from saying more. Sora realized that the last of the non-Fireworker nobles had already left, and Lima Ruminor was striding toward them, eyes blazing. "Be careful, and let me know if you need anything."

He strode from the council chamber before Sora could say another word. She wanted to stamp her foot. She *was* being careful. And she needed information, not coddling.

"What are you doing?" Lima said as she reached her.

"Just talking to my friend's father."

"You are not here to talk," Lima said. "We won't have you attending another council meeting if you can't follow instructions. Wait for us in the library. We have business to discuss."

Sora lifted her nose in the air and glided regally toward the door—or as regally as she could when she'd been summarily dismissed. She would not apologize or make excuses to her captors. They wanted her in the castle so they could maintain the illusion that there hadn't been a coup. They'd just have to accept that she wasn't a stuffed doll. She had a right to talk to her subjects.

Sora's guards fell in on either side of her as she left the council chambers. They only had a few minutes before Captain Thrashe joined them.

"Any word?" Kel asked, striding a little closer to her than a typical guard would. His polished boots tapped smartly on the stone floor.

"Lord Roven is loyal," she whispered, "but he thinks I should keep my head down."

"I can't say I'm surprised."

"There's dissent amongst the Fireworkers, though," Sora said. "The Workers from Square want to set up their own guild—and they're not as afraid of the Lantern Maker as the others. Daz Stoneburner is the head of their faction." She thought of Rafe meeting with Daz Stoneburner right now. He would try to lure him back to his side before the dissent got out of hand. She hoped Daz wouldn't fall for it.

"Interesting," Kel said. "We can use that."

"There's more." Sora looked back, but the corridor was deserted. "The Lantern Maker wants to experiment with Fire Weapons. And I don't think he's talking about new Fire Blades."

She heard a sharp intake of breath from Telvin. "That's not good."

"I agree," Sora said. She'd read about the weapons Firewielders made in ancient days. Even if half the legends were fabricated, they had a lot to fear from an arsenal of Fire. "We don't want them to start down that road."

"I wonder what General Pavorran thinks of all this," Telvin said.

Pavorran was the head of Vertigon's army. He had supported the Rollendars in their coup effort, so Sora wasn't inclined to trust him. Yet...

"He's based on Square Peak," she said. "It's possible he's part of the Square faction. It could be bad news for the Lantern Maker if he opposes this effort."

"I'll see what Berg Doban can tell me about Pavorran and Stoneburner," Kel said. "He knows everyone on Square."

"Don't get caught," Sora said anxiously.

"Are you worried about me, my queen?" Kel said with a grin. "You shouldn't be. I'm a master spy now."

Telvin snorted. "Didn't you get caught last time?"

"Only for a brief moment," Kel said. "Have no fear. I will—"

"Here comes the captain," Telvin said.

The two guards fell silent as Captain Thrashe joined them in the corridor. The Soolen with the eye patch was a quiet man, a malevolent presence who stalked her every move. It had been harder than she thought to communicate with her trustworthy guards under his watch. Captain Thrashe surveyed the trio for a moment and then dismissed Telvin, who snapped off a salute before marching in the direction of the barracks. Sora was sad to see him go. He was always a solid, comforting presence, with his military demeanor and his sharp appearance. He had sworn to be her loyal man, and his straightforward chivalry made her feel that the mountain could be good once more.

As they climbed the castle's central stairwell, she peeked at Kel out of the corner of her eye. He swaggered alongside her, face impassive, giving no indication that they had formed an alliance. He was harder to understand than Telvin. He was friendly and relaxed, but she got the sense that he was a more-complex person than he let on. He had perfected his image as a dueling heartthrob who surely would have no trouble securing another patron, enjoying the adoration of his fans, and living an uncomplicated life. Yet he had decided to take her side too. She hoped she would be worthy of both men's loyalty.

Captain Thrashe marched her to the library, where she'd be meeting with the Ruminors. He took up the guard post outside the door and dismissed Kel. The guardsman sauntered away without so much as a backward glance.

Sora waited for the Ruminors for almost an hour. They didn't speak to her very often, but they would likely need her to sign a few things after the council meeting. That seemed to be all they used her for: her signature and her name.

Sora paced around the library, trying to ignore the memories it conjured of her father and her brother. Both had loved this room as much as she did, with its soft carpets, shelves stretching all the way to the ceiling, and papery aroma. She ought to be studying the history texts for solutions to her current situation, as she'd been doing often since becoming queen. The Lantern Maker had cancelled her usual lessons, so she had only the books in the library to help her. She wished for a mentor or a teacher, someone who could help her know what to do next.

She went to the window looking out on the courtyard. Fresh snow had fallen overnight, pure and bright. The walls were coated in soft lamb's wool and the trees trimmed in diamonds. She leaned on the sill, mulling over what the Fireworkers had discussed during the council meeting. Weapons of Fire. Weapons that would make it impossible for her grandfather or anyone else to challenge them. Vertigon had long relied on its position on the mountain for safety, but the unspoken possibility of Fire Weapons had dissuaded other nations from turning their ambitions this way. That the weapons did not currently exist had never mattered. A few smiths made Fire Blades, weapons that were faster and deadlier than pure-steel swords, but how would the Fireworkers expand their efforts now? She imagined burning cages of Fire, rivers of suffocating heat, beads of light exploding as they entered the bodies of enemy soldiers, devices that could melt steel and burn through wood, potions more deadly than the Firetears that had killed her father. There was no telling what the Lantern Maker could create.

Why was he risking opening that door, though? Vertigon was still secure. Did he anticipate that her grandfather would retaliate for Siv's usurpation? It seemed unlikely. Her grandfather knew how protected Vertigon was—even without Fire Weapons. Rafe couldn't be worried enough to produce these weapons just because of the Amintelle allies and the nebulous threat from distant Soole.

But there was another possibility, one that scared her far worse. What if the Lantern Maker intended to take these Fire Weapons *off* the mountain? What if it was the other nations that had to worry about Vertigon reaching beyond its boundaries? Could that be why he was sowing seeds of discord between Trure, Soole, and Pendark?

Sora leaned her forehead against the cold glass. She wished she could talk over her suspicions with someone, if only to have her fears alleviated. She had no idea how isolating being queen would feel. She still wasn't permitted to speak to her maids, and the Ruminors were hardly good company. The stolen consultations with her loyal guards weren't enough.

Snow began to fall outside, drifting gently over the mountain. Movement caught her eye beneath the window. A short figure with thick arms crossed the courtyard, leaving footprints in the fresh snowfall. Daz Stoneburner must finally be finished speaking with the Lantern Maker. When he reached the gate, a cloaked figure stepped out of the shadows to join him. Judging by their respective heights, Sora was pretty sure that was the Metalworker, Madame Pandan.

The Workers left the courtyard together, deep in conversation. Interesting. Madame Pandan had waited for an awfully long time in the cold to speak to Daz. He had been a Ruminor ally during the coup. Could the tendrils of discord she had noticed during the meeting be gathering strength, or had Rafe already secured the Square Workers' continued cooperation?

A few minutes after the Workers disappeared through the gates, the Ruminors entered the library together. Both looked more relaxed than they had in the council chambers, though they weren't a particularly warm or affectionate couple.

"I have a new task for you," Lima said without preamble.

"Yes?"

"Lady Zurren has informed me that people in the city are worried about you. The rumors suggest you were killed, and we're parading around a decoy. You must go out in public more often to keep people from asking so many questions."

"I'll see if I can fit it into my schedule," Sora said.

"Don't speak to me like that, child," Lima said.

"I am the queen," Sora said. "If you want people to believe it, then maybe *you* should practice speaking to me with more respect."

"Come now, ladies," Rafe said expansively. "We have an understanding. Let's not sully our positive working relationship."

"I've had quite enough of being disrespected for one day," Lima said, not quite under her breath.

A flash of irritation passed over Rafe's face. It was gone quickly, but Sora knew she hadn't imagined it.

"Your hostility does not help matters, my dear."

Lima's expression took on a stony tint, and she didn't respond. Was it possible there was strife in the Ruminors' marriage? *I can work with that.*

"Now, I wish to ask you about Trure, Soraline," Rafe said. "I understand you have spent time in Rallion City. What can you tell me about its defenses?"

"Its defenses?"

"Yes." Rafe smiled. "The army, the wall around the inner city, how quickly the outlying nobility would be capable of sending soldiers to its aid."

"You want me to tell you the weaknesses of my grandfather's kingdom?" Sora couldn't keep the incredulity from her voice. Did they think she was stupid? She may be young, but she wouldn't simply hand over that kind of information to a man with Soolen allies—especially one who'd announced that he'd be experimenting with Fire Weapons that very day.

Rafe sat and folded his broad hands in front of him on the table. "You can start with Rallion City, but I want to know all about the Land of the Horse Keepers."

"I'm not telling you anything," Sora said. She jutted out her lower lip and stared them down.

Faster than she thought possible, Lima crossed the library and grabbed Sora by the hair. She barely had time to scream before Lima hauled her over to a chair and forced her to sit. When Lima released her, she ripped out a few curly strands of her hair.

"You seem to be under the mistaken impression that you have a choice," Lima hissed. She put her hands on the arms of the chair and leaned in close. "Give us the information."

"No," Sora said. Her voice shook, and it took all her willpower not to pull back from Lima's menacing stare. Her mother and sister were in Rallion City. She wouldn't make them vulnerable to Soole or the Fireworkers or anyone else. "You need me to cooperate? Fine. I'll keep Vertigon from worrying about me and making trouble for you, but I won't betray my family."

Lima drew back a few feet and slapped Sora across the face. The hit was completely unexpected, and her head cracked into the back of her chair, making her see stars.

"You can't—"

Lima slapped her again. Both cheeks stung with the force of the blows. Sora's eyes fill with tears. She stared at Lima in shock. No one had ever hit her before. She could hardly believe what was happening.

"Do not make me ask you again."

Lima's face twisted with bitterness. Sora had never felt such hatred directed toward her before. She didn't know what to do with this sudden change in tactics. She stared at Lima, not wanting to blink even though her face stung. Lima raised her hand again.

Desperately, Sora looked to the Lantern Maker. He was a calm, rational man. He couldn't approve of this, could he?

But Rafe was still sitting at the table, a piece of parchment spread before him, poised to begin writing.

"The information?" he said pleasantly.

Sora swallowed hard, her shoulders hunching despite her best efforts to appear unafraid. And she began to talk.

18

THE WILD

SIV groaned as his captors dumped him on the ground. It must be nighttime again. The days had started to run together. At least the sack over his head protected his face from being scraped in the dirt. He flopped to the side with a grunt, trying to ease the incessant pain in his wrists.

"Quit complaining," Charn growled.

"You'd complain too if your skin had started to grow in around your ropes," Siv muttered.

"Impossible," Charn said.

"I saw a fellow it happened to in Rallion City once," Siv said. "The man was afraid of knives and refused to have the rope cut out of him, so he just lived like that."

"How did he use the john?" asked Tech.

"Don't talk to him," Charn snapped.

Siv shrugged. "Some things you just don't ask a man, Tech," he said.

The fourth member of their party chuckled somewhere to Siv's left. His name was Resha, and Tech had let slip that he was related to the mysterious Commander Brach. Perhaps a second cousin or something.

The farther they'd gotten into the wilderness, the less the Soolens had worried about speaking in front of Siv. He'd been filing away every bit of information he could without asking too many suspicious questions. He wanted them to think he was the most-agreeable prisoner ever—at least until he made his escape.

It seemed to be working. Chala joked around with him as they rode along, his voice a welcome departure from the relentless creak of the wagons. Once, when they'd made camp inside a cave for the night, he even took the sack off Siv's head so he could join them in a game of cards.

"I figure one cave is just like the next," he'd said. "You won't be able to figure out where we are from a wall of stone."

Siv had played along, soaking in every detail about his captors while pretending to focus on the cards. That had been two days ago, and he went over the pertinent information in his head as his captors set up camp around him.

Chala Choven led this particular mission, but the other three had known each other for longer. Resha was a noble of modest means, and it sounded as if he'd been a bit of a rake before joining his cousin's force. Tech was as dumb as a stump, but he was bigger than Berg Doban after a feast. Siv was most worried about Charn. Resha and Tech deferred to him and seemed to respect his leadership more than Chala's. More importantly, Charn's quick, powerful movements suggested he was an experienced fighter—with or without weapons.

It was fights *with* weapons that interested Siv the most. His own sword had been taken from him the first time he got knocked out back in Rallion City, of course, but he took a careful tally of the Soolens' weaponry during the card game in the cave. They favored short swords rather than the rapiers he was used to, and each one carried a knife. Charn had additional knives strapped to his back with a harness. Siv had heard him throwing them into tree trunks at night, no doubt honing his aim.

He wouldn't stand a chance against all four at once, and it seemed unlikely that any of them would join forces with him. His best option would be to sneak away. The men had a regular watch rotation, but if Siv could ever slip his bonds, he may be able to overpower the watchman without too much noise and make his escape.

Then he'd have to get far enough away that they couldn't overtake him on horseback. He'd try to steal one of their mounts if it didn't make too noise, but he'd have no idea which way to ride. For all he knew they were almost to the Ammlen Ocean by now. He could accidentally flee smack into the sea. At first he'd tried to estimate which direction they were traveling by judging where the sun hit him, but the damn thing had been elusive lately. The winter sun barely provided any warmth at all, let alone enough for him to make any meaningful deductions about where they were heading.

The other thing he had determined through the bits and pieces he'd overheard was that he did not want to meet up with Commander Brach. The men spoke of him with respect bordering on reverence. To hear them tell it, Commander Brach could fight harder, run faster, dance better, and spit farther than every other man in Soole. He inspired natural devotion in his men, which made him an enemy Siv didn't particularly want.

He could try to get Commander Brach on his side, but Siv's confidence in his diplomacy skills had taken a beating lately. Nothing like a coordinated coup against your kingship to make you question whether you had the chops to be a diplomat and a ruler.

Siv had had a lot of time to think about what had happened during his interminable hours in the wagon—not to mention while he was trying to fall asleep on the icy ground each night. He had thought he was on the right path until Lady Tull betrayed him. Clearly he'd been wrong. He'd also thought he and his men could handle the mysterious swordsmen and whatever the Fireworkers threw his way. His sister had paid the price for his overconfidence. The farther they got from Vertigon, the more he felt it was best he was no longer a king.

One of the men—from the body odor, he suspected Tech—hoisted him up by the elbows and dumped him beside their latest campfire. He set him down too close to it, and Siv had to scramble back to avoid the heat. As it did every time, the warmth of the fire reminded him of Dara. He missed her reassuring presence with a fierceness that surprised him. He wished their last conversation hadn't been an argument. She deserved better than that. She probably deserved better than him.

He wondered if she was still searching the city. She wouldn't give up on him, but they had been traveling fast. She would have no idea at all where to look. He daydreamed about her sweeping in to rescue him, blade and Fire blazing, but the chances were vanishingly slim.

Besides, Dara had saved him enough times. He had to figure a way out of this on his own.

"There's been trouble on the Low Road," Resha said. Judging by his voice and the faint crackle of footsteps, he had just returned from somewhere away from the campsite. The Low Road? Had they come that far east? They would reach Cindral Forest soon if they kept up their current pace.

"What kind of trouble?" Chala asked sharply.

"Bandits. Spies. Just spoke with a courier from the commander. He had it from a group of scouts a few days ago."

"Well, were they bandits or spies?" Tech asked.

"Unclear."

"We'd best keep our eyes open," Chala said. "Did the courier say anything else?"

"Not for our friend's ears," Resha said. "I'll tell you later."

Siv muttered a curse under his breath. He wished they'd forget he was there more often. He might actually learn something useful one of these days. How many bands of Soolen scouts had already crossed into Trure? This was not good.

Branches snapped somewhere to Siv's right, followed by a suspicious rustling sound.

"What was that?" Tech said.

"Probably just an animal," Chala said. It sounded as if he'd taken a seat to Siv's left.

"Sounded big."

"Some animals are big," Siv said. "You ever seen a cullmoran?"

"There are no cullmorans this far south," Chala said.

"If you say so. That's not a risk I'd want to take," Siv said.

Another snap sounded, followed by a sharp intake of breath from one of the men.

"What if it's hungry?" Tech said.

"I'm sure it's nothing," Chala said, his words breezier than his tone. Siv distinctly heard the sound of a knife being drawn from its sheath. Chala must not be taking any chances.

"How are you sure?" Tech asked.

"Go make the rounds again, you big baby," Resha said. His voice came from the opposite side of the campfire now. He must have taken a seat across from them.

"It's dark out there," Tech said.

"Take a damn light."

"Charn has the Everlight on watch," Tech said.

"Did it occur to you that Charn's the one making the noise?" Resha said.

"That you, Charn?" Tech called, his voice sounding a little thin.

"Maybe it ate him already," Siv said. "Cullmorans have really big teeth. I have a scar from one on my arm. Want to see it, Tech?"

"You're lying."

"I'd never lie to you," Siv lied.

"Where's the scar?"

Tech shifted a little closer to Siv on his right-hand side. Could he risk making a move when Tech came within reach? He still didn't know where Charn was.

The rustling sound came again. Tech stopped moving. Silence surrounded them for a half a heartbeat. Then there was an almighty shout, and footsteps crashed out of the brush.

"Look out!"

"To your weapons!"

"Argh!"

Commotion erupted around them, all the sounds garbled. Siv wasted no time. He rolled onto his back and aimed a kick at where he thought Tech's knees were. His feet collided with something solid. The general chaos masked Tech's pained exclamation. Siv quickly flipped over and rolled the other way to where he estimated Chala had been. Though he didn't time it perfectly, he managed to barrel into the man's legs and send him crashing to the ground.

Steel clashed, and the sounds of a fight rioted around Siv. There had to be half a dozen men around the campfire now, their curses and shouts filling the air.

Siv scrambled for a grip on Chala, who was trying to stand up and flee. He couldn't do much with his hands and feet tied, but he could at least make it harder for the man to escape. He rolled on top of him and brought his knees up, digging them into the man's stomach. Chala grunted and cursed, finally managing to force Siv off of him.

"She stabbed me!" Tech hollered through the din. "I need help!"

She? Dara was here! He knew it! Siv got in one more good kick before Chala scrambled out of his reach. The sound of something metal hitting the ground accompanied his grunt. That was what Siv had been waiting for. He gave up trying to hold onto Chala and felt around for the knife the man had dropped. Chala was a drinker and gambler, not a fighter, but Siv knew he'd had a knife in his hand. Dirt, rocks, and leaves met his fingers. It had to be here somewhere.

The fight raged around the campfire, the clang of steel and voices filling the air. It sounded as if his captors were putting up a good fight. Damned if Siv was going to let Dara save him again without his help!

His fingers closed on cold steel. He had the knife! He stretched around and sawed through the bonds on his ankles. Someone stumbled nearer to him, and he tossed out a rapid kick as he went to work on his wrists. The sack still covered his head.

"Here she comes again!" someone yelled.

Damn it! Dara was going to get all the bad guys before Siv even had a chance to fight. Maneuvering the knife with his hands tied proved difficult, especially when he couldn't see. He nicked his wrist as he finally managed to cut through the rope. With a triumphant yell he ripped the sack off his head and leapt to his feet.

Cloaked figures darted around a clearing in a dense wood. Burning brands spread across the ground where someone had kicked the campfire. Steel flashed in the firelight. Tech was on his knees, perhaps unable to stand, savagely waving a short sword at a muscular, broadsword-wielding opponent. An athletic female figure was engaged in a vicious duel with Resha on the opposite side of the scattered fire. Siv barely had time to take in all the details before Charn leapt out of the darkness and rushed at him, short sword raised.

Siv ducked and drove his shoulder into Charn's stomach. The man flipped right over him, managing to get an arm around his neck as he fell. Siv landed on top of him and rolled, trying to avoid Charn's blade. His limbs were shaky from being tied up for so long. He lost his grip on his knife, and it dropped to the ground, lost in the darkness.

They grappled in the dirt, both trying to gain control of Charn's short sword. Siv threw punches whenever he could, ignoring the twinge of pain in his wrists. Pins and needles shot through his limbs.

Charn performed another sneaky flip move and ended up on Siv's back with his arms wrapped around his head. He tightened his hold, beginning to cut off his air supply. Siv rolled, trying to squash Charn beneath him. He couldn't quite get a grip on him. The man was as slippery as a panviper.

A sudden heat near Siv's arm warned him they were too close to the remnants of the campfire. He rolled the other way, managing to loosen Charn's headlock at last. Siv scrambled around, getting on top of his opponent before Charn could get him in another clinch. Siv reared back and landed a few good punches. Charn seemed momentarily stunned, and Siv laid into him, hammering his face with both fists.

An instant later Siv was flying through the air. He hit the ground with a painful thud. Charn had thrown him, catching him off balance while he whaled away at his face. Sneaky bastard. Before Siv could figure out which way was up, Charn leapt on top of him again. This time he had his short sword.

Siv grabbed desperately for the cross guard as Charn drove the blade toward his throat. The sword was shorter than Siv's arms, but the tip hovered dangerously close to his neck. It took all Siv's strength to hold Charn back. Then the man uttered a guttural snarl and threw his weight on top of the blade.

Siv twisted to the side at the last instant, allowing the blade to slice straight past his neck and into the ground beneath him. The sudden shift threw Charn off balance, and all his weight came down atop the hilt, bringing his head so close that Siv could have kissed him.

Instead, Siv snaked his arms around Charn's neck and pulled one of the knives from the harness on his back. He sliced it across Charn's jugular before the man had time to pull back.

Charn's eyes widened as his blood spurted out over Siv's chest. Then he collapsed on top of him, his last breath leaving his body along with his blood.

The world was utterly quiet for a moment, and all Siv could hear was the beat of his own heart. He was alive! What a pleasant surprise that was.

He shoved Charn's body off of him and got shakily to his feet.

"See, I'm not totally incapable of taking care of myself, Dara," he said, striking a relaxed pose and turning toward his favorite swordswoman.

But the woman cleaning Resha's blood off her blade wasn't his Dara after all. Dara was nowhere to be seen in the clearing. Instead, four complete strangers turned toward Siv, standing over the bodies of his erstwhile captors. Every single one had a weapon in hand.

19

STORM CLOUDS

DARA wondered what Vine would do if she left her behind. It was tempting. Vine had been leading them over the Truren plains for days, weaving back and forth across the windswept land whenever she felt the Air urging her to turn. It was taking twice the time it should to travel this distance. Their meandering path had led them across miles upon miles of farmland, followed by miles upon miles of wilderness.

They were back to farmland again. Occasionally they'd encounter farmers or other riders and ask for information, but no one had seen a man matching Siv's description. The strangers were all curious about the two women traveling alone with nothing but two horses and a cur-dragon for company. Rumy tried to fly away whenever they met other travelers, but sometimes there was nowhere to hide. The plains offered little cover.

Dara probably could have traveled through Trure without drawing too much notice, but Vine sat her horse like a lady, and her elaborately embroidered clothes drew all the attention Dara had been hoping to avoid. Vine also had an unfortunate habit of stopping to chat amiably with everyone they encountered, sometimes for half an hour at a time. Dara grew increasingly nervous that whoever had kidnapped Siv would hear about the two women asking questions. And her father still may have sent men out to find her. She could be in as much danger as Siv was.

Dance of Steel

Maybe Dara should set out alone after all. She'd have no idea which way to go, but she was beginning to think Vine didn't know either.

"The Air is not a slave to any woman's wishes," Vine had said when Dara asked whether she thought this strategy was working on the third day outside of Rallion City.

"I thought you could ask things of it," Dara grumbled.

"I have asked. I have been bringing my supplications to the Air each morning when I wake, and it is helping to guide our steps for the day."

"Are you *sure* you know what you're doing?"

"I first learned to commune with the Air many years ago," Vine said.

Dara sighed. "That doesn't answer my question."

"You met Meza. You saw what the Sensors did with the water. Surely you don't doubt it still."

"They did something, all right," Dara said. "They moved a bit of water. You're trying to find a missing person. That's a little different."

"It is all the same to the Air," Vine said.

She had resumed staring across the plains without seeing them, letting the breeze flow through her hair, and communing with the uncooperative Air. Dara had gone back to doing footwork across the dirt and trying not to make eye contact with her horse.

When they weren't riding, Dara kept up with her training. She had fully recovered after the Fire fight, and she was regaining her former fitness level. The clean slices of her blade and the pulse of her feet on the earth soothed her worries about what could be happening to Siv. They used Rumy's dragon fire to build campfires in the chilly evenings, but she avoided touching the flickers of true Fire within it. She wasn't ready to embrace that power again yet. She focused on the practical aspects of their travel as much as possible and on ensuring that she would never be made weak again.

On the afternoon of their fifth day since leaving Rallion City, they stopped beside an old stone stable to eat lunch. The roof of the structure had caved in, and plants grew wild within it. After a lunch of flatbread and jerky, Vine perched atop the stone wall with her legs crossed to meditate. Rumy napped in the dirt beneath her, and Goldenflower and Storm grazed nearby on long leads.

Dara felt uneasy, though she wasn't sure why. She scanned the plains around them. The road they'd been following that day curved toward the south. She thought she saw buildings to the southeast, but it was hard to tell across the hazy expanse. The dark smudge of a grove of trees was visible to the northwest. She felt exposed in this wide, flat land. She missed the dramatic peaks of Vertigon. There was nothing like standing on a bridge over the Fissure and being able to see all the way to the Burnt Mountains.

Storm clouds gathered in the north now, ominous and heavy. She shivered, though it wasn't nearly as cold as Vertigon at this time of year. It must be almost midwinter. Tomorrow, Siv would have been gone for a full week. Her heart gave a painful stutter at the thought. She clutched the pendant in her fist and pushed away the anxiety. She had to focus on the task at hand.

She turned in a slow circle, alert for signs of trouble. Vine claimed she'd be able to Sense danger through the Air, but Dara had the sneaking sensation they were being followed. The feeling had lasted for days now, but she hadn't yet seen any evidence that her worries were founded. The open land didn't seem like a place where someone could follow them easily. She shrugged off the feeling. Those storm clouds presented a different, more-immediate problem.

Vine still perched atop the stable wall. She gave no sign of stirring from her meditation. Her hands rested on the knees of her embroidered trousers, and she breathed steadily, eyes closed, as the wind ruffled her hair.

"Are you almost ready?" Dara asked when she couldn't wait any longer.

"Hmm? Oh, hello, Dara." Vine blinked slowly at her.

"Did you find anything?"

"No . . . not at the moment."

Something in her tone made Dara pause. "What do you mean?"

"This is becoming rather challenging," Vine said. "I do love a good challenge. Only . . ."

"What?"

Vine frowned and combed her fingers through her long hair. "Well, I'm finding it harder to grasp onto him than before," she said.

"What are you saying?"

"The Air doesn't want to cooperate."

Dance of Steel

"Are you . . ." Dara swallowed hard. "Are you sure he's still alive?"

"I do hope so, Dara. It would be a shame to come all this way if he wasn't."

Abruptly, Dara had had enough. She gripped Vine by the arms and hauled her off the low stone wall. Rumy started up from his nap and scrambled a few feet away.

"I need you to be more specific," Dara said, making Vine look her in the eyes. "We can't keep wandering around like this. Can you find him or not?"

"Dara, you have so much tension in you sometimes," Vine said. "Have you considered—"

"Vine!"

"Okay." Vine sighed, slumping against the rock wall. "I'm . . . I'm not sure. I thought I could use the Air well enough to do this, but for the past few days I haven't been sure whether I was following the trail or merely wanting to follow it."

Dara fought against a sudden constricting fear in her chest. She had to stay calm. "Explain."

"It's an imprecise feeling, Dara. I know a bit about how the Fire works, so I understand you must be expecting more clarity, but the Air just isn't the same. You have to trust the feelings and yourself. I'm afraid of messing up because I know this is important. It's making me lose confidence, and the Air respects confidence." Vine's brown eyes filled with tears. "I don't want to let you down. That makes it even harder to get centered."

Dara sighed and released Vine's shoulders. She understood what it was like to struggle to control a power. She'd had an especially hard time Working without using her hands. Zage Lorrid had been a patient teacher, but it took her a while to grow accustomed to the mysterious connection with the Fire that allowed her to Work with her mind alone. It had required a different kind of diligence than dueling—and the confidence of a long-suffering instructor.

Vine was trying to help. Dara shouldn't blame her for her difficulties, even though she was worried they were running out of time to find Siv.

"I'm sorry for snapping," she said at last. "I've never known you to lose confidence in yourself. You're Vine Silltine! You can do it."

"Thank you, Dara." Vine sniffed and blinked back her tears. "I didn't want to say anything. I wasn't sure you'd understand, but it feels good to get it off my chest." She took a deep breath and smiled. "I feel much better now. I truly have no idea where we're going!" And she waltzed back to her horse.

Dara gaped at her. Fortunately, there was no Fire in the land here—otherwise she'd be tempted to set Vine's hair alight. Dara swallowed her irritation, told Rumy it was time to go, and scrambled back into her saddle. Storm snorted but didn't dance around beneath her as much as usual. Maybe she was getting the hang of riding at last. From the sounds of things, she and Vine would be stuck wandering through the wilderness for the rest of their lives. She might as well get comfortable on horseback.

Gloom threatened to pull her under as they resumed their journey. Vine didn't know where they were going, and the Air wasn't helping. The trail—if there had ever been one in the first place—had gone cold. Siv was in the wind, and Dara didn't know what to do next. She wished Vine hadn't shared her misgivings after all. At least when she'd been pretending to know where she was going, there had been hope. What were they going to do now?

The storm clouds amassing in the north grew darker, denser. Lightning spiked in the distance, striking more frequently as darkness fell. A cold wind swept across the plain, carrying hints of rain. With it came the familiar sensation that someone was watching them. Dara didn't fancy spending another night sleeping in the mud. She felt on edge, and Vine wasn't likely to make any progress on her Air Senses if she was exhausted. They needed shelter and a warm bed for the night.

They were approaching the boundaries of a sprawling farm. A house was visible in the dusk, lights glowing from half a dozen windows. Dara heeled her horse forward to catch up with Vine, whom she hadn't spoken to since their conversation by the old stable.

"Let's see if we can stay at that farm for the night," she said.

"Are you sure?"

Dara nodded. "Maybe these folks have seen someone passing by." She was always reluctant to ask strangers for help, but they were getting desperate.

Vine began to look hopeful. "They *are* right by the road."

"If nothing else, maybe they have a map."

"All right, then." Vine studied the farmhouse for a moment. "We'd better tell them you're my bodyguard. Trurens never believe when a noble lady travels without attendants."

"Maybe we shouldn't mention your noble status," Dara said. "It raises too many questions."

"Dara, people love to help ladies." She patted Dara's arm. All hints of her former uncertainty had vanished. "Leave the talking to me."

Vine spurred Goldenflower toward the farm, not waiting for a response. Dara waved at Rumy to hurry along and trotted after her.

The farmhouse was a short, sprawling building off the main road. Constructed of humble materials, its single-story structure appeared to contain room for a lot of people. Dwellings in Vertigon were typically set into the mountainside, sometimes making use of natural caves. It was difficult to tell how large a Vertigonian house was from the outside. But here in Trure, land was available in abundance.

A stable nestled beside the farmhouse, and a broad field spread out in back. The field looked brown and lifeless thanks to the winter chill, but warm light spilled out of the windows of the house. Dara felt a glimmer of hope as they approached. They should just make it indoors before the storm hit.

But as they entered the yard in front of the farmhouse, a piercing scream shattered the quiet evening. Dara froze, her hand going to her sword.

"What is that?" a voice screeched.

"It's a giant lizard!"

"Mummy, come see!"

"No! Make it go away!"

Tiny figures started popping into view all around the farmyard. Dara counted three, four, at least five of them. The gaggle of children drew nearer, all pointing and staring at Rumy, who was trundling along beside the horses.

"Don't go near it, Jin!" shouted a high-pitched, frightened voice. A little girl stood on the farmhouse porch, peeking over the railing.

A boy of around ten, who'd been approaching them cautiously, looked over his shoulder and shouted. "I ain't afraid of no lizard, Shir!"

"Don't say 'ain't,' Jin," said another girl, who followed close on his heels. She examined Rumy with almost as much excitement as Jin.

"Why's it so big?" asked a smaller boy. He had crept to the porch steps but didn't get any closer.

"Maybe it got magicked!" said Jin.

"You mean 'someone used magic on it,'" said the girl beside him.

"Or it magicked itself, Kay," Jin said.

"*I've* never heard of a magic lizard," Kay said. She turned bright-green eyes on Dara and Vine. "Is it magic?"

In answer, Rumy reared up on his hind legs, making the children start, and blew a jet of flame straight into the air.

The children squealed, some in delight and some in fear. The little girl on the porch—Shir—screamed and disappeared inside the farmhouse. A second later, the door opened again, and a short, round woman with pale-blond hair hurried out.

"What is all this ruckus? Jin, are you scaring your sisters again?"

"Mummy, look!" cried the little boy sitting on the porch step. "It's a magic lizard!"

"I think it's actually a dragon," said Kay knowledgeably. "I've read about them."

"Goodness me! Why didn't you tell me we had visitors?" the woman said. She disentangled the small boy tugging on her skirts and hurried down the porch steps. "And a lady, no less!"

"Good evening, ma'am," Vine said. "We were traveling by your lovely home, and we wondered if you might have a room to spare for the evening?"

"You can stay in our room!" called another girl. She looked to be about the same age as Kay, possibly her twin. She stared at Vine's elegant clothes with wide eyes and twisted her hands in her skirt.

"Hush now, Kol," said the woman. "I'm afraid we don't have much, my lady," she said. "I'm sure you'd be more comfortable if you press on to the village. They've a decent inn off the square."

"I fear we won't make it there before the rain begins," Vine said, glancing up at the storm clouds looming nearer to the farmhouse. Lightning flashed as she turned back to the woman. "Your children are absolutely delightful. We'd be honored to stay in your home."

"Please let them, Mummy," begged Kol.

"What about the dragon lizard?" Jin said. "What if it eats the baby?"

"He's a cur-dragon," Dara said. "He doesn't eat people."

"Too bad," Jin said.

"A cur-dragon?" said Kay. "Neat!"

"Can you make him spit fire again?" called the other little boy, who still hadn't relinquished his position on the porch steps.

"He has a mind of his own," Dara said. "I can't really make him—"

Rumy squawked at her and sent another burst of flame into the air. The children cheered.

"Oh dear," said their mother. "Is it safe?"

"He's harmless, ma'am," Dara said. "He can sleep on the porch, if you allow us to take shelter here tonight."

The children turned to their mother, giving her wide-eyed, pleading smiles.

"Oh, very well," she said with a sigh. "We'd best get those horses into the stables before the rain comes. Jin, go find your father."

"Thank you for your kindness," Vine said, dismounting gracefully. "I am Vine Silltine, and this is my bodyguard, Dara. What may we call you?"

"I'm Roma," she said. "And I don't reckon these ones will stay still long enough for you to get them all straight. Please make yourselves at home."

In short order, Roma's husband, a quiet man called Yen, whisked the horses off to the stables, and Dara and Vine were settled at the huge round table inside the farmhouse with steaming mugs of tea. Rumy had been instructed to wait on the porch, and the children alternated between watching him through the windows and darting back to Dara and Vine to ask questions about him.

A natural fire crackling in a stone hearth warmed the cozy farmhouse. Doors led to various bedrooms off the main room, which was kitchen, dining room, and living area combined. Roma bustled around the farmhouse, picking up stray boots, socks, and wooden toys from the floor.

"Sorry about the mess," she said.

"We don't mind at all," Vine said, somehow looking just as at home in the farmhouse as she did in a palace. "We're so grateful for your hospitality."

"Are you a real lady?" asked Kol. She and her twin, Kay, were the oldest of the children. There were seven including the baby, who was fast asleep in a bassinet despite all the commotion, and a toddler, who waddled around, generally getting underfoot. They all had bright-green eyes and pale-blond hair. Kol wore hers long, whereas her twin kept her locks pulled back in a bun at the nape of her neck. Kay had disappeared into one of the bedrooms to retrieve a weathered book, which had roughly drawn pictures of various fanciful creatures in it. She and Jin were busy poring over the entry about dragons in all their varieties while Kol hung around Vine's chair.

"Do you live in a palace?" she asked.

"I am a lady," Vine said, "but I live in a greathouse, not a palace."

"Is that like a manor house?" asked Kol.

"Just like a manor house," Vine said.

"Have you ever been to a ball?"

"Oh yes. Balls are lovely."

"I wish *I* could go to a ball." Kol sighed dramatically. "Have you ever danced with a prince?"

"Indeed I have. And so has Dara. A wonderfully handsome one too."

Dara shot Vine a warning glance. She felt safe here, but it probably wouldn't be wise to share too much about themselves. Vine did love being adored, and Kol was fast becoming her biggest fan.

Dara felt a tug on her sleeve. The little boy who had stayed on the porch steps while his siblings investigated Rumy stared up at her with wide eyes.

"You have a sword," he whispered.

"Yes," she said. "Would you like to see it?"

"Yes, please."

Dara looked up at Roma. "Is it all right?"

Roma nodded. "Be careful now, Ber. Do what Miss Dara tells you."

"It's very sharp," Dara warned as she carefully drew her Savven blade from its sheath. "It's heavy too, so you'd better hold it with two hands."

She placed the black hilt in Ber's hands and made sure he had a good grip before letting go. He stared at the sleek steel blade, eyes wide, and didn't move an inch.

"Why is it so hot?" he asked after a moment.

"What do you mean?"

"It feels like a poker in the fire," Ber said. "I didn't know swords got hot."

Dara took the blade back from him, surprised. "You can feel that?"

"I want to feel!" Jin shouted. He charged over to Dara, knocking against his little brother as he reached out to touch the sword. "What are you talkin' about, Ber? It feels cold to me."

"I want to try too!" The other children lined up to touch the blade. Only Kay could feel the heat like Ber.

"What does it mean?" she asked, fixing Dara with intelligent eyes.

"It's a Fire Blade," came a quiet voice from the door. The children's father had returned from the stables. Rain fell behind him in a quiet rush. Yen wore a broad-brimmed hat, and he took it off to shake away the water as he came inside. For the first time, they could see that unlike Roma and their children, Yen's hair was a deep-bronze color.

"You're from Vertigon," Dara said.

"Aye," Yen said. "It has been a long time since I last saw a Fire Blade."

"Do you want to see if you can feel the heat too?" Kay asked her father.

"I already know I can," Yen said, meeting Dara's eyes steadily. *A Fireworker.* What was a man with the Firespark doing in a farmhouse in Trure? "I think Miss Dara can feel it too."

Dara inclined her head, watching Yen warily. He said nothing more. What would he do now that he knew they shared this ability? It shouldn't matter to these people, but the sudden exposure of Dara's secret made her uneasy.

"Well!" Vine clapped her hands, breaking the tension between them. "I'm starving! May I help you with supper, Roma?"

The children rushed to assist Vine and their mother as she assembled a simple meal of root vegetables and roasted plains pheasant. Dara returned her Savven to its sheath and avoided making eye contact with Yen. She helped Jin and Kay feed Rumy some raw pheasant, and then they joined the rest of the family at the large round table.

The children chattered over each other as they ate, asking Vine and Dara endless questions about Vertigon, Rumy, and what it was like to be a noble lady. Visitors didn't come this way very often, and the children were curious about the world outside their farm. Roma kept busy feeding the baby and preventing the littlest ones from dropping food on the floor. Yen didn't say much, but he listened carefully to everything they said. Dara stuck to a vague outline of their mission to find a lost friend, almost wishing they had given false names. Naturally, they left out the part about Siv being the king.

Rain pounded the roof of the farmhouse. Distant rolls of thunder punctuated their conversation, making Dara grateful they didn't have to stay outside tonight. After they finished eating, Vine gathered the children around her on the rug by the fire and told stories. She gave animated renditions of classic tales, like the Legend of Teall and Daran. The children requested their favorites, some of which Vine knew and some she confessed she'd never heard before. Kay volunteered to tell these ones, her voice strong and sure as she entertained her young siblings.

Dara glanced at Roma. She rocked the baby on her lap and cooed, watching her brood with soft eyes. A lump formed in Dara's throat at the sight, and she found herself thinking about her own parents. They'd never created such an atmosphere of warmth at home. Her father was often preoccupied with his work, and her mother was too practical for stories. Dara mourned what her parents had become almost as much as she mourned her sister's death.

She often relied on what her parents had given her to keep moving forward—her mother's practicality and her father's intensity had become some of her greatest strengths—but she didn't want to develop her mother's coldness too.

"May I have a word?"

Dara started. Yen had appeared beside her. He beckoned with a calloused hand, and she followed him to the window. The rain blurred the details of the yard out front. Rumy slept on the porch beneath the window, snoring contentedly.

"My children like you," Yen said softly. "I don't think you'll harm us."

"Of course not! We—"

"I have to know what you're running from before you stay the night under my roof."

"We're not running from anything," Dara said. "We're looking for a friend, like we said."

"A friend." The skepticism was plain on Yen's weathered face.

"He was kidnapped."

"I see." Yen frowned, still waiting.

"That isn't the full story," Dara said. "But the less you know the better, wouldn't you agree?"

Yen considered this statement for a long time, his expression cloaked. Dara steeled herself for refusal. Maybe they'd be sleeping in the rain after all.

At last, Yen spoke. "There were riders behind you on the road. They never passed the farm. I looked away for a moment, and they had disappeared. Are you sure you aren't running?"

A chill went through Dara that had little to do with the cold night.

"How many were there?"

"Three at the least." He tugged at his earlobe and looked back at the group gathered around the fire. "I can't put my family in danger."

"I don't know who's chasing us—if that's what they're doing," Dara said. "We'll leave if you want us to, though."

Lightning flashed outside, followed an instant later by a peal of thunder. The storm was intensifying. It must be right on top of them now.

Yen sighed, the tension in his shoulders loosening. "I won't turn you out in this." He looked back at his family, safe in a pool of light around the hearth. "Is this friend you're looking for a Fireworker too?"

"No," Dara said. "Just me. And I'm not even a full Worker. I discovered my Spark late in life."

"I see."

"And you?" Dara said. "Did you remain in Vertigon long enough to train in the Work?"

"Aye," Yen said. "I was a Metalworker's apprentice. Made silverware mostly. I traveled to Rallion City to sell my master's wares in my early twenties. That's where I met Roma. I fell in love and haven't returned to the mountain since."

"Do you miss it?" Dara wished she could take back the words as soon as they were out of her mouth. She didn't want to let on that she missed the rush of heat, the way the Fire made her feel invincible. Not Rumy's spurts and the trickle of Fire she'd drawn from the Works back in the palace, but the vast, unrestrained flood of it. Sometimes she imagined that if she Wielded the Fire in the magnificent quantities she'd experienced that night in the Great Hall, she would be able to find Siv. It was nonsense, but she hadn't been able to shake the thought. Siv and the Firespark had entered her life at the same time. The power would always be linked with him in her mind. She wasn't sure she could be whole without either one of them.

And her desire for that furious, burning torrent was the thing she'd inherited from her father that scared her most of all.

Yen met her eyes steadily, seeming to understand. "When I first moved to the Horseplains, I craved it worse than anything," he said. "The desire never goes away."

"How do you cope?" Dara asked. If she truly never returned to Vertigon, she needed some way to resist the incessant itch.

Yen gestured toward his family. "This here makes it easier," he said. "Find something you love more than the power, and hold on to it with everything you have."

Dara reached for the pendant around her neck. She thought she understood.

Dara and Yen returned to the warm circle of his family. Yen dropped a kiss on top of Roma's head and took the baby so she could rest her arms. Dara sat on the floor, and seven-year-old Shir climbed onto her lap and started playing with the end of her golden braid, comparing the color to her own pale hair. Dara smiled at the little girl, hoping that one day she'd figure out how to fill the ache inside her as Yen had.

Lightning crashed outside, and Dara's thoughts turned to Siv.

Was he caught in the rain somewhere? Was there any chance Vine would Sense his trail again? Thunder boomed, making the windows shudder. Shir squealed and threw her arms around Dara's neck. She hugged her tight, hoping Siv wasn't out in this storm—or in worse danger.

20

THE FIGHTERS

SIV faced the four strangers across the scattered remnants of the campfire. He still had Charn's knife in his hand and a substantial amount of Charn's blood on his clothes. Adrenaline from the fight coursed through him, but he wouldn't be able to take four people at once, especially when they'd made short work of his Soolen captors. Even Chala Choven was dead—the poor bastard. Stabbing his way out of this wasn't an option.

"Hello," he said, trying out his friendliest grin. "Thanks for the rescue."

"Rescue?" The swordswoman snorted and pointed her blade at him. "Guess again."

"Hey now," Siv said quickly. "There's no need for that."

"Who are you?" asked a tanned, muscular man, who was even bigger than Tech. All four strangers were decidedly fit and muscular. And they held their weapons as though they knew how to use them.

"Just a hapless traveler," Siv said. "I was taking the High Road from Rallion City to Fork Town when I was set upon by these miscreants."

"We're a long way from the High Road," said the big man.

"It's been a rough week." Siv tightened his grip on Charn's knife, keeping it close at his side. The woman's eyes flickered to it instantly.

"What were you going to Fork Town for?" she demanded. Too

late, Siv realized her accent had a particular lilt for which Fork Town was famous. He'd have to be careful with his story.

"I'm a wine merchant," Siv said. "Going to pick up new stock. Fork Town makes the best wine this side of the Bell Sea."

"Got any left?" asked the big man.

"Sadly no, not after being kidnapped by these unsavory characters." Siv prodded Charn's body with his toe.

"Curious. Very curious indeed." The oldest of the four took a step closer, studying him intently. He was short, with a deep tan and curly, graying hair. He wore a rich-looking red baldric, and Siv got the immediate impression that he was the man in charge here. "What would a group of Soolen scouts want with a Truren wine merchant?"

"He doesn't look Truren to me," said the big man. His hair was flaxen, and despite his bulk Siv guessed he was from the Horseplains himself.

"My mother is Truren," Siv said. "My father was born in Vertigon, but he returned to the mountain when I was young. I grew up in Rallion City, not far from Valor Racing Grounds."

"Thanks for the life story," the woman muttered. "Can I kill him, Kres?"

Siv winced. He shouldn't talk so much. Of course they'd realize he was lying.

"Hold on, Gull, dear," said the leader in red—Kres. "I've never seen a wine merchant fight like that. He's scrappy. I like it."

"He got lucky," said the fourth—and youngest—man. Siv gave a start when he realized this fellow was Soolen. He had the characteristic dark complexion and sleek black hair, but he wore it short, unlike Chala Choven, who'd always been so proud of his long ponytail. He wasn't wearing Soolen clothes either.

"That was more than luck," said Kres. He fixed Siv with an intelligent gaze. "This one's got fight in him."

"Uh, thank you." Siv cleared his throat. "I'd better be on my way if you don't mind." He surveyed the clearing, wondering if he'd have a chance to make a break for it. He probably wouldn't get ten feet. His limbs were still shaky after being tied up for so long. "Could someone point me in the direction of the High Road?"

"Don't move," snapped Gull, brandishing her sword. "I say we kill him."

"Come now," said Kres. "No need for all this hostility. Why don't you tell us why you're really here, lad? And exactly who you intend to report to on the High Road."

"I don't know what you mean." *Great. They think I'm a spy. They're going to kill me.*

"He was with the blasted Soolens," Gull said. "That's answer enough for me." She glanced at their Soolen companion. "No offense."

"In case you didn't notice, I killed one of them." Siv nodded at Charn's corpse. "Would have done the others if you hadn't come along."

"Indeed." Kres smiled, revealing a shiny row of perfect white teeth. "The enemy of our enemy is our friend."

"You're not thinking about keeping him, are you, boss?" asked the woman—Gull. "Don't we have enough misfit projects for one squad?"

The Soolen boy scowled at her. He must be one of the projects.

"As it happens, we are one short for the Dance." Kres tapped his knife against his perfect teeth, scrutinizing Siv—and the body on the ground beside him. "What do you say, friend? Ever wanted to be a pen fighter?"

"A what?"

"You've never heard of pen fighting?" said the young Soolen scornfully. He was right around Siv's age—twenty—a little wider in the shoulders, but not quite as tall.

"I've heard of it," Siv said. "But never in Trure. As far as I know, Pendark is the only place where pen fighting is still legal."

"Sounds like someone got an education in what matters," Kres said. "I could use a decent fighter like you on my squad. Trust me: the gold is better than anything you'd earn peddling Fork Town wine."

Siv blinked. "You . . . you think I could be a pen fighter?"

A wild light flitted through Kres's eyes for an instant. "If you stick with me, I'll make you a pen *champion*. In any case, we can't have you running off and reporting what you saw here. You will travel with us until we can be sure of who you really are."

"Thanks for the offer, but I should be—"

Abruptly, Kres had a knife in each hand, and he'd closed the distance between them. He had barely moved! One of the blades lay cold against Siv's neck before he could even gasp. The other rested on the wrist of his knife arm.

"That wasn't a request."

Yes, Siv definitely wasn't walking out of this one alive. He didn't know what sort of spy Kres thought he was, but they wouldn't let him leave in a hurry. He took a breath, and the knife bit into his throat. Okay, no breathing. Maybe he could pretend to go along with this pen-fighting scheme—at least until they found their way to a road. He could try fighting his way out there. His knees picked that moment to wobble, reminding him that he didn't stand a chance against them alone right now.

"All right," he said. "I'm in."

A slow smile spread across Kres's face. "I had a feeling you would be. What's your name, son?"

"I'm Siv—ren." He cleared his throat. "Sivren Amen."

"Welcome to the team, Sivren Amen." Kres removed the two knives from Siv's arteries at last, making them disappear in an instant. He stuck out a hand. "I'm Krestian March, the best damn pen fighter ever to spring from the fetid swamps of Pendark. You've met Gull Mornington, swordswoman extraordinaire—and a wicked dancer if you're lucky enough to see it."

Gull spit on a burning brand at her feet and took her time sheathing her blade. Siv resolved never to ask her to dance if he wanted to keep his head attached to his shoulders.

"And this magnificent colossus," Kres continued, patting the huge blond Truren on the shoulder, "is Fiz Timon. He's smarter than he looks."

Fiz stuck out his meaty hand. "A pleasure," he said.

"And last but not least is my protégé, my heir-apparent if he doesn't screw up too badly: Latch."

The young Soolen man jerked his head in what was probably the least-friendly nod Siv had ever seen.

"Best clean up this mess and get some sleep, children," Kres said. "We leave for Pendark at dawn."

Siv almost grinned. He'd always wanted to see Pendark. Of

course, there was no way he'd get that far. He'd return to Dara and his family as soon as he could slip away—or convince the pen fighters he wasn't a spy. Still, he'd love to see the famous city by the sea one day.

The pen fighters hauled the bodies away from the encampment and rearranged it to suit them. Gull kicked the burning brands back into some semblance of a campfire. They didn't seem overly concerned about guarding their supposed spy as they worked. Maybe they realized just how little chance he'd have against them if he tried to run. It sure beat having a sack over his head, though.

Fiz disappeared into the trees and returned leading a quartet of horses.

"They've got a wagon, boss," he said. "Shall we take it?"

"I expect it would only slow us down," Kres said after a moment's consideration. He shot a sharp look at Siv. "That must have been quite laborious, lugging you through the woods in that thing."

"I was blindfolded for most of it," Siv said neutrally. He wanted to ask why this group of traveling fighters had attacked his captors in the first place, but he was worried that would inspire more questions about his own shaky origin story—and more speculation about his career as a spy.

He suspected the group might be bandits or mercenaries in their spare time. Resha *had* mentioned trouble on the road. Pen fighters sometimes took alternative employment. They didn't get sponsors like Vertigonian duelists, and they had to rely on prize purses for their living. This bunch certainly didn't have any qualms about appropriating the Soolens' belongings and divvying up their weapons.

Whether they were bandits, mercenaries, or spies in their own right, at least they didn't feel the need to tie Siv up. After dealing with the bodies, Kres and Latch disappeared into the darkness, saying something about scouting the perimeter. Siv flopped down onto the ground beside the campfire and rubbed his wrists and ankles. Angry red bands encircled each of his limbs. How long had he been a captive? A week? It was sure nice not to breathe through that grimy sack anymore. It had started to smell like a dead zur-sparrow.

"Here." The big man, Fiz, sat down beside Siv and handed him a wineskin. "You look like you could use this."

"Thanks." Siv accepted the skin and tipped his head back for a long gulp.

"Can you tell where it's from, wine merchant?" Fiz asked.

"This side of Kurn Pass, I reckon." Siv passed it back to him. "It's similar to Fork Town wine, but not quite as oaky. Tollan?"

"Correct," Fiz said. He took a huge swallow. "You pass the test."

"If there's one thing I know, it's wine," Siv said. "So how long have you been a pen fighter? You're from Trure, aren't you?"

"Yes," Fiz said. "Tollan, in fact. I've been in Pendark for nearly seven years now. None of the horses wanted to carry me, so I had to find something to do outside the Horseplains." Fiz lifted his massive shoulders in a shrug.

Siv laughed. "I wouldn't want to carry you on my back either."

Gull joined them at the fire, folding her long legs beneath her. She immediately took out a knife and began sharpening it with a whetstone, looking at Siv without blinking.

"She's not so mean when you get to know her," Fiz said, not bothering to keep his voice down. "Just don't ask her to cook for you. Made that mistake once." Fiz gestured to a long scar down the side of his cheek, not far from his ear.

"Thanks for the warning," Siv said. "So you're a duelist?" he asked Gull. He figured he'd had decent luck getting female duelists to like him. No sense in having any enemies amongst his newest team of captors.

"This look like a frilly Vertigonian rapier to you?" Gull demanded, and suddenly her sword was in her hand, the tip hovering not an inch from Siv's nose. *How do all these people move without seeming to move?* He wanted to learn that trick. Gull's sword had a wicked curve and a guard that wrapped forward over her hand to join with the pommel.

"I'd say that's a mighty fine saber," Siv said. "Good craftsmanship."

Gull studied him for a moment, then a faint smile crossed her face. "Aye. I had to win a month's worth of solo fights to buy this beauty."

"Looks worth every copper," Siv said. "I take it you're good?"

Gull arched an eyebrow and returned her sword to its sheath at her hip. She picked up her whetstone and knife again and resumed her work.

Fiz chuckled. "She's good. There aren't a lot of women I'd trust to watch my back in the Dance, but she's one."

Siv had never seen a Pendarkan pen fight, but he knew the competition was divided into solo fights and the five-person melee known as the Dance of Steel. Five different weapons. Five fighters on each side. The melees took place in arenas called Steel Pentagons, usually built on islands in the swamps around the city-state of Pendark. Fighters could win huge prize purses—if they made it out alive. Unlike the Vertigonian duels, the Dance of Steel was a dance of death. This group must be skilled indeed if they had survived this long. Or at least most of them had survived.

"So what happened to your fifth?" he asked.

Fiz spit into the campfire, sending up a jet of steam.

"Soolen scouting party. Got more than they bargained for with us. But Shreya was a little too slow. We killed some, but four of them got away."

"Is that why...?" Siv gestured to the bodies of his former captors, indeterminate lumps beyond the warm ring of firelight. He wondered if the scouts had been part of Commander Brach's vanguard. How much longer before his whole army crossed into Trure?

"Aye," Fiz said. "By the time we realized they were the wrong group, we were too far into the fight to back out."

"I'm grateful for it," Siv said. "Sorry about your friend."

"Didn't get a chance to know her," Fiz said. "She was why we came all the way out here in the first place. Kres heard about her skills back in Pendark and just *had* to have her for this season. He's been in an ugly mood since it happened. We're lucky he took out his aggression on this bunch, or he might have killed us all before we made it back to the High Road. She's got to be the most-expensive recruit of all time, and we didn't even get to see her in action."

"Don't joke about her." Latch had returned from scouting—and he did not look happy.

"Easy there, Latch," Fiz said. "I meant no disrespect."

Latch glared at him for a moment and then stalked to the other side of the fire. He sat beside Gull and reached for a share of her wineskin.

"Kres has first watch," he muttered. "If I were you I'd sleep with one eye open." He fixed Siv with a level stare. The look was full of animosity, but Latch didn't even come close to being the scariest person Siv had met lately. He simply shrugged and tipped his head back for another drink.

He'd have to tread lightly while he traveled with this team. He resolved to be as friendly as possible in hopes of convincing them he was who he claimed to be. It looked as if he had his work cut out for him with Latch. He didn't fancy the idea of standing back to back with him in a Steel Pentagon anytime soon. Not that he'd be going all the way to Pendark, of course.

Siv studied the pen fighters lounging around the fire. They had a breezy confidence that Siv found surprisingly appealing. They looked ready to take on any comers with nothing but their blades and their wits. What would it be like to go wherever he wanted, to fight for gold and glory with no one to answer to but himself?

The prospect was actually kind of tempting. Siv hadn't done much good as king. His sister was dead, his crown lost, and he'd been stupid enough to get himself captured. What if he started over completely, as his Uncle Tem had suggested? Would it be possible for him to begin an entirely new life?

Dara's face rose before him, her intense eyes, her fierce smile. The thought that he might never see her again was like a burning coal in his skull. But what had he ever done but let her down? She had given up everything to be there for him after his father's death, and he hadn't even managed to keep his throne. She deserved to follow a superior king. Firelord knew he had never deserved her. Maybe she would be happier if he was out of her life forever.

Siv's father had always told him to take care of his duties. Well, his father was gone. It was almost liberating to know he had failed so completely. He could fall no lower than this. And for the first time, perhaps in his life, he had a real chance to leave it all behind. He could go anywhere. Do anything. Be anyone.

Not that he would really do that. He'd remain with the pen fighters until they reached the High Road. He'd pretend to join their team and prepare for their Dance of Steel, and then he'd return to

Rallion City as soon as he could leave without being hunted down and slaughtered as a spy. But it was interesting to imagine what it would be like to take this path.

As he settled in to sleep, the skies opened and soaked them with rain, but he didn't care. For now, he was Sivren Amen, responsible for no one but himself.

21

ROAN TOWN

DARA awoke to the sounds of children laughing and Rumy squawking. She emerged from the cot where she'd spent the night, still stiff from all the riding, and discovered that Roma had relented and allowed Rumy to come inside the farmhouse. A ring of children in their nightclothes surrounded him, all giggling and reaching out to touch his scaly hide. Even little Shir had overcome her fear enough to place a tentative hand on the hard knob of scales at the end of Rumy's tail.

"Good morning," Vine said brightly as Dara joined her and Roma at the table. Sturdy mugs of tea sat before them. "I took the liberty of letting you sleep in."

"Thanks." Dara accepted a cup of tea from Roma and rubbed her eyes. "We should get back on the road soon, though."

"We needn't hurry," Vine said. "I need time to calm my mind and reexamine my Senses. Roma has offered to let us stay another day."

"But what about—"

"It would be better to get a feel for his position than to continue running about in the wilderness, don't you think?"

As much as Dara hated to admit it, Vine was right. They could wander the plains forever unless they got some guidance. Vine needed time. She thought about the three riders Yen had seen on the road behind them yesterday. Hopefully they would bypass the farmhouse without causing trouble. She didn't like the idea of sitting around doing nothing, though.

"Yen is taking the three oldest into Roan Town today," Roma said, seeming to sense her restlessness. "Why don't you go with him? You can ask after the news. You may learn something useful."

"Oh yes!" Kol said, abandoning the group around Rumy to skip over to the three women. "Please come with us! Mummy promised to make me a new dress, and I've been saving coins for the fabric. Lady Vine, you can help me pick it out!"

"I must spend the day in meditation," Vine said. "I need time and space to calm my mind and petition the Air. Dara can help you, Kol." She leaned toward the girl conspiratorially. "She pretends not to care about pretty dresses, but she secretly loves them."

Dara's mouth dropped open, and Vine gave her an innocent smile.

"I want to go to town too!" little Shir whined.

"Not this time, love," Roma said.

"I'll bring you back a new bow, Shir," Kol said. "Miss Dara can choose the color!"

Vine grinned at Dara. There was no point in contradicting her. Maybe Dara *did* like wearing dresses sometimes. Only on very special occasions.

She finished her tea in one gulp and went to sit on the floor beside the children. Rumy gently nudged his way through them and stuck his snout into her hands to greet her.

"Good morning to you too," she said. "I hope you're feeling suitably spoiled."

Rumy snorted and turned his head so she could see the purple ribbon one of the children had tied around his neck. He huffed out a contented sigh and went back to being patted and prodded by his pile of fans.

The children tore their attention away from Rumy for a breakfast of dried winterberries and fresh brown bread. Afterwards, Vine settled onto the porch for her Air meditation session, and Dara set out with Yen, the twins Kol and Kay, and Jin.

They left the horses behind to rest for the day and approached Roan Town on foot. Farmland lined the road on either side. The houses became more numerous as they got closer to town. The children identified which of their friends' families owned each one as they skipped along. Occasionally they passed riders and wagons on the road, and Yen called out greetings to everyone they passed.

"Roan Town is a trading hub for all the farms in the region," Yen explained. "It's the biggest town east of the High Road. Not far south of here, you reach the foothills beneath the Linden Mountains." He nodded toward a dark-purple ridge on the horizon.

"That's the border with Soole, right?" Dara asked.

"Aye. The mountain range protects us, or it did until the Soolens made their move on Cindral Forest."

"Do you know what happened?"

"Only rumors. Better they went through the forest than marching through here, though." Yen frowned and looked back in the direction of his farm. "I'll warn the townsfolk about those three riders. Could have been Soolen scouts."

"Perhaps," Dara said. Siv had plenty of enemies, and she wouldn't be surprised if she and Vine weren't the only people searching for him. Soolen scouts could be the least of their worries. She hoped Vine would be able to pick up a hint of Siv in the Air today.

The children paid little heed to their conversation. They darted ahead, getting more excited as they reached the borders of Roan Town. Like every settlement Dara had encountered in Trure, it was a rambling, spacious place. The odor of horses rose on the wind, along with the smell of mud and damp timber. The town had a small walled segment in the center of the sprawl, with just enough space for a grassy square, a ring of shops, and a small cluster of houses. Wooden guard towers oversaw the open gates.

"Just in case Soole comes this way," Yen said, nodding at the towers. "Everyone from the town and surrounding farms could fit inside the walls. It wouldn't be comfortable, but it's enough to reassure people there's somewhere to run if Soole crosses our border. We have no high cliffs or Fissure to protect us here."

Dara frowned, thinking of her safe childhood atop the mountain. The Peace of Vertigon was unique on the continent. Yen's children lived with the threat of Soole almost on their doorstep. Whatever her father was doing in Vertigon, Dara hoped he would find some way to renew the Peace.

"Can I go to the sugar shop, Papa?" Jin asked, tugging on his father's sleeve.

"Don't eat anything unless you pay for it," he said.

"I got my coppers." Jin darted off across the town square.

"Be back by high noon!" Yen called after him.

Jin waved without looking back. A group of boys converged on him, popping out from all around the square and shouting his name. The whole pack entered the sugar shop together. Yen chuckled.

"Madame Halder will have my hide for loosing those boys on her shop."

"Will you come to the fabric store with me now, Dara?" Kol asked, grabbing her hand.

Kay latched onto her other hand. "And then visit the blacksmith with me? I want to show Master Mell your sword!"

"If it's okay with your father," Dara said.

"I'll meet you back here in a few hours," Yen said. "Watch out for each other."

He disappeared in the direction of a tavern at the edge of the square. Dara would have preferred to go with him to hear the news, but the twins were looking up at her with wide, eager eyes. She let them pull her across the square to a cozy shop with a slanted roof and a green door. Inside, an explosion of colors and textures met their eyes. Princess Selivia would have squealed in delight.

Dara wasn't much help with Kol's fabric selection. She favored the black, soft gray, and blue textiles, which were too boring for the young girl. Kol eventually settled on a bolt of vivid-green wool she was sure would impress Vine. While Kol chatted with the shopkeeper, Kay asked Dara endless questions about sword fighting. They hadn't hidden the fact that both Dara and Vine were duelists, and Kay had already declared that their visit was the best thing that had ever happened to her.

Dara was wary of the shopkeeper, though, and she answered the questions with care. She avoided using any names. The sensation that she was being watched had returned. She was probably being paranoid. Who could be interested in her all the way out in Roan Town? Her parents probably didn't even know this little town existed.

By the time Kol completed her purchase and they reemerged into the sunny square, it was nearly lunchtime.

"Can we go see Master Mell now?" Kay asked.

"It's almost high noon," Kol said. "Papa will be looking for us."

"But I want him to meet Dara!"

"Maybe we'll have time after the noon meal," Dara said. "I'm hungry. Is your father—?"

She stopped abruptly. Yen stood in the shade outside the tavern across the square, speaking to a lean man with sandy hair and a sharp nose. The stranger wore a red coat. For a moment, Dara thought it was Bolden Rollendar. But that was impossible. Siv had killed Bolden when he attacked the Great Hall with a squad of swordsmen. His body had been on the floor when Dara returned to confront her father. So who was this man?

Yen looked up then, his eyes going straight to Dara and his daughters, his face unreadable. When Dara glanced back at his companion to get a closer look, the man had disappeared.

"There's Papa!" Kol said. She broke into a run across the square, eager to show him her purchase.

Dara followed more slowly with Kay, scanning the square for any sign of the sandy-haired stranger. Why had he disappeared so quickly? His clothes had looked finer than those of the other townsmen, out of place. It *couldn't* have been a Rollendar, could it?

"Good shopping?" Yen asked.

"It was grand," Dara said. "Did you learn anything?"

"No news that would interest you," Yen said.

"Who were you talking to, Papa?" Kay asked.

"I wasn't talking to anyone," Yen said brusquely. He didn't meet Dara's eyes. "Let's order up some stew."

They ate lunch at the wooden tables outside the tavern to make the most of the winter sunshine. Jin soon joined them, his fingers sticky with sugar. Yen said nothing about his mysterious companion, and Dara couldn't coax any additional information out of him.

"Did anyone in town see those three strange riders?" she asked.

"Afraid not," he said. "Perhaps I imagined them."

"Imagined."

Yen shrugged. "It was growing dark."

Dara didn't press him further. Yen seemed fidgety. He kept

looking up at the tavern and, apart from answering direct questions from his children, he didn't talk for the rest of the meal. It was as if a shadow had been cast over him despite the bright noon sky. The children didn't notice, but by the time they headed back toward the farm, Dara had to wrap her hands around her sword hilt to keep them from quaking. She expected disaster to rain down on them at any moment. Something had changed in Yen after speaking to that stranger. He was no longer the unassuming farmer who had welcomed them into his home last night. The sooner she and Vine could get back on the road, the better.

The younger children ran out to the road to greet them when they returned to the farm, Rumy trundling along in their midst. Shir had apparently warmed up to him in Dara's absence, because she rode on his back, giggling madly.

"He's so cute," she said as she tumbled off into the tough winter grass. "I love him!"

"Did you buy anything or see anyone, Dara?" Ber asked solemnly.

"I didn't see anyone," Dara said. She looked directly at Yen, and he met her gaze without blinking. The children scrambled around them, still giggling and chattering, but a chill laced the air that had little to do with the wintry breeze. What had he been talking about with that stranger? And what had the stranger told him about her? She couldn't wait around to find out.

Vine rose from her cross-legged position when Dara entered the farmyard.

"Dara! I'm so pleased you're back. I found him!"

"What?" Forgetting about Yen, Dara hurried up the porch steps to grab Vine's hand. "Where is he?"

"I sensed him at high noon," Vine said. "I believe he is traveling west toward—"

"Let's go west, then," Dara interrupted before Vine could go into more detail about their movements. She didn't look at Yen. "We should leave now."

"Aren't you going to stay for dinner?" Kay said.

"Yeah, and teach us how to sword fight!" Jin shouted. He waved a stick in the air, making clanging sounds.

Dance of Steel

"Meditation is tiring work, Dara," Vine said. "And now that I have a direction, I'm sure we don't have to r—"

"We should leave now," Dara repeated, widening her eyes and hoping Vine would get the hint. "He already has a head start, and we don't want him to get too far away."

"Very well." Vine still looked puzzled, but she helped Dara extract herself from the children and gathered her belongings in preparation for their departure.

Dara was sorry to disappoint the children, but she no longer felt safe in the warm little farmhouse. They packed quickly and finished saddling their horses before the afternoon shadows stretched much farther across the farmyard. Roma insisted on packaging up extra food for them, and Vine pressed a few coins into her hands in thanks. Roma looked as if she wanted to refuse the money, but she accepted after a glance at her large brood.

At some point while they were preparing to leave, Yen disappeared.

All the children gathered in the farmyard to say good-bye. Dara and Vine accepted several rounds of hugs and promised to give Rumy extra treats from each of the children. Dara climbed into her saddle while Vine went back for a final bout of good-byes. Yen was nowhere in sight, and Roma didn't comment on his absence.

A harsh wind blew across the farmyard, whipping through the dry, dead grass. Dara felt that itch between her shoulder blades again. It was past time they were on the move.

"Thank you for your hospitality!" Vine called. "Do let us know if you're ever in Vertigon."

"Bye, Lady Vine! Bye, Rumy! Bye, Dara!"

The children ran out to the road and waved vigorously as Dara and Vine rode away toward Roan Town. When Dara turned back for one more look at the little group, a tall, thin figure emerged on the road behind them. She was pretty sure it was Yen, walking back from wherever he had gone. *Someone* knew they were on the move.

"Dara, darling," Vine said as soon as they were out of earshot of the family, "would you like to explain why we departed in such a hurry? Was fabric shopping that bad?"

"I think Yen gave us away," Dara said. She explained what she had seen in the shadow of the Roan Town tavern and how Yen had treated her coldly following the conversation. "My theory is that was one of Von Rollendar's brothers and Yen is his informant."

"Goodness!" Vine said. "I can see why you wanted to leave so quickly. He looked like Bolden, you say?"

"Could have been his older brother."

Vine tapped a finger against her lips. "That sounds like Lord Vex. He's the youngest of the three. His nephew always did resemble him."

Bolden Rollendar's three uncles had left Vertigon without warning shortly before Bolden and his father launched their coup attempt. There was a pretty good chance they'd recognize Dara. They would definitely remember Vine. And they'd be eager to know Siv was on the loose in Trure even if they hadn't been sent out to find him. The Rollendars had always been remarkably well informed about what was happening in the Lands Below. Why wouldn't they have an informant here?

"I think we should cut around the outskirts of Roan Town and take the road west from there," Dara said. "I don't particularly want any Rollendars to see us strolling through town."

"I quite agree," Vine said. "Have no fear. I believe King Siv is moving to the southwest. My Senses suggest he's angling toward Kurn Pass. If we take the Ridge Road straight west to the High Road, we'll have a chance of catching up with him."

"Kurn Pass?"

"It's where the High Road cuts through the Linden Mountains. If he's taken through the Pass, he'll be beyond the boundaries of Trure."

"Why are they taking him southwest?" Dara said. She would have expected the trail to lead them southeast toward Soole.

"I haven't the faintest idea," Vine said. She clucked to Golden-flower and spurred her off the road to begin the detour around Roan Town, appearing in good spirits despite this new threat. Dara almost envied her nonchalance.

After a final look to make sure they weren't being followed, Dara rode after her, one hand resting on her Savven blade. She wished Yen hadn't found out it was a Fire Blade. Could he truly be one of the Rollendar informants? He *was* Vertigonian, and he had a lot of mouths to feed. What would the Rollendar uncles do with the information he sold them, though?

And why in all the Firelord's realm was Siv moving southwest? Who besides her father and the advancing Soolen army could want him? Dara squared her shoulders and rode back into the wilderness. Whatever else happened, she had to find him before anyone else did.

22

TRAINING

It turned out that when you were responsible for no one but yourself, people could still tell you what to do. Siv should have anticipated that.

Kres woke them before dawn, chipper as a furlingbird, and demanded that they all stretch and do a set of exercises (squats, push-ups, pull-ups on a sturdy tree branch) before they began the day's journey. It was nice to be able to move around again, and Siv almost didn't mind the workout. He also enjoyed the smell of the tree grove, the sun on his face, and the fact that he didn't have to lie around like a hogtied greckleflush. Being a hostage had gotten old fast.

Kres set a grueling pace when they finally mounted their horses and set off into the trees. Siv adopted Chala Choven's dun stallion for himself, figuring Chala was the type to splurge on a quality steed. It wasn't long before they reached the edge of the grove and looked out on the rolling expanse of the eastern Truren plains.

"It will be a brisk ride from here," Kres said. He breathed deeply, gazing out over the plain as if it were his own personal dominion. "Have to make it back to the city before the season begins. I don't want to miss a single Dance. We'll have a winning team this year, children. I can feel it."

"How far is it to Pendark?" Siv asked.

"We are a week from Kurn Pass," Kres said. "We'll spend a few days traversing the Pass, then we'll drink until dawn in Fork Town as tradition demands. After that it'll be less than a week to Pendark if we don't encounter any trouble in the Darkwood."

"I'm out of practice," Siv said, rubbing the red marks on his wrists. "I'll need to work on my dueling to be ready to fight in less than three weeks." Not that he'd still be with them in three weeks. But a little training wouldn't hurt. He could impress Dara when he returned to her.

"Who said anything about dueling?" Latch said. He heeled his horse forward to ride beside Kres. "You're not giving him my spot."

"Have no fear, Latch, my boy," Kres said. "I pegged you for a knifeman, Sivren."

"A knifeman?"

"All you have to do is take down your competitors the way you did your erstwhile captor."

Siv scratched his chin, where his usual casual stubble was becoming a proper beard. Hopefully it would keep people from recognizing him once he made it back to the High Road. A knifeman, eh? He recalled when he and Dara had been attacked in the tunnels near the secret dueling cavern in Vertigon. He had killed a man with a kitchen knife to prevent him from stabbing her. Charn made two. Maybe he *could* handle himself in a knife fight.

With the memory of that night came the image of Dara's face, her eyes on his, the way it had felt to hold her face in his hands, the powerful urge he'd felt to kiss her. He fought to clear the image from his mind. He missed Dara with the intensity of a thousand Fire Lanterns. Yet guilt accompanied her memory. He'd brought her nothing but trouble.

"Don't look so serious," Kres said with a laugh, jerking Siv's attention back to the pen fighters and the fields of Trure spreading before him. "I intend to train you with knives starting right after lunch. I won't throw you in unprepared."

"I'm supposed to have the after-lunch training slot," Latch muttered. "And isn't he a spy?"

Quick as lightning, Kres seized Latch by the coat, hauling him halfway out of his saddle. Latch yelped in surprise.

"I've had enough of your attitude, son," Kres said, his cheery demeanor replaced by a sudden, dangerous quiet. "Do we have a problem?"

"No, sir." Still halfway off his horse, Latch kept himself from falling with a death grip on the saddle.

"I made allowances after what happened to your sweetheart, but I will not have you questioning my decisions. Is that clear?"

"Yes, sir." Latch's eyes flitted to Siv for an instant. He looked away quickly, pretending to be very interested in a bird passing overhead, but it was too late. Latch had seen him watching. This likely wouldn't do anything to improve their friendship.

Finally Kres released Latch and rolled his shoulders with a crack.

"Now then," he said pleasantly. "I wonder what kind of bird that is. The plumage is lovely."

Latch regained his balance in the saddle and broke into a canter to catch up with Gull, who was already riding into the plains. He didn't look back. Siv was relieved Latch hadn't decided to fall in behind him instead. He'd have to watch out for the fellow. He'd also be careful not to question too many of Kres's decisions. Knife fighting it was—until he made his escape.

They rode for several hours after leaving the grove behind. The Truren plains spread around them, nothing but rustling, silvery grass interrupted by the occasional copse of trees and distant farm. It was an idyllic, empty land, not at all like the carefully divided farms around Rallion City. Siv had never been this deep into eastern Trure before. The vast expanse was a relief after his long captivity. It made him feel like a new man.

At high noon, they stopped at the ruins of an old stable to eat lunch. The rain of the night before had turned the ground to mud, so they sat on the low stone wall of the stable while they ate. The roof had caved in, leaving only wild brush and the shadow of a morrinvole burrow inside. They shared an unidentifiable jerky and rock-hard flatbread, and Siv found himself remembering the castle cooks with fondness again. Still, eating flatbread and jerky with the wind in his face and no sack over his head was a far cry better than being force-fed with his hands bound. He was feeling positively cheerful.

"So where are we exactly?" Siv asked. "I'm still a little disoriented after my stint in captivity."

"We're less than a day's journey from Roan Town to the south," Kres said. He brushed flatbread crumbs off his red baldric and pulled a silk handkerchief from his pocket to dab at his mouth. "We'll find nothing but farms along this road. After Roan Town—which has a delightful tavern on the main square, I might add—the Ridge Road turns to the west and eventually joins up with the High Road in Tollan. We'll take the High Road through Kurn Pass and all the way south to Pendark."

"Roan Town is the last settlement before then?" Maybe that would be a good place for him to lose them.

"There are farms and villages here and there." Kres swept his hand over the rolling plains. "It's not an especially exciting country."

"You know, Kres," said Fiz. "We could skip Roan Town and cut straight across the plains to the High Road." He leaned casually against the ruin. He had elected not to sit on the wall in case it collapsed under his weight. "It's easy countryside the whole way. No point going through Roan Town if we can shave a day or two off our journey by cutting straight."

"Are you sure you're not just trying to avoid Roan Town?" Gull said.

"Why would I do that?" Fiz said innocently.

"Doesn't Zenny live there with that new fellow of hers?" Gull leaned toward Siv. "She's his wife. Or was."

"You were the one complaining about the delay yesterday," Fiz grumbled, his wide face reddening.

Kres chuckled. "Very well. I fancy the overland route myself. We'll head straight for the High Road, then. Now, finish up, lad. It's time for your first knife-fighting lesson."

A breeze blew strong across the plains, and for a moment Siv felt a sinking sensation in the pit of his stomach. He got the feeling they should go through Roan Town for some reason. He rolled his shoulders to shrug it off. He'd probably just been looking forward to sleeping in an inn that had ale and hot food. There'd be plenty of time for that when they reached the High Road. He might as well stay with the team until then. He'd head back to Rallion City from there.

He finished his jerky and hopped down off the stable wall. In the meantime, Sivarrion the King was no more. It was time to make a knife fighter out of Sivren Amen.

23

WINTER MARKET

THE crowds parted before Sora and her companion as they meandered through the Winter Market. Lady Zurren was a harsh-tongued woman, with a hawkish nose and dark hair. Lima had assigned her to "keep the queen company" and make sure she behaved herself during her public appearance. The noblewoman held Sora's arm as they strode among the stalls, complaining animatedly about a set of stoneware she had purchased here last year.

Winter Market was a three-day affair held in King's Arena each midwinter. Tables covered in handicrafts, textiles, preserves, and Fireworks filled the wide dueling floor. Winter Market was one of the most-popular festivals of the year, designed to break up the monotony of the long Vertigonian winter. Vendors large and small had a chance to display their wares inside the warm hall, followed by dancing and drinking each night.

The atmosphere was more subdued than usual this year. The people of the mountain were still wary after what had happened the night of the engagement feast. Few knew what had occurred within the castle, but everyone had seen the wall of Fire burning around Square and entrapping a third of the populace. They were loath to trust the Fireworkers after that. The Workers' stalls had less business than the others. People shied away from the glittering Firegold, burning Heatstones, and shining Everlights, focusing on the jars of soldarberry and apple preserves and the stone and wooden crafts at other stalls.

People seemed pleased to see Sora, though. Women stopped to curtsy and squeeze her hand, and men bowed low and offered her their service. Their statements of support were blatant, even fervent. Sora wondered how much the Vertigonians knew about her current status. Even if there was nothing they could do about it, at least they wished her well.

It was nice in a way. Sora had often faded into the background at public events. Her father and brother had been charismatic men, tall and attractive and likable. Selivia was the perfect little princess: adorable, friendly, and easy to love. Sora had always been more interested in what was going on behind the scenes in the kingdom. She'd spent her time having tea with influential ladies and sniffing out possible alliances between the businessmen and the nobles. She knew a lot of people, but she had always drawn less attention than the other members of her family.

Now, though, she felt the affection and concern of the crowds as she made her way through the market. A woman selling colorful silk scarves pressed an Amintelle-blue one into her hands and refused to accept payment. A cider vendor offered her a steaming mug and bowed almost to the floor. An elderly woman cupped her face in her hands and told her she was "a precious child."

Lady Zurren eyed the commoners distastefully when they crowded in on the pair, but Sora did her best to respond to all the attention with grace. She waded through the throng, trying to appear brave and strong, like a queen the people could trust.

Inside, she felt like nothing of the sort. Lima Ruminor hovered at the edge of the crowd, watching her. Sora ducked her head, trying to ignore the fear that wormed through her at the sight of the woman. She was ashamed at how easily Lima had cowed her. Sora had told the Ruminors what she could remember of Trure's defenses after they threatened her with violence. At first she'd tried to tell outright lies, but Lima had realized it and smacked her again while the Lantern Maker sat there and did nothing. Sora had managed to hold back some information only by feigning ignorance. From then on, Lima had used more-aggressive tactics to control her behavior. Sora had begun seeing the harsh, cold woman in her nightmares.

Dance of Steel

She shuddered, trying not to look at Lima, and made sure her friends were still around her. She had four guards today: Kel, Telvin, Yuri, and Lieutenant Benzen, the leader of the Vertigonian contingent of her Guard. Benzen still believed Kel would help him keep an eye on Telvin and Yuri in addition to guarding the queen. Captain Thrashe and one of his countrymen lurked in the crowd too, disguised as traders.

"My queen, may I offer you a salt cake?" Kel moved in closer to her. Lady Zurren was busy grilling a vendor about his clockworks, and she wasn't paying attention to the queen.

"I've already had one," Sora said.

"Are you sure you don't want another?" Kel said. "Salt cakes always cheer me up." He held one out to her. The cake had a fine dusting of sugar on top, and some had gotten on the sleeve of his blue Castle Guard coat.

"All right, then." Sora was surprised Kel had noticed she needed cheering up. She accepted the cake and bit into it, enjoying the mix of sugar and salt on her tongue.

"Are you well, my lady?" Kel asked. "You seem a little subdued lately."

"I'm okay." A lump formed in Sora's throat without warning, and she did her best to swallow it down with the salt cake. She hadn't told her allies that Lima had hit her. They would only try to talk her into leaving Vertigon again. She still didn't want to do that, not when the people seemed to want her. Whenever she was allowed outside the castle, they gathered around her, offering their condolences and telling her how pleased they were to see that she was well. She may feel like a terrified child on the inside, but she wanted to become the queen they deserved. She could never leave them in Lima's hands.

"Sora." Kel rested a hand on her shoulder and gave her a gentle squeeze. She looked up, surprised. The gesture was brief, but it was surprisingly comforting. "You can tell us if you need anything. We're here for you."

"Thank you," Sora said, swallowing again. "I will."

"There's someone we want you to meet." Kel lifted a salt cake to his mouth to hide his words. "Go with Yuri as soon as the distraction begins."

"What distraction?"

But Kel had already put distance between them again, staring idly around the crowd like just another guard.

A moment later there was a loud crash, followed by a chattering, squawking sound, and a dozen juvenile cur-dragons burst into the arena.

Chaos erupted immediately. The knee-high dragons rushed through the crowds, making men jump and women snatch their children out of the way. The cur-dragons scrambled over tables, knocking food and crafts and colorful bolts of fabric to the floor. A few let out little bursts of flame as they gamboled through the market. A display of expensive papers imported from Cindral Forest went up in flames.

"Stop, you burning hell lizards!"

"Who's going to pay for this?"

"Catch them!"

Screams and shouts—and a fair amount of laughter—echoed around the arena. A bucket of Firesticks fell off a table and scattered light across the floor in a wide arc. The cur-dragons were chasing something. Sora caught a glimpse of bright-red fur before she felt a hand beneath her elbow.

"Quickly, my queen."

Yuri led her through the heaving crowds. She glanced back to see Kel stepping forward to block Lieutenant Benzen's view of her, waving frantically as the cur-dragons ran toward them.

Yuri hurried her toward the athletes' trunk room, which wasn't being used while the market was in full swing. A few people called to her as she passed, their words snatched away in the chaos. She couldn't see Lima or Captain Thrashe. The crowd quickly became a stampede as half the attendees tried to get out and the other half joined the fray, trying to catch either the cur-dragons or the creature they were chasing. Sora had a brief moment to wonder where her friends had gotten the dragons before she and Yuri rounded a corner into the trunk room and the arena disappeared from view.

Sora caught a whiff of old sweat and rusting metal as they made their way into the darkened trunk room.

"Apologies, my queen, for bringing you into the men's side," Yuri said, blushing as red as his beard. "We figured it would be the last place they'd look if they notice you're gone."

"I don't mind at all."

The trunk room was a long, thin space where athletes prepared for their duels during the competition season. Sora spotted a large, hulking shape at the far end and made her way toward it, trying not to trip over any trunks or benches.

The dark figure pulled back his cloak and uncovered a small Fire Lantern on a nearby bench, throwing his features into sharp relief. The man was big and bearish, with strong shoulders, salt-and-pepper hair, and a bit of a gut.

"Coach Doban!"

"Hello, my queen," Berg grunted. "You are okay?"

"Yes. It's good to see you." Sora smiled shyly at the sword master. Berg Doban had coached her brother for many years, but she had always been a bit scared of him. He had a gruff manner, and she'd heard him yelling at Siv often for being lazy, his foreign accent twisting the words.

"We have not much time," Berg said. "I am thinking you must leave the mountain. Go to Trure, my queen."

"I can't," Sora said. "Like I told the others, our only chance to defeat the Lantern Maker is to work against him from the inside." She didn't add that she wouldn't be safe in Trure either. It was only a matter of time before the Ruminors put the information she had given them to use.

"It is not worth the danger, my queen." Berg stepped forward and took her small hands between his big, meaty ones. "I have seen too much of this Lantern Maker. Your father and your brother did not respect the danger. I could not save them. Please, my queen, let me take you from this city."

"Why?" Sora asked. "I thought you wanted to help Vertigon. Don't *you* think it would be better for me to stay?"

"My queen, it is not Vertigon," Berg said. "This land is my home, yes, and it has been a place of peace for me. But the Amintelles made it so. I am owing a debt to your father far greater than my debt to the mountain. I failed to protect his son. I must save his daughter, or I no longer deserve to live."

"What debt?" Sora asked.

"My queen, your father gave me mercy many years ago. He gave me a life and a second chance when I was a broken man."

"We need to go back soon," Yuri said nervously. He was keeping watch on the door at the other end of the trunk room.

"Do not interrupt me!" Berg roared, making Sora jump.

Yuri's face paled, and he ducked his head obediently.

"Sorry, Coach Berg."

Berg rounded on Sora again, lowering his voice. "Your father made me whole once more," he said. "He is doing the same for others. He was the good king in more than name."

Sora didn't know what to say as the big man clasped her hands, his palms calloused and rough but his grip gentle. She wished she could let him carry her away to safety, leaving the Ruminors to the mountain they wanted to control so much.

It would be the easy option, and it might even be wise. But it wasn't right. Rafe was creating weapons of Fire, and he was already gathering information on the Lands Below. He was a conqueror in the making with a cruel partner at his side. The Ruminors needed to be stopped—and she was the only one left to do it.

"I can't go," Sora said. "If you truly owe my father a debt, I need you to help me drive a wedge through the Fireworkers. We can't defeat them outright, but we can keep them distracted and fractured so they can't do further damage. I think the Lantern Maker has ambitions beyond holding Vertigon."

Berg's jaw set, and he studied Sora. Then he inclined his head. "I will do what you ask of me."

"I need you to see if you can sway Daz Stoneburner to our side. I think he's the key to splitting up the Workers."

"I can try, my queen," Berg said. "But Daz is strong, and he aided the Lantern Maker before. We must take care with him."

"I trust you," Sora said, squeezing Berg's big square hands.

"I am in your service," Berg said. "But trust no one."

Sora nodded, though she didn't entirely agree. She had to trust a few people if she was going to get anything done around here. She only hoped she had picked the right allies.

"I'd better get back out there before anyone notices I'm gone," she said. "Are we all clear, Yuri?"

"Yes, my queen," he said. "It's still a bit mad out there."

"Good."

Sora crossed the trunk room but stopped to look back at Berg as he covered up the light again, plunging the room into darkness. If people like him were willing to risk their lives for her father even after his death, she was surer than ever that she wanted to be the kind of ruler he had been. Not only was she going to get rid of the Lantern Maker and his terrifying wife, she was going to rule Vertigon well enough to inspire that kind of devotion.

All but one of the cur-dragons had been captured by the time Sora and Yuri slipped out of the trunk room and rejoined the crowd. They surveyed the jumble of debris spread across the floor of the dueling arena, trying not to draw attention to their return. It looked as if the cur-dragons had had plenty of fun in their absence. A barrel of cider had burst, and children were splashing in the resulting puddle. More Fireworks had fallen to the ground. Sparks spurted from one unfamiliar Work and spattered across an unfurled bolt of black cloth like stars in a night sky. A woman was screeching hysterically at her husband for laughing at what looked suspiciously like cur-dragon dung on her shoe. Yuri couldn't quite hide a grin at the results of their diversion.

Sora caught a glimpse of Lima, but a familiar—and very tall—man kept casually stepping in front of her, making it difficult for her to move closer to Sora and Yuri. Kel and Lieutenant Benzen joined them soon after their return. Benzen gave Sora a suspicious look, but he seemed more worried about the remaining cur-dragon than whether she had been up to anything in the brief moments when he'd lost sight of her.

The creature in question perched on top of a hat rack in the center of the arena, hurling small bursts of fire at the men trying to catch him. The cur-dragon looked more scared than angry, and it was making spitting sounds like an irate kitten. Sora's brother would have said it sounded like a panviper with its tail in a knot. The hats from the rack had tumbled across the floor. A puff of red fur peeking out from beneath one of them suggested the creature the dragons had been chasing hadn't been caught yet either.

It was another five minutes before a salt-cake seller managed to toss a blanket over the final cur-dragon and wrestle it out of the arena, leaving relative calm in its wake.

"Seems we ought to start the party early this year!" Kel shouted over the crowd.

Murmurs of agreement quickly followed. The frazzled vendors began gathering up their remaining wares and putting them away for the night rather than bothering to set everything up again. After the mess had been cleaned up, the tables were pulled back, clearing room for dancing. The cider vendors heated up fresh vats, and barrels of ale were rolled down the athletes' entrance. A gaggle of musicians began tuning their instruments, and the conversations spreading through the arena grew festive. Sora smiled at the warmth and good cheer that had replaced the chaos. She loved Vertigon with a fierceness that surprised her sometimes. There were good people here.

"It's time we returned to the castle," Lima said, appearing so suddenly at Sora's elbow that she jumped. "I've had enough of this foolishness."

"Shouldn't we stay for the party?" Sora said.

"I have work to do," Lima said.

"I'm supposed to be reassuring the people. They'll wonder if I leave too soon," Sora said. "You go ahead. The Castle Guard can watch me."

Lima frowned at her, and Sora flinched. She couldn't help it, even though Lima's arms remained firmly at her sides. She shouldn't push the woman.

But to her surprise, Lima said, "Fine. Be careful what you say. I will hear of it later." She gave a pointed look at the many Fireworkers around the hall. None of them looked as if they'd be leaving in a hurry.

"I'll be home by my bedtime," Sora said, meeting Lima's eyes despite the fear worming through her. The other Vertigonians were becoming increasingly wary of the Workers. She should set a better example and not let them intimidate her—at least where anyone could see.

Lima gave a sharp nod. Then she turned to Lieutenant Benzen.

"I want you to report back to me with a list of everyone Queen Sora speaks to this evening. Do not let her out of your sight."

"Yes, Madame Ruminor."

Lima swept away, her dark skirts rippling around her like a storm cloud. Sora breathed a little easier as soon as she was gone, and muscles she didn't know she'd been tensing relaxed. She caught Kel giving her a quizzical look and turned away from him. It was about time for a third helping of salt cakes.

Before long, music trilled through the arena, and the open space that had been cleared between the stalls filled up with dancers. The musicians played livelier tunes than Sora was used to at royal feasts. She'd never actually stayed for the dancing at Winter Market before. The occasion was more popular among the common people. She couldn't have schemed with the nobility even without Lieutenant Benzen monitoring her every move—and Captain Thrashe, though he was more discreet about it. Most of the nobles left after the market closed and held their own midwinter gatherings in the parlors. Lady Zurren was nowhere in sight. She'd probably left the arena when the cur-dragons made their entrance. She hated inconvenience.

Sora was glad Lima had let her stay. There was a warmth and camaraderie to the festival that had been missing from her life of late. She'd been far too isolated up in the castle. She may have made more political progress by attending one of the parlor gatherings, but this was nicer. And there was less risk of anyone reporting back on exactly whose parlor she might have visited.

The music swelled around her, and soon she was tapping her feet and clapping along as the dancers whirled across the dueling floor. They skirted around the wet patch where the cider hadn't been completely mopped up, and Firelight glimmered on it like a mirror. Glasses clinked, and laughter mixed with the musical notes. Sora felt almost happy for the first time in weeks.

Telvin Jale strode up to her through the crowd. Sora smoothed her skirt self-consciously as he offered her a deep, formal bow. Telvin wasn't on duty, and instead of his New Guard uniform, he had opted for the traditional army dress uniform. He'd been enlisted for the standard four years, during which he'd never engaged in so much as a skirmish, but he still managed to look every inch the war hero.

"Would you do me the honor of a dance, my queen?"

Sora accepted his hand, flushing in spite of herself. Telvin was a good five years older than her, and she was sure this was nothing more than politeness. Still, she couldn't help the butterflies that whirled through her stomach as he led her to the middle of the floor. He was terribly gallant. And he had invited her to dance *first*.

Sora smiled shyly as Telvin placed one hand firmly on her waist, took her hand with the other, and began the steps. She followed the movements easily, letting him guide her around the floor. He was an adequate dancer, every bit as proper as she had expected. But as colors and lights swirled around them, a blush warmed her cheeks.

Telvin drew her in a little closer, and her heart skipped a beat.

"I spoke with General Pavorran, my queen."

"Huh? Oh, when?"

"There was a memorial ceremony for veterans this afternoon," Telvin said. "That is why I'm in uniform."

"Of course. Good." Sora focused on the Firegold knot on his shoulder, rapidly realigning her thoughts. Of course he hadn't gotten dressed up for her. And he was dancing with her to share information. He was her sworn man and ally, not her suitor. She cleared her throat, raising her head regally. "What did the general say?"

"He admires the Lantern Maker," Telvin said. "He thinks Ruminor is an efficient man who could do great things for Vertigon."

Sora grimaced. "That wasn't quite what I wanted to hear." So much for her hope that they could persuade everyone on Square to form a faction against the Ruminors. "Did he say what kind of great things?"

"No," Telvin said. "We spoke about Soole. General Pavorran thinks the Soolens are acting above the capabilities of their army. If they try to advance beyond Cindral Forest when spring comes, the general thinks they'll find more opposition than they bargained for."

"Interesting." Sora frowned. She'd once planned to become the Queen of Soole. Much had changed since then, but she agreed with the general's assessment. There had to be more to Soole's actions. The campaign must have left their home cities vulnerable. Why had they taken the risk? "The Lantern Maker has been asking questions about Trure's defenses," she said. "He may intend to help Soole with their campaign."

Telvin's high forehead furrowed, and he fell silent for a moment. They skipped through the dance, trying to keep up with the rapid beat. His movements weren't quite as crisp while he considered this news, and he missed a few steps. Once, he even stepped on Sora's toe.

"I apologize, my queen," he said quickly. "Do you wish to take a break?"

"It's all right. I haven't gotten to dance in a while."

"Allow me to cut in," came a voice at her shoulder. "Poor Jale here can't dance and think at the same time."

Sora turned to find Kel grinning at her. He took her hand and smoothly shouldered Telvin out of the way. The soldier didn't have a chance to object before they were off, sweeping around the dance floor and hitting every step. Sora grinned in spite of herself.

"There's that smile we've been missing," Kel said.

Sora looked up at him, startled, and he squeezed her hand. "You should get to enjoy yourself at least some of the time," he said.

"Thanks. I guess it's been a tough winter."

The music changed. Sora didn't know this dance as well as the previous one, but Kel showed her what to do, his steps as sprightly as they must have been when he dueled. He had an easy smile, and she didn't mind making a few mistakes as they tried out the moves.

"That's it," he said. "Now let's do a twirl."

Sora spun, her curly hair flying around her face, and nearly tripped over his feet. Her caught her around the waist and lifted her off her feet before setting her down and spinning out into a twirl of his own.

"You dance like a girl, Kel!" called Oat, who was waltzing with a pretty redhead nearby.

"Why should the ladies get to have all the fun?" Kel said with a wink. Then he spun Sora out and twirled again, throwing out a foot to trip his friend while he was at it. Oat stumbled, his long limbs windmilling. "Oh look!" Kel said. "You dance like a girl too."

Sora giggled as Oat tried to recover his dignity in front of the redhead. It had been way too long since she'd had any reason to giggle.

She wanted to ask Kel about his life outside of dueling and guard duty. Was there someone special he was hoping to dance with tonight? Kel was a favorite among the female dueling fans of the mountain. He had countless admirers. Some were already edging closer to them, angling for the next dance with the popular duelist.

But none of Kel's rabid fans would dare cut in while he was dancing with the queen. Sora doubted she was the sort of girl he would be interested in anyway. In her own practical assessment, she was too bookish and plain for someone so handsome and charming. But she didn't get to enjoy herself very often, and she was free of Lima Ruminor tonight. She moved a little further into his arms and let the dance sweep her away.

By the time the song ended, she was laughing. Her heart felt lighter than it had in weeks. She moved to the side of the dance floor to catch her breath as Kel's fans closed in on him. He gave her a wink and a bow before the rustle of curls and skirts enveloped him.

"Sora!" a high voice squealed. Jully Roven burst through the crowd to clasp her hand. "I mean, Queen Soraline. You got to dance with Kelad Korran! He's soooo dreamy."

"Hello, Jully." Sora was surprised—but pleased—to see Lord Roven's daughter. Jully wore a long-sleeved dress in a brilliant shade of pink.

"I've missed you," Jully said. "Father won't let me visit anymore."

"I'm afraid the castle isn't much fun right now."

"Yes, I've been listening in on Mother and Father," Jully said. "The Lantern Maker sounds dreadful."

"Are your parents here?" Sora scanned the throng, but there weren't many nobles left. "I'm surprised they let you stay this late."

"Oh no!" Jully burst into a fit of giggles. "They think I'm at Maraina's greathouse." She indicated another young woman, who was dancing with a gangly young bridgeworker her noble parents definitely wouldn't have approved of. "Isn't it grand?"

"As long as you're careful," Sora said.

"You sound as worrisome as Maraina's parents. They're afraid the Lantern Maker will eat us or something. They think we're at *my* greathouse."

Sora glanced at Lieutenant Benzen a few yards away, but he didn't seem interested in her conversation with another young girl. She lowered her voice. "Maraina's parents don't like the Lantern Maker either?"

"Of course not!" Jully threw her arms wide. "Lots of folks don't."

"Do you know of any others for sure?"

"Well, Lord Farrow of course, but he doesn't like anyone. The

Nannings think the Fireworkers are on the right track, though. I overheard Father arguing with Lord Nanning about it the other day."

"Hmm." That was good information. Sora would have assumed that the Nannings were on her side. She moved them from one column to the other on her mental list of allies and enemies, adding Maraina's parents in their place. "Anyone else?"

Jully shrugged. "I can ask around if you like."

"That would actually help a lot," Sora said. Excitement buzzed in her stomach, faint at first but building quickly. There was an opportunity here she never would have anticipated. "But don't mention it to your father."

"Sure," Jully said. "I can ask Maraina and a few of the other girls too."

Sora remembered when she had asked Lord Roven for help working against the Lantern Maker. He had told her to keep her head down until she was married off. Well, if she couldn't get the older lords to help her, she'd start with the young ladies. They deserved to live in a peaceful Vertigon as much as everyone else. And even though she had the Guard on her side, she was going to need the nobility too.

"Just don't let anyone know what you're doing," Sora said.

"Of course. I'm great at keeping secrets," Jully said. "Now, you have to tell me what it was like to dance with the famous Kelad Korran!"

"He's actually really kind," Sora said. A feeling of warmth and bravery began to spread through her, something she'd been missing since the first time Lima raised a hand against her. She wasn't alone. "I'm sure he'd be happy to dance with you too." She grinned, feeling less like a queen and more like a young princess again. "In fact, let's go ask him."

24

RIDGE ROAD

SIV landed in the dirt with a thud. He scrambled to his feet, barely keeping a grip on his knife. His shoulder ached from hitting the packed ground. It had been a few days since the last rain, so at least he hadn't been thrown in the mud.

His opponent darted in with a succession of quick jabs. Siv met each one with a rough swipe of his short steel blade, a block with the forearm or elbow, or a duck. Knife fighting was mostly about grappling and movement. There was very little blade contact involved. The rare clang of knife against knife was different from the ringing of swords: muted, but no less dangerous.

He barely caught the last swipe. His muscles strained as he kept the point from touching his skin with a death grip on his opponent's wrist. Sweat dripping down his face, he forced the knife away bit by bit. Then his opponent punched him in the nose.

The next thing Siv knew, he was on his back, looking up at a cloudless winter sky.

Kres loomed into view. "I told you to watch out for that."

"I thought this was a knife fight," Siv grumbled.

"Knife. Fist. Either one will fell you if your guard is down," Kres said. "Technically, a victory only counts in the pen if you stab your opponent or bring your blade to his throat, but nothing says you can't knock him unconscious first."

Siv lurched to his feet and picked up his fallen blade. The knife

Kres had given him was twice as long as his hand from hilt to tip and had a wicked edge. It was heavier than it looked, made from quality steel. He'd only been practicing for a few days, but Siv already felt as if the blade were part of him.

He didn't have time to admire it, though. Kres rushed in for another attack before he even assumed his guard position. Siv avoided the swipe and leapt backward, dropping into a crouch. He circled Kres, watching for weaknesses. The man didn't have many.

The stance had been the hardest part to get used to as he made the transition from sword to knife. Siv had good reflexes, but it felt strange to crouch as he danced around and around his opponent. Knife fighting could make a man dizzy.

Siv had been with the pen fighters for five days. They traveled the wild Truren countryside, only occasionally passing remote farms and hovels. They trained every day, sometimes with individual weapons, sometimes going two-on-two or two-on-three, sometimes with fists. Whenever they could manage it, they picked a location with trees or ruins to use as obstacles. In Krestian March's world, there was no such thing as an easy practice session. Dara would love him.

"You almost done over there?" Gull called. "I need my practice dummy."

"Patience," Kres said. "We're still—"

Siv struck, barreling into Kres from his low guard position. He lifted the shorter man right off his feet and dropped him in the dirt. An instant later, he brought his blade to Kres's throat.

"I think we're done," Siv said.

"That was a dirty move," Kres said, sounding winded from the throw. "I liked it."

Siv stood and pulled Kres to his feet. The man laughed, brushing off his red baldric.

"That's the first time you've dropped me like that," Kres said.

"It won't be the last."

Kres chuckled. "I knew I picked a winner. I can't wait to see you in the Steel Pentagon. Now run along and play with Gull."

Siv grinned, a remarkable feeling of pride spreading through him. It was a long time since he'd actually been good at something.

"Give me a quick breather," he said, dropping into the dirt beside the swordswoman.

"You're always taking breathers," Gull said. "You'd think you never worked a day in your life."

"Selling wine involves a lot of sitting and drinking," Siv said.

"Sure it does." Gull leapt to her feet and pulled Siv up by the arm. She had warmed to him since discovering he was a decent swordsman to practice against. He ached from the workout, but overall he felt in better shape than he had since the battle in the Great Hall. Apart from his impressive collection of scars, it was as though that had happened to another man in another life.

Gull handed him a saber, and Siv assumed his guard position. He shook off the razor-sharp image of Dara, something he had to do every time he faced Gull with a blade in hand. Though ten years older than Dara, Gull had a similar long-and-lean build, and when she put on a mask and raised a sword, he could almost imagine that her hair was long and golden instead of shoulder-length and brown as ale. But her fighting style was nothing like Dara's, and as soon as the duel began, the illusion shattered.

The clash of steel on steel filled the air once more, quickly dissipating across the plains. Their camp from the night before was at the edge of a vineyard a stone's throw from the Ridge Road, which they'd be rejoining at last. They had made good time across the open countryside despite the training breaks. They would arrive in Tollan and stay with Fiz's mother that very night if all went well.

Siv planned to leave the pen fighters in Tollan. It was directly on the High Road, and it would be a straight shot north to Rallion City. He'd been lulling his companions into complacency as they traveled. There was no sense in running away from them in the wilds. He was unlikely to escape with his life, much less a horse and enough food to make it through the wilderness on his own. They had to accept his story about being a wine merchant by now, though. He was damn convincing. Come to think of it, they never actually let him take watch at night, but he *must* be making progress. Surely they didn't still think he was some spy who'd sell them out to—whomever they were so worried about. He still hadn't figured that part out yet.

The only problem was the more he pretended he was joining

them, the more it felt as though he truly had. He couldn't help picturing himself in a Steel Pentagon, knife whirling, the crowds hollering his name.

He didn't intend to travel all the way to Pendark, but he found himself wondering what would be so bad if he did. He could do nothing for Vertigon. When he returned, he'd spend the rest of the winter locked inside the palace in Rallion City. What was the point? Everyone there spent the whole time telling him to forget Vertigon and start over anyway. He might as well enjoy being his own man for now.

Siv and Gull managed a few decent matches before Fiz returned from scouting and rounded them up to start the day's ride. He was eager to visit his home, and Siv had no chance to rest from his bouts before Fiz hurried him onto his horse and led the way onto the Ridge Road.

The morning was bright, with a fresh winter breeze gusting over a scattered patchwork of vineyards. The sun warmed Siv's face as they rode west. The purple outline of the Linden Mountains rose beside them, the road already beginning its gentle ascent into the foothills. He could make his escape as soon as they reached the High Road, but it would almost be dark by then, and he fancied the idea of a night in Tollan before he turned north once more. Besides, he'd have a better chance of eluding the pen fighters there than if he made a run for it at the fork. He was a good rider but not *that* good.

Fiz hummed as he rode at the head of the group on his massive stallion, which looked more suited to hauling wagons than carrying riders. Kres soon picked up the refrain, his confident tenor ringing out across the plains. Even Gull hummed along, a bit tuneless but still cheery. Siv grinned. Despite the fact that he was figuring out how to escape from them without getting killed, Siv was starting to like these people. It probably had something to do with them rescuing him from a far less-pleasant bunch of traveling companions.

He fell back to where Latch trailed behind the others. Siv had tried to make friends with everyone on the team in an effort to prove he wasn't a spy, but if anything, Latch had cooled toward him throughout the journey. He got particularly grumpy whenever Siv practiced swordplay with Gull. It didn't matter whether he used a rapier or a saber. Latch did not like that there was another skilled duelist among them now.

But damned if Siv was going to let the surly Soolen get the better of him. If he was going to survive long enough to make it home, he couldn't pick up any new enemies. Firelord knew he had enough of those already.

"He sounds like a burrlinbat when he sings that song," Siv said, putting on his friendliest grin and nodding at Fiz up ahead. "Have you ever heard—?"

"I don't care," Latch said through gritted teeth.

"Just making conversation," Siv said.

Latch rolled his eyes. "I've never heard a burrlinbat."

"How about a bullshell?" Siv said. "I hear they make a pretty powerful noise. They live on the Soolen—"

"I know where they live."

"Ever seen one?"

Latch gave him a flat look. Then he sighed. "Once."

"Was it as big as Byrd Brelling says in his Soolen travel journals?" Siv brought his horse closer to Latch's, unable to hide his excitement. "He writes that if you find an empty shell, there's enough room for ten men to camp inside."

"Brelling exaggerates," Latch said. "You'd be hard-pressed to fit the five of us inside an empty bullshell."

"Really? But Fiz is as big as two men. You reckon you could fit six normal folks inside in a pinch?"

"Sure. Six." Latch looked at him out of the corner of his eye. Was that curiosity? That could be a good sign. "You ever read about Brelling's visit to Cindral Forest?"

"That was my favorite," Siv said. "That's where I first read about gorlions and—"

He froze as Latch whipped out his rapier and laid it across his throat so fast it could have been a Fire Blade.

"Easy there," Siv said. The tip of the blade was cold against his skin. They had dropped back far enough that none of the others would be able to do anything before Latch rammed the tip through his neck. None of them looked back or noticed Siv's plight anyway.

"You've read Brelling's travel journals," Latch said, his voice dangerously quiet.

"Yes." Siv gulped, his throat bobbing against steel. "No one's ever drawn a blade on me because of my preferred reading material before."

"You read a lot?" Latch said softly, pressing his sword harder against Siv's neck.

"Yes . . ." Siv had no idea where this was going.

"You don't seem to know how rare and expensive Brelling's travel journals are," Latch said. "They're too pricey for your average Truren wine merchant to afford *one*, much less enough of them to have a favorite."

"I didn't own them," Siv began, thinking fast. "I once met a—"

"Save it," Latch said. "Who are you really?"

"I'm a wine—"

"I know a lord's manners when I see them. And I know those Soolens didn't kidnap you by chance. I thought you were a spy, but spies aren't any richer than wine merchants."

Siv cast about for a way to salvage his story. He couldn't tell the truth, naturally. He may be getting along with the others, but they wouldn't bat an eyelash if Latch killed him. He wished people would stop pulling swords on him, even if it was just because of his reading habits. Come to think of it . . .

"How do *you* know about Brelling's journals?" Siv said. "You said Brelling exaggerates. You've read them too, haven't you?"

Latch's face twitched, and that was answer enough.

"You're some kind of secret lordling, too, aren't you?" Siv said. It may not be the best idea to annoy Latch right now, but he was short on options. "Don't think I didn't notice that no one uses your surname. And your dueling style is remarkably refined for a pen fighter. I'd say you've at least worked with a Vertigonian coach. Those don't come cheap either."

"Is that why you're here?" Latch demanded. And he looked genuinely scared for the first time. *Interesting.* "What do you know?"

"I don't know anything," Siv said. "I'm not a spy, and I'm not here for you."

Latch frowned, but he didn't remove his sword from Siv's neck.

"Can we agree to keep our own secrets?" Siv said.

Latch didn't answer. A bead of sweat slid down Siv's face and into his scruffy beard. He did not like having a sword at his throat one bit.

That never happened to him back when he was king. Well, *almost* never.

"I don't want any trouble," he said. "I swear it."

At last, Latch relaxed and withdrew his sword.

"Thank you." Siv resisted the urge to rub his neck. "I don't think Kres would be too happy about having to find yet another knife fighter."

It was the wrong thing to say. Latch spat a curse at him and heeled his horse forward again. Right. He'd been close to Shreya, the knife fighter who was killed before Siv joined them. He sighed. So much for bonding with Latch over their shared reading interests and secret noble pasts.

Still, he wondered if the rest of the squad knew about Latch. Were they hiding him from some sort of trouble? Was that why they'd been so determined to keep Siv lest he give them away? Was it possible Latch had even more people after him than Siv himself? He would keep Latch's secret, but that didn't mean he couldn't try to find out more.

He could only hope it all had nothing to do with him.

25

SHADOW

DARA clutched the hilt of her Savven blade. It kept her hands warm, and its solid weight at her hip was reassuring. She turned in her saddle to scan the road behind them for the hundredth time that day.

They were being followed. She'd been sure of it for a while now. She had expected to be attacked after they bypassed Roan Town. Yen must have reported their departure to his mysterious sandy-haired friend. He must have disclosed everything he knew about them.

They had ridden late into the night, and when they finally made camp, she'd spent sleepless hours waiting for dawn, hands tight on her sword, expecting an assault at any moment. Vine had slept soundly after her hard day of meditation, trusting Dara to keep them alive until morning. An attack didn't come that night, nor the one after it. But they had a shadow. The wraithlike presence never got too close, but it was always there.

They were still traveling on the Ridge Road, which ran alongside the Linden Mountains until it reached the High Road to the west. The Ridge Road meandered through groves of bare-branched linden trees, slowly drifting closer to the foothills. Unlike on the plains, the hills and trees provided ample hiding places for their shadow.

Dara felt on edge. She wanted whoever was behind them to attack already. At least then she could do something about it.

Vine showed no signs of concern. Ever since she picked up a hint of Siv in the Air, she'd been following it like a hound. Her confidence had returned with interest, and she seemed certain they were going the right way. Rumy charged onward as eagerly as Vine, as if he too could smell Siv on the breeze. Dara was the only one who still worried.

"Why aren't they attacking?" Dara said—not for the first time.

"I expect they want us to lead them to King Siv," Vine said.

"And then what?"

"Who knows?" Vine tossed her hair over her shoulder. "I'm sure plenty of unsavory people would pay for knowledge of his whereabouts, including your parents."

"Do you . . ." Dara swallowed. "Do you think we should draw them in another direction? They must not have the Air Sense, or they wouldn't need us."

"That is a reasonable guess," Vine said. "It's your decision, Dara."

Dara looked back at the empty road again. She had been considering that possibility for days. According to the clues in the wind, Siv had traveled overland at an angle toward the High Road, whereas Dara and Vine were riding due west. They moved quickly, but Siv was making good time too. It would be a race to get to him before he reached Kurn Pass, if that was where his captors were taking him. Vine had reported that she sensed pain and struggle in the Air—sometimes multiple times a day. Whoever had Siv, they were hurting him regularly.

Those hints of pain were enough to make Dara abandon the idea of guiding their shadow off on a false trail. Whoever was following them to Siv might not be as bad as the people who had him right now.

Movement flickered at the edge of her vision, and she whirled in her saddle. The road was still empty, but she'd had enough. She wasn't going to lead anyone to Siv. It was time to end this.

"Rumy," she called. "Come here, boy."

The cur-dragon banked sharply and glided down toward her. She'd sent him to try to get a glimpse of their pursuer more than once over the past few days, but he hadn't had any luck yet.

Rumy came in for a landing, startling up a puff of dust. Storm shifted nervously. Their steeds had gotten used to the cur-dragon, but it still unsettled them when he soared down, wings flaring, and landed close by.

Dara slid off her horse's back and knelt beside Rumy.

"I need you to give me some Fire, boy," she said.

Rumy snorted and looked up at her in surprise. She had only tried to Work with the residual Fire in his flame once since that day on the mountain path. She worried that if she started using the Fire again, she wouldn't be able to stop. She missed the sensation of heat beneath her skin almost as much as she missed the sound of Siv's laugh. Yen had said time and distance would help. Even though she was fairly certain Yen had sold them out, he was probably right about that. But she couldn't sit here and let some unknown enemy follow them straight to Siv while she still had this tool at her disposal.

Dara readied herself for the blast as Rumy reared back on his hind legs. She was a little out of practice in Working. How long had it been since they left Vertigon? Four weeks? She wondered what was happening up there. Was Sora still sitting on the throne as a puppet, dancing to Dara's father's wishes? Or had he decided there'd been enough time for the transition? Dara shook off the thought of her father, trying to focus on the task at hand.

Rumy blew out a jet of flame, and Dara stuck her hands into it all the way up to her elbows. The heat of the dragon fire warmed her, but it was nothing like the Fire that mixed with Rumy's flame in little spurts. It could be her imagination, but there seemed to be more Fire there than last time. Dara clutched at the spurts, soaking them up like a sponge.

She lost all awareness of the world around her as the Fire seeped into her skin and coursed through her veins. The rush was incredible, even in this small quantity. She had missed this. It was raw power. Pure. Blazing. Indestructible. The Fire from Rumy's flame was somehow wilder and more difficult to control than the molten power flowing from Vertigon Mountain, but she welcomed it, burning feral beneath her skin.

A gust of wind buffeted her face, sharp and cold, drawing her attention back to the dusty road. Rumy's flame had started to weaken.

"That's enough," Dara said. "Thanks, boy."

She wrapped her hands around her Savven blade to help her focus. It was still easier for her to control the Fire when touching steel. The Work she was about to attempt was a delicate thing. Rumy lay down on the ground, winded from expelling so much flame. She would only have one chance to get this right.

She eased the Fire out of her skin, letting it pool in her hands. They were the only travelers on the road here, but she scanned their surroundings once more in case the searing light drew unwanted attention. Then she closed her eyes and reached out with her senses.

She'd been thinking a lot about Vine's Air Sense on their journey. Vine had felt something when she neared the pool of Fire collecting in the secret cavern on Square Peak, even though she had no Firespark. And Dara had been sure she felt something of the Air once, some sense of Siv on the wind. At the time she had brushed it off, assuming it was her own desire to find him playing tricks on her mind.

But what if there was a connection? What if having the Firespark gave her the ability, however limited, to make use of the Air magic that flowed freely on the plains of Trure? Zage Lorrid had once said the Fire was the raw material, but the magic within her was something else, something distinct. How much could she do with it?

She closed her eyes and let the breeze caress her skin, feeling for some hint, some presence. She was aware of Vine and Rumy and the horses beside her. She smelled the horseflesh, the leathery saddles, the dry aroma of dead linden leaves. She heard the rustling, sighing, ever-present wind.

She reached further, trying to grasp onto something just beyond the edge of her senses. She groped blindly, as if she were feeling for residual Fire. She tried to leave herself open to all sensations, hopeful she might feel something through the Air even if she couldn't bend it to her will. *Please let this work.*

Then she felt it. A flicker. A shadow. A hint of nuisance.

She struck.

The Fire she'd gathered shot away from her like an arrow. Thin spirals of power snaked into the shadows behind them. She'd practiced the action before, but she'd never relied on blind feeling to guide its trajectory. She felt the stream of Fire bend and coil, following the hints from the Air. It was like the sensation on her scalp when she curled her hair around her finger, a mere hint of movement.

A gasp came from deep in the trees, followed by a muffled curse.

"Got you," Dara said.

"What are you doing back there?" Vine asked. Intent on her own senses, she hadn't noticed what her companions were doing.

"I caught our shadow," Dara said. "Let's see who we're dealing with."

She left her horse with Vine and backtracked, following the pull of the Fire she'd sent blindly into the trees. The dry leaves crunched beneath her boots as she pushed through the dense grove. A few dozens yards off the road, she found the Fire, Worked into shackles and holding a prisoner tight.

It was a man, though not the sandy-haired Rollendar lord she had expected. This fellow was younger, probably no more than twenty-five. He wore rough clothes in the Truren country style, and he had tanned, freckled skin and light-brown hair. He stood utterly still, staring at the shackles of Fire as if they were live vipers.

"Who are you?" Dara demanded. She drew her sword, but she didn't threaten him with it directly. The Fire ought to scare him enough.

"Let me go," the man wheezed. "Are you one of them Air Witches?" He had a coarse voice, and Dara got the impression that he was farmer, a country boy. Could he be here by chance?

"Why are you following us?"

"I ain't following you."

"You are," Dara said. "You have been since Roan Town."

"Let me out of these blasted things," the man repeated.

"I don't think so," Dara said. "Who hired you?"

"Release me, Air Witch."

"Does that look like Air to you?" Dara took a few steps closer to her prisoner, adopting a menacing tone. "Fire is a lot more dangerous than Air."

"Now, Dara, that is debatable," Vine said, pushing through the trees to join them, both horses in tow. "Air can surprise you, and I daresay it can be just as lethal as Fire with the right technique."

"Tell her to let me go," the man said desperately, turning to Vine as much as he could without brushing against the Fire that held him. Sweat broke out on his forehead, and he looked on the verge of panic.

"Dara doesn't respond well to commands," Vine said. "It's a rather endearing quality, I find." She walked in a wide circle around their prisoner, stepping lightly over the brush and fallen tree branches. "Now then, you aren't what I was expecting," she said. "Are you a local?"

"I'm Truren, if that's what you mean," the man said. "I ain't answering any more questions until you free me."

"I'm afraid that wouldn't be wise," Vine said.

"Tell us who hired you," Dara said.

"I work on a farm near Roan Town." The light from the Fire made his eyes glow as he stared at his shackles. He tore his gaze away and looked pleadingly at Vine, perhaps thinking her a more-likely ally than Dara. "Farmer Wells hired me to care for the horses is all."

"We're pretty far from Roan Town," Dara said.

"Dara is right," Vine said. "And you've been following us rather closely for several days."

Dara looked up. "You sensed him?"

"I didn't think him worthy of concern," Vine said. "We are on a tight schedule."

"Wait a minute," the man said. "You're an Air Witch too? They didn't tell me . . . oh, I never should have left the farm. That's what I get for talking to strangers. Farmer Wells ain't that bad."

"Ah," Vine said pleasantly. "Now we're getting somewhere. Dara? I don't believe this man will hurt us. Perhaps you could make him more comfortable?"

Dara hesitated, but her captive was starting to look quite distressed. Her shackles of Fire, a Work she'd seen both Zage Lorrid and her father perform, were less smooth and stable than they should be. The Fire from Rumy flickered in a way that the pure molten power from the mountain did not. Little sparks, almost as fine as mist, spurted off them. The captive was probably in pain. She released her hold, pulling the Fire back into her body, and brought the point of her sword to his neck instead.

"Better?"

The man rubbed at his wrists, already looking happier despite the blade at his throat.

"Dung-eatin' witch," he said.

"There's no need for that language," Vine said. "Now, will you tell us who hired you and neglected to mention what you were getting yourself into?"

The man straightened his back.

"I wanted a few extra coins for a new horse," he said. "Ain't nothing wrong with that."

"Not at all. Please continue," Vine said pleasantly. "And do tell us your name."

"Tann Ridon. Friends call me Rid." He eyed Vine up and down, as if hoping she might become one of those friends. "It was a man from Vertigon. Met him in the tavern in Roan Town."

"Did he have sandy-blond hair and a long nose?" Dara asked. "And a red coat?"

"That's him," Rid said. "Probably about thirty-five? Forty? Wouldn't tell me his name."

"That sounds like our Lord Vex," Vine said. "What did he hire you to do?"

"I was just supposed to follow you and report back," Rid said. "No harm meant."

"What did he tell you about us?" Dara asked.

"Nothin'. Said you weren't supposed to be so far from home, and he wanted to know what you were up to." Rid gave Dara a sidelong glance, easing away from her blade.

"He didn't say what he wanted with us?" Dara asked.

"Naw. Wasn't all that talkative. Paid up front, though. That was nice."

"Interesting." Dara wondered if Vex Rollendar might only be curious. Perhaps his presence in Roan Town had been a coincidence. On the other hand, there had been those three mysterious riders behind them, and Dara had felt as if they were being followed earlier in their journey as well. "Did he have any men with him?"

"Two bodyguards. They pretended to be his friends." Rid shrugged. "I ain't stupid. I wouldn't trust the guy as far as I can throw him, but I was blasted tired of sitting around waiting for Farmer Wells to take the final ride."

"Well, we'd appreciate it greatly if you don't tell him where we're going," Vine said. "That would be ever so helpful."

Rid blinked. "You . . . you mean you're going to let me go?"

"Vine, I don't think that's a good idea," Dara said.

"You don't wish to kill this nice young man, do you, Dara?" Vine said.

"No, but . . ." Dara frowned. Rid was probably harmless, but he was still a Rollendar informant. They couldn't just let him walk away, but she couldn't stab someone in cold blood either.

"He is a spy," Dara said slowly.

"Nonsense," Vine said. "He's an enterprising young man who aimed to improve his fortunes in the world." She reached into her saddlebags for the coin purse she kept there. They were running low on coin, but she didn't hesitate to pull out a few glittering bits of gold. "If we give you some money, will you kindly pretend you lost us?"

Rid's eyes widened, and he stared back and forth between Dara and Vine. "Just like that?"

"I don't see why not," Vine said.

"But . . . you're just going to go on down the road all by yourselves?" Rid said.

"Worked out well enough so far," Dara said.

Rid cleared his throat gruffly. "I'm not sure I can let two women travel by themselves without a protector. I keep hearing there's gonna be a war. And if you already have crooked folks trying to follow you . . . I could come along . . . maybe be your bodyguard. I ain't expensive."

Dara snorted. "I'm not sure you're bodyguard material."

"You used witch magic to get me," Rid said. "It ain't fair."

"We're not taking recruits," Dara said.

"Hold on," Vine said. "He has a point, Dara."

"What?"

"I do?"

"When we reach the High Road, we'll encounter more travelers. They will wonder about two women gallivanting through the wilderness alone. It has doubtless caused us to stick in people's memories already. Perhaps if we had a strapping young bodyguard such as this, we would make less of an impression on the world as we pass."

Rid's cheeks reddened when Vine called him strapping, and he stood a little straighter.

"I can protect you," he said. "I win all the staff fights against the other farmhands." He nodded toward a thick walking stick he had dropped when Dara wrapped him in bonds of Fire.

"I don't like it," Dara said. She still held her Savven blade to Rid's throat, but he didn't seem nearly as afraid of it as he was of the Fire. Still, they could hardly trust him if he switched sides that easily.

"I have a good feeling about this," Vine said. "And I wouldn't mind having someone else to talk to. You are far too worried about our friend to make good conversation, Dara."

"What friend?" Rid asked.

"You don't need to know," Dara said.

"Come now, Dara, no need to be hostile." Vine stepped up to Rid and delicately lifted Dara's blade away from his throat. She smiled up at him, widening her big brown eyes. "Don't betray us, and I daresay you'll have a chance to see the world. That's what you want, isn't it?"

"Aye, m'lady." Rid looked down at her, already showing a hint of the devotion that Dara had seen Vine command in more than a few men—and women. "I don't want to be stuck on the farm forever."

"I think you'll make a lovely traveling companion," Vine said. "Let us go. We don't want to let our friend get too far ahead."

And she turned and waltzed back toward the road.

Dara landed her blade on Rid's shoulder before he could move two steps.

"I'll have no problem killing you if you try to hurt us," she said. "Just because she's decided to trust you on a whim doesn't mean I do."

Rid's jaw tensed, but he nodded. "Just don't do that fiery thing again." And he followed Vine back onto the road.

THEY TRAVELED ONWARD, getting closer to the High Road every day. The disquiet that had filled Dara while they were being followed was replaced by worry that Rid would betray them. Even if he didn't, Vex Rollendar might have sent more than one shadow after them. There was no telling where the elusive lord himself was now.

Keeping an eye on Rid was annoying at first, but as they continued their journey, Dara began to see what Vine had recognized on instinct. Rid was harmless—a young man who'd jumped at the opportunity to change his fortune from a mysterious stranger in a tavern. They might not keep his loyalty forever, but at least Vex Rollendar didn't have it either.

Rid asked endless questions about Vertigon and the parts of the world he'd never seen before. Vine had traveled and read more than Dara, and she answered his queries patiently. It quickly became clear that Rid considered himself Vine's bodyguard, not Dara's. He strode beside her horse, scanning the countryside for threats and boasting about how he'd protect her. Dara wondered how he'd react the first time he saw how good Vine was with a sword.

By the third day after Rid joined their party—the sixth since they'd left Roan Town—it was as though he'd always been with them. He had a guileless energy that helped to relieve some of the tension of the journey. He also took over the duty of caring for the horses with enthusiasm. That alone was enough to make Dara warm to him.

She couldn't help teasing him with the Fire, though. Once she had a taste of Working again, it was as if a dam had been broken. That rush of power and heat in her blood reminded her just how much she'd missed the Fire. She took to asking Rumy to share more of his flame each morning. He obliged, producing burst upon burst of dragon fire mixed with Fire. If Dara wasn't mistaken, each time, he produced a little more of the true power. She was dying to know whether this was something all cur-dragons could do, or if Rumy was unique.

As they rode, Dara practiced, twirling the Fire above Storm's neck, pooling and spooling it in her hands, building Fire Blossoms and sending them spinning into the trees—or around Rid's head. She experimented with holding Fire while she did her dueling forms, and she was sure it made her aim more accurate and her connection with the Savven blade more complete. And the heat! The pure heat flowing within her body was better than the most-satisfying run across the bridges or the sweetest soldarberry bursting on her tongue. She'd once insisted she never wanted to touch the Fire again. She knew the dangers of her father's power. But all too soon she was asking Rumy for more.

Rid hated these practice sessions, at least at first. He had never seen Fire Wielded like this before. In truth, Dara had never seen many of the things she tried as they rode farther and farther toward the setting sun. But he couldn't help the awe that crept onto his face as she filled the air around them with light and bled Fire out of her pores. It always faded eventually, though. Rumy's Fire was still nothing compared to the raw power she'd left behind on the mountain. The raw power that called her home.

On their sixth day, they decided to keep riding onward after dark. The Ridge Road smoothed out as it began the final approach to the High Road through a patchwork of vineyards. The vineyards meant people, and they wanted to avoid strangers for as long as possible. Siv was still ahead of them somewhere, but they were slowly making up the distance.

Dara occasionally asked Rumy for a bit of light to make sure they hadn't strayed off their path. He obliged, looking extra pleased with himself any time his bursts of flame revealed little creatures creeping across the road in the dark.

Rid walked with his hand resting on Goldenflower's neck, his staff tapping the dirt at regular intervals. He chattered on as usual, sharing a long and convoluted story about horse training back on the farm.

"And then Farmer Wells takes a lump of honeycomb out of his pocket, and the mare—this is the one I told you about yesterday with the bum leg—the mare gets a sniff of the honey, and she—"

"Wait!" Vine said. She stopped abruptly and turned in her saddle, the consternation on her face just visible in the darkness. Rid lifted his staff, whirling it wildly as if he expected attackers to materialize from the air around him.

"What is it?" Dara heeled Storm forward, shoving Rid out of the way. Rumy circled over their heads, providing a burst of illumination.

"He's gone." Vine's face was deathly pale.

"Siv?"

"The Air is still carrying whispers, but I can't feel him anymore."

"He's not . . ."

"I don't know, Dara." Vine fidgeted in her saddle, struggling to calm herself enough to listen to the Air.

Dara took Vine's reins and held her horse steady while she concentrated. Their saddles creaked, and a creature chattered in the darkness. Dara could barely breathe. What did Vine mean Siv was gone? After all this time, had his captors finally decided to kill him? The thought made her want to throw up.

"What's going on?" Rid asked.

"I'm not sure," Dara said.

"Is Lady Vine okay?"

"It's not her I'm worried about."

Vine sat very still for a long time. Dara tried to sense whatever she sensed, but she was too afraid of what she might find. She felt nothing but dread.

Wind rustled ominously through the vineyards. The rows of bare vines stretched away from them, eerie and empty.

Finally, Vine slumped and held out a hand for her reins.

"Vine," Dara said, unable to keep the desperation from her voice.

"I'm sorry, Dara. He's just . . . gone."

26

THE VINTNER'S REST

SIV and the pen fighters made decent time on the Ridge Road, still stopping to spar whenever Kres said the word. He wanted to train when the mood took him, and no one dared tell him otherwise. Siv had acquired a steady supply of bruises during their journey, and he ached in a different part of his body every mile. He had definitely improved, though. He was working harder than he ever had in his life. Surprisingly, he kind of liked it. He could hardly wait for Dara to see what he'd learned.

Riders passed them regularly now, going in both directions, but they mostly kept to themselves. When Kres asked passersby for news of the world, they responded to his inquiries with suspicion. Unease had plagued Trure since Soole's invasion of Cindral Forest. Rumors of troop movements spread like wildfire, but no one seemed to have real information.

The High Road was even more crowded when they joined up with it and turned in to Tollan. It was the last village before Kurn Pass, serving as a way station for the miners who worked in the Linden Mountains and the farmers who cared for the vineyards in the southern reaches of Trure. Wagons creaked by sometimes, carrying bushels of dried grass and teetering stacks of barrels. Siv avoided looking at the wagons lest they remind him of his miserable days with the Soolens. He had been enjoying his (relative) freedom too much to think about his unplanned departure from Rallion City.

The sun sat low on the horizon as they entered Tollan. The buildings were mostly constructed of wood in the single-level style prevalent throughout Trure. Dead leaves caught in the thatched roofs, and bare linden trees spread their branches overhead. The purple shape of the Linden Mountains loomed beyond the village, with a distinct dip where Kurn Pass cut through them.

Fiz's mother kept an inn just off the High Road, not far from the northern edge of town. As they turned into her yard, she burst out of the doors and ran full-speed toward them.

"Fiz! My boy! You are late!"

Fiz swept his mother into a hug, grinning widely.

"We ran into some excitement," Fiz said.

"It's bad enough I have to worry about you in the pen. Now I have to worry you'll find trouble in the wilds too? Hello, Gull, dear. And Krestian, so good to see you again."

Madame Timon was as wide as her son, though not quite as tall. She had the same flaxen hair and broad smile, and thin wrinkles spidered from the edges of her eyes. She shook hands all the way around the squad. Kres introduced Siv and Latch by first names only. So she hadn't met Latch before? *Very interesting.*

"They are proving to be fine recruits," Kres said. "We shall win every Dance this year, I'm sure of it."

"I thought you were going out to pick up a young lady?" Madame Timon said.

"Fortune had different plans." Kres looked at Siv with a calculating gleam in his eyes. "Better plans, I daresay."

"Fortune? I rather think the wind brought them to you," Madame Timon said. "You must listen to the Air."

"Now, now, let's not get into that old debate again." Kres offered his arm to Madame Timon and escorted her toward the door of her inn. "You argued me under the table last time I was here."

Madame Timon chuckled. "I believe that was my house ale."

Fiz and Gull followed Kres and Madame Timon, who were still talking animatedly. Siv caught Latch's eye as they crossed the yard—and received a scowl for his troubles.

The inn, called the Vintner's Rest, was a fine establishment of smooth black stone, apparently one of the few buildings in the village not constructed from linden wood. Fiz greeted the stable boys by name, slapping backs and asking after wives and girlfriends before they whisked the horses away.

The pen fighters climbed the steps of a broad porch at the front of the inn and trooped inside. They found a well-kept common room, with a fireplace of black stone and a single large table filling most of the floor space. Madame Timon ushered them to seats at the table and commanded them to relax. Before long, they each had a foaming mug of ale and a steaming plate of roast vegetables paired with an unfamiliar dark meat. Siv tucked in, letting the babble of conversation unfold around him. He was so hungry he could eat a mountain bear.

"What's the news, Mother?" Fiz asked as she set a final plate on the table and joined them.

"All rumors, I'm afraid," Madame Timon said. "I was hoping you'd know what's happening up north."

"We've been off the High Road for most of our journey."

"Well, every traveler that comes through here has a different story about what that Soolen army is up to." Madame Timon glanced at Latch, taking in his Soolen features. "You may want to keep your head down while you're in Tollan, my friend."

"You don't need to worry about our boy here," Kres said. He glanced pointedly at Siv as if to hint that he didn't trust *him* quite as fully. It didn't matter. If all went well, Siv would be far away by morning.

"I'm not," Madame Timon said, "but the army might. I had a pair of Soolen merchants in here a few days ago, and they were questioned more than once. They're good customers. Stayed here now and again for years, but the soldiers don't know that."

"Soldiers?"

"Aye. There's a new company stationed here to watch the Pass. They're still letting people through for now, but the whole town is on edge."

"Perhaps we shouldn't linger," Kres said. He adjusted his red baldric and glanced toward the window.

"Nonsense," Madame Timon said. "You all need a hot meal and a good night's sleep."

Siv was heartened to hear about the increased military presence. It ought to make his defection from the group easier—after that hot meal and good night's sleep. Would the average Truren soldier recognize the grandson of their king? He didn't want to be hung as an imposter before he made it back to Rallion City. On the other hand, given how his luck had been lately, maybe it would be better if no one recognized him at all. Being caught by someone who *wasn't* loyal to his grandfather—such as the treacherous Lord Bale—would be much worse than roaming around with the pen fighters.

Madame Timon smiled and patted Kres's hand. "Don't you worry about any trouble."

"I am sure we are safe under your roof, my dear Madame Timon." Kres skewered Siv with another incisive look. He grinned back.

"You mentioned you were out near Roan Town." Madame Timon suddenly rounded on her son, eyes sharp as a furlingbird's.

Fiz paled. "We didn't go in—"

"Did you see Zenny?"

"There was no time—"

"I told you to look her up when you were in the east," Madame Timon said.

"Can we not discuss—"

"You two are still married, you know. I never thought a son of mine would abandon his commitments just because his wife looked twice at a fellow with a pretty face. What was his name again?"

"Does it matter?" Fiz tugged at his collar. "And she did more than look."

"Perhaps. But a strong fellow like you should fight for his woman." Madame Timon thumped her son's huge shoulders. "Show that dandy what you're made of."

"I'd rather not talk about that right now." Fiz looked at the others imploringly. Gull and Kres just chuckled, but Siv figured he ought to help the man out.

"This meat is excellent, Madame Timon," he began, putting on his most-charming smile. "Is it goat?"

"That's horsemeat, of course," Madame Timon said. "You're not from Trure, are you, dear?"

Siv nearly choked. Horsemeat? They definitely didn't eat that in his grandfather's palace.

"It's delicious," he said, hoping his eyes weren't watering.

Latch reached across the table for the pitcher of ale and muttered, "Thought you said you grew up in Trure."

He didn't speak loud enough for the others to hear, but Siv stiffened anyway. He had to be more careful. This whole false-identity thing was harder than he expected.

"You didn't know it was horsemeat either," he whispered, nodding at Latch's plate, which he'd pushed away after Madame Timon's words.

Latch snorted. If Siv didn't know better, he'd almost think it was a laugh.

The group continued to chat and drink, cleaning their plates and holding them out for seconds of everything except the horsemeat. It was still early for dinner, and they had the communal table to themselves. Siv wished he could ask Madame Timon what was happening in Vertigon without arousing the suspicions of his companions. She must know a lot of what was going on in the world with so many travelers coming through her doors. Siv still worried about his former kingdom, even though it seemed less likely than ever that his grandfather would lend him men to retake it. He wouldn't treat the threat of Soole lightly, even if only half the rumors were true.

As nice as it was to see new lands, Siv missed the dramatic cliffs surrounding his homeland, the bridges disappearing into the mist. But he couldn't think about the mountain without remembering how he had failed it. He had been dragged out of his former life, but Vertigon might not have been sorry to see him go.

More travelers entered the inn while they ate, and Madame Timon alternated between fussing over her son and serving the newcomers. Her patrons were mostly workers from the surrounding vineyards and merchants transporting goods through Kurn Pass. Siv kept his head down in case he was recognized, though that seemed unlikely this far from Rallion City. Latch made an effort to remain equally inconspicuous. Only Kres and Gull were as relaxed as the Timons.

When everyone had finished eating, Fiz stood and stretched.

"I have a few people to visit this evening," he said. "Old friends and the like."

"Don't be out too late," Madame Timon said.

Fiz chuckled. "She forgets I'm a thirty-year-old man. I'll always be a boy in my mother's eyes."

Fiz headed out into the town, but the others remained in the inn. As tempting as it was to go carousing with the big Truren, Siv had to prepare for his escape. Besides, he couldn't wait to sleep in a bed again—at least for a few hours. He'd had no idea how much he appreciated his bed before going on the run for his life.

Madame Timon showed them to rooms up a rickety wooden staircase from the common room. Siv and Latch had to share a garret furnished with two narrow cots and an oddly contorted candlestick. Latch wasn't enthusiastic about the prospect, but Siv was too tired to care either way. Besides, if he had to bet, he figured Gull was the more likely of the two to sleep with one eye open.

"Please don't stab me in my bed," Siv said. "I'm looking forward to a nice long rest."

Latch rolled his eyes and climbed into his cot—the one closer to the door, unfortunately. He turned his back on Siv without so much as a good night. The fellow was a puzzle. He was downright surly—understandable after the death of his friend—but Siv got the impression that there was more to him than that. What was he running from? Siv wished he could have found out before he had to leave the team.

He sighed and snuggled underneath his blanket. That kind of problem was better tackled after a good night's sleep. And he intended to sleep like the dead. He'd need his strength when he snuck away before dawn. He had it all planned out. He'd wait until the whole inn was asleep, and then he'd retrieve his horse and be a solid few hours north before the pen fighters were any the wiser. He was counting on their safe lodging in Madame Timon's inn to guarantee that one of the others wouldn't be awake and on watch—as they always had been throughout the journey. And with the first Dance of the season happening so soon, they wouldn't waste time searching for him. He hoped.

No sense in lying awake worrying until then, though. Siv snuggled deeper into his blankets, trying to ignore the eerie shadows cast by that bizarre candlestick.

He had barely drifted off when Kres pounded on the door.

"Quickly! We must leave at once," he called.

Siv sat up, disoriented. "What?"

"Rise and shine, children. The army is about to close the pass."

"Why?" Siv rubbed his eyes, every muscle aching from his knife training sessions. Latch sat up too, looking considerably more alert.

"Word just arrived," Kres called. "The Soolen army has crossed the border into Trure."

"Why?" Siv said again, still crawling his way out of whatever nice dream he'd been having when he was so abruptly awakened.

"Don't be stupid, lad," Kres said. "Invasion! Fiz heard the news while he was out. An official rider from the capital."

"But—"

"There will be time for questions later. If we don't leave now, we'll be stuck on this side of the mountains until spring."

Latch scrambled out of bed and began gathering his things. Siv followed his lead, still feeling sluggish. He wanted to ask Latch's opinion of what Soole might have in mind by advancing in the dead of winter, but as usual, Latch ignored his attempts to start a conversation.

They stumbled down the stairs to the common room, said a groggy good-bye to Madame Timon, and headed out into the night. Siv didn't relish the idea of entering Kurn Pass in the dark, but he'd like being stuck in Tollan even less.

They rode through town, their horses' hooves pounding the dirt, and Fiz filled them in on what he'd heard. The Soolen army was moving across the Truren plains to the northeast, heading for Rallion City.

Siv pulled up short as the last of the mist cleared from his brain. Rallion City. Where his mother, his sister, and his Dara were staying. Moreover, *Kurn Pass*? What was he *doing*?

He was going the wrong way, that was what he was doing. He began to turn his horse.

Suddenly Gull was directly in his path. "What is it?" she said.

"I'm not leaving Trure." Siv's horse danced beneath him, sensing his agitation. "I have to turn back." *So much for sneaking away.*

"This is no time for cold feet," Fiz said.

"It's not—"

"Why'd you change your mind now?" Latch demanded. "As soon as we hear about the invasion."

"Yeah." Gull narrowed her eyes, and her hand strayed to her sword hilt. "Are you *sure* you were a prisoner of those Soolens?"

"It seems someone's true colors are showing at last," Kres whispered. A gleeful light flickered in his eyes. And off his knives. How did he get those out so quickly?

"I'm not on Soole's side," Siv said. He looked to Fiz, who was staring at him with furrowed brows. He didn't draw his broadsword, but with his strength, he hardly needed it.

"You're in an awful hurry to run off," Fiz said.

"This isn't about you," Siv said. "I'm sure it would be fun to be a pen fighter and all, but I have duties."

Latch snorted in disbelief, and Gull looked equally suspicious.

"And what, pray tell, are these duties?" Kres asked, his voice taking on that dangerous quiet tone again. He edged closer, so their horses' flanks were nearly touching. "Sivren Amen."

The others drew closer too, backing Kres up, cutting Siv off. He swallowed. Kres's right knife hovered near his knee, mere inches from his main artery. He'd seen how Kres could move. He'd never get his own blade out before Kres sent his lifeblood spilling over his saddle. Even if he did, he'd have the others to deal with next. Apparently he hadn't made as much progress with the team as he'd thought. He *knew* he should have tried to sneak off sooner. He'd been too busy playing pen fighter to get away when he had the chance.

He studied the four fighters crowding in around him, thinking fast. The rest of the street was deserted. No one would even see the confrontation. Kres knew he wasn't telling the whole truth about himself. Why else would he have said his name like that? But did Kres know his true identity? Or was he more worried about what Siv could reveal about their squad?

Kres's knife twitched nearer to his leg. *Think, Siv! What are your options?*

He'd have to fight his way out of this after all. He had seen these four in combat. If they wanted to prevent him from leaving—and possibly giving them away—they would. Still, his hand strayed toward his knife hilt. Faces sprang up before him: Dara, Selivia and his mother, Sora and his father. So many people he had let down in one way or another. He had to get back to them. It was his duty.

But if he drew his blade, he would die before he got two steps nearer to Dara and his family. What would that accomplish?

He hesitated. His family was safe in his grandfather's palace, protected by the Truren army. He couldn't stop the advancing Soolen force. If he somehow fought his way through Kres and the others, he might not even make it back to Rallion City. And what use would he be if he did?

Kurn Pass was about to be sealed. If he didn't leave Trure tonight, he would not have another chance. What if he really did start again? What if he stopped pretending and joined the pen fighters in earnest? What if he rode for Pendark tonight?

"Well?" Kres said. The other three watched him, faces stony. "Planning to sell wine on the front lines, are we?"

Siv cleared his throat, and the images rose before him again. Dara. His father. Selivia and his mother. Sora.

It was Sora's face that decided it for him. He had gotten his sister killed. The single most-important duty he'd ever had, and he'd failed. He couldn't help anyone. The others would be better off without him.

"Nothing," Siv said at last. "I was confused. Not enough sleep. We'd better keep moving before the pass closes."

"Agreed," Kres said. He dug his heels into his horse's side and led the way into the darkness. Siv followed, kicking up dust as he left Trure behind.

27

THE LIBRARY

SORA sat in the library, fiddling with a quill made from a thunderbird feather. The Lantern Maker sat beside her, poring over a crumbling tome. He had asked Sora here to sign another round of edicts, but he had become engrossed in his studies and hadn't spoken to her in nearly half an hour. To her immense relief, Lima hadn't joined them today.

Sora studied the Lantern Maker's profile. His high forehead furrowed, and his thick salt-and-gold hair was unkempt. While his wife became bolder and brasher by the day, Rafe had adopted a brooding focus of late. He was still as charismatic and imposing as ever during council meetings, but she had begun to see more of his other side. While his wife ran the castle and struggled to keep the Workers and nobles in line, he focused to the point of obsession on a secret project of some kind. For good or ill, his true passion lay with the Work.

Her growing ring of informants had been helping her put the puzzle pieces together. Berg Doban had told her in a note smuggled in Oat's pocket that Rafe had ordered a handful of Fireworkers to begin forging Fire Blades in large quantities over on East Square. The army was keeping the curious eyes of the nobility—and their daughters—away, but the duelists couldn't help noticing how busy their favorite smiths had become.

She suspected Rafe's mysterious project had more to do with Fire

Weapons than the relatively commonplace Fire Blades, though. He was seen leaving the Fire Warden's greathouse multiple nights per week, where the ancient Well bubbled beneath it, the source of all the mountain's Fire. Sora herself had encountered him in the castle corridors smelling of smoke and metal and looking as if he'd spent hours doing strenuous exercise. Whatever he was developing, it was separate from the army and the other Workers. It was in Rafe's hands alone.

Sora wished she could find an excuse to visit the Well herself, but that may arouse suspicion. Lima already got angry whenever she caught her asking questions. She shuddered, touching her tender cheeks. Lima's rough treatment of her had continued. Sora couldn't antagonize her further.

She wouldn't necessarily know what she was seeing inside the Fire Warden's greathouse anyway. The more her tiny circle of influence grew, the more she understood she needed help from someone who knew the power well. Her brother hadn't stood a chance against Rafe's Fire, and she wouldn't either. Unfortunately, the Fireworkers seemed to be thriving with their new status, if Jully's reports were any indication. That worried her too.

She spun her thunderbird quill, twirling the rough feather against her palm. The Lantern Maker sighed deeply and placed the book on the table.

"You've studied Vertigon's history, haven't you?" he said.

Sora started, surprised out of her reverie. "Yes, it was an important part of my education."

"Do you know the story of Sovar, the first Amintelle king?"

"My great-grandfather? Of course. He was a Firewielder. The last in my family."

"Indeed he was." Rafe folded his arms on the table and turned toward her. "Tell me: do you know why he had to fight to overcome his rivals in the first place?"

Sora placed her quill on the table, lining it up perfectly with an empty piece of parchment.

"The previous ruler was a tyrant who worked the people too hard," she said, recalling Zage Lorrid's papery voice as he told the story. She missed Zage's looming, morose presence in the castle. He had been an excellent teacher. "The Last Tyrant was little better than a slave driver. The Firewielders had to remove him for the good of the mountain. Sovar was the strongest, and he was also the most noble and good. The people rallied behind him to defeat the Last Tyrant and the other Firewielders, and when it was done, Sovar established the Peace of Vertigon." She couldn't help smiling at the thought of her ancestor's greatest work.

"That is the story, yes," Rafe said. He studied her with a piercing intensity. "Do you believe it?"

"Of course," Sora said. "Vertigon has been peaceful and prosperous for a hundred years thanks to Sovar Amintelle. And he was just. We don't call him the First Good King for nothing."

"True," Rafe said. "He was a just ruler. But do you really believe he was the strongest Wielder?"

"What?"

"There were other Firewielders who could best Sovar in a direct contest. Did you know? That is why he instituted the restrictions on the Fire in the first place."

Sora frowned, sorting through everything she had been told about him. "I thought that was because his son—"

"Yes, his son couldn't Wield, but he actually began the task of containing the Fire long before his son was born without the Spark."

Rafe stood and walked to the window. He faced the courtyard, silhouetted against the afternoon light. Sora had always pictured Sovar Amintelle looking like her father, but now she imagined him with the Lantern Maker's shape and intense eyes. Imagined him binding up the Fire instead of freeing it.

"He was afraid the other Wielders would take the mountain back from him," Rafe said, his back still to her. "He weakened all of us through his actions in the end."

"But if he wasn't the strongest," Sora said, "how did he win the succession battle?"

"The King of Trure sent men to assassinate Sovar's biggest rivals in their beds."

"I—*what?*" Sora wasn't sure what she had expected, but it wasn't that.

"Oh yes." Rafe turned to face her. "This 'Good King' achieved his final victory through treachery."

"How would you know that?"

"Some legends aren't written down in books," Rafe said. "I was apprenticed to one of the oldest Fireworkers on the mountain in my youth. His memory was long."

Sora heard a crunch and realized she'd crumpled her thunderbird quill in her fist. She dropped the fragments on the table, confusion rushing through her. She had always assumed her family was the best and noblest one on the mountain. She had never questioned whether they should be the ones to rule. The people had been prosperous under the Amintelles. And she *knew* her father had been good, even if his grandfather was not. But there was another part of Rafe's story that didn't sound complete.

"Why would the King of Trure help Sovar if he wasn't the strongest candidate?" she asked. Trure and Vertigon had been allies even then. It didn't make sense that that old ruler—also her great-grandfather—would want to weaken his closest supporters.

"That is the correct question," Rafe said. He returned to the table and tapped on the book he'd been reading. It was a journal of roughly scrawled notes and diagrams that must be over a hundred years old. "The Worker who *was* truly the strongest had interesting ideas. I believe he was preparing for a Work that would have altered the balance of power in the continent." Rafe fell quiet for a moment, as if lost in thought. When he spoke again, Sora was no longer sure he was still addressing her. "He had to have been close. The King of Trure protected his interests by installing a less-powerful Wielder on the throne. Sovar must have swayed him by promising to further limit the Fireworkers. He *must* have known it was possible. And now Vertigon is not as strong as it could be thanks to our 'First Good King.'"

Rafe stared at the journal, and Sora was surprised it didn't burst into flames under his gaze. He didn't say anything else, apparently losing himself in the obsession that had gripped him lately. Sora was starting to figure out what it was.

"And you want to make Vertigon strong again?" she prompted.

Rafe smiled. "You are perceptive. The mountain is enduring a painful transition right now. I'll be the first to admit that it hasn't been as smooth as I'd like. But you have no idea how strong we could be."

A fierce light blazed in the Lantern Maker's eyes, and Sora shivered. He may respect her understanding and speak to her like an adult, but she couldn't forget how dangerous this man was. Rafe with his slow-burning ambition and his utter dedication to his goals was a greater threat than his harsh wife. And far more was at stake here than Sora's own safety.

"What Work was the strongest Wielder preparing?" Sora asked.

A slow, deadly smile spread across the Lantern Maker's face.

Someone banged on the door, making Sora jump.

"Come," Rafe called.

Captain Thrashe marched in and offered a gruff salute. "The Soolen army has crossed the border into Trure," he announced. A gleam of anticipation and triumph lit his single eye. He tugged his eye patch straight. "My countrymen are marching to Rallion City!"

"Now?" Sora gasped. "I thought they wouldn't move until spring." It may not snow in Trure as much as it did in Vertigon, but it was still an inhospitable place for an army used to southern climes.

"They are expected to reach the capital before the week's end," Captain Thrashe said, still directing his comments to the Lantern Maker. "Commander Brach will set a brisk pace."

"Good," Rafe said. "Tell me as soon as the siege has begun."

A siege? Fear sent Sora's heart racing. Her mother and sister were still in Rallion City as far as she knew. Her grandfather had estates all across the plains where they could retreat if needed, but what if they didn't escape the capital in time? The locations of those estates were among the few pieces of information Sora had managed to keep from Rafe and Lima, despite their abuse. But what if they found out some other way? Sora already felt guilty enough about telling the Ruminors what she knew about the size of the Truren army and how many of their forces were typically stationed in the capital.

She hoped her grandfather had called reinforcements and extra provisions in from the countryside, but he too must not have expected the army to begin a siege in the dead of winter. Had they really been able to carry enough supplies halfway across the continent? It didn't seem like a wise strategy, especially in light of what Sora knew of Rallion City.

Captain Thrashe departed, the door snicking shut behind him, and Sora looked at the Lantern Maker. He had returned to his studies. He wasn't nearly surprised enough by this news.

"How do you know the Soolens are going to lay siege instead of launching an assault on Rallion City?" she said, hoping Rafe's chatty mood would continue for just a little while longer.

"I have been in contact with Commander Brach for some time," Rafe said.

Sora frowned, arranging the quill fragments around the empty parchment in front of her. Commander Brach? He came from one of the richest and most-influential houses in Soole. He was supposed to have a brilliant military mind. Something didn't line up.

"But you know Rallion City is vulnerable to a direct attack," she said. "The army needn't bother with a lengthy siege. I told you so myself." Hope bloomed in Sora's chest. Was it possible she hadn't betrayed her family as thoroughly as she feared? "You didn't pass on all the information I gave you to the Soolens?"

"Of course not," Rafe said. "That information is for me to use, not Commander Brach. Don't mention it to good Captain Thrashe, if you please."

"I don't quite understand," Sora said. Rafe was communicating with the Soolen commander, but he'd held back a critical piece of information. Why? And why had his wife gone to such lengths to get the information out of her? He must plan to use it himself. Which meant . . . "You want to attack the Soolen army while they're occupied with the siege and take Rallion City yourself!"

"You are a clever girl," Rafe said.

Sora stood, sending the quill fragments fluttering across the table. "You're not going to stop with Trure, are you? You want to conquer the Lands Below. All of them." Sora could hardly believe it. She knew the Lantern Maker was ambitious, but this?

"With the full use of its Fire, Vertigon Mountain is the single most-powerful entity on this continent," Rafe said. "We have the potential to truly use our strength. I will not allow it to languish as a single petty kingdom. It is time the Lands Below acknowledge our rightful supremacy."

Sora could see it now: Rafe bringing his Fire down on the lowlands. Rafe destroying all who opposed him in a torrent of Fire and smoke and blood. No wonder he wasn't worried about petty factions on the mountain. No wonder he spent all of his time studying the Lands Below and whatever mysterious Work had led the old King of Trure to help her great-grandfather murder its original creator. Her eyes fell on the ancient journal that had arrested his attention once more. What if Rafe figured out how to replicate this great Work himself? Could anyone stand in his way?

She had to stop him. Not just for the sake of Vertigon. She had to stop him for the sake of the entire world.

28

TOLLAN

TOLLAN simmered with activity when Dara, Vine, and Rid arrived. They reached the fork where the Ridge Road met the High Road the morning after Vine lost Siv's trail. They turned south to ride into town, joining a steady stream of travelers: traders, miners, local vineyard workers, and even a few noblemen surrounded by hard-eyed bodyguards. Every party was abuzz with rumor and speculation.

"Soole has crossed the border!"

"They're marching on Rallion City."

"I can't believe it. Cindral Forest is one thing, but Trure?"

Mistrust of strangers warred with the travelers' desires to hear the latest gossip and share their own theories about what would happen next. Dara and her friends could hardly ride a hundred yards without another passerby calling out to exchange news.

"It's an army of tens of thousands!"

"The king has sent soldiers to protect us."

"The capital is days away. We have nothing to worry about."

"We'll never lose to those rockeaters."

"There could be Soolen spies everywhere!"

As Dara listened to the speculation, she realized they'd made the right choice in allowing Rid to accompany them. He may not be a particularly imposing bodyguard, but at least they were no longer two women wearing foreign clothing on the road alone. It was more important than ever to avoid attracting attention. Rumy drew far too many eyes, though. Few cur-dragons ever traveled this far south.

Dara felt out of her depth as the rumors of the hostilities spread. She had grown up in a peaceful land. Even though that had changed of late—and she'd been right in the thick of the action—she had no experience of true warfare. Were they in danger because they were outsiders, even though Vertigon wasn't involved in the conflict? She wished someone could advise them. Vine and Rid were only a few years older than her, and neither one acted particularly confident in these circumstances. They both moved closer to her as they rode through the outskirts of Tollan. Somehow she had become a protector, first of Siv and now of her companions. But she wasn't sure what to do herself.

After Vine lost track of Siv the previous night, they had agreed to continue toward Kurn Pass, hoping Siv might still be moving that way even though Vine could no longer feel him. Vine postulated that if Siv had been killed, she would still sense some residue of him instead of this gigantic nothing. Perhaps he had moved beyond the range of the Air somehow.

Though they'd stopped to regroup, Dara barely slept. The trail had gone cold once more. The situation was almost as bleak as when Siv disappeared from Rallion City without a trace. They could only hope to find some clue in Tollan.

As they rode amongst the thatched houses and trees of the busy town, a company of Truren soldiers marched past, apparently returning from patrol. Some neglected their strict formation to turn and admire the two women on horseback. One of the men had big ears, like the handles on a cider mug. There was something familiar about him . . .

Dara stiffened, resisting the urge to duck. That mug-eared soldier had helped search the capital for Siv after he disappeared. He must have been reassigned. He was sure to recognize her, and he'd been in the room when Vine arrived at the palace too.

"Let's stop for a meal," Dara said quickly, wheeling Storm toward a black stone inn beside the road. The soldier would send them straight back to King Atrin if he spotted her.

"It's like you read my mind," Rid said. "I'm starving!"

Dara wished his voice were a little quieter. She lowered her head, hoping the familiar soldier wouldn't look up. Fortunately, Vine didn't say anything. Wearing a vague expression of concern, she followed Dara off the road without objection.

They found themselves in the yard of a cozy-looking establishment called The Vintner's Rest. A pair of stable boys jogged out to take their horses. Vine handed over a few coins to coax them to look after Rumy too. She assured them he wouldn't bite.

"I am so looking forward to a hot meal," Vine said.

"Ain't that the truth!" Rid said, starting toward the inn. "Oh, uh, beg pardon, m'lady. Should I eat with the stable boys, or . . . ?"

"Nonsense," Vine said. "You must eat with us."

Rid grinned and offered Vine his arm to escort her up the inn steps. A large woman with hair like fine-spun straw met them at the door and introduced herself as Madame Timon. She ushered them to seats at one end of a communal table before bustling off to the kitchen at the back of the inn.

A few locals sat at the other end of the table, near a large fireplace. They eyed Vine and Dara with some interest, and Rid quickly positioned himself between the two women and the strangers. He was hardly intimidating with his homespun clothes and youthful air, but it was a commendable effort. Dara had half expected him to run off to report their whereabouts to more Rollendar informants as soon as they reached the town. Apparently Vine still had his loyalty. And probably his infatuation as well. It wouldn't be the first time.

The innkeeper returned, a sprightly serving girl in tow, and asked about their travels as she set steaming bowls of hot porridge in front of them.

"We are riding to Pendark to visit the great city by the sea," Vine said.

Dara bent over her bowl to hide her surprise. Pendark? Surely Vine didn't think this chase would take them that far.

"I'm afraid that won't be possible right now," Madame Timon said. "Kurn Pass has been closed to protect Trure."

"Closed?" Dara said.

"Yes. Soldiers and Sensors both are blocking the passage."

"Sensors?" Vine said.

"Yes, my dear," Madame Timon said. "Air Sensors. You may think it's superstition, but we must protect our land in all ways, including using the ancient discipline."

"You can put up a barrier with Air?" Dara asked. She met Vine's eyes. Could that be why she suddenly lost track of Siv last night? He could have entered Kurn Pass before the barrier went up. A ray of hope worked its way into her. They could be close!

"Of course," Vine said. "That would be a magnificent undertaking. Do you also Sense the Air, Madame Timon?"

Madame Timon inclined her head. "When it grants me the gift, I do."

"Could you help us find someone?" Dara asked before Vine and Madame Timon could start rambling about gifts and requests—or suggest daylong meditation sessions. "He may have passed beyond the barrier last night."

"If they are on the other side, my Senses won't help you," Madame Timon said. "But I am an innkeeper." She chuckled. "A lot of people come through here. What does your friend look like?"

"He's tall," Dara said. "And handsome. He has dark hair, high cheekbones, and a scar on his temple. He may or may not have a beard."

"How old is this friend?" Madame Timon asked. Dara thought her voice sounded sharper than before, but when she looked up Madame Timon's face was smooth.

"He's twenty," Dara said. "We don't know who he's with, but we think he's traveling against his will. He was kidnapped."

Madame Timon's eyebrow twitched. It was a tiny gesture, but Dara immediately sensed a coldness to her manner that hadn't been there a moment ago.

"I haven't seen him," she said. "Now, will you be taking a room?"

Dara and Vine exchanged glances. She must have picked up on the sudden chill too. But they couldn't travel any farther until they learned more about the barrier. Besides, Madame Timon might offer more clues. They agreed to take rooms in the Vintner's Rest.

After lunch, Vine retired for a nap. Dara checked on Rumy to make sure he wasn't causing too much trouble in the inn stables. She found him gnawing a bone, surrounded by a pile of feathers. He snapped his jaws contentedly at her.

Satisfied that Rumy wasn't going to make the inn's horses stampede, Dara decided to investigate the barricade at Kurn Pass. If Siv really had been taken beyond it, they had to catch up with him soon. Kurn Pass only had a single outlet, but they didn't know which way he'd go from Fork Town on the other side. If they picked the wrong fork, he'd be gone for good. Unless Vine could Sense him in the Air outside of Trure? None of that mattered if they couldn't get out of Tollan, though.

Rid jogged up to her as she crossed the inn yard. "Where are you going?"

"I want to look around town," Dara said.

"Can I come?"

"Are you sure you don't want to rest?"

"I ain't never been to a town like this before," Rid said. "I can sleep when I'm dead."

"Fine," Dara said. "Try not to draw attention to yourself."

"Not a problem." Rid fell in beside her as she headed up the road, arms swinging. "I reckon you stand out more than I do with your fancy sword."

Dara frowned, but she didn't contradict him. Her weapon was unique, and it looked much finer than her travel-worn Guard coat. She was not exploring a strange town without her Savven blade, though. They could meet any number of suspicious characters around. She needed to be on her guard, especially after the news of the invasion.

The town of Tollan was basically one long stretch of shops and taverns lining the High Road. A few smaller streets turned off into the foothills, with a scattering of houses and tree groves along each one. The Linden Mountains dwarfed the town with purple-blue shadows. Even so, these mountains weren't nearly as tall as Vertigon Mountain or the vast, wild range of the Burnt Mountains in the far north.

The narrow gap of Kurn Pass knifed the Linden Mountains in two. The range was an effective barrier protecting the southern border of Trure. Unless you traveled through Kurn Pass, you had to make a difficult trek over the heights or travel far to the east where the mountains gave way to the badlands between Soole and Cindral Forest.

Rid sauntered along beside Dara, taking in the details with wide eyes and chattering away. She appreciated his eagerness to help, but he did ask an awful lot of questions. She didn't know anything more about Tollan than he did. She may have grown up in a larger city than Rid, but she was just as naive in the ways of the world.

"Where'd you get your sword?" Rid asked after they passed a smithy, with clangs and hot air emanating from its open doors.

"It was a gift."

"They have a lot of black swords in Vertigon?"

"No."

"Lady Vine was saying it's a Fire Blade. Is that true?"

"Yes," Dara said. "It wasn't always that way. I imbued it with a Fire core myself." It had been an accident, and Dara still wasn't sure how her Savven blade compared to other Fire Blades. The torrent of power blazing through it during the confrontation in the Great Hall had been far greater than Firesmiths normally used when they Worked Fire Blades. She could wield the sword faster than was natural—as with any Fire Blade—but it also contained more heat than any Fire Blade she had encountered. Moreover, she felt connected to it in a way that was difficult to describe. Yes, Siv had given it to her, so it was special for that reason, but this was something different. Something more elemental.

"Can you do that with other things?" Rid asked. "I reckon a Fire staff would be darn useful."

"If it was made out of metal, I could try," Dara said. She glanced at Rid. "I thought you didn't want anything to do with Fire Witches."

"I don't know about that," he said. "You don't seem so bad. Folks around these parts get nervous around Air Witches, but Lady Vine is probably the nicest gal I ever met."

"I guess she is," Dara said. "I hope she can do something about this barrier of Air."

As they approached the Pass, they discovered that the Air wasn't the only barrier they'd have to face. Soldiers camped on both sides of the road. They had erected a wall of fresh-cut timber taller than any horse could jump directly across the pass. It smelled of new sap and sawdust. Less-pleasant odors drifted from the army camp: latrines and sweat and burnt stew.

They drew nearer, hoping to see whether or not it would be possible to climb over the wall. Dara frowned up at the sharpened stakes jutting out from the top. These were angled toward the pass, clearly meant to keep out invading forces. If they were careful, they might be able to climb over, though she wasn't sure what they'd find on the other side.

"Hey you!" called a voice. "What's your business?"

A young soldier approached them, hand on the hilt of a saber.

"Nothing." Dara started to walk away, hiding her face, but Rid didn't follow.

"Hi there!" He strode directly up to the soldier, arms swinging. "I'm just in from the countryside. What are you fellas up to?"

"Up to?" the soldier said incredulously. "Haven't you heard?"

"Not so much traffic down in Roan Town," Rid said. "Everyone in Tollan seems more skittish than a spring pony."

"The Soolen army is marching on Rallion City," the soldier said.

"Aye. We heard *that*. But what's all this?" Rid indicated the barrier, studying it with a guileless curiosity that was actually pretty effective. His country-bumpkin act was significantly less suspicious than Dara's efforts to assess the barrier's weaknesses. Probably because it wasn't really an act.

"We're here to make sure no enemy soldiers get through Fork Town," the soldier said, puffing his chest out importantly. He looked younger than Rid, with a pattern of blemishes marring his cheeks.

"What are the chances of that?" Rid asked. "I heard they got plenty of men camping in Cindral Forest."

"You can never be too careful," the soldier said. "We *could* see some action here. It's an important posting." He sounded as if he was trying to convince himself. Being sent south when the invasion was happening to the north must not sit well with him.

"What's this barrier made out of?" Rid asked, moving closer to the logs.

"What's it look like? Wood."

"Just wood? That burns easy, don't it?" Rid looked at Dara significantly. For a man who had been afraid of the Fire just a few days ago, he seemed pretty excited about the prospect of burning things down.

"So what?" the soldier said. "We got fifty men here. They're not going to let anyone through without a fight."

"Fifty, eh?" Rid said. "I heard there were Air Witches up here. We don't hold with their kind in Roan Town."

"Those bags of wind are harmless. They came out here and stared at the Pass while we were putting up the logs, all humming and swaying. I didn't see anything. Apparently the Air will warn them if anyone comes, but I figure our scouts are good enough for that."

"I'm sure they are," Rid said. "I wouldn't like to meet an Air Witch."

"They're not dangerous," the soldier said with a shrug. "They're peace-loving folk. *We're* the dangerous ones."

"Yeah?" Rid leaned against the log wall as if it were a pasture fence. "So this wall won't suck the life out of the Soolens if they touch it or try to get past?"

"It doesn't work like that," the soldier said. "You Roan Towners don't know much, do you?"

"Hey now," Rid said pleasantly. "I only wish I could be in the army one day. You keep up the good work here."

"We most certainly will." The soldier stood a little straighter.

"Say . . ." Rid began, his voice almost too casual. "You think my friend and I could climb up the barrier for a look at the other side? I'd sure love to see it. I ain't never been to Kurn Pass before."

"Climb the barrier?" The soldier chuckled. "I can think of better things to do with a girl. There's this—"

"Sunders!" A harsh voice snapped toward them, and the young soldier paled.

"Oops. It's the captain. You'd best be on your way."

Rid didn't move. "You were saying we could try climb—"

"Sunders! What are you doing? Who are those two?"

"We'd better go," Dara whispered, tugging on Rid's sleeve.

Rid hesitated. "He's almost—"

"We can't draw attention to ourselves," Dara said.

"But—"

It was too late. The owner of the harsh voice marched up to them, making it impossible to steal away.

"What do you want?" he demanded.

Sunders raised his hands placatingly. "They were just asking about the barrier, Captain Fr—"

"The barrier?" The captain's hand went to the saber at his hip.

"Just curious," Rid said. "We'll get out of your way, sir."

"Be quick about it," the captain said. "And don't let me catch you near here again."

Rid and Dara nodded and tried to edge around the captain before he changed his mind. They were *not* supposed to be attracting the notice of the local cavalry. But just when Dara thought they were free, the captain shot out a hand and grabbed her arm.

"Don't I know you?" he said.

"I don't believe so." Had he been part of the group searching for Siv too? Dara didn't remember him, but she'd had more-important things on her mind at the time.

"You aren't from Trure," he said, his grip tightening on Dara's arm. "That's a foreigner's accent. You some sort of spy?"

"She's no spy," Rid said. "She's my lady love. We're just up from the country for a visit to Tollan. I ain't never been to a city before."

The captain snorted. "This backwater is hardly a city." His grip on Dara's arm didn't ease. "That's a mighty fine blade for a country boy's lady love."

"Captain Frem!" another soldier approached from the camp. "There's a message for you. Direct from King Atrin!"

Captain Frem's mouth tightened.

"Where are you staying in Tollan?" he asked.

"The Vintner's Rest," Dara said, figuring it would be all too easy for him to check her story. She met his gaze steadily, daring him to try something.

"I don't want to see you sniffing around the barrier again," he said.

"You won't."

Finally, Captain Frem nodded and released Dara's arm. "Move along."

"Yes, sir!" Rid said. "Come, my love, let's go get us some pie." He looped his arm through Dara's and with a brief nod at Sunders escorted her back toward the town.

"That was too close," Dara said, dropping Rid's arm as soon as they were out of sight of the soldiers.

"If only that Captain Frem fellow hadn't turned up," Rid said. "Sunders might have given us a boost over the wall himself."

"That was a good effort," Dara said. "Maybe next time you could warn me before you waltz up and start talking to soldiers."

Rid shrugged. "No problem."

"We'd better get Vine," Dara said as they hurried back up the High Road. "That captain isn't going to forget us."

"He wouldn't hurt her, would he?" Rid said. "We have to hurry!"

Dara caught his arm before he could take off down the street. "I'm sure that message from the king will keep him busy. We don't want to draw attention to ourselves by running through the streets."

Even so, Dara picked up her pace too. She didn't like the idea of staying in Tollan for long now that they'd alerted Captain Frem to their location. But how were they going to get past that barrier with a whole company of soldiers watching it? From what she had seen, it would be a slow climb if they managed it at all. And burning through the wall with Rumy's dragon fire—or anything she could Work—would draw far too many eyes. They needed another option.

Dara mulled over the problem as she and Rid hurried back along the High Road. Not fully aware of where she was going, she accidentally jostled against someone.

Someone tall, with sandy-blond hair and a long, thin nose. For the second time that day, an iron grip closed around her arm.

"There you are," said Vex Rollendar. "I've been looking for you."

29

THE CELLAR

DARA tried to twist out of Lord Vex's grip, but one of his men appeared and grabbed her other arm. She struggled frantically against both of them. The newcomer forced her arm behind her back, and Vex took control. He was surprisingly strong. Dara's joints screamed in protest as he tightened his hold on her elbows.

The other man yanked her Savven blade from her sheath. He groped for more weapons, not being subtle about what else he pawed in the process. Blind panic jolted through her like lightning. She wasn't going down without a fight!

Dara threw her weight backward into Lord Vex, knocking his jaw with the back of her skull, and used the momentum to kick at the other man's kneecaps. He grunted and stepped back out of her reach.

She started to scream, but a hand clamped over her mouth. She smelled old leather and sweat as rough fingernails dug into her cheek. A third man had joined Lord Vex and was helping him regain control of her from behind. He seized her head by the base of her braid so she couldn't try another headbutt.

"We must get off the street," Lord Vex hissed. "Quickly."

The two men lifted her up between them. Dara flailed violently, trying not to let terror overcome her, trying to break free. It was futile. She'd held her own against bigger and stronger swordsmen, but wrestling was a different matter. She had no chance as Lord Vex's men overpowered her and steered her out of the crowd.

Shadows fell over them as they entered an alley. It happened so fast that many of the passersby probably hadn't noticed the young woman being carried away by three grown men. No one did anything to help. Dara struggled wildly, her heartbeat frantic. Where was Rid? Had he betrayed them after all?

Taking little notice of her efforts to escape, the men hauled her through the alley and around the corner of a massive, windowless building. Dara wanted to keep fighting, but she forced herself to go limp and drag her feet along the ground. She may not be a match for these men, but she wouldn't make it easy either.

They approached a trapdoor set in the base of the building. Dara started thrashing again, fear lending her strength. Rough hands pulled her closer and closer to the door. It couldn't end like this. She scraped at the dirt with her heels. If she left signs of a struggle, maybe Vine could come after her. Her Air Sense should still work on this side of Kurn Pass. That might be Dara's only hope. She couldn't defeat three men unarmed.

Lord Vex relinquished her arm to the man who'd taken her Savven blade and pulled open the trapdoor. The opening gaped like a wound. After one final glimpse of the sky, Dara was yanked into a darkened cellar. The door banged shut, cutting off the light.

They descended a flight of wooden stairs. The two guards lifted Dara right off her feet to keep her from thumping against every step. When they reached the bottom, there was a scraping sound, and a light flared to life. Lord Vex held a lantern aloft.

They were in an earthen cellar packed with barrels of wine. A sweet, oaky smell permeated the cramped space. Lord Vex led the way down an aisle between stacks of barrels, a pool of light surrounding his broad shoulders. The bodyguards dragged Dara after him. She felt panic tightening around her chest the farther into the cellar they got. They must be after Siv. Would they kill her when they found out she didn't know where he was? She'd be dead long before Vine could follow the Air to her.

Then Lord Vex's light reached the back of the cellar. Sitting in a chair against the packed dirt wall was Vine herself. Dara's heart sank. Vine sat upright, regal as a queen, but her ankles and wrists were bound. She wore no shoes. They must have snatched her straight from her bed in the Vintner's Rest.

"Tie her up," Lord Vex said.

"Yes, sir." The man who'd grabbed Dara's braid shoved her roughly into a chair beside Vine. Dara wasted no time. She kicked both boots straight into his groin the moment he loosened his grip to reach for a rope.

The momentum shoved her chair back into the wall, jolting her painfully. Her captor doubled over, cursing vilely. She lashed out with her fists as he bent forward. Her first strike landed on the side of his cheek. An instant later she flew out of her chair and hit the floor. The other guard had smacked her across the face. He moved so fast she hadn't seen him coming. Darkness oozed across her vision as she tried to get up, but a boot landed on her back, forcing her to the ground.

"Enough," Lord Vex said. "Can't you two brutes handle one girl without dramatics?"

The guard Dara had kicked fell to his knees on the cellar floor, still wheezing, but the other quickly tied her arms and hoisted her into the chair. Her head rang like a bell at the jerky movement. The guard who'd hit her had hairy arms and a broad, knobby forehead. He wasn't gentle, and he leered as he pulled apart her legs to tie one ankle to each chair leg.

The other managed to climb to his feet again. He wore a battered leather vest, and he had a rough pattern of pockmarks across his face. He spit in the dirt at Dara's feet, but he stayed well away from her, hands still hovering over his groin.

"Are you all right?" Vine asked as the hairy-armed man finished tying her up and stepped back.

"I've been better." Dara's head pounded, and sparks blossomed in front of her. She blinked until her vision cleared.

Lord Vex stepped closer, holding up his light. It was an ordinary lantern with a wax candle and mirrors inside the casing. Dara had already tried reaching for Fire, but there was none to be found nearby. Vex must have known about her ability and brought her to a place without easy access to Fireworks. He was tall and lean, like his deceased brother and nephew, but his movements were quick and decisive, unlike the indolent Bolden and the cold, stiff Von. This was a man of action. He was dressed for travel, with a cloak covering his red coat. Dara was certain he was the man she had seen talking to Yen back in Roan Town. And he had hired Rid. The boy must have decided to betray them after all.

"Well," Vex said. "That was even easier than expected. Your reputation may have overstated your competence, Miss Ruminor."

"What do you want from us?" Dara demanded.

"I'd very much like to know where our former king is hiding," Lord Vex said. "He killed my favorite nephew. And my new liege is interested in seeing his face—with or without his body."

"We don't know where he is," Dara said.

"I doubt that very much," Lord Vex said. "We've been following you for some time. I understand you have some sort of Air connection to him."

Damn it, Rid. He must have told Lord Vex everything. But when had he found the time? While she was checking on Rumy? It didn't matter now.

"The connection is gone," Dara said. "We don't know where he is."

"That's not entirely accurate, my dear Dara," Vine said.

"What?"

"I believe I found the connection again," she said. "I'd have told our fine hosts earlier, but we were waiting for you to join us."

Vex exchanged glances with the pockmarked bodyguard and took a step closer to Vine.

"Is that so?" he asked, his voice dangerously quiet.

"I can't feel it down here in the cellar of course," Vine said, "but as soon as we're back in the Air, I can lead you straight to him."

Dara stared at Vine, wondering if she had been hit in the head too. If she truly had regained the connection, why would she tell Lord Vex? Was she hoping to lead him astray? She would have to be careful. The Rollendars were too cunning for that kind of trick.

Vex certainly didn't look convinced. "Why would you do that?" he said.

"I don't want to die." Vine's eyes widened pleadingly, and she fluttered her thick eyelashes, leaning forward as much as she could when tied to a chair, somehow managing to push her chest out despite her bonds. A single tear clung to her lashes like a diamond. Dara nearly rolled her eyes. There was no way that would work.

But Lord Vex stared at Vine for a moment as she looked up at him with her big, brown eyes. Then he cleared his throat. "We shall see," he said gruffly.

He walked away from them, jerking his head to draw the pockmarked man with him. They spoke in low voices while the one with the hairy arms loomed over Dara and Vine. He had buckled Dara's Savven blade at his waist, and the sight made hot anger rush through her. He also carried a broadsword on his back and knives in his boot and his belt. His fists were weapon enough, though. Dara's face still stung from his blow.

She glanced at her fellow captive. Vine appeared composed, but she kept biting her lip, something she didn't do very often. She must be more scared than she was letting on. She gazed at Lord Vex and his companion, who were still conferring in the pool of light from the lantern. When Vex glanced over at her, she gave him a tremulous smile. Dara hoped she had a plan.

She tested the strength of her bonds, racing through their options. She had to assume Rid wouldn't help them. He was probably already spending his payment for selling them out. But what about Rumy? If Vine had been taken from her bed in the inn, Rumy might still be sleeping away in the stables at the Vintner's Rest. Unless the Rollendar men had killed him first. Dara tried not to dwell on that possibility.

She remembered Madame Timon's reaction when she described Siv to her. She was sure the woman knew something. What if she had alerted the Rollendars that Dara and Vine were separated and vulnerable?

However they'd been found, Vex and his men had captured them without much difficulty. Vex must have decided this would be more efficient than following them. Dara tugged harder against her bonds, but they didn't budge.

Vex returned from the other side of the cellar and looked down his long nose at them. His sandy-blond hair swept neatly to the side over piercing blue eyes. He might have been handsome for an older man, if Dara didn't want to stab him so badly.

"You may live, providing you lead us to Amintelle," he said.

"That sounds like a fair arrangement," Vine said. She met Lord Vex's eyes steadily. "I will help you in any way I can."

"What?" Dara choked.

"Can't we kill the blond?" asked the pockmarked man. His hands strayed toward his groin, which must still be in pain.

"I won't help you if you kill my friend," Vine said quickly. "We come as a pair."

"We can use her as bait when we find the boy. I understand he's fond of her." Lord Vex leaned in closer. A harsh shadow cut across his face, making him look ghoulish rather than handsome now. "But if either one of you tries to escape, we will kill both of you. Is that understood?"

"Of course, Lord Vex," Vine said.

Dara only glowered at him.

"Come now, Dara," Vine said. "Let's reassure the nice man."

The other guard snorted.

"Fine," she said. "I won't try to escape."

"There," Vine said. "Now, won't you loosen our bonds a bit, my lord? I do think my arms have gone to sleep."

Lord Vex ignored her. "Go gather our provisions, Mertin," he said to the pockmarked man. "We leave at dusk."

"Yes, Lord Vex." Mertin fixed Dara with one more glare before heading toward the cellar stairs. She was satisfied to see he walked gingerly, slightly bowlegged from her kick.

"I'll be back in a few hours, Grelling," Lord Vex said to the other man. "I have arrangements to make. Don't let these two talk to each other." His eyes flitted back to them, lingering on Vine for a moment. "I won't have them scheming against us. And remember: no Fire."

The man with the hairy arms—Grelling—bobbed his head in a rough bow and took up a position in front of the two chairs. Lord Vex followed Mertin out of the cellar, leaving his candle lantern behind.

Dara desperately wanted to ask Vine about her plan. Had she really managed to Sense Siv on the Air again? If she had, they couldn't escort these men to him. But would Lord Vex realize she was taking them in the wrong direction? He had to figure it out eventually. He struck Dara as far too intelligent for simple schemes.

Of course, Vine may simply be buying time. If that was the case, Dara would do her part to figure out a way to escape.

If only she had access to some Fire! Despite their distance from the mountain, she had come to rely on it for comfort. Even the trace amounts she could get from Rumy's dragon fire were enough to lull her into a false sense of security—even invincibility. But she was still a swordswoman. She had to figure out a way to get her hands on a weapon.

Unfortunately, Grelling proved to be a diligent guardian. Every time Dara tried to whisper to Vine, he growled at her to be quiet. On her third try, he smacked her across the face. Dara tasted blood in her mouth and resolved to wait until they were on the move to sneak a private word with Vine. She didn't want to provoke him further. She was all too aware of the way he leered at the two women bound to chairs in front of him. It made her feel vulnerable in a way she hadn't throughout their travels. She would rather have a cullmoran watching over them than this brute.

Mertin and Lord Vex returned after a few hours and hauled them back up the cellar steps. Vex didn't hesitate to help his men with the task. Apparently he wasn't the type of lord who made his subordinates do all the dirty work. He made Dara decidedly uneasy. She hadn't paid much attention to him when he was the youngest of a group of brothers. He'd had no real power compared to Lord Von and his scheming son. She already regretted that oversight.

Outside, they found a dark, moonless night. They could barely see the outlines of the buildings surrounding their erstwhile prison, apparently some sort of warehouse. Skeletal trees loomed over them, their branches stretching patterns across the sky. Four horses were tied up beside the cellar entrance, one laden with supplies for the journey. Dara had held out some hope that they could escape if they had their own mounts. Instead, the two henchmen hoisted Dara and Vine onto their horses, tied them securely to the saddles, and climbed up behind them.

Mertin still refused to come near Dara, so he put Vine on his horse, and Grelling took Dara. She looked straight ahead as he settled himself in the saddle behind her, pressed far too close, and reached both arms around her to take her reins. She wanted nothing more than to throw her head back and break his nose, but she had to be strategic. She would treat their captivity like a dueling tournament. She needed a tactic to deal with each opponent, and she couldn't make any rash moves, or she'd be eliminated.

Lord Vex strode over to Mertin's horse. "Here you are, Lady Silltine," he said. "I took the liberty of purchasing you some boots."

Vine looked down at him, surprise crossing her face, as Lord Vex put the shoes on her bare feet and tied them himself. The shoes were exactly the right size, and Vex took care lacing up the soft leather. Vine appeared distracted by the unexpected act.

Don't let him play games with you, Dara thought. Vine was the one who distracted and entranced people. She shouldn't fall for a stray act of consideration.

When Lord Vex finished with Vine's feet, he mounted his own horse. "Now then. What does the Air tell you? Where is our missing Amintelle?"

Vine looked unsettled, but she closed her eyes and adopted a serene expression. Her breathing slowed gradually. Dara still wasn't sure whether or not she was faking it. She certainly looked as if she was Sensing in earnest. Lord Vex's piercing eyes never left her face, his long nose giving the impression of a bird of prey watching a mouse.

Vine was quiet for so long that Dara wondered if she'd gone to sleep. Grelling shifted impatiently behind her, and she tried to ignore the stale stench of his breath and the feeling of him pressed against her back. A cold wind blew through the darkness, rattling the branches over their heads.

Finally, Vine's eyes popped open.

"I have him!" she said. "He is traveling through Kurn Pass."

"I figured as much," Lord Vex said. "Let's go."

He heeled his tall, black stallion forward, and the others followed. Vine and Mertin rode behind Vex, and Dara and Grelling took up the rear, leading the packhorse. It was dark enough that passersby probably wouldn't be able to tell that the two women were tied in place, but they kept to the shadows behind buildings anyway.

All of Tollan felt tense. The news of the invasion to the north had sent the townsfolk into the warm confines of home. The only people about wore uniforms. The soldiers let their party pass unhindered.

They drew near the barrier across Kurn Pass. Torches burned

alongside the wall, revealing the shapes of soldiers on guard. The camp beside the road was well lit too. They would have had a difficult time climbing over without being seen by a dozen men.

Vine drew in a sharp breath.

"What?" Vex asked, twisting quickly to face her.

"I . . . I am sure this is it," Vine said. She sounded strained, not at all like she usually did when she was Sensing. "Yes, he passed through here. I can feel him on the other side of the barrier."

"I anticipated he'd be taking the Pass," Lord Vex said, "so I've made arrangements with Captain Frem. We'll need you again when we get to the Fork. Come."

Lord Vex rode directly toward the camp full of soldiers. He spoke to the sentries posted at the entrance, and they waved him through. Campfires burned at regular intervals, and men huddled outside neat rows of tents. Dara prayed someone would realize the two women being transported through their camp were prisoners, but none of the soldiers paid them enough attention to see that their hands were bound. Either that, or they had strict instructions from Captain Frem not to interfere.

The western end of the log barrier jutted into the camp. As they approached it, an older man in uniform stepped out from a large tent. Dara recognized Captain Frem. He didn't speak to them, but he nodded at Lord Vex as they passed.

What had the Vertigonian lord done to get this Truren army captain to let him pass unhindered? The Rollendars had been a wealthy family before their fall, but had Captain Frem's cooperation really been bought with such ease in a time of war? Dara didn't understand it, but she was more certain than ever that she didn't want Lord Vex coming anywhere near Siv.

A small sally port cut through the log barrier in the heart of the soldiers' camp. They never would have been able to reach it on their own. But Lord Vex rode straight up to it, and the sentries opened the gate to let him through. Dara looked around frantically for aid. She didn't want to enter Kurn Pass with these men. But the soldiers looked the other way—all except one.

Sunders, the private she and Rid had met earlier that day, stopped short as he passed them with a cook pot in his hands. His uniform was damp, and he looked as if he'd spent the past few hours scrubbing pots. He stared at Dara, mouth slightly ajar. He recognized her! Dara widened her eyes and grimaced, trying to communicate that she needed help. Sunders blinked at her. She jerked her head, trying to draw attention to her bound hands.

"Eyes forward," Grelling hissed in her ear. "And stop your fidgeting, or I'll give you something to fidget about."

Dara froze, still not wiping the fearful expression from her face. Sunders stared at her like a baby goat.

"I'm warning you," Grelling said, and he dug his fingers in her thigh, low enough so the soldiers couldn't see. Pain spread from his hand. Still, Dara didn't stop looking at Sunders until they passed through the sally port, leaving the camp of soldiers behind.

The gate closed with a thud.

The other side was even darker than Tollan had been. Cliffs rose on either side of the Pass. The gap was far narrower than the Fissure into Vertigon Mountain, and it was man-made. Miners had blasted straight through the mountains hundreds of years ago, leaving a serviceable trade route between Trure and the coastal lands of Pendark and Soole. It had opened up the north to trade from beyond the Bell Sea and had ushered in an era of prosperity and luxury in the Land of the Horse Keepers.

But in the dark of night, the Pass was an eerie black portal into the unknown. A shiver went through Dara that had little to do with the cold wind whistling around her. Their captors could decide Dara and Vine had outlived their usefulness at any moment. There'd be no one around to help if Lord Vex decided to slit their throats and leave their bodies in the Pass.

Dara desperately wanted to get her hands on a blade. She could feel the heat from her Savven, still buckled at Grelling's waist, but she couldn't do anything without touching it. Unlike a Fire Lantern, she couldn't simply pull the power out of the sword. It was an integral part of the metal now, and she needed to hold it in order to make use of its magic. She was trapped.

Lord Vex turned to Vine, his features indistinct in the darkness. "Can you still feel him?" he asked. "Is there Air outside Trure?"

"Oh yes," Vine said breathlessly, not taking nearly as long with her "Sensing" now. "I believe he was here a day ago at most." She met Dara's eyes, and Dara immediately got the sense that Vine was telling the truth about this part. Siv had been here. He was still alive. Despite their perilous position, a little of the tightness in Dara's chest eased.

"We should continue straight ahead," Vine said.

"You're certain?"

"Quite," Vine said. "But you may encounter more trouble than all this is worth on the other side of the pass. Our dear king can be very ornery."

"Amintelle won't escape," Lord Vex said.

"Perhaps," Vine said. "I expect we shall see in a matter of days."

"My liege will be pleased." Lord Vex moved his horse closer to Vine and Mertin, blocking Dara's view of her friend. "There may be a reward if you lead us true, Lady Silltine."

"I'll keep that in mind," Vine said. "I do wonder why you serve the Lantern Maker after he betrayed your brother, though."

"The Lantern Maker?" Lord Vex looked back at Dara and grinned, the expression feral. "My new liege has more to offer than a jumped-up craftsman. Shall we?"

Lord Vex kicked his horse forward, and they rode into the dark. Dara breathed steadily, fending off the fear that tried to descend on her with the darkness. So Vex wasn't working for her father. But whom would he deliver Siv to if not her parents? Somehow, she didn't think Siv's chances of survival would be any better with Vex's new liege.

Dara sincerely hoped Vine knew what she was doing. If she had told Lord Vex the truth about her Senses, they would catch up with Siv in a few days. As much as Dara was dying to see him, she hoped they didn't find him. She only wished she could warn him a storm was coming.

30

THE PEACE

LADY Jully pressed a bundle of paper into Sora's hand. It was bulky, composed of four or five sheets, but Sora managed to tuck it into her belt before Lima saw. She would have to warn Jully to be a little more discreet next time. The young lady waltzed away through the crowd, her pink skirt fluttering around her. So much for stealthy communication.

Sora strolled more slowly amongst the visitors in the Great Hall. Today they celebrated the founding of the Peace of Vertigon, a move that struck Sora as ironic given the events of that winter. Nobles and Fireworkers alike had turned out for the reception in all their finery. Servants meandered through the crowds with platters of soldarberry tarts, tiny minced pies, and goblets of wine. A dueling exhibition was scheduled for later in the evening, organized by Lord Zurren. He'd offered to host the event in his own greathouse down by Thunderbird Square, but Lima had vetoed that idea. The streets of Vertigon were not as safe as they used to be, and the reports of war in Trure only heightened Lima's caution.

Sora rested a hand on her belt, eager for an opportunity to sneak off and read Jully's notes away from Madame Ruminor's watchful eyes. A core group of young noblewomen had been passing her information for several weeks now. They mostly reported conversations they overheard between their parents and their noble friends, but they had taken to eavesdropping on people on the streets and bridges too. She was dying to know what everyone thought of the news from Trure and the Lantern Maker's subsequent decision to increase the size of the army. She'd have loved to see Lord Farrow's reaction when that edict was announced.

The notes from her spies gave Sora a fascinating perspective on what was happening in her city. She had hated being out of the loop during the earlier days of her reign. Public opinion shifted and morphed as people grew used to the new distribution of power in Vertigon. The nobles grumbled about the Fireworkers swaggering around as if they owned the place, sometimes in surprisingly coarse language, and the Fireworkers scorned anyone who couldn't match them for strength. The common people eviscerated them all—at least in private—and lamented that the mountain would never be the same. Jully reported every curse and complaint in her loopy, girlish handwriting and passed it to Sora whenever she had a chance.

The Fireworkers certainly seemed to be enjoying their new status. The ones attending this reception, for example, carried Fire openly, some spinning and twisting it above their hands as they made idle conversation, others wearing loops of the molten power as if they were bracelets.

The sheer excess of Fire on display spoke volumes. The Workers previously exercised careful stewardship of their finite shares, dedicating all of it to the production of useful objects to sell and trade. But with the loosening of restrictions, some were already taking in more than they needed. Sora had received reports that lesser Fireworkers were already being forced out of business. If they couldn't draw the power and hold it strongly enough, it was simply taken from them by more-powerful Workers. These Workers gloried in the surplus and took every opportunity to flaunt their dominance before their contemporaries. Some of the disgruntled weaker Workers had retaliated with physical violence. The mountain had been knocked out of balance, and Sora wasn't sure how to fix it.

She listened to snippets of conversation as she mingled with her guests, her guards hanging back by the walls. She heard the usual gossip about parlor antics and scandals, but a serious tone permeated many exchanges. Vertigon was balanced on a cliff's edge, and fancy dresses, expensive wine, and idle gossip wouldn't change that.

Sora wore black today, unwilling to appear overly festive. She mourned the destruction of the Peace of Vertigon, and she didn't care who saw it. Her long sleeves hid her bruises, remnants of Lima's most-recent reminder of who was in charge. She felt increasingly aware she was running out of time before the Lantern Maker decided he didn't need her anymore. She had to stop him from completing his mysterious Fire project before she was silenced for good.

"Good evening, Your Royal Highness."

Sora stopped as Lady Tull Denmore swept into a deep curtsy before her, blocking her path.

"Tull," Sora said. This was one noble she didn't feel compelled to treat with diplomacy. She hadn't forgotten how Lady Tull conspired with the Rollendars against her brother, even becoming engaged to him to further her aims.

"I wanted to congratulate you on this occasion," Lady Tull said. "The Peace of Vertigon is—"

"Thank you. Excuse me."

Sora turned her shoulder to Lady Tull, hoping she would get the hint. But the woman wasn't deterred.

"Wait! My queen, I would speak with you, if you have a moment."

Sora grimaced. Lady Tull was a two-faced traitor. The longer Sora spent in her company, the more she wanted to scratch the woman's delicate, pretty face. She had never had a remotely violent streak before, and she didn't intend to start on the anniversary of the Peace, no matter how much of a farce it was.

"What is it?" she said at last.

"The other heads of noble houses and I are concerned," Lady Tull said. "We are worried there aren't enough smaller Fireworks being produced this winter. We fear for the impact it will have on our houses when the export season begins in the spring."

"You don't even own any Fireshops," Sora said. Lady Tull controlled the large Denmore and Ferrington estates, but most of their business was in agriculture and livestock husbandry. One of the major access roads did cross through their land, however, and they maintained close relationships with everyone who dealt in imports and exports.

"Several heads of houses have spoken to me about their concerns. It was my idea to approach you," Tull said. "You have the Chief Regent's ear."

Sora thought that stretched the truth a bit, but she appreciated that Tull didn't dismiss her entirely. It was good to know the heads of houses were openly discussing their dissatisfaction with the Lantern Maker—and turning to her for solutions. She should encourage those cracks to grow.

"I will discuss it with the Chief Regent," she said. Rafe had been spending more time in the library with her. He seemed to enjoy having someone to discuss his research with, especially since he and his wife had been less than warm to each other lately.

"Thank you, Your Majesty." Lady Tull apparently read too much encouragement into Sora's diplomacy, because she offered another elegant curtsy and placed a hand on Sora's arm. "My queen, I wanted to apologize for my involvement with Lord Bolden. It was ill advised and—"

"Ill advised?" Sora said flatly. "Bolden killed my brother and attempted to take my throne." She still held out hope that Dara and Siv had escaped the mountain, but Lady Tull didn't need to know that.

"I was blinded by my affection for him," Lady Tull said with a delicate sigh. "The romance of youth was—"

"You mean your ambitions backfired, and now you're trying to salvage your position." That young-love act might work on the old lords, but Sora knew better. "I'm not interested in anything you have to say on the subject."

Lady Tull blinked, and Sora couldn't help feeling smug. She recognized an ambitious and calculating young woman in Lady Tull, even though many of the noblemen wouldn't see past her pretty face. Sora had long thought that one of her distinct advantages in not having a particularly pretty face was that people weren't distracted by it. Lady Tull used the distraction to great effect. Even her brother had underestimated her. But Sora wouldn't fall for it.

"Enjoy the rest of the party."

She turned her back on Lady Tull and spotted Lima approaching. The Lantern Maker's wife was never far away in a crowd. As she crossed the Great Hall, she had to force her way through a group of

Fireworkers. Her face darkened when they didn't move out of her way immediately. She still wore a scowl when she reached Sora.

Before Lima could ask what Lady Tull wanted, Sora said, "I have to use the water closet."

"Be quick about it," Lima said. "You must give your speech shortly. The sooner we can be done with it, the better."

Lima escorted her to the door of the water closet, which was located off a corridor outside the Great Hall. She had been more careful about leaving Sora alone in mixed company ever since the Winter Market. Sora had a feeling someone had noticed her sneaking away and reported back to Lima. Either that, or one of her noble informants wasn't as trustworthy as Jully thought.

Using the young girl and her friends to gather information wasn't ideal, but every time Sora tried to put out feelers amongst the older nobles, they told her to stop trying and keep her head down. It frustrated her that people wouldn't take her seriously. She may be shy of her eighteenth birthday, but she was still a queen. More importantly, she might be the only one who knew the scale of the Lantern Maker's plans. She had to make people understand how important it was to get rid of him.

Lima halted in the corridor outside the water closet, and Sora shut the door firmly behind her. The woman made for an uncomfortable shadow, and she didn't want to spend any more time with her than necessary.

She pulled the paper Jully had given her from her belt and sat on a low bench inside the cool, dimly lit room to read. Jully had a rambling writing style, and she erred on the side of repeating everything she heard, useful or not. In this note, Sora found the usual complaints about the Fireworkers, rumors of Soolens lurking around the mountain, fears about the war in Trure, and more complaints about the Fireworkers. But one line stuck out to her:

There are always lights in the Fire Warden's greathouse. Sometimes frightful rumbling noises too. No one knows what's going on there.

Sora frowned. Could Rafe be making progress with his Fire

Weapons? Did it have something to do with whatever he was studying in the ancient Firewielder's journal? The mysterious Work that was supposed to make the mountain strong. She needed to win some of the Workers to her side eventually. She'd debated confiding her suspicions about Rafe's secret project to Daz Stoneburner, but she worried the Lantern Maker had regained his full cooperation. Daz hadn't spoken against him in the last two council meetings.

She'd learned a key piece of information about Daz Stoneburner from Berg Doban on one of the rare occasions he had been able to get a message to her. It was harder to get in contact with him than with the harmless-seeming young noblewomen. But was the hint about Daz enough to allow her to trust him?

She turned over the next sheet of paper, looking for clues about the mysterious Work being carried out in the greathouse.

The door burst open, banging against the wall hard enough to make the lone Firebulb shudder, and Lima strode in.

"What are you doing?"

Sora leapt up, trying to stuff the papers back into her belt, but it was too late. Lima crossed the small space and snatched them away from her. A dark cloud oozed over her features as she read the notes.

"Where did you get this?" she demanded, her voice icy.

"It's nothing. I was just—"

Sora should have seen the blow coming. Suddenly she was on the floor, crumpled against the bench. Flecks crossed her vision like the Orange Star, and her face stung.

"What is the meaning of this?" Lima hissed.

"I was just scribbling some—"

"This is not your handwriting. Do you take me for a fool?"

Lima grabbed Sora's arm and hauled her off the ground, dropping her roughly on the bench.

"No," Sora said, trying to project meekness.

"This isn't a game." Lima leaned in close, her breath hot on Sora's face. "You may think you're playing at a conspiracy, but you have no idea what you're dealing with."

"And you do?" Sora straightened, pressing her back against the cold wall behind her. "Look at that note. The mountain is in turmoil. It's going to erupt if you don't rein in the Fireworkers. You are going to ruin everything that makes Vertigon great."

"Careful, girl," Lima whispered.

"I am the queen." Sora lifted her chin, the stars in her eyes making her reckless. She'd had enough of cowering. "You cannot continue to treat me like this. You're not the Chief Regent. You're not even a Fireworker. You are nothing."

Lima smacked her hard across the face. Sora tasted blood on her lip.

"You need me," she said, fighting to keep her voice from trembling. The anger helped. They were going to destroy everything. "You'd have killed me weeks ago if you didn't. Maybe you should try listening to me instead of parading me around at parties every few days."

Lima smiled, and the expression was utterly terrifying. Then she swung at Sora again.

It was worse than it had ever been before. The blows rained down, two, three, four. Fury and frustration gave Lima's fists strength. Sora could sense the rage that she was certain came from more than just anger at Sora's words. Lima had to be deeply frustrated by her position. She must have expected things to be different when she and her husband finally took power.

But that realization did little to help Sora now. She tried to avoid the blows, to fend them off with her arms, but Lima was too strong. Sora's resolve not to cry broke, and tears mixed with the blood on her face as Lima took out her rage on her.

She was about to break down and beg for it to stop, when the door crashed open.

"What are you doing?" came a horrified voice.

Tears blurred Sora's vision, and she could hardly see as someone rushed forward and caught Lima's arm before she landed another blow.

"Unhand me."

"Don't you dare touch her."

Sora was aware of a struggle above her. She pulled herself into a sitting position, waiting for her eyes to clear. Whoever had entered strong-armed Lima over to the door. She shook loose her assailant.

"Come, girl, you have a speech to give."

"She's not going anywhere with you. And you don't want anyone to see her like this anyway. Find someone else to give your burning speech."

Steel rasped in the sudden quiet following the words.

"Fine," Lima spat. "Take her to her chambers. I'm done with her."

The door slammed shut. Still shaking uncontrollably, Sora looked up at her rescuer.

It was Kel, his face as white as death. He knelt beside her and reached a tentative hand out to touch her cheek. Sora winced at the sting.

"How long has this been going on?" he said quietly.

"It doesn't matter. It's—"

"It does matter. You should have told us what she was doing."

"You can't d-do anything about it." Sora shuddered, unable to stop the tears pouring down her face. "You broke your c-cover."

"Hey, it's all right." Then his arms were around her, and he held her gently against his chest. Sora buried her face in his coat and let the tears fall.

"It wasn't so bad at first," she whispered. "But she's . . . she's getting worse."

"I know what's it like," Kel said softly, his breath ruffling her hair. "My old dad used to hit me all the time."

"Really?"

"Dueling was the only thing that saved me. You know what I learned? It's never about you. It's not your fault."

"I thought I could handle her."

"You shouldn't have to handle anything on your own."

"I just wa-wanted to be a strong queen," Sora said.

"You're wonderfully strong," Kel said. "Firelord knows this is a hard situation, but you've been damn brave."

Sora sniffed, aware that she was dripping tears and blood on Kel's uniform. But she didn't pull away. Maybe she didn't have to be as strong as she thought when she had friends on her side. Gradually, her tears subsided.

"That's better," Kel said, sitting back on his heels. "Now, I'll be right back."

"Where are you going?"

"To kill that evil woman, of course."

"Wait!" Sora gasped. "The Lantern Maker will burn you to ashes. That won't help anything."

Indecision crossed Kel's face, and for a moment she thought he was going to carry out his threat anyway. Then he sighed. "Okay, my queen. What do you want me to do?"

Sora dried her eyes on her sleeve, considering her options. Lima was clearly coming unhinged. Could they divide her from the Lantern Maker without doing further damage to the mountain? He seemed more interested in his secret projects than in Lima's power plays most of the time. Those projects were still the greatest threat. But maybe Lima had given them an opportunity.

"I need you to bring me Daz Stoneburner," Sora said at last. "If Madame Pandan is with him, she can come too."

"Right now?" Kel asked.

Sora pushed a strand of hair back from her face. She could tell a black eye was already forming, and blood crusted her lip. The Workers needed to see what kind of people they had put in power.

"Right now."

It was time for drastic measures. If she was going to split the mountain, she'd split it. Maybe that was the only way to put it back together again.

Kel helped her onto the bench. He brushed a gentle hand along her cheek before departing to fetch the Square Workers. As soon as she was alone, she took deep, shuddering breaths to calm herself. She wouldn't let Lima terrorize her any longer. She needed to go on the offensive. And now she had leverage.

She'd been focusing on the nobility, but it was becoming clear that Rafe's efforts to raise up the Fireworkers had been a little too successful. They were claiming power fast, and even Lima seemed to be struggling with the new reality. But they also might be the only ones who could stop Rafe from unleashing his secret project on the Lands Below.

Sora was going to have to fight Fire with Fire.

She pulled a cover down over the Firebulb in the water closet, casting the small room into shadow. She moved into the darkest corner, mulling over her plan, putting the actions she had to take next in their proper order.

The door opened with a scrape, and fear jolted through Sora's heart once more. But it wasn't Lima. Kel had returned with Daz Stoneburner and Madame Pandan the Metalworker. Sora stayed back in the shadows as the two Workers shuffled in, scanning the water closet suspiciously. Kel stopped behind them, managing to look menacing despite being shorter than both. Sora caught a glimpse of Telvin Jale guarding the corridor before the door closed again.

"Thank you for coming to see me," she said regally.

"This is a rather . . . unconventional place for an audience, my queen," Madame Pandan said.

"This won't take long," Sora said. "I want you to work with me against the Lantern Maker."

Daz coughed. "My queen! You must have the wrong idea about us. We are loyal to the crown and the Chief Regent."

"The crown's and the Chief Regent's interests are at odds," Sora said, gaining confidence as she spoke. "You must know that he doesn't want what's best for Vertigon."

"My queen, I don't—"

"You don't truly want the Lantern Maker to create Fire Weapons to invade the Lands Below, do you?"

The two Workers exchanged shocked glances.

"That's what he wants," Sora said. "And I'm guessing you don't like it. My question is: can you stop him?"

"He has overstepped the bounds of wisdom," Daz said. "But what you are suggesting—"

"That's not the only bound he has overstepped," Sora said. She pulled the cover off the Firebulb and emerged into the light, revealing her battered face.

Madame Pandan gasped. "Did he—?"

"Not him," Sora said. "It was Madame Ruminor."

Daz stared at her, his face ghostly in the light from the Firebulb.

"But you're just a child," he said.

"I can't think this is what you wanted when you helped the Lantern Maker overthrow my brother."

"No," Daz said. "It most certainly is not."

Sora recalled the key piece of information Berg had provided her about Daz Stoneburner, the one reason the Firesmith might be her only hope. He hated violence. He hated it even more than the average Vertigonian. He was talented at crafting sport dueling rapiers, but he abhorred bloodshed. He had helped create the wall of Fire around Square Peak during the coup because he believed it to be the safest way to achieve what he wanted for the Fireworkers without further violence.

But according to Berg, Rafe's actions since then did not sit well with Daz. And he wouldn't like the idea of Rafe as a conqueror either. Now, Sora was counting on his conscience to get the better of him at last.

"You must know the Ruminors are not good for Vertigon," she said. "The balance that keeps our mountain peaceful has been disrupted ever since he freed the Fire. People are being hurt, and it is only going to get worse. Will you help me stand against them?"

Daz and Madame Pandan looked at each other then back at Sora. Daz's gaze lingered on her battered face. At last, he bowed his head.

"What do you need us to do?"

31

FORK TOWN

SIV and the team rode into Fork Town at dusk. The journey through Kurn Pass had been a blur of shifting shadows and creaking saddles. They had entered the Pass as a company of Truren soldiers was constructing a log wall to block it. Their rush to get far enough away to avoid trouble meant they'd had a long ride in the dark after a tough day's journey. They slept for a few hours at a time beneath the sheer rock cliffs of Kurn Pass and continued through the next few days in a tired haze.

"I'd rather get to Fork Town and rest there than sleep on the rough ground," Kres said when they complained. "And I want to put some distance between us and Trure."

The arduous pace struck Siv as unnecessary. The Soolen invasion had happened far to the northeast. Obstructing the pass had been a precaution to protect the border, but they were hardly in danger here. Still, he figured he'd appreciate Fork Town even more when they finally arrived.

Siv remained wary of his companions. Their reaction when he tried to leave had confirmed his somewhat dubious status amongst them. They didn't trust him, no matter how friendly they acted on the road, and they didn't plan to let him walk free. He hoped the strain of leaving in the middle of the night had contributed to their open hostility. They worried he would give *them* away, not the other way around. They didn't know who he was—or who he used to be.

For good or ill, he was bound for Fork Town, leaving his past farther and farther behind.

The thought of Dara was a blade in his gut with every step. He could hardly sleep with her face before his eyes. He told himself again and again that he'd had no choice, but he couldn't help feeling that she'd have fought anyway. She wouldn't let a petty thing like a knife to her veins and enemies on all sides keep her from returning to him. But unlike Siv, she hadn't gotten her sister killed. Unlike him, she could still bear her own name with pride.

By the time the sun rose over the Linden Mountains that first morning, the pen fighters had fallen back into the same camaraderie they'd enjoyed while traveling the plains. Latch grumbled. Gull and Fiz teased each other. Kres expounded on how the team was going to make him proud in the Steel Pentagon. By their second day in the Pass, Siv started to wonder if he had imagined the way they crowded in around him and brandished their weapons when he tried to turn back. He had to remember these people were not his friends.

At least their destination didn't disappoint. Fork Town—it should really be called Fork City—was one of the most-important trading hubs on the continent. Located on the southern side of the only reliable route through the Linden Mountains, it was the primary access point to Trure this side of the badlands. The fork that gave the town its name was a busy roundabout alive with snorting horses and creaking wagons. Dust rose over it, shimmering gold in the setting sun, as they rode in from the north. A brick platform stood at the center bearing an ancient iron statue overlooking the traffic. The main roads branched off to Trure, Pendark via the Darkwood, and the Soolen Peninsula. Inns and taverns lined each fork, eventually giving way to warehouses and tenements farther from the center. Beyond the city boundaries, vast vineyards crept up the slopes of the mountains and edged across the landscape.

Famous as a trading center, Fork Town was infamous for its nighttime activities. Most travelers stayed more than a day to allow for both rest and recreation. With the closure of the Pass, the town nearly overflowed with stranded merchants and restless mercenaries. It promised to be an especially raucous night.

The pen fighters took rooms in an inn just off the main fork called Teall's Traveler. Kres warned them they'd resume their usual training soon, but he gave them the night and the next day off. They all napped for a few hours and reconvened in the inn's common room to prepare for a night of proper Fork Town carousing.

For his part, Siv was looking forward to drowning his regret in the famous Fork Town wine. He'd spent restless hours worrying about what was happening back in Rallion City during the journey. Now that Trure had been invaded, it was more important than ever to send word to the royal palace. Even if he couldn't escape the pen fighters, maybe he could at least let his family know his whereabouts.

But as he debated how to return, he always circled around to the reality that he couldn't do anything against the Soolen army even if he escaped. He was just one man. His grandfather had a wall and a palace and a world-famous cavalry. The Soolens probably wouldn't make it halfway to Rallion City before the Trurens stopped them. Selivia and his mother would be fine.

Besides, look what happened to Sora in your care. Siv couldn't keep the ugly thought from rearing its head like a cullmoran—and he knew firsthand how ugly those were. His shame at failing his most-important task was enough to keep him moving further away from who he used to be. He didn't much like that fellow anyway.

As he started on the first of what he hoped would be many goblets of wine in the inn's common room, he couldn't keep Dara's image from coming to him. He could walk away from his former self, but he couldn't walk away from her as easily. He couldn't drink away the memory of her intense eyes, her proud mouth, her self-assurance, her passion. Sure, he mused about starting fresh and relieving her of the burden of protecting him, but he still missed *her*. The woman. The friend. Dara had been on his side more than anyone in his life except his father and sisters. Only she could scold him for being immature while still showing far more faith in him than he deserved. She had stayed with him through his darkest moments—and she made it a thousand times harder to walk away.

He was also sure she felt more than loyalty for him. There had been no pretending after that kiss. He wanted nothing more than to kiss her one more time, to tell her she was the most-beautiful woman he had ever known, to offer her every broken shred of the world. Yet he had let the events of the past few weeks carry him away from her. And now he was stuck on the wrong side of the Pass.

Siv scowled into the ripples in his goblet. Dara didn't need to guard a fallen king. And she probably didn't even want to be with a man like him.

"Got a girl on the mind?" Gull asked, nudging him with her bony elbow. She'd let down her ale-brown hair, and it fell in a sleek curtain beside her cheek.

"You could say that."

"Ease up a little," Gull said. "No woman wants a man who mopes."

"I'm not moping."

"Pouting, then." Gull took a long gulp from her goblet. "Even your sexy lips don't make a pout like that enticing."

Siv's jaw went slack. Sexy lips? Fiz threw his head back and laughed louder than a hecklebird. People at other tables looked over at the sound.

"Close your mouth, pretty boy," Gull said. "Have another drink, and tell us about your girl."

"I don't want to talk about her," Siv grumbled, his face reddening.

"Don't turn into Latch," Gull said. "I had all the first-love sighs and giggles I could take while Shreya was still with us."

"How long were they together?" Siv asked. Latch hadn't come down from his room yet. Maybe he could finally get something out of Fiz and Gull about their surly Soolen. He was becoming more and more certain that Latch was the reason they were all so worried about spies.

"A week at most," Fiz said. "Latch had it bad for her from the first day. And she liked him back, though I can't imagine why. Watching them spar was like seeing an unlicensed fan show in the Gutter District of Pendark."

"Speaking of which," Kres said, coming over from where he'd been chatting with the innkeeper and setting a new pitcher of wine on the table, "there are plenty of girls in Pendark, lad. And men. I'll show you beauties beyond your most-elaborate and colorful dreams in the great city by the sea."

Siv poured himself more wine. He didn't want to see these

Pendarkan beauties. He wanted to see Dara. But as Kres launched into a bawdy tale of fan shows and Waterdancers, he tried his hardest to put her from his mind. Firelord knew she should forget about him.

Latch was the last to join them, and he nodded at everyone except Siv. He had bathed more thoroughly than the others and donned a clean shirt and long vest. Even his tall boots had a fresh shine. He looked more like a young lord and less like a rough-and-tumble pen fighter without the grime from the road. Whatever had enticed him to join the pen fighters, it seemed he too was having a hard time giving up his former identity completely.

"Catch up, mate." Fiz pushed the pitcher toward him. "We're in for a big night."

Latch poured himself a drink but didn't take more than two sips. That was no way to enjoy a man's first night in Fork Town. Siv tried to ignore his crankiest companion as the pen fighters worked their way through more wine. The common room grew hot, packed to the walls with travelers eager to speculate about the closure of Kurn Pass and what it meant for trade. Those transporting goods bound for Trure from Pendark argued over whether to wait it out, try to sell their shipments right there in Fork Town, or even take the southeastern fork road down to Soole itself. They squabbled, loud but festive, and shouted for more wine.

A few people in the common room knew Gull. They called out greetings or bawdy suggestions, and she responded in her usual dulcet tones, apparently not too enthusiastic about reconnecting with anyone in her hometown. When Siv asked if she had any family here, she gave him a flat stare and refused to answer. He returned to his cups. Better to let sleeping velgon bears lie.

The general consensus among the travelers was that Pendark remained safe—or as safe as it ever was—so the gossip didn't alter the pen fighters' plans. Before long, Kres stood and banged his goblet on the table.

"Let us make the rounds, friends!" he said. "No wayfarer in Fork Town ought to spend their whole night in a single tavern. It's bad luck."

"Hear! Hear!" Fiz called.

They tumbled out of the Teall's Traveler's door and tramped

through the streets, footsteps already weaving. It was long past dark, but the streets were as lively as if it were high noon. Laughter and multi-accented voices from other revelers filled the air. The crowd was rougher than in the parlors and taverns of King's Peak where Siv had spent many an evening carousing, but he didn't care. He wasn't a prince or a king anymore. He was just another anonymous vagrant lurching through the throng.

Kres, Fiz, and Gull led the way through a succession of inns (The Laughing Pullturtle, The Waterlord's End) and taverns (The Sodden Soolen, Kurtle's Kettle, The Goblet and the Girl). Latch and Siv ambled along after them as the night whirled, confusing their senses.

Revelers milled around the main fork, which was no longer crammed with horses and wagons. The winter chill didn't dissuade the people from dancing in the streets, clutching at each other as their feet kicked up dust. Three fiddlers, triplets by the looks of them, pranced on the raised brick platform in the center of the roundabout, where the age-darkened statue stood. Decades of scrawled signatures and lewd pictures vandalized every inch of the figure. Its battered head appeared to have more than one face. A pimply boy banged on a kettledrum at its feet. The sound was wild and joyous, the cacophony almost overwhelming. Despite himself, Siv grinned, tapping his feet to the rhythm. He'd always wanted to see this. As king he never would have had a chance except on dull diplomatic excursions. But regular people were free in the Fork. No matter where he came from or what he'd done, a man could strike out in any direction to seek his fortune. He could join a mercenary band, assume a new identity, disappear into the night with the right enticement. Every branch of the fork suggested new possibilities.

Women wearing colorful Truren scarves and wide skirts skipped toward them, beckoning them to join the dance. The youngest among them was short, with auburn hair and dark eyes full of promise. She carried a wineskin under her arm and when she tipped it back, berry-red dripped down her chin like blood. She giggled and wiped it with her sleeve then held the wine out to Siv.

He stared at it for a moment. Maybe it was time he truly left his former self behind. Maybe it was time to forget. The dark-eyed girl nodded encouragingly.

"Come along, Siv, Latch!" called Kres. "We don't want to lose you to the Fork. It has happened before."

Siv frowned. That fate was less tempting than it ought to be for a man of his age and physical condition. For some reason, a Fork Town revel with a stranger did not strike him as appealing a diversion as it once might have. He didn't want to get lost with the dark-eyed girl. He declined the offer of wine. The girl blew him a kiss and disappeared with a toss of her auburn hair. Siv turned away from the dancers and jogged to catch up with his companions. He didn't look back.

The streets weren't quite as wild as they meandered away from the main fork. They ended up in a small, less-crowded tavern called The Lightning Bug's Revenge two blocks from their inn. Fiz informed them the tavern keeper sourced her house wine from the best vineyards in the region. He leaned against the bar to chat with the woman while she poured them another round. The tables were arranged close to the common room wall, leaving an open space in the center with a platform for a fiddler. It was empty now, and Siv spotted the fiddler snuggled in a corner with a buxom woman on his lap.

A retired pen fighter Kres and Gull knew from Pendark waved from another corner, and they went over to greet him while Siv and Latch found a table by the wall opposite the bar. Fiz was still engrossed in his conversation with the tavern keeper. They caught snippets as they took their seats.

"... always miss this red." Fiz banged his goblet on the darkwood bar.

"As you ought." The tavern keeper chuckled, pouring him another. "It's better'n anything vined this side of the Bell Sea."

"I've heard that claim more than once tonight," Siv said. He leaned toward Latch, who had ended up sitting beside him despite his usual efforts to keep a table between them. "My favorite wine is still from the Purlen fields, though."

"Oh, Purlen is quality," Latch said with a wistful sigh. "It's so good it's almost . . ." He trailed off, staring at Siv with horror.

"Got you again!" Siv said. "Purlen wine is the most-expensive vintage on the continent. And you've had it often, have you?"

"You bastard."

"I'm not out to expose you." Siv topped up Latch's wine goblet for him and grinned. "I reckon we have a lot in common. So can you stop being so damn grumpy?"

Latch scowled, but the expression didn't have its usual wrath. It was hard to be cranky with a belly full of good food and wine, clean clothes, and a warm bed waiting for you at the inn. At last Latch sighed and accepted the refilled goblet. That was progress. Siv might get through to him yet. He raised his own drink in a toast—and the tavern doors crashed open.

With a thunder of footsteps, a dozen armed men poured into the common room. Fiz shouted a warning, but Siv and Latch barely had time to stand up before the first foe reached them.

The man swung a curved blade so fast it whistled through the air. Siv ducked and heaved the table forward to stop the assault. He and Latch scrambled in opposite directions, drawing their swords as they went. Then the rest of the attackers were upon them.

The men had the look of mercenaries: mismatched bits of armor and no colors to signify their allegiance to lord or land. They were a mix of nationalities too, not unlike the team of pen fighters. These men weren't quite as well trained, but they had the advantage of numbers.

Two enemies converged on each member of the pen-fighting team. Kres uttered a war cry and brandished his knives. Gull fell into her silent, practiced fighting stance, staring down her opponents with a vicious intensity. Fiz had left his broadsword behind at their inn, but he bellowed and swung his fists at anyone that dared get near him.

Siv had his own pair of opponents to worry about. Fortunately, he'd worn his sword when they went out. He drew the knife Kres had given him and wielded both weapons, using every ounce of training he could muster. Despite all the wine he'd consumed, he managed to keep his feet, dancing in and out of his opponents' range, daring them to strike.

Fighting two men at once required more agility than it took for a morrinvole to cross a bridge line. He finally understood why they called it the Dance of Steel.

His first opponent fell with a deep slice to the wrist. The man scrambled away, desperately trying to hold in his lifeblood with his other hand. The second was tougher, but Siv had been practicing hard over the past few weeks. The fight felt surreal, as if it were taking place underwater. That was probably the wine.

His opponent struck, and Siv moved on instinct, countering the hit with a strong parry—not his most elegant ever—and then he sliced his attacker's ribs with his knife. He nearly lost an eye to the riposte, the jab missing him by a hair. He leapt back, stumbling over a fallen chair. He kicked the chair forward to deter his opponent and edged around a table near the wall.

He had time for a quick glance around the tavern as his opponent assessed his new position. The common room had emptied of everyone except the pen fighters and their attackers. The pen fighters—who were professionals after all—had already dispatched several of the mercenaries. Kres and Gull moved back to back to combat their remaining two attackers. The clash of steel and a colorful array of curses in several languages filled the air.

Siv had been correct about the two attackers for each pen fighter —except for Latch. Four men had cornered him, and they were trying to force him toward the door.

That was all Siv had time to see before his own opponent closed with him again. This one was better than his companion, but as Siv met his slashes with parry after parry, he got the impression the man wasn't trying to kill him. He pressed Siv hard, but he didn't take any risks that might get him close enough to deliver a killing blow. It was almost as if he was trying to distract him. So this was a kidnapping, not a murder, was it?

Siv risked another look at Latch. Why were twice as many men going after him? Siv had assumed the assailants were here for him at first. What mercenaries wouldn't want a chance to capture the former King of Vertigon? But Latch was the one being herded toward the door.

Well, whatever this was about, Siv wasn't going to let his new teammate be taken. He bellowed a war cry and threw his knife at his opponent. The man raised his blade in time to block it, giving Siv the opening he needed to ram his sword straight into the soft flesh of his adversary's armpit. He let out a bloody gurgle and dropped to the floor.

Siv snatched his knife up from where it had skittered away and hurtled over his fallen opponent, not pausing to watch him die.

Latch was putting up a good fight across the room, but too many men surrounded him. He had taken down one with a stab to the thigh, but the other three edged in and managed to disarm him. Two of them grabbed Latch's arms and hauled him toward the door.

Siv launched off the fiddler's platform and hurled himself into one of Latch's captors at full speed, causing all four of them to tumble to the ground. Siv's wild hit struck true, and the first man died. Siv shoved his sword into Latch's newly freed hand and leapt up to deal with the man who'd stayed on his feet.

Latch tangled with his other would-be captor on the ground while Siv faced off against the final foe. Too late, he wished he'd given Latch the knife and kept the sword for himself.

His opponent was armed with a short sword and a dangerous grin. Siv crouched, knife at the ready, and watched for an opening. He took a few swipes to test the man's defenses. The short sword caught the knife every time. At least the man was biding his time, exercising caution. If he went for a direct attack, Siv wouldn't be able to stop him without taking a cut or two. Or a gaping wound to the gut.

Siv bounced on the balls of his feet, staying agile just as Kres had taught him. Sweat beaded on his forehead, and it occurred to him that he might throw up the night's libations on the man who was trying to kill him. This was why he should never drink. Why did people always try to kill him when he drank?

Despite the wine distorting his senses, he kept his head. His opponent attacked, and Siv met the short sword with a quick parry, the blow sending vibrations up his arm. Before his opponent could riposte, Siv jumped back. He aimed a kick at the man's fist, his foot coming up beneath his sword arm. The man grimaced, but he kept his grip on his sword. *Damn it. That should have worked.*

Siv advanced for a series of quick jabs. Perhaps surprised by the kick, his opponent didn't react as quickly as he had before. Siv swiped at his elbow and was rewarded by the sight of a thin strip of blood on the edge of his knife.

He leapt back to avoid the short sword again. Not giving his opponent a chance to breathe, he kicked his knee with a hard crunch. Before the man could do more than curse, Siv tackled him, grabbing his wrist to deflect the sword from his stomach.

They hit the ground, Siv grasping the man's sword arm in his left hand. He forced the weapon away from his body and drove his knife between the man's ribs. He gave a surprised grunt. Siv kept his blade in until the body relaxed under his hands. Silence reigned at last.

Siv cleaned his blade on the corpse's tunic and climbed to his feet, still feeling slightly off balance. He looked around for his friends and any remaining enemies.

"Now that's training for the Dance if I've ever seen it!" Kres had a wild glow in his eyes, and his hands were drenched in blood. He stood triumphant over the bodies of the mercenaries, Gull at his side. Blood soaked her sleeve as well as her blade. Fiz had taken refuge behind the bar, and it looked as if he'd wielded a pair of stone pitchers in lieu of weapons. Two unconscious men lay before him. At least one looked as though he'd never wake.

Latch had dealt with the last of his would-be kidnappers. He held Siv's blade out to him by the hilt. He met his eyes and gave him a respectful nod so brief Siv would have missed it if he blinked.

"Better keep it until you're safe," Siv said. "Wouldn't want them to carry you off."

Latch stared at him for a moment without expression then withdrew his hand. He didn't argue with the assertion: they had been attacked by a group of mercenaries intent on kidnapping Latch. The fellow got more interesting by the day.

The tavern patrons began to reemerge from underneath tables now that the fighting was over. The fiddler clutched his instrument as though he expected he'd have to beat someone over the head with it. The tavern keeper looked on the verge of exploding over the mess—as soon as she figured out whose fault the fight had been.

"We'd best move on before the Town Watch arrives, lads," Kres said. "Seems a man can't even enjoy a night of carousing in peace anymore."

Fiz sighed. "We're never going to get a decent night's sleep in an actual bed, are we?"

"Shouldn't we see if the Town Watch knows anything about these goons?" Gull asked. She cut a strip of cloth from the edge of her shirt and began expertly binding up the wound on her arm. She didn't even wince as she pulled the cloth tight with her teeth.

"I daresay we know enough," Kres said.

"There'll be more of them," Latch said with a sigh. "They won't give up."

"Have no fear, my friends," Kres said. "Pendark awaits!" He turned as if he meant to sweep dramatically toward the door.

"Hold on a minute," Siv said. "Don't we deserve to know what the Firelord all that was about?"

Kres smiled benignly. "All what, son?"

"The attack! If I'm going to risk my neck with you people, isn't it fair I know why?"

With a few lightning-quick steps Kres put himself between Siv and Latch. The latter still held Siv's sword, so he wasn't in much danger, but Kres's intentions were clear.

"You're a smart boy, Sivren Amen," he said softly. "You saw who they were after. Don't you think if I was going to tell you more, I would have already?"

"It's all right, Kres," Latch said. He still sounded brusque, but his voice had taken on a commanding tone. "It's only fair that he knows. He saved my life just now. If he were really a spy, he wouldn't have done that." He sighed heavily. "I think we can trust him."

Kres shrugged. "It's your secret. But know this: I protect the members of my team. You're new here, Siv lad, but you'll get the same protection as long as you don't cross any *other* members of my team. Is that clear?"

"Clear as a krellfish eye," Siv said. He was starting to understand. The pen fighters had tried to bring vengeance on Shreya's killers. They had prevented him from leaving when they fled Tollan because they didn't want him to reveal Latch's whereabouts. All for the team. Their loyalty—once won—might not be a bad thing to have. "So what's the big secret?"

Latch lowered his sword. "My surname is Brach," he said. "I'm Commander Brach's son."

"The commander of the Soolen army?" The news wasn't quite as juicy as Siv had hoped. Latch hadn't even been a king before? How disappointing.

"Among other things," Latch said evasively.

Siv tried to remember the long conversations he'd had with Sora about the noble houses of Soole. Sora had mostly talked *at* him while he counted the minutes until his next dueling practice. The thought of Sora created a tight knot of pain in his stomach. He ought to be able to remember *something* she had told him. *Brach*. That was the commander his original captors had served, but there was something else important about the name. They had a fort in the badlands, and...

"Wait, isn't Brach the richest and most-powerful house in Soole?"

"You forgot stuffiest," Latch said.

"That's why you wanted to get out of Tollan so quickly? Because your father is leading the invasion?"

"Brach isn't exactly a popular name in Trure right now," Latch said.

"And you're the rebellious scion?" Siv said. "You figured you'd join the pen fighters rather than follow in your father's military footsteps, and now he's sent mercenaries to get you back?"

"Something like that."

"It was sure nice of Kres to take you under his wing." Siv had a feeling they were leaving something out. So what if Latch was a rich kid from a well-known house? It was not as if *he'd* ever had his kingdom stolen from him by a powerful sorcerer. But what was in it for Kres? The man was risking death by keeping young Latch out of his father's clutches. "You must be great friends."

A slow smile spread across Kres's face. "The best."

If anything, the response left Siv more confused than ever.

"This is all very heartwarming, gentlemen," Gull said. "But aren't we supposed to be getting out of town?"

"Right you are, Gull darling," Kres said. "We can continue sharing life stories on the road. Let us retrieve our horses and leave the blessed Fork in our dust. We only have a week before our first Dance. We'd best move on before word of our exploits spreads."

32

CHASE

DARA'S wrists ached from her bonds, and her back felt sore from sitting bolt upright on Grelling's horse to avoid touching him as much as possible. She wanted to slam her fists into his ugly chin. Despite all her efforts over the past weeks, they were still leading Siv's enemies straight to him. She spent her nights plotting ways to escape, but Kurn Pass left her with limited options. There was nowhere to go but onward. Even if she managed to break free of her ropes, her captors would catch up long before she reached Fork Town. She didn't want to contemplate what they'd do then. Grelling treated her with a casual brutality that warned her not to underestimate him. These were no bumbling henchmen—and Lord Vex was as vigilant as his men.

Dara was realizing the most-dangerous Rollendar of them all was still alive. Vex and his two companions trained with sword and fist every morning and evening. Vex himself proved the most skilled, and Dara wondered whether he might have had a solid career as a duelist in other circumstances. He'd certainly landed on his feet after the disgrace of his house. He had assumed control of the Rollendar informants and found a new lord to serve—one who wasn't her father—and still had time to capture them. Unfortunately, he gave nothing away about the identity of his new liege as they traversed the pass.

Starting on their second day, Lord Vex insisted that Vine ride with him on his horse while Mertin galloped ahead to scout their path. Dara thought her efforts to charm him might be working, but he quickly proved he was very much in control. He questioned her closely about the Air, no doubt trying to catch her in a lie. Vine tried to deflect his attention with smiles and strategic eyelash-flutters, but Lord Vex was proving resistant to her wiles.

"Have you ever visited the Far Plains, my lord?" she said as they approached a gap between two cliffs on the third morning of their trip. They'd leave Kurn Pass behind in a matter of hours.

"Once."

"Did you see the remarkable cliff paintings on the Rock?"

"Yes. I'd question the sanity of a man who went all that way without looking."

"I quite agree with you." Vine smiled up at him. Her smile was remarkably charming given that she was tied to a saddle. Vex shouldn't have stood a chance against her. "I first visited in my youth, and I cried all afternoon at how beautiful they were. Did you know they were created with Air? It took seven years to coax the Air to give such a magnificent gift."

"I know the story."

"You must know the Air chooses to help whomever it wishes." Vine sighed, and her voice took on a calculated dreaminess. "Beyond the bounds of the plains, one can only hope there will be enough of an Air presence to Sense the truth."

"If you are laying the groundwork to tell me you've lost him once we reach the Fork, you are wasting your time," Vex said, a touch of amusement in his voice. "I have confidence in your abilities, my lady."

"Why, thank you, my lord." Vine laughed tremulously. "I've no idea what you mean by groundwork, though. Oh, look! Don't the shadows make a lovely pattern on the cliff face?"

Vex allowed her to chatter on. Dara tried to get a good look at his face to judge his reaction, but by his expression, he might as well have been listening to a report on the harvest from an orchard worker.

"Going somewhere?" Grelling grunted, his thick fingers tightening on her arm.

Dara realized she'd been leaning forward in the saddle and sat back. She was used to Grelling's smell by now, but she'd never be comfortable with the press of his body against hers. She hoped they'd acquire extra horses in Fork Town so she wouldn't have to ride with him anymore. She actually missed Storm.

She still wasn't sure whether or not Vine was lying about Sensing Siv beyond the boundaries of Trure. She had given regular updates on his supposed progress as they rode through Kurn Pass. According to her, they had gained ground, but Siv would still reach Fork Town before them. Despite the presence of their enemies, Dara half hoped Vine was telling the truth. Siv would be lost for good if they couldn't figure out which fork he'd taken.

She hated to contemplate the idea that she might never see him again. Her life had entirely revolved around dueling until she met Siv. Protecting him, making up for her parents' actions, and learning to Work had consumed her since the previous autumn. But she'd left her parents, the Fire, and her dueling career behind in Vertigon. Siv was all she had left. Could she find a place in the Lands Below without him? The prospect of being utterly without a purpose scared her almost as much as the thought of never seeing him again.

She shifted in Grelling's saddle, pushing away the fear as she pushed away the looming presence behind her. She wouldn't let that happen. She was going to win somehow.

On their final morning in the pass, Mertin left them to gallop ahead. He consulted briefly with Lord Vex while they watered the horses before disappearing. At high noon, they exited the pass and rode into Fork Town to meet him. When they discovered the nature of his errand, Dara's heart sank so far into her boots that she couldn't even take in the sights of the infamous fork.

An entire company of fighting men was waiting for them. Mertin stood proudly at their head. Rollendar gold no doubt already lined their pockets. The ten men were mercenaries, a mix of Pendarkans and Trurens, and one looked Vertigonian, though he was dressed in a Pendarkan style more suited to the warmer climate. They carried themselves with easy confidence in their movements and swagger in their steps. Numerous weapons decorated hips, backs, and boots. They had the air of men who knew how to kill and didn't much care who their targets were—providing they got paid. They waited in the shade of an inn off the roundabout carrying riders and wagons through the Fork, ready to join their swords to Vex's.

Dara swallowed hard. They were in trouble.

Mertin approached to introduce their leader, a tall Pendarkan man with the hilts of two mismatched broadswords rising above his shoulders. Vex broke off his conversation with Vine about Fork Town wine and gave Dara a victorious look. He clearly believed he had already won. He was probably right. Dara had hoped she, Siv, and Vine could take Vex and his cronies despite the fighting prowess they had demonstrated in their daily training sessions. She had watched them closely, learning their fighting styles and planning out what strategies she would use against them. She and her friends were more than competent—especially if they could get their hands on some swords. But these new arrivals changed the game entirely. Siv wouldn't stand a chance if they caught up with him.

After consulting with Lord Vex for a few minutes, the mercenary leader—who was called Wick—led the way into the yard of the finest inn on the main fork called the Laughing Pullturtle. They dismounted, planning to use the tall darkwood inn as a headquarters while the mercenaries gathered information on their quarry. Apparently Mertin had promised them Lord Vex would pay for the company's lodgings in only the best inns for the duration of their service. Dara couldn't imagine where his resources came from. Did he still have access to the Rollendar wealth? If not, his employer must really want the former King of Vertigon dead to go to all this expense.

A jumble of dust and voices rose in the inn yard as the mercenaries prepared to scour the town on behalf of their new employer. Apparently Vex wasn't willing to rely solely on Vine's word. After hauling Dara off his horse, Grelling turned his attention to the sole Vertigonian mercenary to grill him on where the best brothels and dancing houses could be found. The young man had a mish-mash of an accent that suggested he hadn't grown up on the mountain. He wasn't likely to be of any help to the two women.

Lord Vex was still talking to Wick, the leader of the mercenary company. Dara eased closer to them. No one stopped her in the midst of all the activity in the inn yard. With the presence of Vex's hired reinforcements, there was nowhere for her to run anyway.

"He should have arrived sometime yesterday," Lord Vex was saying.

"Saw a fellow matching his description in here last night," Wick said. His lantern jaw churned steadily as he chewed on something between his words. "Can't imagine he's the only tall, dark-haired young man in town, though."

"Who was he with?"

"A group of pen fighters, if I read 'em right."

"Pen fighters?"

"You heard of the Steel Pentagon?" The mercenary spit a jet of dark-brown juice in the dust. "That's what we call the combatants down in Pendark. There were five of them going on a tear."

Lord Vex touched the hilt of his sword. "So he could still be in town?"

"Most folks stay two nights all told to get in a proper bout of carousing," Wick said. "It's Fork Town tradition." He eyed Lord Vex up and down. "He know you're after him?"

"Find these pen fighters if they're still in town," Vex said, ignoring the question. "And have your men bring any information directly to me."

"Consider it done, my lord." Wick spit out more brown juice and snapped his finger at his second-in-command. "You didn't hire a bunch of amateurs."

"Good. There's a handsome bonus for the man who brings him to me."

"Now you're speaking our language."

The mercenary offered a casual salute and strode away. Vex's gaze shot to Dara before she could pretend she hadn't been listening. He waved her over.

"What do you think, Miss Ruminor?"

"Sorry?"

"Would Amintelle take up with a squad of pen fighters?"

"I don't know," Dara said. "They're for some sort of competition?"

"The Dance of Steel." Vex rubbed a hand along his chin. He had shaved every morning on the journey through the pass, and it was still smooth. "It's a gladiator competition. Men fight with sharp weapons in the Steel Pentagon. Sometimes to the death. Do you think our young friend would get mixed up with that?"

Dara hesitated. Joining a competition where you fought to the death seemed like a foolish thing to do. On the other hand, Siv had always wished he could compete in the duels. Now that he wasn't king, would he be tempted by the prospect of a fight for death and glory? She wondered whether *she* could win such a contest. The very thought sent an unexpected buzz of excitement through her. Her competitive side wasn't always the wisest part of her, though—or of Siv.

She picked at the ropes digging into her wrists, avoiding Vex's gaze. "I couldn't say."

She could certainly see Siv considering it. But if he'd truly joined a group of pen fighters, did that mean he hadn't been kidnapped after all? That couldn't be true. He would have come back to Rallion City to find her if he were able, wouldn't he? Wick must have seen some other young man with the pen fighters last night. She glanced at Vine, hoping she might be able to Sense some trace of Siv if he had truly been at this inn, but she was busy charming a pair of mercenaries who had been assigned to guard her while Vex was busy.

Lord Vex soon took charge of Vine once more, escorting her into the darkwood inn himself. Grelling, meanwhile, dragged Dara after them with far less consideration. As he hauled her across the common room, she brushed against the sheath of her Savven blade hanging from his belt. A jolt of warmth electrified her senses. Grelling shifted the blade away from her before she could do more than feel the latent Fire in the steel. She nearly dove for it, but the busy Laughing Pullturtle common room was far too crowded for her to move freely. She'd have to wait for the right moment.

Vex arranged for a private dining room up a rickety wooden staircase, and he and Grelling brought Dara and Vine up there to wait for news of the mercenaries' progress. Grelling left at once, and Dara caught a glimpse of him ordering one of the mercenaries to guard the door as it swung shut.

The women weren't allowed to speak to each other as usual, but Vex cut their bonds with an ivory-hilted knife and allowed them to relax within the confines of the private room. It was large enough for a rough table made of the same dark wood as everything else in the inn. A pair of low couches formed a sitting area, and a small, round window let in a bit of light. The innkeeper himself brought in a platter of wild rabbit sandwiches and mugs full of clean water. He offered them a pitcher of wine too, but Lord Vex waved it away.

Dara tried to appreciate the soft couch and not having to drink from a canteen while she could, but the anticipation made it difficult to enjoy anything. She didn't want Siv to be caught, but the possibility that she might finally see him sent a thrill through her more powerful than a jolt of Fire. He could have been in this very building less than twenty-four hours ago. Wick had said people usually stayed two nights in Fork Town. Was he still here somewhere?

She paced at first, and Lord Vex did not stop her. But as the hours passed, she eventually settled in to wait on one of the couches. Lord Vex sat on the opposite one next to Vine, and they chatted as if they were attending a royal reception. They mused about art, literature, courtly gossip from Vertigon, even fashionable dining. Vine's efforts to ingratiate herself with their captor were valiant. She even scooted closer to him on the couch, looking up at him with a soft smile on her lips. She showed no signs of making a move to incapacitate him, but Dara figured she was biding her time. She couldn't help noticing that Vine and Vex were becoming almost friendly. She hoped Vine wouldn't hesitate to dispatch him if she ever managed to get her hands on a weapon.

At last, the Vertigonian mercenary with the strange accent returned with the first piece of news. A young man matching Siv's description had been seen with a company of well-known pen fighters by multiple people in an inn called Teall's Traveler. The mercenaries soon brought in others who claimed to have seen him the night before too in half a dozen other drinking establishments. The informants were bleary eyed and worn looking after a night of Fork Town revelry, but their descriptions left little room for doubt.

One dark-eyed girl with auburn hair described Siv down to the new-looking scar along his temple, which few people knew about as far as Dara was aware. Like the others, the girl had seen him with three or four companions. He had been drinking in the Fork, not looking at all like a prisoner. Dara recalled Vine's assertions that he was experiencing pain on a regular basis and wondered if she'd gotten it wrong somehow.

Wick delivered the biggest piece of news himself, extracted from a local tavern fiddler. The man who looked like Siv and the mysterious pen fighters had been involved in a brawl at a tavern called the Lightning Bug's Revenge. They'd been attacked by another group of mercenaries and left town shortly before dawn. Dara and the others had missed them by mere hours.

"Firelord take him," Lord Vex muttered. "Who were these mercenaries?"

"Not a company I'm familiar with, sir," Wick said. "Weren't alive enough to tell me much."

Lord Vex frowned, no doubt wondering who else knew the King of Vertigon had been available for kidnapping in Fork Town.

"And these pen fighters survived?"

"Yes, sir. Put up a good fight by the sounds of things." Wick reached a hand over his shoulder to touch his broadsword. "Got the names of a few of the pen fighters out of the tavern keeper, but she didn't know the younger fellow."

"Hmm." Lord Vex studied Dara and Vine, who still sat on opposite couches. "It sounds like our young friend is on quite an adventure. But I won't be beaten to my prize." He looked back at his mercenary. "Gather your men, Captain Wick. We leave within the hour."

"Right away." Wick stomped from the room, already barking orders to his second-in-command.

"Now we know we're chasing the right man, it's time to figure out which way he went." Lord Vex crossed the room and offered Vine his arm in a manner that brooked no argument. "We're going out to the Fork. Are you ready to use the Air again, Lady Silltine?"

"Of course, Lord Vex," Vine said. "I do hope I can still Sense him. The Air is temperamental at times."

"You'll find a way," Lord Vex said. "I'd hate for someone else to beat me to my prize."

"Truly, that would be disappointing."

Vine didn't resist as Lord Vex steered her toward the door. She looked back at Dara and gave her a wink as they left the room.

Wick assigned the young Vertigonian mercenary to guard Dara, and he took up a position by the door as the others departed. Grelling and Mertin hadn't returned yet. They wouldn't get nearly as much time to rest now that Lord Vex knew Siv was on the road again—possibly with other mercenaries in pursuit.

Dara fidgeted in her seat, wishing she knew what was going on outside. What would Vine do at the Fork? If she knew where Siv was going, would she tell Vex the opposite route? Or would she tell him the truth, hoping Vex wouldn't believe her? Dara would hate to be caught in that particular mind game—but mind games were Vine's specialty. She'd have Lord Vex eating out of the palm of her hand before too much longer.

The news Wick had brought worried her. Why was Siv getting into tavern brawls? He couldn't possibly know the danger he was in from Lord Vex and his men. And who else was after him? Would her father have hired a crew of mercenaries to attack Siv all the way out in Fork Town? Or was there another player in the mix? She drummed her fingers on the arm of the couch, wishing she could do some footwork or go for a run to clear her head.

The mercenary by the door studied her curiously. He had dark-brown hair, common for Vertigonians, and the paler strip peeking out beneath his collar suggested his deep tan wasn't his natural skin tone. He couldn't be more than a few years older than Dara. He kept a hand on the curved sword at his belt, and his stance was loose and relaxed. Clearly he didn't think she was a threat. Vine was better at charming people than Dara was, but maybe she could take advantage of Lord Vex's temporary absence.

"Excuse me?" she said, putting on what she hoped was a friendly smile. "Would you mind if I look out the window?"

"Don't see why not." The mercenary's accent had a foreign lilt, and again Dara got the impression that he hadn't spent much time on the mountain.

"Thanks." Dara rose, moving slowly to avoid alarming him. She strode to the small round window overlooking the road. It was too small for her to fit through, and the mercenary didn't react when she pulled open the shutters for a better view.

The main fork itself spread before her, its three roads branching off at even intervals from a circular road. A brick platform in the center bore a heavily-graffitied statue of a man with his hands on his hips, his face gazing blankly at the Linden Mountains to the north. Or at least, she thought he was gazing north. On closer inspection, he appeared to have another face on his rusty metal head looking to the east.

"Two faces?" she mumbled, leaning her forehead against the smoky glass.

"Three."

"Sorry?"

The young mercenary had taken a few steps closer to her, still effectively guarding the door.

"He's got three faces. One for each fork. You can see 'em better up close."

Dara looked back at the statue, just making out the shadows of features on its head. Just then, Lord Vex and Vine emerged from the inn beneath her and strode toward the center of the roundabout. The road ran around the brick platform in a complete circle. A constant flow of traffic moved through it: horses, carriages, foot traffic, even a drove of cattle not much bigger than goats hurried through the fork.

Vine and Vex waited for a wagon drawn by four horses to pass before crossing to the center platform. Dara could tell Vex had Vine's arm in an unyielding grip. To passersby, though, they could have looked like an attractive couple out for a stroll.

"You're from Vertigon, aren't you?" the young mercenary asked behind her.

"Yes."

"I was born there, but I don't remember a bit of it," he said. "My parents left when I was a babe in arms."

"Did you grow up in Fork Town?" Dara asked, not looking away from the road below. Vine and Vex had reached the center of the roundabout. None of his bodyguards accompanied them, but Vex was armed. Dara had seen him spar enough to know he was more than capable without them.

"I grew up here and there," the young mercenary said. "Fork Town is home for now, but who knows later? Got to make my fortune first."

"There's good money in mercenary work?"

"If you get with the right team, there is. It's all in your team and your blade. We don't usually guard kidnapped women, though."

"Hmm." Dara thought of Siv apparently joining up with a squad of pen fighters. She knew how much of a burden the kingship had been for him. Maybe he too was enticed by the idea of making his fortune with his blade alone. She didn't like the possibility that he wasn't trying to get back to her, though. There must be more to the story.

Dara tensed as Vine climbed onto the brick platform at the center of the fork. She closed her eyes and adopted the familiar cross-legged Sensing posture. Lord Vex alternated between watching her and scanning the three forks. Could she feel anything? She'd used the Air on occasion in Vertigon. She must be able to do it here too. But what would she tell Lord Vex?

"You all came in from Trure, right?" the young mercenary asked affably. He clearly hadn't been given orders not to talk to her.

"Yes."

"Did you see any Soolens? I hear they invaded. Came bursting right out of Cindral Forest in the middle of a rainstorm."

"I don't know any details," Dara said. "The news broke while we were in Tollan."

"Tollan's a decent town. We go through there all the time."

"I don't know when people will be able to travel through there again," Dara said. "They walled up Kurn Pass when we left."

How long could Vine keep it up down there? She was excellent at stalling, but Siv needed as big a head start as possible. Even from this distance, Dara could see Vex tapping his foot impatiently. How long before he decided to follow the rumors about the Pendarkan pen fighters regardless of Vine's Senses?

"That's what I hear," the mercenary said. "Say, could you tell me more about Vertigon? It's so far away. I don't meet many folks who've actually been there."

"What do you know about it already?"

On the platform beneath her, Vine shifted her position with a sudden, jerky manner. That was unusual for her during meditations. It was as if she had just realized something. Or Sensed something. Dara clutched the edge of the windowsill as if it were a weapon.

The young mercenary launched into a fanciful description of Vertigon where the people rode on dragons and all the bridges were made of Firegold. Dara let his words wash over her as she concentrated on Vine, looking for another movement like the one before. Had she Sensed Siv just now?

Suddenly a dark shape blurred through the air above the fork and collided with Lord Vex. A tall figure hurtled across the street after it, dodging carriages and riders, and tossed something to Vine that glinted in the sun. A sword.

33

THE FORK

THE thing that had hit Lord Vex spread its wings wide and launched into the air again. A cur-dragon! It swooped and swerved around Lord Vex's head. He drew his sword and took a swipe at it. While Lord Vex was distracted, the tall figure leapt onto the brick platform with Vine. At first Dara thought it was Siv, but then she recognized Tann Ridon's gangly frame. Rid had followed them! And he had brought Rumy.

The cur-dragon heaved dragon fire at Lord Vex. The Rollendar lord dove out of the way just in time. Rumy breathed more fire, herding Vex farther away from Vine and Rid.

But Vex's mercenaries kept a close watch, and they charged across the busy road to join the fray. People from the town ran to watch the fight, and curses and shouts rose as mercenaries and spectators got in the way of the riders and carriages trying to make their way through the fork.

Steel flashed in the center of it all. Vine and Rid could barely fend off Vex's men from their position atop the brick platform, the three-faced statue at their backs. They needed Dara's help.

"What's going on out there?" the young Vertigonian mercenary asked, his voice suddenly sharp. Dara hadn't noticed when he stopped babbling. He strode closer to her but not too close, his hand firm on his sword. Despite his youth, he was no amateur.

But Dara wasn't either. She pressed her face to the glass again, acting absorbed in the fight down in the street. Vine was an excellent swordswoman, and she held off the mercenaries—barely. Rid's staff whipped through the air, occasionally connecting with a head or a weapon. It was only a matter of time before the blades made it through. They were outnumbered six to two.

"There's a fight in the street," Dara said. "I think your team is involved. They're losing."

"Eh?" The young mercenary took a few steps closer. When he was near enough for Dara to feel his breath on her cheek, she drove her elbow backward into his gut.

He grunted and reached for her, but Dara was already moving. She darted across the room, grabbing the water pitcher from the table and hurling it behind her at the young mercenary without breaking her stride. She burst out of the private dining room and into the narrow hallway. Another mercenary waited there, but she ran past him before he could get his sword all the way out of its sheath.

Dara threw herself down the narrow stairs to the common room of the inn and out the front door before anyone could react. Shouts rose behind her, but she ignored them. This was their only chance.

When she emerged into the sunlight, Vine still held her ground atop the brick platform. She danced back and forth, jabbing and twirling with all the grace and speed that had made her such an excellent duelist. Dara was still unarmed. She needed a distraction.

"Rumy!" she shouted as she dashed across the road. A pair of riders pulled up sharply, cursing at her as she rushed in front of their horses. "Rumy! I need Fire!"

The creature heard. With a joyful squawk he flew over Lord Vex's head and streaked toward her, a bright flame already building in his throat. Dara raised both hands as Rumy soared above her and let loose a burst of dragon fire. Screams rose from the onlookers that had gathered to watch the battle in the fork.

Rumy's flame felt like a warm breath of summer wind on Dara's skin. Within it, flickering jets of true Fire spewed through the air—noticeably more than the last time they tried this. Dara sucked the flames to her as if they were her last breath. The Fire soaked into her skin, into her blood. She gloried in the familiar sensation for an instant. She had missed this. She didn't want to let it go. But there was no time to delay.

Dara Worked the Fire within her, pulling the wild, flickering residue into a cohesive stream. Then she dove onto the brick platform, scraping all the skin off her elbows as she went. She touched the foot of the ancient statue and forced the Fire into it.

"Get ready to run!" she bellowed to Vine and Rid. The fighting men pressed them hard, and she wasn't sure if they heard her. The clash of steel filled the smoky air as their weapons whirled, frantic now. They wouldn't last much longer.

The metal beneath Dara's fingers began to melt. Working with Fire from Rumy still wasn't smooth, but she didn't need this to be elegant. The Fire flowed through the statue like blood through veins, melting its ancient iron. Rust and paint flaked off and fell around Dara like snow. Then with a squeal and a hiss, the statue moved.

Gasps rose from the crowd gathered outside the roundabout. The statue turned on the platform, guided by Dara's power. Fingers of molten iron snaked out from it, supported and directed by the Fire. The fingers thickened, draining more iron from the figure and sharpening into spikes. The writhing mass of spikes and white-hot metal shifted with a groan. Then the statue began to walk.

Dara rolled out of the way, directing its lurching, ungainly steps with the Fire like a hand inside a puppet. She had no idea what she was doing, acting on instinct and desperation. The iron spikes flailed dangerously close to Vine, but she simply danced out of the way, getting in a quick jab to the wrist of one of the mercenaries as she went. The man was too busy staring at the moving statue to notice.

In fact, all the mercenaries were staring at the statue as if it were a devil made flesh.

"Now!" Dara gasped.

Vine grabbed Rid—who was gaping as much as the mercenaries—and took off running across the street. None of Wick's men raised a hand to stop her.

Dara closed her eyes for a moment, Working the hunk of iron so that it was no longer quite so supple. She solidified it as she'd done with the bars of her cage back in King Atrin's dungeon. Then she used the last bits of Fire to make it spin.

The statue dropped off the platform and whirled, moving

Dance of Steel

toward the men who'd been fighting Vine and Rid. The men shrieked and leapt out of the way as the spikes of iron sliced the air like a hundred razor blades. Dara stared after it for an instant, shocked that it was actually spinning. She'd practiced Working Fireblossoms on their journey, and she used the same principle to spin a knot of Fire and shove it into the iron figure with a prayer. And it was working!

She jumped off the platform and ran after Vine and Rid. She didn't know how long the thing would spin, but she wasn't taking any chances. She couldn't see her companions anymore. The Fork was a wild jumble of gaping onlookers, fretting horses, and carriages. Where were they?

Something thudded into Dara's shoulder, and she stumbled. The small ivory hilt of a knife stuck out of the back of her shoulder. She chanced a look back. Lord Vex hadn't been distracted for long. He had slowed to throw the knife, but now he ran toward her at full speed. Dara yanked the knife from her shoulder. It would have to do for a weapon. She planted her feet in her dueling stance. Vex was almost upon her, sword in hand. Maybe she could hold him off while Vine and Rid escaped.

Suddenly a huge shape shot in between Vex and Dara, sending up a cloud of dust. A black carriage drawn by two wild-looking horses pulled between them and skidded to a halt. Before Dara could move, the carriage doors opened, and Vine's face appeared.

"Quickly, Dara!" she said.

Dara didn't stop to wonder where the carriage came from. She dove inside, and the door shut behind her, plunging her into darkness.

The carriage took off with a lurch, jostling and bouncing her on the floor. She rolled into a pair of boots with sharp steel toes then rolled the other way and found herself looking up at Rid's knobby knees. The butt of his staff rested on the wooden floor by her head.

"Oh, we've left such a mess." Vine sounded delighted. The carriage bounced around too much for Dara to get up, but she could see her friend peering out the window, calmly watching the commotion in the fork as they sped away.

"Where's Rumy?" Dara said.

"He's riding on the roof," said an unfamiliar voice. "He refused to join us until you were safely inside. Not that I'd have left you behind after that brilliant display."

Dara finally managed to sit up and look at the owner of the voice —and the wearer of the steel-toed boots. It was a stately woman wearing a full skirt that just covered her knees. She had an olive-skinned, animated face, and her hair was white as snow.

"Who are you?" Dara asked.

"I'd very much like to ask you the same question," the woman said. "I haven't seen a Firework like that in decades. Where did you learn to do that?"

"I've never done that before," Dara said. "It just seemed like a good idea."

"Magnificent."

"This kind woman offered us refuge in her carriage," Vine said. "I daresay she saved our lives."

"My pleasure." The woman was still staring at Dara as though she were some kind of exotic creature. A very valuable one.

"You're bleeding, Dara," Rid said. "Oh, you're bleeding real badly."

"I don't think it's too deep," Dara said. She scrambled onto the carriage seat beside the strange woman and across from Vine. Rid's face had gone a little pale, and Dara glanced down at her arm. Okay, maybe the knife wound was deep after all. Now that she was looking at it, the pain hit her hard. It was like being stabbed all over again. A patch of blood spread down her sleeve.

"Let me," the strange woman said. She reached for Dara's arm. The deep-olive skin on her hands was wrinkled, but her grip was firm as she peeled off Dara's coat to get a better look at where Vex's knife had struck her. Blood seeped steadily from the wound, darkening her blouse.

Suddenly the woman's fingers went as cold as ice, and water oozed from her fingertips into the stab wound. Or at least, the substance was like water. More blood welled up for a moment as silvery liquid rushed through the cut. A second later it stopped bleeding altogether. The neat incision pulled together, and the silver substance filmed over it like a wax seal. It still hurt, but much less than it had before.

Vine leaned forward with a sharp intake of breath and examined the wound.

"Oh, that was beautifully done," she said.

"You're a Waterworker?" Dara asked, looking up into the woman's luminous brown eyes.

"I prefer the term 'Watermight Artist,'" the woman said. "But yes. My name is Wyla."

"Why did you help us?" Dara asked.

"It's not often I get to meet a Firewielder," she said. "I thought you might like to chat for a little while."

"You took an awfully big risk for a chat," Dara said. "Lord Vex has a dozen armed men with him."

"I have a rather competent bodyguard myself," Wyla said. "But that's why we're moving in such a hurry. I can, of course, drop you off somewhere when we are a safe distance away."

"We are traveling to Pendark," Vine said. "I don't suppose you could take us part of the way there?"

"Yes," the woman said with a smile. "In fact, I can get you all the way there. Pendark is my home."

"If it isn't too much trouble," Dara said slowly.

"Not at all." Wyla leaned out of the window on her side of the carriage and rapped on it. "Change of plans, Siln. Take us straight home."

"Yes, my lady."

"Pendark?" Dara asked Vine in a low voice.

"If he's with a group of pen fighters, it seems the best option," she said. "I Sensed hints of him in the fork, but I couldn't determine which way he went from here. The Air is too muddled in these parts."

Dara frowned. "Lord Vex will guess he's going to Pendark too." She imagined Vex and his dozen fighting men thundering down the road, getting closer and closer to an unsuspecting Siv.

"We'll just have to get there first," Vine said. She ran her fingers through her dark hair and settled in as if she owned the elegant carriage. She hardly looked like a woman who'd been wielding a sword a moment earlier—or one who'd spent the past three days as a captive.

Rid looked considerably less at ease in their new surroundings.

He stared at the sleek canvas walls and the discreet lantern as if they were made of gold.

"Where did you come from?" Dara asked him. "I thought you sold us to Lord Vex."

"Sold you?" Rid looked genuinely hurt. "Of course not. That soldier let me through the barrier back in Tollan. Sunders. Decent fellow. Rumy and me have been behind you the whole journey. Kurn Pass was darn spooky, but we made it through all right."

"I'm sorry I doubted you," Dara said.

"It's all right." Rid glanced around the carriage and grinned. "This is a lot better than walking to Pendark, don't you think?"

"I guess it is." Dara studied the mysterious Waterworker's profile. Wyla's hands were folded on her knees, and she looked harmless enough. Dara couldn't guess how old she was. Energy seemed to emanate from her, but her white hair and the thin pattern of wrinkles around her lips and eyes suggested she was older than she seemed.

"How far is it to Pendark?" Dara asked.

"A mere three days by carriage. Where are you staying in the great city?"

"We'll take rooms in an inn," Dara said. She wondered if they even had any coins left after their time in captivity. Vine had always carried their purse—indeed, they had mostly been using Vine's money throughout their travels—but Mertin seemed like the type to relieve her of it in short order, whether Lord Vex approved or not. Dara couldn't quite believe they had escaped. That had been very close.

"You must stay with me, then," Wyla said.

"We don't want to impose," Vine said.

"Nonsense. I have plenty of room in my manor," Wyla said. "I insist." She looked over at Dara and smiled. There was something predatory in her eyes. Dara had a feeling she'd been planning on having them stay with her from the moment they entered her carriage. She hoped they hadn't exchanged one kind of captivity for another.

34

THE PLAN

SORA sat on the floor of Selivia's bedroom amidst a pile of cats. A litter of kittens had been born in the kitchens that summer, and Selivia hadn't made good on her promise to their mother to find them homes before leaving for Trure. Now the cats had taken over the absent princess's bedroom. Selivia would be delighted when she returned.

If she returns. Sora frowned and trailed an old scarf across the floor for the cats to chase. News had reached Vertigon that the Truren cavalry had engaged the advancing Soolen army—and lost. The siege of Rallion City was imminent. She'd heard nothing of her mother and sister. Sora hoped they'd get out of the city before the Soolens arrived. Captain Brach would never let them walk free if his assault succeeded, and she worried the Lantern Maker would have something more sinister in mind for them.

She didn't know when he planned to move against the Soolen army. His next step hinged on the completion of the mysterious Work beneath the Fire Warden's greathouse. Her alliance with Daz Stoneburner and the Square Workers might be her only chance to delay his aggressions. Hopefully, they could stop him before he unleashed his power on the Lands Below.

A rustle of feathers and a squawk drew her attention away from the cats. Lima had moved Selivia's pet furlingbird here. It used to live in a parlor in a lower level of the castle, but the Lantern Maker's wife had taken over the room for her own use, and she hated the chattering noise it made at all hours. At least it wasn't a thunderbird.

Sora knew the servants had discreetly continued to feed the rest of Selivia's pets for her. She hoped Lima never discovered the greckleflush that lived in the dungeon. Selivia thought it was adorable, but she was the only one. It wasn't nearly as useful as the cur-dragons, who still carried on their usual tasks of melting snow from pathways and delivering messages. Sora had heard that they were less cooperative for the Ruminors than they used to be for her family, though. They acted oddly restless, spewing more flame than necessary and constantly pulling at their leads. Good for them.

Rafe had been busy with his project, and Sora hadn't seen much of Lima lately either. She had mostly been confined to her room or the library since Kel stopped the Lantern Maker's wife from hurting her. Lima must sense she had lost her power to terrorize Sora into submission, and she refused to risk any outings or audiences lest Sora defy her in front of the Fireworkers. Sora rarely saw her Castle Guard friends anymore because she didn't need Vertigonian escorts. And Kel was surely being watched after his intervention, so he wasn't assigned to her inside the castle anymore either. She'd been enjoying the company of Captain Thrashe and Lieutenant Benzen too often of late.

But today, her friends had finally managed to coordinate a meeting without drawing the attention of their commanding officers. The door opened, startling the furlingbird, and the three men she'd been waiting for sauntered into the chamber. Oat, Yuri, and Kel could still move freely as Castle Guards, even though they weren't allowed to take her outside the castle. Sora's heart swelled at the sight of their faces, and she leapt to her feet. She had missed them.

"Hello, my queen," Oat said, giving the chamber a quick scan. "Are we all clear?"

"Yes. The Lantern Maker has a meeting with Master Corren, and his wife is entertaining Lady Zurren."

Lima hadn't bothered to invite Sora to that particular tea. Lady Zurren's social position had improved greatly since ingratiating herself with Lima. She didn't even pretend to be the young queen's friend anymore.

"That's a lot of cats, my queen," Yuri said. He crossed the chamber and picked up one of the creatures. It swatted at his red beard with a white-tipped paw.

"You can have one if you like," Sora said. "My sister doesn't need this many."

"It's all right." Yuri chuckled as the cat crawled beneath his beard and started to purr. "I'm sure it's having more fun here than it would out in the barracks."

A ginger cat latched onto Oat's boot. Two others chased each other over the brightly colored cushions on Selivia's couch and around the guards' ankles.

"I went to Daz's forge to order some new dueling rapiers," Oat said, delicately detaching himself from the ginger cat. "He spoke with the last of the Square Workers. They will help stop Master Ruminor's secret Work."

"Good. With the news from Trure, I don't want to delay," Sora said. She didn't add that Lima's recent habit of excluding her from meetings meant her days had to be numbered as well. She picked up another cat and cradled it in her arms. "How soon can they move?"

"Daz says they won't know what they're dealing with until they see it."

"This might help." Sora shifted the cat to her shoulder and pulled out the old journal the Lantern Maker had been studying. She'd liberated it from the library yesterday, hiding it in her skirts when Rafe wasn't looking.

"You're becoming a pickpocket?" Kel said. "Nice one."

Sora blushed with pride. She'd overheard Rafe asking Lima if she'd seen the journal, but she didn't think he suspected her. Her unassuming presence had its advantages at times.

"Did you see Berg too?" Sora asked Oat.

"I'm going there tonight," Oat said. "Daz wants some non-Worker backup in case they run into guards or something inside the Fire Warden's greathouse."

"That's a good idea. And the army?"

"Jale says they're still focused on recruiting," Yuri said. "Half the young duelists on the mountain have enlisted. At this rate there won't be any competitors left come the start of the season."

"More trophies for us," Kel said.

"Do you think there will even be a season if we go to war?" Sora asked.

Kel winced. "Let's hope we never get that far. I'd hate to disappoint the fans."

"As long as they can see you, I don't reckon they care whether you're actually dueling or not," Oat said.

Kel shoved him lightly and sighed. "True. True. There are advantages to being this handsome."

"Have any of you seen Lady Atria lately?" Sora asked, not wanting to get off track.

"I spent a nice long time in her parlor last night," Kel said. "I don't want to alarm you, but she has been entertaining a high percentage of Ruminor supporters lately."

Sora frowned. "Is she trying to get information?"

"Maybe," Kel said. "But you have to understand that she's addicted to influence. She has always cultivated ties with the most powerful people in Vertigon regardless of their politics. The Fireworkers grow more powerful by the day. I'm not saying she'll betray you, but we need to watch out for her."

"Maybe we shouldn't use her parlor when we make our move," Oat said.

"It's in the perfect spot, though," Yuri said. "We won't find a better place to hide on that street."

"I think we're safe to wait in the parlor while we keep an eye on the Workers," Kel said. "Just don't be surprised if Lady Atria pretends not to know us if things go poorly."

"Understood," Sora said.

Oat scratched his chin, where a shadow of a beard roughened his jaw. "It's up to Stoneburner now. Let's hope he learns something from this stolen book of yours."

"I reckon that just might save us," Kel said.

Sora smiled. She felt vindicated for not taking advantage of the rescue attempt earlier that winter. She could never have stolen the journal or found out Rafe was working on something dangerous if she had fled the castle. She hoped the others were starting to see the wisdom of her decision.

"We need to move quickly," she said. "The Lantern Maker is building a weapon and an army. I'm pretty sure both those things are easier to fight when they're still in progress." Sora could almost admire the Lantern Maker for his tenacity. He was making the move from usurper to aspiring conqueror with remarkable speed. She wondered how long he'd been planning all this. She understood he had originally sought revenge for the long-ago death of his first daughter. But that had ceased to be his primary aim.

The furlingbird gave a squawk, pulling Sora's attention to the sun slanting sharply through the three tall windows. She'd be expected for dinner soon, and the Guards shouldn't linger either.

"Is there anything else we need to discuss?" she asked.

"The Workers are still causing problems, my queen," Yuri said. "I broke up a fight the other day between one of the weaker Workers and a tavern keeper. The Worker can't get enough Fire for production anymore, but he said the tavern keeper should give him free ale on account of his status. That didn't go over well."

"I've heard about fights too," Oat said. "It's not always the non-Workers starting them either. The Fireworkers like to show off."

"Is the Lantern Maker doing anything about it?" Sora asked. That wasn't on the list of things he discussed with her during their hours in the library.

"The army patrols the rougher streets at night," Yuri said. "Not sure that helps things, though."

"The sooner we can restore the balance, the better," Sora said.

"I agree," Oat said. "I miss the old Vertigon."

Sora missed it too. The Peace had been special. She hoped their plans with Daz and his friends would help them bring it back soon.

Yuri put the cat down, gave it a final scratch, and said, "We'd better go our separate ways before Captain Thrashe notices we're in here."

"Does he suspect anything?" Sora asked.

"He's had his eye on us from the beginning as original members of the New Guard," Oat said with a shrug. "He doesn't trust us anyway, so I'm not too worried. With all due respect, they seem to think you're not a threat, Your Majesty."

"That's fair enough." Sora grinned. "I'm only a little girl, after all."

"That's right," Yuri said. "And you're a girl we're damned proud to serve!"

"Hear! Hear!" Oat said.

Sora stood a little straighter, despite the cat in her arms choosing that moment to latch onto a curl of her hair. "I can't tell you how much it means to have you all looking out for me."

"It is a pleasure, my queen."

"And an honor!"

"Let's not be too sappy," Kel said. "You two are getting as bad as Telvin Jale. Let's hit the practice hall before dinnertime."

"We'll let you know as soon as Daz gives us a date for the big move, my queen," Oat said. "We'll ask him to hurry."

"Thank you."

Oat and Yuri saluted and sauntered out. Kel hung back a bit and moved closer to her instead of following his friends out the door. The cats still rolled around on the floor, and the furlingbird rustled its feathers irritably, but a sense of quiet descended on the room. Somehow, Sora felt calm in Kel's presence. Safe.

"Your Highness," Kel said. "I wanted to ask if you've had any more problems with Her Giant Horribleness?"

He reached out to scratch the head of the cat purring comfortably against her shoulder. The sensation made her think of lazy afternoons spent with her little sister, playing with the kittens in this very room. She felt years older now. She hoped Selivia had been spared that. She deserved to enjoy her youth while she could.

"Lima has stopped with the physical violence," Sora said, "but she's also not involving me in meetings as much as she used to."

"Is that bad?"

"I get my best information when she puts me in front of people who need to see me acting the queen. She has either decided she doesn't want to risk me speaking out of turn, or she doesn't need me as much anymore. Neither possibility is particularly heartening. I can't have all my information streams drying up."

"I had a hand in that, I'm afraid," Kel said slowly. "We had another small chat after our last encounter."

"What?"

"I may or may not have threatened her within an inch of her evil old hide if she ever touched you again."

A bout of conflicting feelings rushed through Sora. She was grateful Kel was trying to protect her, but it put them both in a more-precarious position. Lima would know he was loyal to her. And if the Ruminors decided they didn't need a figurehead after all, she'd be in even bigger trouble. But something else wasn't right.

"Wait, you threatened Lima Ruminor, and she didn't fire you then and there?"

"Nope." Kel shrugged, as if the prospect of being on the bad side of the second-most-powerful person in the kingdom didn't bother him.

"But why? What's her angle?"

"Not sure. Maybe she's afraid I'll tell people what she has been up to. I gather she's not popular."

"Hmm." Sora didn't think that explanation fit. Lima could be biding her time, planning revenge. That *was* her specialty. "You need to be careful."

"Always am, my queen." Kel grinned and gave the cat one more scratch, his hand brushing Sora's hair as he pulled it back. "Well, I'd better go wipe the floor with my dueling partners." He offered her an elaborate bow and turned for the door.

"Kel!" Sora said before he disappeared.

"Yes, my queen?"

She blushed, feeling shy as he met her eyes.

"Thank you."

"You're welcome, Sora."

And he closed the door behind him.

Sora shook her head, fighting down the army of butterflies cavorting in her stomach. This was *not* the time for that. Kel protected her because he was a decent man, not because he had any interest in her. She had never been under any illusions about her alluring qualities. But she couldn't help looking up at the door a few times as she sat back down on the floor, just in case it should open again.

No, she should focus on the plan. Attacking the core of the Lantern Maker's power was a bold move. But if Rafe was dangerous now, who knew what he could become if he completed his mysterious Work? They had to stop him before the consequences stretched to the edges of the continent. And she knew her own days were numbered, no matter how much Kel tried to protect her. She had to make those days count.

35

STEEL PENTAGON

SIV didn't know where to look as they rode into Pendark. It was especially magnificent after traveling through the Darkwood for days, staring at nothing but bland stretches of leafless trees. The Darkwood wasn't nearly as spooky and mysterious as its name implied. The skeletal trees let through plenty of light at this time of year. Dead leaves crackled underfoot, and unfamiliar creatures sang in the barren branches. It grew warmer as they made their way south, and Siv could hardly believe winter was still in full swing up in Vertigon.

After three monotonous days, they emerged from the Darkwood and descended a gentle slope to the lowlands. As they left the musky smell of dead leaves behind, Siv caught his first good whiff of the salt-tinged coastal air. The great city-state of Pendark spread before them, nestled against the coast of the Black Gulf. Farther out, the Gulf opened into the vast, rolling expanse of the Bell Sea.

Pendark was a swampy land, its only city built around the delta of a muddy, slow-moving river. The border between the Black Gulf and the marshland was hard to distinguish where the delta fanned out around the city's structures. The Waterworkers had spent years directing and redirecting the flows of the delta into canals to carve out their territory. Little islands had been created all over the city, some stretching out into the gulf. Waterworkers controlled the islands, and they fiercely protected their domains. Their king kept a tenuous hold on his own island, his power over the city-by-the-sea little more than ceremonial. The Waterworkers were the true powers in Pendark.

They were also notoriously territorial and violent. Siv had read some dramatic (possibly exaggerated) stories set in the city. Frequent civil wars and skirmishes broke out between the powerful Waterworkers, who constantly tried to expand their domains. All Pendarkans were supposed to be violent, come to the think of it—and fiercely competitive. No wonder the bloody Dance of Steel was the most-popular sport.

The Pendarkans might have destroyed each other long ago if not for the fabulous trade opportunities offered by their seaside location. The chance to earn serious coin outweighed the desire for victory in every contest. Traders sailed from across the Bell Sea and into the welcoming arms of the Black Gulf day and night. Once in Pendark, they hawked their wares to merchants who transported their goods all across the continent.

Soole had sea access too, inspiring more competition between the two lands. But while Pendark fostered trade from across the Bell Sea alone, the Soolen Peninsula also bordered the Ammlen Ocean. The Soolens enjoyed exclusive access to goods from the East Isles. This was the primary source of income for the larger of its two port cities. As much as the Pendarkans resented Soole's supremacy in this area, more than enough ships arrived from the Bell Sea for them to thrive.

Siv had read a lot about Pendark, but the most-elaborate travel accounts were nothing compared to riding into its muddy streets for the first time. Colorful flags waved from every rooftop, representing whichever Waterworker currently held sway in that area. The salt-air smell mixed with the fetid aromas of mud and moss. Hawkers shouted at them from all sides, offering exquisite carvings, rare seafood, and lucrative trade deals. Women waved from houses on stilts, advertising their own kind of wares. A large percentage of the buildings in the city perched on stilts. Some had stables on the ground beneath them, while others were built directly over the mud-brown river, complete with docks for canal boats underneath. Floods threatened the city several times a year, and the Pendarkans had gotten tired of rebuilding their homes. The Gulf actually protected the city from the worst of the storms on the Bell Sea, but the warring Waterworkers were storm enough.

The road from the Darkwood extended all the way through the city to the Black Gulf. They would have to cross several bridges from island to island to reach the true coast. Siv could hardly wait to dip his feet in the sea for the first time. Kres had a different destination in mind for them, though.

"Let's stop to watch a solo match or two," he said, heeling his horse in between Siv and Latch, who had been too occupied by the sights to notice they were riding side by side. "No sense in wondering what the Pentagon is like so much that you lose your nerve when it's your turn to do battle."

"We've both fought to the death before," Latch said.

"Yeah, it'll probably be easier than our average afternoons have been lately," Siv said. "I'm not nervous."

He liked the idea of stopping by a match, though. He did want to see what a Steel Pentagon looked like before he fought in one. Their first Dance of Steel was scheduled for the very next day. He wiped his palms on his trousers, no doubt damp from the swampy air. He *definitely* wasn't nervous.

Kres chuckled and led the way to a small dock where they could tie up their horses for a price. A scrawny old man took their coins and handed Kres a pair of oars that had seen better days. The team loaded into a rickety, flat-bottomed boat and rowed across the murky river to a small island. Kres explained that a few of the islands in the city of Pendark had been set aside for use as Steel Pentagons, often after the warring of the Waterworkers had rendered them useless for other purposes—or not worth fighting over.

They scrambled out onto the soft earth as a horrible scream filled the air. Shouts and jeers followed. Siv and Latch exchanged wide-eyed glances as they approached the fighting ground.

He had imagined halls, like the vast King's Arena where the biggest dueling tournaments in Vertigon took place. But the Steel Pentagons were open-air spaces no more than fifty paces across. The one in the center of this island was on the smaller side, perhaps twenty paces across, with a few barrels and logs scattered across it to form obstacles. Spectators pressed in around the five sides of a wooden barrier, making bets and cheering for their favorites. The rough-looking men drummed on the railing or propped their elbows on it, eating shriveled squids on sticks. The smell of blood and sweat mixed with the fusty aroma of swampy water and mud. The Dance was a muggy, intimate sport—both for the spectators and the competitors.

Fiz elbowed through the crowd, using his bulk to secure a spot for them near the Pentagon. Siv's blood pounded in his ears as he squeezed between a pair of grimy spectators to get a better look. The press and the shouts and the stink heightened his excitement. At last he was going to find out what the fuss was all about.

The first thing he saw was a man being dragged out of the arena. In two pieces. Siv had killed a few men by now, but this? This was new.

The victor strutted back and forth across the bare ground, holding aloft a broadsword edged with blood. He was as big as Fiz, but where Fiz was a cuddly blond bear, this fellow was pure monster. He shouted his own praise so loud the veins bulged in his thick neck. Drops from a cut on his muscular arm left red pools in his muddy footprints as he stomped across the Pentagon, gloating over his victory.

The crowds hollered, hoarse and vicious. Some called for the fellow to cut his defeated opponent into even tinier pieces. Siv had known his fair share of rabid sporting fans, but these Pendarkans were a whole new breed.

A scrawny man wearing a mud-spattered tunic hurried to the center of the Pentagon and hollered, "That's the third victory this week for Hadrachia the Hammer! Let's hear it, friends!"

The crowds roared as Hadrachia accepted a coin purse from the scrawny man and hauled himself over the edge of the wooden barrier to exit the Pentagon. His fans instantly closed in on him, so only his clean-shaven head was visible above the throng.

"Now then," called the scrawny announcer. "Who's next?"

"I will fight!" shouted a short, powerfully built man from across the arena.

"Well, if it isn't the Murderer of Mud Island!" called the announcer. "Do we have a challenger?"

"The matches aren't set in advance?" Siv asked Kres, leaning in close so he could be heard over the hollers of the crowd.

"Not at a gutter fight like this," Kres said. He had the wild glint in his eyes that Siv had come to recognize as a frenzy bordering on bloodlust. He should remember that Kres was Pendarkan. He shared the insane competitiveness for which the land was famous.

"We have a set match tomorrow as part of the league," Gull added. "These bruisers fight for prize purses wherever they can."

"Now, shut up and watch," Kres said. "Plenty of the gutter fighters compete with us in the league. You'll learn a thing or two."

Siv pressed up against the barrier as the Murderer of Mud Island fought a taller Soolen fellow who had answered his challenge. The latter attracted jeers from the crowd as he advanced to the center of the pentagon and drew a saber. Soole wasn't growing any more popular as the news of the invasion spread. The Soolen fighter ignored the insults as he raised his blade.

"All ready!" the announcer called. "Let us dance!"

With a savage cry, the Murderer of Mud Island launched himself forward, his saber a whirlwind of steel. The Soolen challenger stumbled over a log obstacle as he danced back. The crowds roared for blood. He managed to find his feet, though, and met the Murderer stroke for stroke.

"These guys are fast," Siv said.

"You haven't seen anything yet, lad," Kres said.

"I fought the Mud Island Murderer back in my saber days," Fiz said. "He's vicious in the pen, but he's not a bad fellow to have a drink with afterwards."

"If you live until then," Latch muttered.

Despite the Murderer's impressive speed, the Soolen fighter clinched the victory. Unlike the previous combatant, he didn't kill his opponent. He executed a brilliant feint and ended the fight with his blade against his opponent's neck. The jeers turned to adoration in an instant.

"We have a new victor!" the announcer called. "Let's hear it for the Rockeater of Soole!"

The crowds roared, all animosity toward the Soolen fighter forgotten. Siv glanced at Latch, but he didn't seem particularly interested in the success of his countryman. If anything, he looked a little green.

"Mud Island might need to get itself a new murderer," the

announcer said with a chuckle. "Now, who's next?"

Two fighters called out their intentions to fight at the same time, and there was a brief, intense struggle between them over who had the right of way. One fighter knocked the other cold with his fist before they even made it into the pentagon. The fist-happy fellow sauntered to the middle, strutting as though he'd already scored an official victory. Too bad he'd miss out on a prize purse for that move.

The fellow was whip-thin, with bulging eyes and long hair hanging lankly around his sharp-bladed shoulders. His weapon of choice was a long-handled knife with a curved blade.

"Looks like the Pendarkan Panviper is back for more," shouted the announcer. "Who will challenge him?"

"I know who I want to fight today," the Panviper said. "I seen just the man in the crowd."

"Have some kind of personal grudge, eh? All right, then. Who is it?"

"Today I challenge The Master, Krestian March!" The Panviper whipped his knife around and pointed it at his chosen opponent. He smirked. "Guess he's back from his winter vacation."

"Kres March?" The name spread quickly through the crowd, and all heads turned toward Siv's companions. Soon Gull and Fiz's names were being repeated back through the crowd too, the voices eager and admiring. So the team had a reputation.

"Can't the bastard give me a chance to rest my boots before another damn challenge?" Kres muttered.

"Well?" the announcer approached them on the other side of the wooden barrier. "Do you accept the challenge, Master March?"

"No, I do not," Kres said. "I just arrived. The Panviper can cool his blood."

"You refuse to fight? I name you a coward!" the Panviper shouted, his face going purple.

"That's hardly the first time you've done that," Kres said. "Words, words. Nothing more."

"Are you turning down the Dance?" the announcer asked.

"Can't you just teach him a quick lesson," Gull said, fingering the hilt of her blade. "The fool deserves it."

Kres sighed in a manner that suggested the whole charade was calculated. "I daresay he does. Very well." Kres raised his voice and addressed the Panviper and the announcer. "I accept the challenge on behalf of the newest member of my squad. The boy's a bit green, but I can't be bothered to fight the Panviper again. Meet Siv the Slicer."

Then, to Siv's utter surprise, Kres grabbed him by the collar and heaved him over the barrier. Siv barely managed to get his feet under him before he hit the mud. When he regained his footing, he stood inside the Steel Pentagon.

"Uhh, Kres?" Fiz said.

"What? Nothing like a quick gutter match to rid the boy of first-Dance jitters," Kres said. "Don't forget to draw your knife, lad."

Siv stared numbly as the scrawny announcer approached him. The shouts of the crowd crashed around him like thunder.

"Welcome to the Steel Pentagon, Siv the Slicer!" the announcer cried, grabbing him by the arm and yanking him toward the center of the fighting ground. Siv had to step nimbly to avoid the obstacles in the mud. His brain hadn't quite caught up with what was happening yet. "That's a fine scar there. This fellow has seen a fight or two, folks!"

"If he got cut up, he can't be particularly good," said the Panviper.

Guffaws spread through the crowd. Siv didn't bother to point out that the Panviper had three times as many scars as he did. He was too busy fighting down the nerves that had finally barreled into him with the force of a charging cullmoran. This was not how he had expected the day to go at all.

"Fine," the Panviper sneered. "I will fight you, but know that you stand for Kres March's honor this day. And I shall destroy you!"

Siv glanced back at the squad. It would be a shame to damage their reputation by falling in his first fight. Latch looked distinctly relieved that he hadn't been sent into the pen as the second-newest member of the team. Fiz gripped the wooden barrier so hard it might crack, and Gull was chewing her lip, making it go white. Only Kres didn't seem nervous. He watched Siv face down his first pen fight without emotion or any particular signs of distress. Maybe he should take it as a compliment that Kres wasn't afraid Siv would lose to the Panviper. That, or Kres didn't care whether he lived or died.

Well, damned if Siv was going to lose his first true competition match. He'd never be able to face Dara again.

He turned back to the Panviper, drawing his knife and hefting it—mostly without shaking. He crouched into his guard stance, and before he could so much as take a breath, the announcer shouted, "All ready. Let us dance!"

The Panviper struck fast, as if he were—well, a panviper. Siv leapt out of his reach. An instant later his boots slipped out from under him, and he sprawled in the mud, banging his head on a nearby barrel. Stars burst across his vision. The crowd roared with laughter.

The Panviper laughed too and strutted back and forth in front of Siv, flinging his lank hair around his shoulders.

"This is your champion, Kres?" he crowed. "Siv the Slicer? More like Siv the Slider! He's as green as—"

Siv didn't hear whatever choice comparison the Panviper had prepared for him. Not bothering to stand up, he kicked out with both feet and knocked the Panviper's legs out from under him. Before the man could rise, Siv scrambled on top of him and put his knife to his throat.

"I win," he said.

The crowds roared, as much laughter as cheering in the din. That had been fast. Siv's hand still vibrated as a rush of nerves and adrenaline tore through his body. And the sweet jolt of victory.

"Danged guttersquid," the Panviper spat, not moving an inch. His rancid breath huffed in Siv's face. Siv couldn't help grinning as he eased the pressure on his knife.

"Looks like we have a victor!" the announcer called, sounding a bit surprised about how quickly it was over. "Siv the Slicer, folks! And Kres March's reputation lives another day."

The announcer patted Siv on the back as he rose to his feet. "Not bad there," he said in a much quieter voice. "Mind you, the Panviper is a terrible fighter, but I've seen worse debuts." He shoved a small bag of coins into Siv's hand. "Welcome to the pen."

"Uh, thanks," Siv said.

He returned to his team on unsteady feet.

"You made it!" Fiz shouted, slapping him on the back as he scrambled back over the wooden barrier. "I was nervous there for a minute."

"I wasn't," Gull said. "No way he was going to lose to the Panviper." Despite her bravado, Gull squeezed his arm tight, her hand coming away muddy.

Latch nodded at him with what could only be described as the most-grudging respect in the world. Siv grinned right back. They were going to be friends yet.

"Not bad, lad," Kres said. "Now, it's high time we got back to headquarters."

"Doesn't Latch have to fight too?" Siv asked. "What if he gets nervous tomorrow?"

Latch gave him a flat look, all signs that he was happy Siv hadn't died vanishing in an instant. *Two steps forward, one step back.*

"Latch will be fine," Kres said. "He's not fighting tomorrow."

"Wait, what?" Latch turned his surly glare on a new target.

"Sorry, my boy. With hired men hunting you, we can't very well put you in the Pentagon in front of hundreds who'd sell out their own mothers for coin, now can we?"

"But—"

"Have no fear. I'll call in a favor with another swordsman. We'll have our five for the Dance."

"But I—"

"This isn't up for discussion," Kres said. And he pushed away through the crowd without another word.

Latch stared after him, his mouth open. Fiz and Gull looked less surprised—or they hid it better. Siv tried to say something comforting, but Latch shot him a death glare and stalked after Kres.

At least Siv could now be sure Kres didn't know who he was after all. If he didn't want to put Commander Brach's son in front of crowds who might recognize him, he'd never allow the former King of Vertigon into the Steel Pentagon. Siv figured chances were pretty slim that someone in the raucous crowd would recognize him. With his new beard and scars, his own mother would have to look twice to be sure it was him.

But he would make sure the people knew him by a different name. Siv the Slicer. Maybe the Panviper wasn't much of an opponent, but he'd finally had a taste of victory—and he liked it.

"So, where's headquarters?" he asked the others. "I could use a bath."

36

THE WATERWORKER

DARA leaned out the window of the Waterworker's carriage, letting the cool wind caress her face. The trees of the Darkwood lined the road on either side like grubby gray sentinels. Watching their identical forms flash past didn't do Dara's stomach much good. She didn't like the rumbling, swaying motion of their current conveyance any better than she liked riding horses.

Vine sat across from her and leaned out too, relying on the wind for information rather than to soothe any motion sickness. She had taken to riding in the grand carriage as though it were the only way she'd ever traveled. Dara had to admire Vine's poise. She handled all these new experiences far better than Dara, who felt as if a bridge had collapsed from under her the moment she left the mountain. She was grasping endlessly for a branch or a root, something to slow her fall and remind her of who she was.

Dara was too used to dealing with certainties—where her hard work produced results. If she trained harder, she'd become a better duelist. If she remained vigilant, Siv would be safe. If she learned the Work, she would one day reconcile with her parents. Those aspirations were gone now, scattered to the wind, and she didn't have Vine's ability to blow where the wind took her.

She hoped her reunion with Siv would ground her once more. If she could rescue him, perhaps he'd help her figure out what to do next. He'd always relied on her. Maybe she needed to rely on him too.

Across from her, Vine closed her eyes, smiling at whatever the Air told her. The farther they got from the confusing muddle of Fork Town, the more certain Vine became that they were traveling in the right direction.

"He passed this spot quite recently," Vine said. "I can still Sense him."

"Are you sure?" Dara asked.

"He's likely no more than five hours ahead of us, if that."

"Five hours?" A low buzz of anticipation began in Dara's stomach. Or maybe that was the motion sickness. They were gaining on him at last. "You can be that specific?"

"Indeed," Vine said. "I think I am becoming more Sensitive the more time I spend communing with the Air on this journey." Vine sat back in her seat, glancing at Wyla, but the woman didn't look up from the knitting needles clacking in her strong fingers. The Waterworker had been unimpressed with Vine's abilities so far. She seemed to consider the work of the Air Sensors to be fairly limited, even mundane.

Dara, on the other hand, continued to fascinate her. Wyla spent their long hours in the carriage questioning Dara about her Fire training and abilities. Dara did her best to indulge her, especially because she'd been so kind as to give them a ride. But she still felt like a morrinvole caught between the claws of a feral cur-dragon when Wyla looked at her.

Dara held back the truth of her parentage, mentioning only that her father was a Fireworker but her training came from another. Once she revealed that her Spark had manifested unusually late, it fascinated Wyla to no end.

"I had an apprentice like you once," she had explained the previous afternoon as they rumbled through the Darkwood. "He first accessed his connection to the Watermight when he was twenty-one years old. His potential was magnificent."

"Was?"

"Alas, he was neither teachable nor patient. He tried to do too much too quickly, and the Might overwhelmed him."

Dara was about to ask more, when Wyla stood and leaned out of the carriage window to speak to Rumy, cooing and chirping at him in a language all her own. Wyla had great affection for the curdragon. Dara trusted Rumy's judgment when it came to strangers, and he had embraced the Waterworker wholeheartedly, making Dara feel silly for being suspicious of her. By the time Wyla pulled her head back into the carriage, Dara had been overcome by yet another bout of motion sickness and hadn't asked what happened to Wyla's former apprentice.

Dara preferred to ride beside Siln the carriage driver/bodyguard on top of the carriage. Having the wind in her face helped with the sickness and took her mind off her throbbing shoulder. Siln was a well-built man in his early forties with intricate tattoos winding around both arms. He was happy to answer her questions about Pendark. He was also a sport-dueling fan—an oddity for a Pendarkan. Discussing strategy and famous duels with him became a welcome respite from talking about the Fire with Wyla.

Wyla offered little information about her own abilities, but the woman piqued Dara's curiosity. She had never met a Watermight wielder before, but she'd heard of their reputations from Zage Lorrid, who had spent years in Pendark in his youth. The main thing Dara remembered from their conversations was that the Waterworkers warred for dominance every few years, throwing the city into turmoil until the strongest magic users drowned all opposition. If Wyla had a fancy carriage and a manor house in the city, she must be powerful. But she asked questions like an academic rather than a great sorceress. On the other hand, Zage had been rather dry and pedantic himself, and he had nearly matched her father for power. He might have won their final confrontation if he hadn't been trying to protect Dara.

Dara shied away from the remembrance. She was far away from the Great Hall in Vertigon, but the memory of what had happened there was as sharp as ever. She had resumed practicing with the Fire on her journey, but she still felt conflicted about it. She craved its intoxicating heat, its power, the feeling of invincibility it aroused in her. But she feared it too. She had seen what it could do, and she had seen how it twisted the father she loved and admired. He had sought more power and abhorred the checks and balances that had been imposed on him for so long. Dara was afraid of what he might be doing now that all the barriers had been torn down, and she was afraid of what would happen if she embraced the Fire the way he did. She wasn't sure she wanted anything to do with her father's magic anymore.

But again, that left the question of who she was now.

The clack of Wyla's knitting needles brought Dara's attention back to the carriage. They were nearing the end of their journey. They should exit the Darkwood soon. If Vine was correct about Siv being here five hours ago, he could be arriving in Pendark at that very moment.

Dara stuck her head back out the window, hoping for a glimpse of Pendark through the barren trees. There was no sign of the city yet, though the road had started to slope downward. She looked back—and saw a cloud of dust rising behind them.

"Riders," she called. "Lots of them."

"Is it Lord Vex?" Vine asked.

"Could be. I can't make out any details yet."

The cloud of dust behind her morphed and curled, taking on shape. Sun glinted on steel. The thunder of hoof beats overpowered the creak of the carriage and their own horses' clamor.

"There are at least a dozen of them," Dara said. "And they're armed."

"Sounds like our friends," Vine said.

Dara concentrated on the company drawing nearer behind them. Yes, the lead rider wore a red coat, and she'd recognize that sandy-blond hair anywhere.

"Rid!" she called, banging on the outside of the carriage to get his attention. The young man was chattering away with Siln on the driver seat up front. "You'd better get in here in case he recognizes you."

"Sure thing," Rid said. He scrambled back toward her on the narrow running board attached to the carriage. He'd become adept at crawling around on the moving conveyance throughout the journey. Still, Dara wished he'd scramble faster. They couldn't be seen.

"Rumy, you too."

The cur-dragon squawked and clambered off the roof to enter the carriage through the opposite side.

Dara sat back while Rid climbed in, almost landing in Vine's lap in the process. That may have been intentional, come to the think of it. Rid continued to worship her, and their temporary separation had only served to heighten his ardor.

The carriage was crowded with the three fugitives, the Waterworker, and the overgrown cur-dragon. Only Wyla didn't look nervous. Her knitting needles continued to clack away as the drumbeat of hooves approached.

No sooner were they all settled in their seats with the curtains drawn than the riders were upon them. A tiny gap in the curtains revealed snippets of the mercenaries, who rode in close, pressing near on either side. Dust bloomed around them. The creak of leather and the smell of horse sweat blew through the window. Dara pressed farther back against her seat, hoping no one would get curious about what hid behind that flimsy, blowing curtain. They didn't know if they'd been seen climbing into Wyla's carriage back in Fork Town.

Indistinct voices rose outside, and Siln called out a greeting. Dara held her breath. They wouldn't dare search a Waterworker's carriage, would they? Hopefully they hadn't noticed the cur-dragon riding atop it a moment ago. Lord Vex wouldn't forget being dive-bombed by Rumy in the fork anytime soon.

Dara was surprised Lord Vex and his mercenaries hadn't overtaken them sooner. Wyla's coach couldn't travel as fast as a dozen mounted riders. Vex must have spent time asking around about the identity of Siv's companions before leaving Fork Town. Dara wished they'd been able to do the same. It would be easier to find him in the vast warren of Pendark if they didn't have to rely on Vine's flighty Air Sense.

The carriage shuddered as the riders surrounded it. She caught a glimpse of the young Vertigonian passing by. Grelling followed close on his heels, Dara's Savven blade still belted at his hip. The sight made her toes curl with anger. She swore she felt a spark of heat from the blade as it passed by, just out of reach.

Dara had dared hope they would beat Vex and his mercenaries to the city. They could warn Siv of these new enemies and spirit him away before Vex's men arrived. There was no chance of that now.

It was taking too long for the riders to pass the carriage. Did they suspect something? Would Wyla be able to fight them off with

Watermight this far from the sea? Dara hadn't seen any more of the silvery substance after Wyla cleaned and sealed her stab wound. Her shoulder still throbbed, though it was healing faster than was natural. She should be able to fight. She gripped the ivory hilt of Lord Vex's knife until her fingers ached.

The last of the mercenaries passed them. The company continued ahead, beating a rapid path toward Pendark. They'd have a head start searching the city after all. Pendark was big, but if Vex had learned the identity of Siv's mysterious companions, he could find them within a few hours. Dara clenched her teeth, ignoring the grit of road dust in her mouth. She couldn't lose him now. Not when she was so close.

"Are they gone?" Rid asked.

"Better wait a few minutes in case they double back," Dara said.

"Sure thing. I don't want that Lord Vex finding me now I switched to your side," Rid said. "He don't strike me as the forgiving type."

"No, he doesn't." Dara knew plenty about the Rollendars' capacity for cruelty and violence. None of what she'd seen during her captivity made her feel any better about Lord Vex. Even without his dozen fighting men, he was a formidable adversary. And he was closing in on Siv.

"Wyla," she said. "Could you use the Watermight to gather information if Vine's Air Sense doesn't cooperate when we reach the city?" She gave her friend an apologetic glance. She didn't want to hurt Vine's feelings, but this was urgent. "Or can you give her power some sort of boost?"

"Hmm, interesting that you ask this," Wyla said. Her knitting needles stilled for the first time all morning. "I do like the prospect of combining the unique powers."

Dara frowned, not quite following. "If you could just help—"

"Some will dispute the wisdom of it," Wyla said. "But I've had different ideas for some time. I'd love to experiment if you're open to the idea."

"What idea?"

"Combining the powers." Wyla leaned forward, an eager light in her eyes. "Fire and Watermight in particular. If a practitioner could harness both, they would have a remarkable edge."

"Wouldn't they cancel each other out?" Dara asked. Her father had taught her that Fire was stronger than Watermight, but she didn't want to insult the Waterworker by saying so. Zage had been less convinced about the Fire's inherent superiority—and he had actually spent time in Pendark.

"Perhaps," Wyla said softly. "But perhaps not. It would be a fascinating area of research."

"I was mostly thinking maybe you could feel him if he's touching water or something," Dara said.

"That may be possible," Wyla said. "But I am interested in bigger experimentation. Perhaps you'd like to help."

"I don't want to get involved in any magical experiments," Dara said. "I just want to find my friend."

"Come now, child," Wyla said, a note of grandmotherly disapproval entering her voice. "I have helped you willingly thus far. You're saying you won't join me in testing out a few theories?"

Wyla sounded pleasant enough, but she put a hand on the door of her carriage as if to emphasize how much they were in her debt.

"No . . ." Dara said slowly, wishing she had some of the political acumen Siv and his sisters were always talking about. She felt as if Wyla had somehow trapped her with this conversation—which Dara had started in the first place. "I can try out some Works with you, but I need to find my friend before Lord Vex does."

"Of course," Wyla said. "After the *tremendous* amount of trouble you've endured to find him, I'm eager to meet him."

Dara exchanged worried glances with Vine, who had been listening carefully to the exchange. Wyla didn't know Siv's true identity. Dara feared what she'd do with that kind of information.

"I'm sure he'd love to meet you too," Dara said at last, smiling with some effort. Siv would be thrilled to meet a powerful Pendarkan sorceress, but then he could be too curious for his own good.

"Good," Wyla said. "I believe my informants will be of more use to you than my Might in this particular matter. I'm glad you brought it up, though." Her knitting needles resumed their clacking. "I had been looking for a delicate way to address the issue of payment."

"Pay-payment."

"For my assistance, of course. I don't offer favors lightly."

Dara should have known this was more than a simple carriage ride, no matter how dismissive Wyla had been when they offered to pay her before. They didn't have a single coin left, and Dara had no idea where they'd get more. Wyla probably wasn't interested in gold, though. Dara had the sudden sensation of the carriage walls closing in on her. She wished for the wide emptiness of a Vertigon bridge over a chasm.

"I wouldn't dream of leaving without repaying you for all you've done for us," she said.

"Excellent." Wyla sat a little straighter in her seat, an unmistakable note of triumph in her voice. "We've been traveling for three days, and I saved three lives. I'll throw in my dear Rumy here for free." Wyla scratched Rumy's head, and the cur-dragon huffed contentedly. *Traitor.* "You will stay with me for three months and assist with me in my research."

"Three months?"

"We shall explore potential collaborations between Watermight and the Fire. That task shouldn't be rushed."

Three months seemed a high price for a three-day ride, but it wasn't as bad as Dara had feared. Time was one of the only things she had to offer—after she saved Siv. It wasn't as if she'd be going back to Vertigon anytime soon, and she doubted anyone would welcome her back in Rallion City after her escape from the palace dungeon. She feared Wyla wouldn't let any of them walk free unless she agreed. It was the least she could do for Vine and Rid after all their help.

"Can we delay this payment until after I find my friend? I don't know how long that will take."

Wyla's mouth tightened. "I dislike waiting."

"Those men will kill him," Dara said. "They're probably searching the city by now. We have to find him immediately."

Wyla sighed. "Very well. You may take as long as you need, but be warned that I am not a patient woman. I will see to it that you uphold our bargain. If the delay becomes too much of an inconvenience, I might add another month, for your friend's life."

"I give you my word," Dara said. "You will have your payment as soon as my friend is safe." She stretched out a hand to shake Wyla's. Vine's eyes widened, and she twitched her head slightly. The warning was clear, but before Dara could pull back, Wyla caught her wrist in an iron grip.

"I accept your word," she said softly. "You will stay with me for three months and assist in my research. You will not leave Pendark in that time. So may it be."

As Wyla said the last words, an icy sensation crept through Dara's hand and up her arm. A thin border of silver appeared beneath Wyla's fingernails. There was no mistaking it. Watermight. Dara's whole arm went numb for an instant, then the sensation faded as quickly as it had begun.

"What did you do?" Dara demanded, snatching her hand back as soon as Wyla released her.

"It is a simple bit of Artistry that will ensure you uphold your end of our agreement," Wyla said. "I haven't gotten as far as I have in this world by taking people at their word. I hope you understand."

Dara rubbed her hand. Her fingers tingled as if a practice blade had struck the nerves in her wrist. "How does it work?"

"If you try to leave Pendark before the agreed-upon three months are over, your sword arm will freeze to the core. This may cause your bones to crack, though I must say I haven't seen it myself. People rarely break their word to me."

Dara clutched the ivory knife hilt to steady her hand, trying not to let Wyla see her alarm. She'd never encountered this kind of Work before. The Fire had been used only to craft practical objects for a century. What were the powers capable of when you ventured beyond simple production?

Vine's face was a mask of unconcern, but Dara knew her well enough to recognize her apprehension about this development. If nothing else, this may dampen Vine's desire to impress the Waterworker. At least Vine could still leave the city if she wished. Dara was the only one implicated in the bargain. The only one Wyla wanted.

She looked at the mysterious Waterworker, wondering what she'd gotten herself into. *I guess I have three months to find out.*

"Now that's taken care of," Wyla said, taking up her knitting needles again, "you may wish to look out the window. We have reached Pendark."

37

FIRE

SORA paced across her tower bedroom, from the window to the Fire Gate to the tapestry-covered wall and back again. She had never moved to the king's chambers in the central tower after being crowned. She normally appreciated the familiar comfort of her neat, orderly space in the midst of everything happening on the mountain. But as she strode back and forth, waiting for news, she hated the room more with each step.

Daz Stoneburner would descend to the Well at midnight to sabotage the Lantern Maker's secret Work. He and a dozen of his trusted Square Peak allies were hiding in Lady Atria's greathouse next door to the Fire Warden's old home until it was time. They still didn't know exactly what form the Work took. They'd have liked more time to prepare, but news had arrived that the siege of Rallion City had begun. They couldn't afford to delay. They would take their stand against the Lantern Maker before his Work was complete—even if it meant going in blind.

Sora leaned on her windowsill to look out over King's Peak. Darkness had fallen over the mountain, but she could just make out the roof of the Fire Warden's greathouse from here. If only she could tell what was going on inside! She'd only been informed of when the operation would take place yesterday morning. Madame Pandan had slipped her a note at a council meeting while pretending to discuss a Metalwork ornament on the council chamber door.

Dance of Steel

Sora had been careful not to hint at her connection with Daz and the Square Workers lest this attempt fail. Sabotaging the secret Work would not remove the Lantern Maker from power, and she still needed to be on the inside to keep tabs on what he was doing. The Square Workers would try to get in and out of the Well before the Lantern Maker was aware. Hopefully he would never find out which Workers were responsible for the interference.

Sora felt frustrated that she couldn't do more to help tonight. Berg and a handful of duelists were guarding the Square Workers' backs while they crept into the Fire Warden's greathouse. Oat and Yuri were watching the Lantern Maker to make sure he and his wife didn't go for a midnight stroll to the Well. Telvin Jale was posted outside Sora's door—along with Captain Thrashe, of course—and Kel lurked outside the greathouse, ready to bring her the news of what had happened.

Until then, Sora couldn't do anything but wait. Wait and pace.

A knock sounded at her door. She froze, her heart leaping straight into her throat.

"My queen?" Telvin poked his head through the door.

"Yes?"

"You have visitors."

"Now?" She widened her eyes significantly, and Telvin gave her a strained look in return. This was not part of the plan.

"Yes, my queen."

"Very well." Captain Thrashe would be right outside the door, so there was nothing more she could say. "Send them in."

Jully Roven entered in a flurry of magenta silk, followed by her friend Maraina in yellow. Telvin offered them each a crisp, military-style bow, making the two girls giggle behind their gloved hands. Each one had a bag slung over her shoulder, and Maraina carried a pale-pink box full of sugared salt cakes under her arm. They darted over to Sora as soon as Telvin closed the door behind him.

"Oh, Sora, it's wonderful to see you," Jully gushed.

"What are you doing here?" Sora asked.

"We told the guards at the front gate that we had planned to stay with you tonight for your birthday, and they let us right in!"

"My birthday?" Sora felt a strange emptiness at the thought. She had completely forgotten what day it was. She had been so focused on the plan for tonight that she hadn't even thought about celebrating. She would turn eighteen when the midnight bell struck.

"We're so sad you're not having a proper royal feast," Jully said. "But we thought we'd surprise you anyway." She skipped over to the couch by the Fire Gate and sat, tucking her feet underneath her.

"Uh . . . this might not be a good night for this."

"Whyever not?" Maraina said. "You only have one eighteenth birthday!"

She sat beside Jully and opened the box of salt cakes, the stiff paper wrapping crinkling softly. Then she dug into her bag and pulled out a dark glass bottle.

"I snuck this from my father's wine cellar," she said. "It comes from across the Bell Sea!"

"I'm sure it does," Sora said. "Thank you for thinking of this, but I'm a little tired tonight."

"But it's your birthday!" Maraina whined.

"I know, but I've been very busy lately."

"Being queen must be so boring," Jully said. "Can't you do something fun for once?"

Sora normally appreciated that her friends didn't treat her differently now that she was queen, but she was beginning to regret that now. These girls could do with some deference. She looked back at the darkened window. Daz and his Workers should be getting into position now. She dearly wished she could see what was going on.

"Staying up late one night can't hurt," Maraina said. "You weren't even sleeping anyway."

Sora forced herself to look away from the window. She wasn't doing any good pacing and staring at a faraway rooftop. She supposed the young noblewomen would give her the perfect cover if things went badly out there. No conspirator in her right mind would have friends over on the same night she had coordinated a sabotage effort. At this point it might be more suspicious to send them away, though. She'd have to play along.

"Okay," she said at last. "You can stay."

"Yes!"

Jully produced a bag of dried soldarberries to go with the wine and cakes, and Sora brought over three goblets from beside the water pitcher and sat, straightening her skirt—Amintelle blue—over her knees. She tried to keep up her end of the conversation as the young ladies chatted and gossiped, but she couldn't help glancing at the window every few minutes.

"You're so quiet today," Jully said. "Are you worried about Sel?"

"What? Oh, yes. But I'm sure she'll be safe in my grandfather's palace."

"My father doesn't think Soole can win the siege," Maraina said. "He thinks they'll give up and go home by summertime."

"I hope so," Sora said.

"Oh, let's not talk about the war," Jully said. "Let's talk about that handsome guard outside the door."

"Ooo, I know!" Maraina gushed. "How can you stand it, Sora? He's so gallant!"

"You mean Telvin Jale? Yes, he's very nice." Sora blushed. She didn't want to let on just how much of a crush she'd had on Telvin Jale when he first joined the Castle Guard. And he was her sworn man, too. Did she still have a crush on him? Despite his straight-backed good looks and his chivalry, he wasn't the young man she found herself thinking of these days. Her gaze strayed to the window again.

"My father hired a few extra bodyguards recently," Jully said, "but they're all old and ugly."

"Why is he hiring more bodyguards?" Sora asked. One was standard for appearance's sake, but most nobles in Vertigon rarely considered a whole company of bodyguards necessary.

"Same reason everyone else is doing it," Jully said around another bite of salt cake. "Vertigon isn't as safe as it used to be. And the army makes him nervous, marching around like they do now."

"What do you mean?"

"Most folks don't go out at night since the army started patrolling the streets to keep the peace. They're always stopping people to ask their business. They say it's by order of the Chief Regent."

"We had to sneak to get here this evening," Maraina added.

"Hmm." Sora had received reports about this, but she didn't know it had gotten that bad. What if someone spotted Kel while he was waiting to bring her news? Fear cut through her, but she pushed it away. Her allies knew the dangers and would be prepared. She was worrying irrationally. She needed to be calm and collected, like a true queen. She trusted her men to look out for themselves. She stopped herself from fidgeting with the folds of her dress. Everything would be fine tonight.

"Did you hear me?"

"What? Sorry, Maraina. I wasn't listening."

"What's his name, then?" Maraina giggled and took another sip from her wine goblet.

Sora blinked. "Whose name?"

"You keep looking wistfully out the window," Maraina said. "Who are you thinking about? You can tell us."

"It's not that," Sora said, a blush creeping into her cheeks.

"You're about to turn eighteen!" Maraina said.

Jully gasped. "That's right! You can choose a king and get married."

"What *else* would you be thinking about tonight?" Maraina said.

"You must have someone in mind." Jully scooted closer to her, eyes bright. She reminded her so much of Selivia sometimes. Sora wished she could spend her birthday with her sister. Selivia would be just as eager to find out whom she was thinking about at night.

"There is someone," Sora said at last. "But he's not a nobleman. He can't be my king."

Jully bounced on her cushion and clapped her hands. "Oh, a forbidden romance!"

"It's not even a romance," Sora said. "He doesn't think of me that way, and I'm too young for him." She had already considered and categorically dismissed the possibility that he might be interested.

"Nonsense," Maraina said. "You're eighteen—and the queen! You could marry Lord Samanar if you wanted."

Maraina dissolved into giggles once more, and even Sora had to laugh at the thought of taking the gruff old man as her king. His former wife would make that awkward if nothing else. She still lived on King's Peak and entertained an assortment of male friends after her salacious liaison with her husband's butler a few years ago. But Sora wasn't prepared to tell her friends whom she'd been thinking about. She was the sensible one in her family. Selivia could sigh about romantic old tales, and Siv could pine after Dara Ruminor, but Sora had always known she would make a politically advantageous match. She certainly couldn't admit to having the tiniest crush on the local dueling heartthrob, even if he *had* shown her unexpected loyalty and kindness. No, she had to be practical.

"Lord Samanar might be a decent candidate," Sora said as lightly as she could manage. "I wonder if it's snowing."

She stood and walked toward the window. She wanted to see what was going on out there, and she didn't want her friends to keep asking about the object of her affections. Her affections were last on her list of priorities—and she always stuck to her lists.

She leaned on the windowsill, expecting to see the same dark shadows cloaking the rooftops. Instead, a glow emanated from lower on King's Peak. It was indistinct at first, but it grew brighter by the second. The illumination changed the shape of the familiar shadows on the peak, and in her confusion Sora couldn't tell where the Fire Warden's greathouse roof was anymore. She realized why a moment later. *It's gone!*

She stifled a gasp and pressed her face against the cold glass. She hadn't heard an explosion, but the roof of the greathouse had been blown—or melted—away. Now Fire was welling up within the building. It rose like water from a spring inside the marble boundaries. Mere seconds after Sora reached the window, the Fire began to spill over the walls. A hint of light spread away from the house, as if Fire was flooding out the front door and pouring down the slope. The glow from the dripping Fire traveled between the greathouses, illuminating the streets farther down the mountainside. Sora clutched the windowsill, her knees suddenly weak. What was happening?

Shouts came from elsewhere in the castle, some confused, some panicked. Others must have noticed the strange light outside. Sora pushed open her window, ignoring the winter chill. A clamor of voices rose in the night, screams and warnings. Every few seconds, she heard a strange sucking, gurgling sound.

The Fire continued to well up from the greathouse. It slipped down the walls, cloaking them in gold. Sora couldn't see the street from here, but she imagined the Fire running down the peak in a molten river. Would it burn through the houses in its path or slip around them like floodwater? Would the people have enough time to flee?

More warning shouts reached her tower window, but she feared they would be too late.

What of Daz and his companions? Had they gotten out of the greathouse in time? Fireworkers were supposed to be immune to the heat, but even they could drown in a flood of Fire. There had been non-Workers inside too: Berg Doban and the fighters he had recruited to watch the Square Workers' backs. *And Kel. Kel was right outside.* Did they have time to run?

"What are you looking at?" Jully asked, joining Sora at the window. She gaped at the sight of the Fire spilling over the walls of the greathouse. "What happened?"

"I don't know," Sora said. Flickers of light across the peak suggested the Fire was overflowing in other places too, though nowhere as bad as at the Warden's greathouse.

Where was all the Fire coming from? The Well was supposed to emit a steady flow, not gush power from every outlet. This was a disaster! There had been a surge of Fire once when Sora was a child, but that had been a problem with the containment system. Rafe had destroyed that system, supposedly to let the Fire run freely. But now weeks' worth of Fire was bubbling forth from the mountain, putting every man, woman, and child in Vertigon in jeopardy.

Sora tried to remain calm. It couldn't be a coincidence that this had happened the night the Square Workers assailed the Well. What had they done?

Suddenly a gurgling noise inside the room caught her attention. Sora whirled around as a torrent of Fire burst from her Fire Gate.

Maraina shrieked and leapt off the couch by the Gate, narrowly avoiding being splashed by the white-hot liquid. The Fire spurted across the floor, burning the carpet and seeping into cracks in the stone. The metal grate melted as the burning golden substance surged through it in far greater amounts than it could handle.

The burst only lasted for a few seconds, but it was long enough to make it feel as hot as summer. The smell of melted metal filled the room.

Telvin rushed through the door, skidding to a stop before his boots touched the Fire on the floor. He had drawn his sword.

"Are you well, my queen?"

Sora's heart raced like a Truren stallion, but she and the other girls were unharmed. The Fire was already slowing to a burble and receding back across the stone floor.

"We're fine. What's going on out there?"

"I don't know," Telvin said. "It's everywhere!"

Sora studied the fiery gold liquid on the floor. It was as if the whole mountain had filled up and erupted from every outlet, including her Fire Gate at its very top. She could only imagine what the pressure had been like farther down the mountain.

"I must go see what's happening out there," she said.

"I'm not sure I can let you do that," Telvin said. He glanced back at the door as his superior officer pushed it open.

Captain Thrashe surveyed Sora and her friends with his single eye. Unsettled by the Fire simmering on the floor, he didn't advance into the room. The Fire was already draining back into the stone like water into dry earth, but Soolens were notoriously wary of the substance. In truth, anyone who couldn't Work tended to be uncomfortable around the Fire. There would be a lot of scared people on the mountain tonight. Sora was one of them, but she couldn't let it show.

"Captain Thrashe," she said, marching past Telvin to face the larger man. "I must go down to the Great Hall."

"I cannot allow it," Captain Thrashe said.

"There must have been surges throughout the castle. I need to be informed about what's going on out there."

"Chief Regent's orders," Thrashe said. His jaw jutted out, but he still didn't enter. They faced each other over the threshold. "You stay in your room at night."

"Fine," Sora said. "Then I want you to send me any Fireworkers currently in the castle. And a messenger. I have work to do."

"I cannot—"

"We are in crisis," Sora said. "Unless you plan to fix whatever has gone wrong with the Fire tonight, you must give me access to people who can."

Before Captain Thrashe could answer, Oat ran up to them, long legs windmilling.

"My queen, the Lantern Maker has gone to investigate." He saluted Captain Thrashe but spoke to Sora right over his head.

There were advantages to being the tallest man on the mountain. "He is leaving the castle right now."

"Thank you. Did he say anything about . . .?" Sora glanced at her companions huddling by the far wall of her room and stopped, trusting Oat would understand what she was asking. Was the Lantern Maker looking particularly triumphant?

"No, my queen. He didn't seem to know what was going on."

"Okay, thank you. I want you to return to the entrance hall to await his return. Let me know as soon as you hear something."

If the Lantern Maker was surprised, he must not have set a trap that would cause this dramatic overflow of Fire. Had the Square Workers done this on purpose? She couldn't imagine how that would help their cause.

"Yes, my queen."

"And send me someone to act as messenger, and a Fireworker to report on the damage."

"Yes, my queen. Captain." Oat leapt to obey, charging off before Captain Thrashe could stop him.

Sora looked up at the one-eyed Soolen, who must have gotten far more than he bargained for when he first allied with Bolden Rollendar and the Lantern Maker. She wondered if he knew that Rafe was planning to double-cross his countrymen.

"I will remain in my room," she said. "But I want to make sure everyone in the castle is safe. You will allow me to send and receive messages in exchange for my cooperation. And order Telvin and his fellow guardsmen to sweep the castle to make sure we aren't facing further threats here."

Captain Thrashe glanced at the Fire glowing on the floor then back at her. She stood firm, not cowering as she once had under his guard. At last he jerked his head in a nod and stepped back to let Telvin follow her orders. As the tap of Telvin's boots faded away, Captain Thrashe saluted, something he had never done for her before, and resumed his post outside the door.

Sora allowed herself a small smile as she turned back to her room.

Maraina and Jully clutched each other's hands, staying as far from the Fire Gate as they could get.

"It'll be okay," Sora said.

"What happened?" Maraina wailed. "Is it the end of the world?"

"No, it's not," Sora said. "But you'd better not go home yet. You're safe here."

"Can Telvin stay and watch out for us?" Jully asked.

"Oh yes," Maraina agreed. "I'd feel much better if he was keeping us company."

"Telvin has work to do," Sora said. "But I'm sure he'll be back." She had to smile at the disappointment on both girls' faces. Their fear hadn't quite overcome their desire to have the handsome guardsman around.

She returned to the window. Fire still oozed over the walls of the greathouse, but with less violence than before. Smoke and light trailed all over the mountain, giving it an eerie aura. The worst of the surge appeared to be over. How much damage had been done tonight? And what of her friends who'd been at the Warden's greathouse? She wished she could run down to see what was happening for herself.

But it was her duty as queen to make sure her people were all right. She may not be able to leave her room, but she would do what she could.

Jully and Maraina finished off the bottle of wine and went to sleep on her bed while she waited for whatever news her messengers and guards could provide and sent them running again with further instructions. She worked to restore order and calm as the hours passed. She made sure no one had been hurt and listened to reports of what had occurred near the various Fire Gates and access points in the castle when they overflowed. If only she could be sure the same was happening in the rest of the city. The Lantern Maker still didn't return.

The Fire gradually drained from the Fire Warden's greathouse. The flood continued down the mountainside, leaving a trail of illumination all the way to Orchard Gorge. As the nighttime mists danced outside her window, Sora wished more than ever that she could leave the castle at will. In the days of peace, no one minded if she and her brother and sister went out into the city. Her brother had taken full advantage of this by patronizing the taverns and parlors all over King's Peak. She'd visited regularly at the noble greathouses, always in the company of her bodyguard, Denn Hurling, whom she still missed terribly. If she'd been royalty in the Lands Below, she never would have enjoyed the freedom of movement she'd had in her childhood. But she was truly a prisoner now—and she couldn't do much for her people from here.

She feared something had happened to Kel and Berg. She had barely begun to get to know the latter. She still hadn't learned what had happened between him and her father to inspire such devotion in the old sword master. If he had been killed, she might never know.

It was hours past midnight when her door opened at last, and Lima and Rafe strode in together. Their faces were grim as iron, and for a moment she feared they'd come to kill her at last. Then Kel slipped into the room behind them.

Sora barely restrained herself from launching across the room to hug him. His hair was sweaty, as if he'd been running, but he looked unharmed. He stayed near the wall, and Sora wasn't sure if Lima and Rafe even realized he had followed them inside.

"We need you," Lima snapped. She wore a cloak pulled hastily over a thick woolen nightgown, and her iron-gray bun hung lower on the nape of her neck than usual.

"Why? What's going on?"

"A crowd is gathering outside our gates," Rafe said. He was fully dressed, and he looked much calmer than Lima. Still, a deep furrow in his prominent forehead hinted at his concern. "The people do not want to hear from a Fireworker right now. You must reassure them everything is under control."

Sora almost laughed. "Is it? That didn't look like a controlled burst of Fire to me."

"Don't take that tone," Lima said. Kel took a few steps closer to her, managing to look menacing despite his slight stature. Lima jumped, finally noticing his presence, and something like fear crossed her face. Kel only grinned at her. Rafe didn't seem to notice the exchange, but Lima cleared her throat and modified her own tone. "The danger is over."

"What happened out there?" Sora said. "I need to know if I'm to reassure people."

"Sabotage," Rafe said. "A group of Workers tampered with a project I've been working on for some time."

"What project?"

"It doesn't matter now. They've destroyed a very delicate balance I worked hard to maintain," Rafe said. He strode to Sora's window. The light playing off the mists created an ominous silhouette around his tall, broad form. "I can only hope we won't see additional repercussions. This surge had incredible power. It could set off a chain reaction at the Spring."

"The Spring?"

Rafe waved a distracted hand. "Where the Fire comes from, child."

"I thought it came from the Well."

"Before it reaches the Well, the Fire flows underground from an ancient spring deep in the Burnt Mountains." He fell quiet for a moment. "The Well has provided for us, and we haven't tampered with it for centuries. But it could give more."

"More Fire?" Sora asked.

"More power." Rafe turned from the window, his face dark against the glow. "I attempted to draw more Fire to the mountain. My project was designed to increase the volume of the Well and enable us to enact truly magnificent Works unlike anything the continent has ever seen. The surge tonight was a taste. A glorious one at that." Rafe's voice took on a dreamy quality, and Sora understood he was no longer speaking to her. "There are still risks, but now that we've seen the potential..."

"Rafe," Lima said. "Even you have said the limits need to be respected."

"Limits, yes." He let out a dark laugh. "There are always limits." He stepped toward his wife, feverish intensity on his face. Sora didn't dare move. He already controlled a vast amount of Fire. How much more could he want?

"You saw it, Lima," Rafe said. "This surge was a fraction of the true power we could tap if we are willing to do what's necessary. The accident tonight only confirms my theory. I wasn't certain before, but now that the dam is broken..."

"This hardly needs to be discussed in front of the child," Lima said. She had begun to play with the edges of her cloak, an unusually nervous gesture for her.

"So you want to pull more Fire from the Spring?" Sora asked

quickly. She couldn't miss her chance to learn more. She needed Rafe to keep talking. "Then what will you—?"

"There are things at the Spring that shouldn't be awoken," Lima said.

"Like what?"

"This doesn't concern you," Lima said. "Get your cloak. You must address the people before they knock down the gates."

Sora didn't argue. She grabbed her cloak, pulling the inner door to her bedroom closed before the Ruminors noticed her birthday visitors. A chill crept through her at the pensive expression on the Lantern Maker's face as he looked out the window once more. The glow from the Fire trailing over the mountain gave it a ghostly quality. She was afraid the events of tonight had awoken something much worse in Rafe than whatever prompted him to tamper with the Well in the first place.

But what terrible power lurked in the wild reaches of the Burnt Mountains? What could make even the formidable Lima Ruminor nervous? Sora had thought Lima would go to any lengths to achieve her goals, but even *she* thought the Lantern Maker had surpassed the bounds of wisdom. Was there any way to stop him?

38

THE BLUE HOUSE

HEADQUARTERS—as Kres had described it—turned out to be a large blue house on stilts in the fish-curing district. Located only a few hundred yards from one of the biggest fish smokehouses in the city, the house had been remarkably cheap for Kres to purchase with the team's pooled winnings. The reason for the bargain became apparent as they crossed a rocky causeway to the small island where the blue house sat nestled amongst a dozen similar dwellings.

"What is that smell?" Latch said.

"I suspect it's this thing called a fish," Siv said, eyes wide.

"Don't be cute," Gull said. "Our poor noble lad here probably never smelled a fish smokery before."

Siv didn't mention that he'd never smelled one before either. He was too busy concentrating on not gagging. It really was unpleasant.

"We eat our fish fresh in Soole," Latch said.

"And raw, if I remember right," Fiz said. "Foulest thing I ever had in my life."

"It's an expensive delicacy," Latch muttered. "It's not foul."

Fiz chuckled, and Gull grinned at Siv. It was almost too easy to rile Latch.

"Come along, children," Kres said. He kicked his heels into his horse's sides at the end of the causeway and rode ahead to the blue house. He vaulted off the back of his horse almost before it stopped moving. A narrow ladder led up to the main house. Kres scrambled up it in a flash and paused on the porch, which had white flags flying from the railing. He flung his arms wide.

"Welcome home!"

Kres looked genuinely happy to be there. He took out a huge brass key and wrestled with the door for a minute before it opened with a pained screech. The others took more time to rub down their horses and secure them in the paddock underneath the house before climbing up after him. Fiz and Gull were already more relaxed than they'd been the entire time they were traveling together. Siv supposed that was what happened when people came home.

He paused at the ladder as images of the home he'd left behind cascaded down on him. His room, where he sprawled on the rug to read, experimented with melting things on the Fire Gate, and slept past noon after nights of carousing. The dueling hall, where he'd spent many happy hours training—and where he first met Dara. The cur-dragon cavern, where he spent time with his sisters. The library, where he could always talk to his father. He avoided picturing the Great Hall, where the Lantern Maker had defeated him and stolen it all away. The heady beauty of Vertigon was lost to him. But could he find another home, perhaps here in this blue house on stilts that smelled like fish? If the pen fighters ever stopped threatening to kill him whenever he tried to leave, perhaps he'd like to stay.

"Are you going up or what?" Latch tapped his foot impatiently behind him.

"Oh yeah, just checking to make sure Fiz didn't crack the rungs when he climbed up."

Fiz shouted a genial curse back down at him, and Siv climbed the ladder to the narrow porch, which ran all the way around the house, those white flags decorating it at intervals. The front door opened into a bright room with wide windows on three out of the four sides. A row of doors on the windowless side must lead to bedrooms. A small, open kitchen bordered the eastern side of the house, with a rough-hewn wooden table and five stools separating it from the rest of the room. The house had no other furniture, and exercise equipment spread around its edges: iron weights, bars for pull-ups, folded rugs for stretching. A large pentagon was marked on the scuffed floorboards with red paint. This was definitely a training house. Kres's fighters truly lived for the Dance.

Siv crossed to the huge windows. The silvery line of the gulf peeked over the tops of the buildings to the south. At this height, the divisions between the different districts in the city emerged. Walls or canals separated many of them, and each region displayed flags to indicate their allegiance to—and possession by—a different Waterworker. The effect from above was of a bright flower garden, complete with lots of mud beneath the fluttering colors. Their white-flag district didn't stretch too far before it gave way to a sea of emerald green to the south and west. Sure, there may not be any sheer cliffs or peaks cloaked in mist, but it wasn't a bad view.

They got settled in their rooms—Siv and Latch had to share, though Latch acted less miserable about it than before—and then they reconvened for an afternoon meal. Kres fixed it himself, humming as he dumped a random assortment of dried and slightly musty ingredients into a giant cook pot. The meal had a distinctly fishy odor. Siv suspected he'd have to get used to the smell of seafood quickly.

Kres was certainly having a good time now that he was home. He hummed and tapped his feet, and by the time the stew reached a boil, he broke into all-out song. Gull rolled her eyes, but she tapped her fingers on the table in time with Kres's song. She seemed younger and less guarded here. Fiz elbowed in to claim the first serving of fish stew the moment it was ready, and Kres playfully whacked him with a damp towel. Fiz chuckled jovially. Siv couldn't help thinking the pen fighters were something like a family. He glanced over at Latch. He could be the grouchy old uncle.

"Now rest up, children," Kres said when everyone finished eating. "I want you all to stretch and do some light exercises this evening to limber up for the Dance tomorrow. Now that we've given the Pentagon a glimpse of our new knife fighter, I want a solid showing in our first melee of the season."

"Have you changed your mind about me?" Latch asked, sounding more eager than he probably meant to.

"Afraid not. We must determine how badly you're wanted by the local hired swords."

"Kres—"

"I'm sorry, lad. After what happened in Fork Town, I'm not sure it's worth the risk to the team."

The look of disappointment on Latch's face was all too familiar. It mirrored how Siv had felt when his father first explained that—as the heir-prince—he wouldn't be allowed to compete in the dueling opens back in Vertigon. He couldn't help feeling sympathetic. Now that Siv had competed in one match—albeit not a challenging one according to the announcer—he wanted more.

"What if we made him a disguise?" Siv said. "We could shave all his hair or get him a hat or something. No one needs to know." Granted, a hat hadn't worked out that well as a disguise for Siv. It felt like a lifetime since he'd been snatched from outside the racing grounds in Rallion City.

"That may be a possibility for the next Dance," Kres said carefully. He pushed back his stool and stood. "I need to locate a backup swordsman in the meantime. Do stay out of trouble while I'm away."

Latch followed Kres out of the house, still arguing his case. Before the door squeaked closed, he looked back at Siv and nodded. Could it be? Could that have actually been a full-on *friendly* nod? Siv grinned. Miracles did happen.

He stood to help Gull clean the bowls and put away the rest of the food while Fiz started on another helping of fish stew. The big man seemed determined to make up for all their lean days on the road in a single evening.

"Do you know who the extra swordsman is?" Siv asked as he and Gull tidied up the kitchen together.

"A few fighters are always asking to join our team," she said. "They were practically breaking down our door to vie for a spot when we lost our last knifeman and the old duelist retired. But Kres wanted Shreya."

"I see. She must have been something special."

Siv had a sudden vivid image of Dara joining the team as their fifth fighter. He could see her doing lunges on the scuffed training floor, debating combat strategies with Kres, smiling at him across the humble wooden table. As soon as the thought formed, he was pretty sure he'd never wanted anything more in his entire life. As soon as he figured out how to send word to Trure, could he invite her to join him? He had little hope of retaking Vertigon, but if Selivia and his mother were okay, he could offer Dara a life. Her presence would make this little blue house a home.

Gull nudged him with her bony elbow. "We'd never have picked you up if we hadn't gone to Trure to recruit her. Funny how things turn out."

"Yeah, funny." The truth was Siv didn't know whether Dara still wanted him anymore. If he were worthy of her, he'd never have been taken in the first place. He certainly wouldn't have been lured by the temptation of a life with the pen fighters. Siv frowned, thinking of when he'd tried to leave and the pen fighters threatened to kill him if he gave them away. All because of the other incognito member of the team.

"And where did you get Latch?" he asked, trying to push away the burning image of Dara.

"Not my story to tell," Gull said. "I reckon he and Kres'll trust you enough to fill you in eventually."

"What about you?" Siv asked as he put the last bowl away in a cupboard. "How did you get into the Dance?"

Gull met his eyes, and something sad shadowed her expression. Before he could react, she stepped in and brushed a kiss on his cheek.

"Wouldn't you like to know?" she said. Then she winked and headed for her room, hips swaying.

Siv tugged at his collar. Had that wink been an invitation? Gull had teased him mercilessly throughout their journey, but the kiss on the cheek had been a step beyond flirtatious. He frowned. He may be joining this new family while he was stuck on this side of the Pass, but he didn't want to take it that far. Despite his best efforts to convince himself she was better off without him, Siv couldn't look at another woman without thinking of Dara. Gull may be willing, but he didn't want her the way he'd wanted Dara almost from the moment she'd first walked into his dueling hall.

"You don't get a wink like that every day," Fiz said. "And Gull isn't a patient woman."

Siv jumped. He had forgotten the big man was still there, sitting at the wooden table with a fourth helping of fish stew, a quizzical look in his eyes.

"I'd better go make sure Latch didn't fall in the canal," Siv said and marched firmly to the door without giving Gull's room a second glance. The door squeaked closed behind him.

He found Latch ambling along the edge of the little island, kicking stones into the muddy water. The blue house wasn't far from the rocky causeway connecting to the main road, and plenty of stones scattered in the soft mud. Siv picked one up and hurled it into the slow-moving canal. It sank like, well, a stone. He selected another, flatter rock and threw it with precision. This one skipped lightly across the water before plopping into the murk.

"Sorry about the Dance," he said to Latch. "I know you were looking forward to it."

"Doesn't matter," Latch said. "I guess it wouldn't be worth it if I got murdered the second I left the Steel Pentagon."

"You'd risk death in the Pentagon anyway," Siv said. "If you care so much about staying alive, what's the big difference?" He wondered if Kres had ever planned to let Latch into the Steel Pentagon at all. He certainly had a vested interest in protecting the runaway lordling.

Latch raised an eyebrow. "The difference? I'd be facing down my adversary man to man in the Dance of Steel, participating in the grand fighting tradition of the oldest city on the continent. The alternative is having hired thugs pack me off to my father."

"I'd give anything to have my father back," Siv said without thinking.

Latch paused. "He's dead?"

Siv grunted, hoping to end the conversation there, but Latch abandoned his effort to kick the entire island into the river stone by stone and turned to face him.

"How?"

"Killed," Siv said.

"In battle?"

Siv sighed. The man was finally interested in having a civil conversation, and this was what he wanted to talk about? On the other hand, Siv knew more of Latch's secrets than was strictly fair already. Perhaps he should return the favor. Maybe he and Latch would be friends by the time they fought side by side in the Dance of Steel after all.

"He was murdered," Siv said at last. "I know who did it, but I couldn't defeat him. That's why I had to leave home. I failed to avenge him." *And Sora.* The Lantern Maker's men had killed his sister too, and he couldn't even give her a proper burial. That was more than he wanted to share with Latch, though.

"I thought Vertigon was supposed to be safe," Latch said. "Didn't realize you had murderers too."

"Yeah, well, it's not as safe as it used to be." Siv felt a wrenching guilt at leaving his people behind. He couldn't imagine the Lantern Maker would be able to resume the Peace he had destroyed so completely.

"Sorry about your father," Latch said gruffly.

"Thanks," Siv said. "So, why are you trying so hard to get away from yours?"

"We have political differences."

Siv snorted. "What, you're friends with different noble houses?" In Siv's experience, politics was mostly about being friends with various powerful houses. And not letting them plot your assassination. He wasn't particularly good at that last part, though. He had the scars to prove it.

"It's a little more complicated than that," Latch said. "When my father invaded Cindral Forest, he led the army without the knowledge or approval of the Soolen royal family."

Siv narrowly avoided tripping into the canal. *That* was not where he thought this was going.

"He just decided to start attacking foreign lands all by himself?"

Latch nodded. "The queen and the crown prince are keeping it quiet for now, but the celebrated Commander Brach—my dear father—intends to conquer Trure for himself."

"I . . . don't even know what to say." Siv eyed Latch, reassessing his decision to run off and join the pen fighters. "You disapprove?"

"I don't think he'll succeed. He planned to lay siege to Rallion City, but when he faces the famed Truren cavalry, he's going to get thousands of his men killed. Most of the ordinary soldiers didn't know they were betraying their homeland and condemning themselves and their children to certain exile. No ambition is worth doing that to so many people. I told my father as much, but he was too eager to destroy the horselovers and establish his own throne. Some secret ally promised information and aid that made him think he could defeat Trure."

"A secret ally?" Siv ran through a list of candidates in his head, wondering who in Trure would stoop to such a betrayal. Sora would have known. *He* couldn't name half the Truren nobility. Unless the help had come from outside of Trure.

"I don't know who it was," Latch said. "My father can be too confident for his own good, though."

Siv remembered how much his first captors had admired Commander Brach. And they at least had already known they were breaking away from Soole. He wondered what Commander Brach had planned to do with him. Lucky he had fallen in with the pen fighters and Brach's estranged son instead.

"So you told him off and ran away to join Kres's traveling circus?" he asked.

"Pretty much." Latch looked up at the blue house on stilts. "Kres promised to keep my secret and look out for me. Gull and Fiz know who I am too because they were there when we met. Shreya didn't know." His expression darkened. "She was Truren through and through. And scouts from my father's army killed her."

"I'm sorry about that," Siv said, hoping Latch wouldn't be offended by his sympathy. No wonder the man was so damn grumpy all the time. That was a heavy burden to shoulder. It was like—well, it was like Dara knowing her father had killed his. *Damn.* No wonder things had been rocky between them when he last saw her. He could have been more understanding. Latch would never see the woman he loved again. But maybe Siv still had a chance to make things right.

"Didn't know her that well," Latch said gruffly. "It's more what could have—never mind." His eyes darted up to meet Siv's, then he looked away quickly.

"I hear you," Siv said. He bent to retrieve another flat stone to give Latch a chance to assume his surly mask once more.

He considered Latch's revelation. So Soole's celebrated general had jaunted off with a large chunk of their army to conquer his own kingdom. They sure lived in interesting times. Siv would have spent more time mulling over what this meant for the continent, but the rumble of hooves on the rocky causeway distracted him from that line of thought.

He looked up as a dozen armed men on horseback thundered across the causeway, heading straight for them. *Not again.*

Siv and Latch exchanged tense glances. So much for keeping Latch out of the Pentagon. They'd been found anyway. And their swords were in the house at the top of the ladder.

39

PENDARK

DARA never imagined a city like Pendark could exist, even in her wildest dreams. The canals and streams divided the land into dozens of marshy islands. Buildings rose from some islands atop rock structures. Others rested on stilts, either above the mud or above the murky water. A handful of towers appeared in the distance, and she glimpsed manor houses centered on some of the larger islands. These had high walls reinforced with rocks, and guards scowled down from the ramparts. The crowds of people tramping through the streets and filling the canal boats paid them no mind.

As in Rallion City, the masses came from many different lands. Winter was almost at an end here, so people walked around without coats, their exotic clothing on display. Dara was beginning to understand just how parochial her life had been in Vertigon. Although it was a large, busy city, its inaccessibility at the top of the mountain meant that few foreigners traveled all the way there. But the port city of Pendark teemed with variety. Children darted through the mud in bare feet without a parent in sight. Barges passed by on the canals, packed with precious wares from across the sea. Strange creatures swam in the canals or peeked out from cages beneath stilted houses or atop other barges. Even the weapons were different, with more curved swords and hilts bedecked with colorful inlays and glittering stones.

Banners flew from every house in a myriad of colors. The patchwork of colors dividing each region was like a quilt spread out beside the sea. As their carriage clattered down the main thoroughfare from the Darkwood, they passed between a pale-blue region and a seemingly endless field of purple.

Wyla explained that each Watermight practitioner had his or her own color. She named the principals as they passed from pale blue and purple on either side, through the purple district, and onward into a field of yellow.

"What's your color, ma'am?" Rid asked.

Wyla gestured toward the full skirt fanning above her steel-toed boots.

"I favor a particular shade of poison green."

Dara hardly listened to Wyla. She leaned out the window, trying to see as much of their surroundings—and as many of the passersby—as possible. They'd all ridden inside the carriage since Lord Vex's men overtook them. Dara wished she could sit up top with Siln for a better view of the muddy walkways and the canal boats of all shapes and sizes floating by. There was a fleeting chance she'd spot Siv in the throng. She feared Lord Vex had gotten to him before they even arrived in the city.

"Huh." Rid stuck his head out of the window on the opposite side of the carriage. "Looks like we're coming up on your land—er, marsh."

"Indeed," Wyla said. "I must say I'm looking forward to cleaning off the dirt from our journey and connecting with my power once more. You will stay with me, of course, even though your three-month term has not yet begun." Her tone brooked no argument.

"I'd so love a bath," Vine said. "And perhaps a swim. I've swum in the Azure Lake in Trure but never the true salt water of the sea."

"We don't have time for swimming," Dara said. "Lord Vex could be locating those pen fighters right now."

"We will soon reach my manor house," Wyla said. "I can send out my informants from there."

"I'd like to get a head start at least," Dara said.

"You may get out now if you insist on searching instead of resting," Wyla said.

"I'll do that, then." Dara couldn't rest. Not when they were this close. Not when Lord Vex had beaten them to the city.

"Very well. Rumy can ride with me. I daresay he'll attract unwelcome attention if he accompanies you."

"Is that all right?"

"I know you won't leave Pendark." Wyla tapped Dara's sword arm with her ice-cold hand. "From here you need only walk straight ahead for another quarter mile to reach the gates of my manor. I shall see you there soon enough."

"Of course." Dara checked the ivory-hilted knife in her belt and Siv's pendant around her neck. She didn't have any other belongings to collect. She put a hand on the carriage door. "Are you two coming?"

Rid looked as if he might protest, but Vine said, "Of course, Dara. We won't leave you to search alone."

Dara hollered for Siln to stop the carriage. With a final look at Wyla's cool, knowing eyes, Dara climbed out. Her boots splashed down in a puddle of mud.

Vine descended with more grace and surveyed the street around them as Wyla's carriage pulled away. Rid had climbed down on the other side, and he nearly got hit by another carriage as he crossed the road to join them. He gaped at the buildings on stilts and the busy canal running alongside the road as if they were made of magic and Fire. Dara could barely take in the details. She was too focused on searching for Siv—or for the telltale red of Vex Rollendar's coat.

"Vine?" Dara said. "Can you Sense him?"

"I shall try," Vine said, "but there is a great deal of interference here. It's partially the crowd, but I believe the Watermight disrupts the vibrations as well. I will ask Wyla about it in more detail later."

"We'll have plenty of time with her," Dara mumbled. Maybe they shouldn't have been so quick to leave her carriage, but she had to get away from those knowing, icy eyes. And she'd hoped Vine would Sense him as soon as they arrived.

She scanned the faces gliding by on the nearest canal boat. They blurred together in a hundred colors, all set against the backdrop of Wyla's poison-green banners rising from the island beyond them. She tried to ask passersby for information, but they shook her off before she could launch into Siv's description, hurrying on their way. The barefooted children didn't seem to understand her, their movements wild as they scurried away. Everyone acted so busy here, almost frantic, as they went about their business. A growing sense of panic clutched her, making it difficult to approach the problem strategically. They were running out of time. *Focus, Dara!*

Vine showed no such anxiety. "Excuse me, good sir." She grabbed a passing stranger by the arm and held on tight even as he tried to shake her off. "Could you tell me where to find the pen fighters?"

"The pen fighters?" the man said blankly. "Which ones, woman?"

"That's just it," Vine said. "I don't know. My dear cousin has taken up with a troupe of them, or a squad, or whatever you call them." Vine gave a simpering giggle, giving the impression that her head was full of more air than it actually was. "I so want to find him, but I don't know where to start."

"There are dozens of Steel Pentagons in Pendark and hundreds of pen fighters," the man said. He tried to walk off, but Vine kept her hold on his arm, her eyes widening plaintively.

"He's tall and athletic with dark hair. *Very* handsome," she said, and something in her voice made it sound as if she were calling *this* man tall, athletic, and handsome. He relaxed and stopped trying to rush off. Dara had no idea how she did it.

The man tipped his hat to a jaunty angle. "That description fits half the pen fighters in this city. You got to be more specific, little lady."

"Oh dear," Vine said. "I so want to find him. Can you tell me where I should start? Perhaps they gather somewhere or live in a particular district?"

"Don't know about that, but the first big Dance of the season is tomorrow," the man said. "There will be a lot of fighters in the audience. You have a decent chance of spotting him even if he's not in the pen."

"Oh, thank you!" Vine winked at Dara. "And where will that take place?"

He gave directions to a Steel Pentagon in the market district ("Bright-red flags. You can't miss them.") and even offered to buy her a drink if they ran into each other there. Vine rewarded him with a pat on the shoulder, and he wandered away, chortling about clueless women.

"There now," Vine said, rejoining Dara and Rid, who was still gaping at everything in sight. "Wasn't that more useful than wandering blindly? I suppose there's not much we can do until tomorrow. We might as well continue on to Wyla's manor."

"But Lord Vex—"

"He'll probably be at the very same Pentagon tomorrow," Vine said. "I'm sure Siv will survive for one more night if he's made it this far."

Dara frowned, worry gnawing at her stomach. Vine was probably correct that asking around about an athletic young pen fighter in a city this size was a waste of time. But she couldn't shake the feeling that Siv needed her today—perhaps this very minute.

"I want to keep looking."

Rid didn't quite hold in a sigh. Dara ignored him.

"Please, Vine," she said.

"We could try going to higher ground," Vine said. "But I'll warn you the Air isn't granting me much assistance here."

Dara sucked in a dense, muggy breath. She could see how Vine might have difficulty getting answers from the Air through all this. She could barely smell the sea here.

"There are taller buildings over there." Dara pointed to the southeast. "Maybe we can climb one to get out of the stink of the swamp."

"It's worth a try," Vine said.

Dara led the way, picking through the streets and trying to avoid any route that would require them to pay for a canal boat. They'd really need to do something about their coin problem soon—unless Wyla was planning to pay for her help with the Fire. Dara didn't want to get further into Wyla's debt by asking for money.

As they squelched through the streets, she kept her hand wrapped tight around her ivory knife hilt. She wouldn't put it past the gutter urchins of Pendark to steal it from her. The blade Lord Vex had kindly given her by throwing it into her shoulder was her only weapon. She missed her Savven so much it hurt to think about it. As far as she knew, Grelling still had it in his grubby, wandering hands.

If she only had her Savven, she couldn't help thinking, she would find Siv. The blade was an inexplicable part of her connection to him. He'd given it to her, and she'd saved his life with it. Then she'd transformed it into a Fire Blade while trying to save him again. That had to count for something.

As she dwelt on the Savven, something moved in Dara's chest. It was like a nudge or a spark. Dara put her hand to her chest, feeling the cool shape of the necklace Siv had bought for her. That hadn't been taken from her at least.

But that nudge. Was it possible?

She concentrated on the Savven again, remembering Vine and Wyla's suggestion that there was a connection between her Fire ability and the other powers lacing the continent. She focused on the Savven, on the Air, on the Watermight that ruled this city, on her desperate need to find Siv before Vex did.

She felt the nudge again, and without thinking turned down another road, leading slightly away from the taller buildings she'd noticed before.

"Dara, where are you—?"

"Shh," Dara said. She let her feet guide her, trying not to think too much, trying not to be distracted by the buildings and boats and rocky causeways around her. Instead of thinking about Siv, she concentrated on the Savven, on the Fire Blade she had created in the moment of the most painful and heightened sensation of her life. As she focused on the Work, the sensation grew stronger.

She followed the feeling, not fully understanding but allowing her Firespark and the tug of the Savven to guide her. She'd felt a glimpse of heat from the blade when Grelling passed her on the road too. It might not take her directly to Siv, but maybe she could still do something about his pursuers.

Dara followed the fragile sensation like a bloodhound after a scent. It may be as fleeting as Air, but Dara held onto it as if it were Fire in her veins. Vine and Rid trailed after her. If they spoke, she didn't hear them. They left Wyla's district. White flags fluttered from the buildings now. The smell of fish and smoke laced the air. She barely noticed it as she walked farther into the strange city. The connection was tenuous, and she didn't dare hamper it with doubt.

Then she heard a rumble. A thunder of hooves traveling far faster than any riders had business to in a crowded, swampy city.

Dara broke into a run, ignoring Vine and Rid's exclamations behind her. She didn't want to be distracted, though now she was following her ears more than that fleeting sensation in her chest. Even before she rounded the corner, she knew what she'd see.

Lord Vex's company was riding along a rocky causeway to an island with a handful of houses on stilts. Grelling rode in their midst, the Savven blade at his waist calling Dara like a beacon.

She ran after them, not yet knowing how she'd get the blade back. But she needed to know where they were going. Perhaps they'd found lodging in one of the stilted houses on the little island. Dara glanced at it across the wide canal, and her heart stopped in her chest.

Siv stood on the shore of the island, almost within shouting distance. Siv, the man she loved. The man she'd crossed the continent to find. He stood on that island, and Lord Vex and his dozen swordsmen rode straight toward him, weapons raised.

Dara couldn't even yell a warning. Siv was facing the riders anyway. Facing down his doom. Why hadn't he drawn his sword? *He doesn't have one.* Another man stood by his side, but he didn't have a weapon either. They didn't stand a chance.

No, no, no, no, no.

The first rider reached the end of the causeway and galloped onto the island, mud flying from his horse's hooves. He drew a night-black sword. Lightning thrummed in Dara's heart. It was Grelling, preparing to cut Siv down with her Savven blade.

Ignoring the pain in her chest, Dara hurled herself down the shallow bank beside the road and straight into the slow-moving waters of the canal. This shortcut wouldn't get her there in time, but she sloshed through the mud anyway. The water got deeper and deeper. It was nothing compared to the wild, icy river back in the Fissure, but she still couldn't move fast enough.

Grelling pulled ahead of the other riders. He was almost to Siv and his companion. She was too far away.

No. Not when I'm this close.

The Savven blade whipped through the air. Siv ducked Grelling's first swipe, a slash that would have taken his head from his shoulders. Steel glinted in his hand. He had a weapon after all—a small dagger. A slash of red appeared on Grelling's leg when he wheeled his horse around for another charge. Siv had gotten in one good slice.

His companion didn't even have a knife, but he wielded a rock in either hand. He threw one to distract Grelling and brandished the other like a club.

Lord Vex and the other riders bore down on them.

The canal water was up to Dara's neck now, putrid and murky. She still couldn't swim. She wasn't going to make it.

Please. At least let me get there in time to go down fighting.

She launched herself forward, and her boots sank deeper into the soft bottom of the canal. Too deep. A hint of silver glittered in the water. *Please. I'll do anything.*

As the water closed over her head, she felt a thump, as if something had smacked her in the back. More silver flashed before her eyes. Then her feet were sucked out of the mud. A surge of water swept in and lifted her up. A furious wave carried her upward, forward. The wave hurled her onto the island, dumping her and a mad rush of mud and seaweed and silver and water onto the company of mercenaries.

A roar of sound. Curses. She smashed into someone and tumbled sideways. Her knees hit the ground. Pain spiked through them, and her vision wavered then cleared.

Chaos filled the island. The strange wave had scattered the riders, breaking their charge. Horses slipped in mud, and men shouted about sorcerers and water demons. Steel and water cast silvery reflections throughout the tumult.

Dara found her feet not ten paces from Grelling's horse, which tossed its head, eyes rolling in fear, as he yanked on the reins. Dara leapt forward and drove her knife into Grelling's thigh all the way down to the ivory hilt.

He cursed and reached for her, but she dragged the knife upward, slicing his leg closer and closer to his groin. The pain must have been intense, because he dropped her Savven and clutched at his leg, trying to hold it together as his artery spilled red over Dara's hands.

She released the knife, leaving it in Grelling's leg, and dove for the sword, narrowly avoiding being trampled by the frantic horse.

Dara's fingers closed around hot steel. She had no idea what had happened. She hadn't caused that rush of water. All that mattered was she had her sword back. And she wasn't going to lose Siv now.

40

DANCE OF STEEL

SIV stabbed furiously, forgetting all the fancy knife techniques Kres had taught him. Blades slashed at him, unwieldy in the confusion, and it was all he could do to keep them from finding his flesh. His clothes dripped from that mad wave, making his fingers slip on his knife hilt. But he was still alive for now.

A horse slid in front him, eyes rolling, as its rider tried to get it under control. The snorting, agitated beast bought Siv a moment's respite. He looked around for Latch. The bastards weren't going to kidnap his teammate if he had anything to say about it!

The frantic aftermath of the wave made it difficult to see what was going on, but there had to be at least a dozen enemy fighters on the muddy island now. And they were quickly getting their animals under control.

He spotted Latch at last. He'd found his feet a few paces away, still unarmed. He leapt back desperately as a man in a red coat lunged straight for his gut. Unlike last time, these men didn't look interested in taking Latch alive.

Siv darted forward, picking up a rock as he went, and hurled it at Latch's attacker before he could stab again. It struck him across the face with a glancing blow. The man's hand flew to his cheek, which was already spattered with a canal's worth of mud, and Latch used the momentary distraction to scramble over to Siv. He gave him a quick nod and picked up another rock. The red coated man started toward them, but a horse flailed into his path before he could take two steps.

Siv put his back to Latch's, and they prepared for the next assault. He fended off a surprise stab from a pockmarked fellow. Siv swung his fist, and the punch missed the man's nose by an inch, but when his feet skidded in the mud, he sliced a deep cut in the man's forearm. The fellow cursed and retreated a few paces. Three more fighters took his place, finding their feet and advancing deliberately on the lone pair. With efficient hand signals, they split up to form a ring around them. Siv knew then that he was going to die. At least he had a friend at his back.

A fourth attacker joined the group closing in on him and Latch. Around them, horses still screamed and pitched across the ground, heedless of their riders. Curses filled the air in a confused jumble. Fiz and Gull would hear the commotion and join the fray—hopefully with extra swords—but too many attackers were still on their feet. And these men knew what they were doing. A fifth joined the ring, drawing inexorably nearer. Siv and Latch weren't going to live long enough for the other pen fighters' help to matter.

Then a roan horse reared up, kicking at the sky. The large man on its back keeled over, clutching at a wound that neither Siv nor Latch had given him. The horse's hooves hit the mud, and it bolted —revealing none other than Dara Ruminor standing behind it.

Dara's eyes found his for an instant, and they blazed with intensity and fire and hope. The whole damn universe narrowed to a single point. *Dara.*

A dazzling smile crossed her lips. Siv was struck dumb by the sight, by the feeling that everything was right in the world for this moment.

Then Dara dropped into her dueling stance, raised a black-hilted sword, and attacked. She took the nearest of the five men in the back, momentarily distracting the others from closing with Siv and Latch. Her blade flashed, swift and brilliant. Siv had never seen anything more beautiful in his life. He could stand still and watch her fight for eternity. He swore he could die a happy man right now.

But if he didn't get moving, he would *actually* die. He tightened his grip on his knife and hurled himself into the fray. Latch uttered a savage shout and followed, rocks and fists swinging. They were outnumbered, and these men were no amateurs. Most had regained their footing after that mysterious rush of water. Even with Dara's help, they were in deep trouble. They tried to stay together, but with each of them facing at least two opponents, it was almost impossible.

Then with a terrific battle cry, Fiz and Gull joined the melee. Fiz whirled his broadsword with brutal intensity, incongruous with his gentle-giant demeanor. Gull wielded two blades, her thrusts precise and deadly. After cutting down two fighters in quick succession, Gull hollered Latch's name and tossed him one of her swords, already dripping blood. The pen fighters danced, proving in a matter of seconds that they deserved their reputations.

Mud and blood flew as the battle raged. Horses and men screamed, and the clash of steel sent shivers like lightning through the air. All Siv wanted was to watch Dara, but the attackers pressed in around him, blocking her from view. Siv spotted a dull hint of silver beside a fallen body. He switched his knife to his left hand and lunged for the discarded sword. He scrambled to his feet, the stranger's blade in hand, and found Latch again. They stood back to back, jabbing and slicing as their opponents tried to break through their defenses. Siv felt energized, alive. He wasn't going to let them slaughter his friend in cold blood!

Abruptly, he realized the man in the red coat he'd noticed earlier had sandy-blond hair and a thin nose. He knew that face. He flashed back to his fight with Bolden Rollendar in the Great Hall. But this man was older—and a far better swordsman. What the heck was Vex Rollendar doing trying to kidnap Latch Brach?

Oh, right. He was probably here for Siv. He'd been found at last.

Vex was fighting Gull—and he wasn't losing. Gull was a talented, experienced swordswoman, but it was all she could do to parry his attacks. Vex advanced, forcing her to give ground. Fiz was too busy swinging his broadsword with the strength of three men to help her. Siv tried to get closer, but more foes surged between them, and he was hard pressed to defend himself, much less anyone else. Gull cursed as Vex's blade sliced across her shoulder.

But then Vex retreated of his own accord, gliding back out of Gull's range before she could counterattack. His eyes went to the rocky causeway, where two more figures were racing toward them. Vex didn't move for a moment, and a strange expression—almost a smile—crossed his face as he watched them approach. He roused himself and shouted a warning to his men as Gull closed with him again, her gaze lethal.

The newcomers were a tall young man wielding a wooden staff and—Siv blinked in surprise—Lady Vine Silltine. They joined the fray, seeming to know exactly which fighters were the enemies in the jumble. Siv redoubled his own efforts. Suddenly instead of a dozen cavalry running down two, it was now a brawl in the mud, seven to eight.

Siv nearly had his head taken off by a swipe from an assailant. He ducked and stabbed at his attacker's leather jerkin as he scrambled out of range. The man cursed and renewed his assault. Siv was pretty sure he'd fought this guy before—and now he was mad. Then an elegant figure danced in to help. Vine finished off the pockmarked man with a neat stab through the chest.

"Pardon me, but I did hate that man, Your Majesty," Vine Silltine said as he slumped to the ground. Then she whirled away, searching for her next opponent.

Another foe lunged at her from behind, but Siv dove between them and parried the thrust. Before the man could riposte, Siv slammed his sword through the fellow's eye. He withdrew the blade, already seeking his next opponent.

"Dirty Soolen," someone growled, and Siv turned as a tall Pendarkan with sickly brown teeth engaged with Latch. He was the most-skilled fighter Siv had seen yet, and Latch struggled to block his attacks.

Before Siv could move to his friend's aid, Gull and Fiz closed in together and finished off the Pendarkan. He dropped in the mud at their feet.

"Captain Wick's dead!" one of the fighters hollered, a young guy who could have been from Vertigon. He looked scared. As well he should. The battle was turning against the aggressors.

"Fall back!" called another. "This fight's too dear already."

"Not until we finish this," Vex Rollendar said. His cold eyes pinned Siv from across the battlefield. You could have iced a fish and shipped it back to Vertigon in that gaze.

"My lord, we can't win," said a large, ugly fellow. He had a massive slice up his thigh, and Siv was surprised he hadn't bled out already. "Mertin's dead, and these men won't stay without Wick."

Vex cursed. He was too far away from Siv to engage him. He'd taken a wound to the side—probably payback from Gull—and he was bleeding heavily.

"Fine," Vex spat. "Retreat." He met Siv's eyes across the blood-spattered field once more. "We'll finish this later." His gaze cut to Vine before he led the withdrawal from the island. She wiggled her fingers in a coy wave as he departed.

The last of Vex's men dragged their wounded onto horses, leaving the dead behind, and galloped back toward the rocky causeway. Only a handful had survived. That was what they got for attacking the best damn pen fighters in Pendark!

Siv didn't wait to see if all the enemies actually left the island. He whirled around, searching for Dara. Vine was on her knees beside the young man with the staff, who groaned feebly. Latch had taken a stab or two, but blood marked his blade, and he looked triumphant. Bodies littered the ground around him. Gull and Fiz were unharmed except for the thin cut on Gull's shoulder. They worked quickly to silence the injured and screaming horses.

But where was Dara? She couldn't have fallen. Not now. Siv searched the muddied and bloodied bodies for a hint of her golden hair, panic seizing his heart like a fist. The last of the horses went quiet, leaving only the groaning of the injured man. Where was she? She couldn't have been hurt protecting him—not again. Siv swore if anything had happened to her, he'd—

There was a tap on his shoulder.

Siv turned, coming face to face with his Dara.

She looked at him, her intense eyes bright with the rush of battle.

"There you are," she said.

"Dar—" Siv couldn't speak. He tried to clear his throat, still hoarse from the exertion, no doubt.

"I've been looking everywhere for you," she said. "I was starting to think you didn't want to be found." Her eyes softened with a thin film of tears.

Siv hadn't realized exactly how much he missed Dara until that moment. The whole Fireblessed world didn't matter now that she was standing before him, covered in mud and blood and looking more beautiful than a thousand lightning bolts. He had failed as a king. He had gotten himself kidnapped. And yes, he'd run away, joining the pen fighters rather than fighting through a hundred Kres Marches to get back where he belonged. But now he knew for certain: he belonged with Dara. She might never forgive him for his failings, but he would follow her across the world to make it up to her. He would do whatever it took to earn back her trust. He wouldn't lose her as Latch had lost Shreya. Not now that she was back within reach.

"Are you hurt?" Dara asked nervously. "You're not usually this quiet after you win a duel. Usually you at least gloat or—"

Siv dropped his knife and sword in the mud and closed the gap between them. He took Dara's face in his hands and kissed her as he should have done every single day they'd known each other. He kissed her as he'd dreamed of doing every single night they'd been apart. He kissed her, knowing they couldn't completely make up for lost time, but damn determined to try.

Dara clutched his coat as if she was afraid he'd pull away and kissed him back.

Siv had no idea how long they kissed. All he could think about was her lips, her teeth, her tongue. Her eyelashes fluttering closed over her beautiful eyes. His fingers in her hair. Her hands around his neck. Really, he couldn't think much at all.

Someone cleared their throat theatrically nearby, but Siv didn't care. He had Dara in his arms, and the whole world could cease to exist for a little longer. He drank her in, living for every second with her. Wanting her to clutch him tighter. Wanting her.

"Ahem," came a familiar singsong voice. "I do so love reunions, but our friend needs medical attention. I don't suppose you two could help? You'll have plenty of time for that later."

With a great deal of effort, Siv released Dara, stopping for a moment to run his hand down her cheek.

"I love you," he said hoarsely.

"Me too."

"Anytime," Vine sang.

Finally, Siv turned to look at the others. Vine had her hands pressed over a wound in her lanky friend's shoulder, and Gull was ordering Latch to stop complaining while she patched up his injuries. Fiz was watching them with a broad grin on his face.

Siv took Dara's hand and went over to help Vine cut a strip of fabric from her friend's shirt and bind up his arm.

"You the fellow we been looking for?" the young man asked woozily.

"I guess I am," Siv said.

"Name's Rid. You got some true friends in these ladies." Rid dropped his head back in the mud and moaned, earning more fussing from Vine.

"Have you been following me all this time?" Siv asked Dara.

"Yes. We thought you'd been kidnapped." Dara glanced at the pen fighters, who'd helped to defend him, and her brow furrowed.

"I was. These folks rescued me—and then sort of threatened to kill me if I left. It's a long story. Meet Fiz, Gull, and Latch."

Gull gave a short nod, her usual mistrust of strangers plain on her face.

"How'd you get here?" she demanded. "And why did those men attack?" She eyed Dara and her friends as if she suspected they'd brought Vex and the others down on their home.

"Wasn't me this time," Latch said. For the first time—probably in his entire life—a huge smile split his face. "Guess I'm not the only one with mercenaries after him."

"I think we all have a lot of explaining to do," Siv said, stealing another look at Dara. Guilt nudged at him again. She must have been through a lot to track him down—even after he was out of his kidnappers' clutches. He would find a way to make it up to her. "Shall we get the wounded inside first?" He also kind of hoped they could get through the stories and go back to kissing soon.

"Clean him up in the water trough over there," Fiz said. "Kres'll have a fit if we get blood in the house."

Half an hour later, they all gathered around the wooden table once more. A rival pen-fighting squad lived nearby, and they agreed to keep watch in case Vex returned with more men. They hadn't joined the fight lest they injure themselves before the big Dance tomorrow, but they didn't mind posting a lookout.

The sun began to set, casting shadows and colors over the city. Gull found a few grimy bottles of ale and shared them around the table. Vine had put Rid to bed in Siv and Latch's room, but the others' injuries were minor. Latch seemed pleased at the prospect of having real battle scars.

As they drank the ale and rested from the fight, Siv explained how he'd been kidnapped in Rallion City, dragged through the Truren wilderness by the Soolens, and eventually fallen in with the pen fighters. He didn't state his true identity. Fiz, Gull, and Latch knew too much by now.

"So I came to Pendark," he finished. "I almost turned back at Kurn Pass, but these folks dissuaded me." He nodded at the pen fighters, remembering the way they closed in around him in the darkened streets of Tollan when he tried to return to Rallion City. He *could* trust them, couldn't he?

"We thought he was going to betray us on account of Latch," Fiz said with a shrug. "No hard feelings."

"Latch?" Vine said.

"Oh, the other member of our squad with a price on his head." Fiz slapped Latch on the back, making the latter grunt. That slap couldn't have been pleasant with the wounds he'd taken during the fight.

"Did you send word to Rallion City that you're all right?" Dara said. "We were out in the wild by then anyway, but your mother and sister are worried sick about you. Your grandfather too."

She wisely didn't mention their names, but the reproach in her words made him cringe. If Dara was upset with Siv for not cutting through the pen fighters to return to her, she didn't show it. He should have tried harder, even if it got him killed. Add that to the massive pile of things making him feel guilty. The weight of regret was getting heavier than a bullshell. But the latest attack only proved that people close to him would always be in danger.

"I was planning to send word when I arrived here," Siv said, avoiding the pen fighters' eyes. "But I can't go back. I couldn't defend my cr—my former position." He swallowed hard and said the words that had been plaguing him: "I got my sister killed. My family is better off without me."

Dara gasped. "Siv!" She grabbed his arm and shook it, giving him a look he didn't understand at all. Some extraordinary mix of intense joy and sadness. Then she said, "Sora is alive. Vine brought word right after you were kidnapped."

"Oh yes!" Vine said. "I nearly forgot. She's..."

Vine launched into some sort of explanation, with Dara adding commentary, but Siv couldn't process anything else. Their voices washed over him like a wave from the Bell Sea. He felt as if he'd been smacked in the head. *Alive.* Sora was alive. Which meant...

"I left her."

"Siv..." Dara began.

"We walked away." An empty cavern opened up in his mind. "We left her for dead. And now she's a prisoner. Until the Lantern Maker kills her."

"We don't know if he'll do that," Dara said.

Siv stood, knocking his stool to the floor. "We have to leave tonight. We can get in a few miles before midnight if you're ready to travel." He barely knew what he was saying. Mist wrapped through his brain, eating away at every nerve. Alive. Alive. Alive. And he had left her behind.

"There may be a small complication," Vine said, giving Dara a meaningful glance.

"I can't go right away," Dara said. "A Waterworker helped me find you, and I need to repay her before I leave Pendark."

"So pay her. I have to help Sora." He imagined his sister alone, scared, cowering before the spectral shape of the Lantern Maker.

"I agree," Dara said. "But the payment is complicated." She took his hand, preventing him from sprinting for the door. "Let's not rush into anything. Besides, this Waterworker might teach me something that could help us fight my father."

"Us? Are you sure?" Firelord knew he didn't have any right to ask her to come with him. If it weren't for Sora, he never would have dared.

"Of course." Grim determination shone in Dara's eyes—and maybe a little fear. "You didn't think I'd let you go that easily, did you?"

"Even though it's your father?"

Dara hesitated, a shadow crossing her face. The prospect still weighed on her. No matter what she had been through while they were apart, she couldn't relish the idea of confronting the man who raised her, the man Siv was certain she still loved.

"We have to make it right," she said at last.

Siv squeezed her hand. He didn't want to put Dara at risk, but he felt incapable of letting her out of his sight ever again. He had business in Vertigon, and he needed her help. He righted his stool and sat beside her once more.

"We don't have to leave tonight," he said. "Tell me more about this Waterworker complication and how I can help."

As Dara explained the dangerous bargain she'd been forced to make, anger began to boil in Siv's stomach. Three months Wielding power with the conniving Waterworker. Three months imprisoned within the boundaries of Pendark. Dara's tone was as practical as ever, but she looked nervous. Siv gently wrapped his hands around her sword arm, the one the Waterworker had cursed, and silently vowed to protect her with every movement, every thought, every breath, from now until the end of eternity. A sense of duty replaced the anger, firm and hot, like new-forged steel. Maybe he had a chance to be the man his father had taught him to be after all. Dara had been ensnared while trying to save him. He would do whatever it took to atone for it—and to earn the loyalty she had already shown him.

There was work to be done, but he felt on firmer footing than he had in months. This, at least, was clear: Dara was his family. And he wouldn't let the Lantern Maker, the Waterworker, or anyone else hurt his family anymore.

He thought of Sora, all alone in Vertigon. He hated delaying his return to her. She must be afraid, perhaps cowering in a dungeon or locked in a tower. She was only a little girl. But he wasn't going to give up on her. And maybe the Waterworker really would teach Dara something they could use. With her help, he would get back to his sister somehow.

41

THE QUEEN

SORA marched down the stairwell from her tower. Lima and Rafe walked ahead, carrying on a rapid, whispered conversation with Captain Thrashe. They paid little heed to the queen trailing along behind them, but she didn't forget that *they* had come to *her* for help. It was time to take back control of her mountain.

Kel fell in beside her. After a quick glance at the trio up ahead, he slipped his hand into hers.

"Are you all right?" he whispered.

"*I'm* fine. What happened out there?"

"Whatever the Fireworkers did backfired," Kel said. "I was keeping watch outside, so all I saw was Berg Doban bolting out of there as if he was being chased by all the fires of hell. And then he burning *was*. The Fire just sort of burst out of the building, overflowing from all the doors, spilling down the walls. I've never seen anything like it."

"Was there an explosion?"

"I didn't hear one. It happened fast, though."

"The Workers would have been pretty far underground if they were at the Well when it happened."

"True," Kel said. "I may not have heard an explosion, but there was plenty of screaming."

Sora shuddered, grateful for Kel's hand in hers. Zage Lorrid, the old Fire Warden, had taken her down the steep stone staircase to the Well once. He wanted her to know just how uncomfortable it was for a non-Fireworker down there. She'd never forget the lake of molten Fire churning beneath a massive stone bridge, the sheer power flowing outward to the Fireshops and access points across the mountain. She still remembered the way sweat had soaked her body and her head had become light and achy within seconds of walking through the door. She had never asked to see the Well again.

"Did anyone else make it out?" she asked.

"Berg lost a few men. Madame Pandan was at the top of the stairs and made a run for it. I think Daz and the rest of the Fireworkers are dead. They underestimated what they were dealing with in there."

Sora's heart sank. All of her Worker allies, gone in one sweep. She shouldn't have let them assault the Well without more research. But they couldn't let Rafe finish his Work—not when the fate of the continent was at stake. She had sent the Square Workers to do a job, and they had paid the cost. But making life-or-death decisions was part of being queen. She had to live with the consequences.

Kel hadn't let go of her hand, and she tightened her grip on him. The Ruminors didn't look back. They probably didn't care whose hand she held anyway.

"Are you sure you're not hurt?" she said.

"Of course not, my queen." Kel smiled at her. "This wasn't nearly as scary as confronting Her Giant Horribleness. It was practically a night off."

His smile made her stomach flutter. No wonder all the female dueling fans on the mountain loved him so much. They had serious things to worry about tonight, but she was glad he was okay.

"Did you hear the Lantern Maker mention the Spring just now?" she said. "I've never heard that term before. I always assumed the Fire came straight from the Well. The idea of disturbing the Spring made Lima nervous—and that makes me nervous."

"I heard," Kel said. He frowned, his steps slowing.

"You know something?"

"Maybe. Only . . . it's silly."

"What?"

Kel glanced significantly at the Ruminors, but they were still busy with Captain Thrashe.

"We need something to go on." Sora eased a little closer, pressing her shoulder against his. "Even a hunch."

"My grandmother used to sing me a rhyme when I was small," Kel said. "She wasn't the most-educated woman, but she had a great memory for the old songs." He bent down to whisper in her ear, and his breath tickled her cheek. "One of them had a line that went, 'In burning range, let not the wild Spring break.' She always said Spring like it was a big thing—and the line just popped into my head when they were talking."

"Burning range?" The Lantern Maker had mentioned the Spring being located in the Burnt Mountains. Kel could be on to something. "Do you remember the rest of the song? What happens at the Spring?"

"That's just it." Kel rolled his shoulders uncomfortably, and Sora pulled away a little, hoping he wasn't objecting to her nearness. But he didn't let go of her hand. If anything, his grip tightened. "The song is about dragons—big ones. The next line goes, 'Lest Fire spread across the land and bid true dragons wake.'"

"True dragons?" Sora almost laughed. He might as well have said painted tarbears. The creatures had been extinct for just as long. Extinct—or sleeping. No one knew for sure. "It has been centuries since the last true dragon was seen," she said. "Do you think meddling with the Spring could really bring them back?"

"It's just a song," Kel said. "All I know is I'd like to see the Lantern Maker try to take down a true dragon after waking them up from their nap."

"If he's planning to take them down." For a moment she pictured Rafe Ruminor astride a giant true dragon like the drawings she'd seen in ancient texts. The creature's eyes blazed with Fire, and it tore across the Truren plains, engulfing them in flames. Rafe himself looked like an ancient Firedemon, consumed by a rush of intoxicating power. The image was far more terrifying than Lima in a rage. Sora prayed Rafe would never be unleashed on the world like that—with or without the help of the fabled creatures.

Sora shook her head. What was she thinking? It was the strain of the night, the shifting shadows of the castle before dawn. She was sleep deprived. Of course the Lantern Maker wouldn't *try* to wake the true dragons. If they were the ancient power that lived at the

Spring, even he wouldn't be foolish enough to risk it. The true dragons had been wild, fierce beasts when they roamed Vertigon long ago. Even the most-ambitious Fireworker couldn't tame them.

No, Sora had to focus on things she could control. Tonight had been a disaster, but she wouldn't stop trying to take Rafe down. And she still had allies left.

Kel didn't drop her hand until they reached the entrance hall. A few Fireworkers awaited them, looking tense and anxious after the events of the night. Some had reported to her in the hours she waited in her tower. They nodded to her, seeming reassured by her presence, even though the rumble of voices outside indicated the castle wasn't out of danger yet.

Lima gave Sora quick instructions on what to say to the crowd gathering outside the gates and then hurried her out into the courtyard.

It was the darkest hour of night, with no moon or hint of dawn. Sora walked carefully, grateful the paths had been cleared since the last snow. As she walked, she remembered the harvest festival her brother had held that autumn. The way laughter and music had filled the courtyard, breaking the spell of gloom that began when their father died. Her brother had charmed the crowds that night, making them love him, making them believe he could be as good as their father. Sora may not have his charm and charisma, but she wanted to be good too.

She heard them long before she saw them. People gathered outside the locked castle gates, talking, crying, shouting. A baby wailed. It was far too cold out for children. But the people needed to know what had happened tonight. They needed to know if the Works that had kept them safe and prosperous might spew forth Fire and put their children in danger. They needed to know if the Workers who had given Vertigon so much were taking it back once and for all.

Sora reached the wall and climbed a narrow staircase to the catwalk at the top. A cold wind blew over the ramparts, carrying smoke and tendrils of mist. She let the breeze touch her face for a moment, remembering that this was her mountain. She would protect it—even if that meant soothing the people who hammered at the gates, calling for the Lantern Maker. He would only bring his wrath down on them. She had to prevent any more deaths from occurring this night.

After a final glance at the Ruminors waiting beneath her, cowering out of sight, she straightened the skirts of her Amintelle-blue dress and leaned over the edge.

"Look! It's Queen Sora!"

"Queen Sora!"

A few pale faces turned upward. The throng outside the walls was larger than Sora expected. At least a hundred people milled in a pool of flickering light. The men, a mix of noblemen and commoners, carried torches rather than Firelights. She wondered where they had even found such things. Steel glinted too. Weapons bared and ready.

"What happened, my queen?" someone called.

"The Fireworkers have gone mad, that's what!"

"Down with the Fireworkers!"

"Please, everyone. I need you to listen to me," Sora said. Her voice was thinner and more nervous than she would have liked. She saw how quickly the crowd could turn to a mob. They were frightened and cold. They had dealt with the domineering behavior of the newly empowered Fireworkers. Their peaceful city now needed army patrols to protect anyone who went out after dark. The world beyond their borders had been thrust into turmoil. And now the Fire had turned against them. They'd had enough.

"Open the gates!"

"Queen Sora, we will take down the Chief Regent for you!"

"Long live House Amintelle!"

"Death to the Firewielders!"

The crowds surged against the gates, and the force shuddered through Sora's boots. She was tempted to urge them to keep pushing until the gates gave way. They could retake the castle and throw the Ruminors off the steepest cliff in the three peaks.

But the people would try to rip apart every Fireworker they found, and the Fireworkers wouldn't stand for that. Too many would die tonight. She had to calm them down.

"I know you are scared," Sora said. She fought for serenity. This was her role, to protect and comfort her people however she could. She may only be an eighteen-year-old girl, but she would show them she was not afraid—and they didn't need to be either. "There has been a terrible accident," she said. "But there was no malice in what occurred tonight. It was an unintentional Fire surge, something that has happened before and will happen again as surely as lightning strikes and blizzards shake the mountain."

"An accident?" someone called. "Are you sure?"

"It's the Fireworkers' fault!"

"Rid the mountain of the Workers forever!"

"Please," Sora said. "We must not let fear have mastery over us. More importantly, we must not take out that fear on our neighbors. This was a natural disaster. We should be helping not threatening each other."

She sought out the eyes of the people gathering beneath her, trying to form a connection with them one by one. She ignored the Lantern Maker and his wife waiting on her side of the wall. These were *her* people first and foremost. She met the gaze of the mother clutching a whimpering baby to her chest, the two teenage boys, probably brothers, with kitchen knives in their shaking hands, the wiry tradesman wearing nightclothes beneath his cloak. She knew some of them by name: a serving man named Hirram. A duelist called Murv. Lord Samanar waited at the edge of the crowd, his arm around Lady Atria. The hem of her skirt was burned away, as if she'd fled through a spreading pool of Fire. Lord Morrven waited on the other side of the crowd, glancing nervously at the flaming torches around him. And Berg Doban stood there too, a hand on his sword. He met her eyes and nodded.

"We need to rally together," Sora said, her voice finding strength. "Some of your fellow Vertigonians have lost homes and livelihoods tonight. A few have lost family members. I will do everything I can to help, as will the Fireworkers in my royal court, but I need you too. Don't turn against your neighbors. Don't let fear take hold. Don't forget that the Peace of Vertigon, even more than the Fire, is what makes us strong."

Some of the anger and nervous energy began to dissipate from the crowd. For once, Sora was glad she wasn't a big, strong man. She was a young woman, and if she hadn't lost her head over a burst of Fire, however catastrophic, they needn't either.

"Queen Sora is right!" someone shouted at last.

"Yes, we should be helping."

"The Peace! Remember the Peace!"

"Thank you," Sora said. "Now, I need your help to keep this process orderly. Since you're all here, perhaps you could lead the effort to rebuild."

"Just tell us what we can do to help, Queen Sora."

"Hear! Hear!"

"Long live Queen Sora!"

Sora smiled, warmth building in her chest, even though a cold wind was blowing. "Thank you. We have a lot to do. I always find it helps to make a list."

She glanced back at the Ruminors huddling anxiously behind the castle gates. Lima held her fur muff tight, as if trying to choke the life from it. She seemed to expect the gates to crash down at any moment. But Rafe watched Sora appraisingly. When she met his eyes, he nodded. He must know they would have had a witch hunt on their hands without her. The mountain would run with blood as well as Fire. Rafe could tamper with the ancient Spring, rile up whatever Fire-blasted creatures he wanted, but she wouldn't let him take the mountain down with him, not while she was queen.

She looked back at the crowd gathering in the darkness beneath her. The sobs had subsided, and the weapons had been returned to their sheaths. Even the flickering torches seemed calmer. Expectant faces turned her way. Sora took a deep breath.

"That's better," she said. "Now, it's time to get to work."

42

SUNSET

DARA felt nearly delirious with joy and weariness as the last threads of light drained from the Pendarkan sky. The pen fighters argued amiably about what to eat for their evening meal. Dara let their voices tumble around her, already feeling comfortable in the strange house on stilts. With its simple kitchen table and dedicated training space, it was somehow both cozy and severe at the same time.

She kept her eyes glued to Siv, watching the thoughts progress across his face. He hadn't spoken in a while, no doubt still processing all the recent developments. The scar on his temple had faded a little, and his new beard made him look older and more rugged. The new look suited him. He had been through a lot over the past few months.

She'd arrived just in time. She could barely contemplate what would have happened if she had agreed to go back to Wyla's manor or resigned herself to looking for him at the Steel Pentagon the next day. It had been far too close.

Without the initial confusion of the water and mud, Siv and his friend never would have survived until the reinforcements arrived. Even though they were technically outside the bounds of Wyla's domain, Dara was fairly certain the Waterworker had conjured the wave that deposited her on the island in time to stop Grelling's killing blow. She doubted she'd imagined the flickers of silvery Watermight in the wave.

Dara knew the additional help would add to her debt. Wyla had already established that her assistance came with strings.

She would worry about that tomorrow. All she wanted to think about right now was Siv's hand in hers at last. The news about Sora affected him deeply, but he didn't let go of Dara, even though he was distracted. It was as if he intended to hold onto her hand for the rest of their lives. That was fine with her.

As the others finally settled on drawing straws and sending someone out for fresh fish and bread, the door flew open with a loud screech.

"Would someone mind telling me why there's a cur-dragon on my porch?" The leader of the pen fighters had returned. He strolled in, studying the group around his table with shrewd curiosity.

"Rumy?" Siv asked.

"Guess he got tired of waiting," Dara said.

Siv jumped up to go see his long-lost pet, tugging Dara with him.

"Kres, Dara. Dara, Kres," he said as they brushed past the new arrival.

"A pleasure." Kres, who was pushing forty, was shorter than both of them, and his strides were loose and self-assured. The intelligence and strength in his demeanor told her in an instant that he was a talented fighter. He would have been a real asset if he'd arrived in time for the fight.

The others introduced Kres and Vine to each other and launched into a dramatic retelling of the fight in the mud while Dara and Siv escaped onto the narrow porch. Rumy reared up on his hind legs on the wooden rail and snorted a happy greeting. Siv finally released Dara's hand and threw his arms around the cur-dragon's neck. Rumy lunged forward, joyously knocking his master over on his back. Siv laughed, scratching Rumy's head and tickling his scaly belly while the creature slobbered on him like an oversized dog.

Dara leaned on the porch rail, looking out over the darkened city. A light breeze caressed her face, carrying the aromas of smoke, fish, and salt. Lights burned in a thousand windows, with the flickering, unsure quality of mundane flame. There must be plenty of Fireworks in the city, but they'd be expensive this far from Vertigon. Most people must use wood and wax fires for their light.

There was Watermight out there too. She wondered if she'd be able to interact with it in some way, as Wyla had implied. Would it respond to her Firespark? Could she combine it with the Fire to create Works of even greater power? She didn't understand the connections between the powers, which were so strongly tied to their individual lands. Perhaps Wyla didn't either, and that was why she had secured Dara's assistance. Being indebted to Wyla made her nervous, but she couldn't deny she was curious. Would it truly be possible to collaborate with a Waterworker? And more importantly, could she discover a way to thwart her father's Fire? She still dreamed she might neutralize him without killing him. She had failed once, but perhaps she could try again.

She had three months to figure it out. She'd report to the Waterworker's manor in the morning. Surely Wyla would give her until then. For now, she wanted to enjoy the sounds of the joyous reunion beside her. For now, she wanted to rest easy knowing the man she loved was safe. In the morning, she would repay her debt.

Siv touched her ankle and motioned for her to sit. She slid down beside him, the wooden porch rough beneath her hands. Rumy nuzzled her face then settled his bulky weight onto both of their legs.

"What have you been feeding this guy?" Siv said.

Dara laughed. "He's gotten bigger, hasn't he?"

"And cleverer, I'm sure," Siv said, patting the creature's scaly back affectionately.

"He's been a real life saver," Dara said.

"You have that in common." Siv leaned over and kissed her cheek. He lingered there, his mouth brushing her skin, and heat spiraled out from his lips. He left more kisses at the corner of her eye, at the edge of her mouth, at the soft place where her jaw met her neck. His fingers traced soft circles on her arm. She didn't dare move, afraid he would stop. Then Rumy grunted and stuck his nose in between them, demanding more attention. Siv obliged, pulling back with a chuckle.

"So what now?" Dara said when she could breathe normally again.

"We figure out a way to rescue my sister."

"And then?"

"We take back what's ours."

"Good." She scooted closer to him, not caring that she was disturbing Rumy's position. She had waited long enough for this. She leaned her head on his shoulder.

Siv didn't move for moment, as if he'd been captured in glass. "Dara?"

"Yes?"

"I'm sorry I didn't return right away." His breathing grew ragged, raw. "I should have fought harder. But with Sora . . . the coup . . . my father. I figured everyone would be better off without me."

Dara couldn't speak for a moment. She had been through so much to get him back. It *did* sting to know that for at least part of the time she'd been chasing him he'd contemplated never coming back. It was hard to accept that the pen-fighting team would actually have killed him if he'd tried hard enough to get away—although she couldn't be sure about that Kres fellow. But Dara understood what it was like to live with guilt, to wish you could go back and do things differently, see things better.

She tugged gently on his beard. "Don't let it happen again."

In answer, Siv slid his arm around her back and pulled her in. He held her gently, firmly, as if he was afraid she'd stand up and walk away. He held her as though she were precious and breakable —or as if what they had together were precious. He rested his face against her hair, breathing her in. Despite the awkwardness of the cur-dragon lounging on their laps, Dara had never felt more at home.

It was much warmer in Pendark than it had been during their travels, but a chilly breeze still blew inward from the sea. Dara snuggled into Siv's chest and breathed deeply, at ease at last. They had work ahead of them. Mysterious magic wielders to appease. War-torn lands to cross. Enemies—Rollendar or otherwise—to fend off. Someone would try to kill them again. That, at least, seemed inevitable.

But all that mattered right now was that they were together. And together, they were strong.

She turned to Siv, taking a moment to memorize every angle of his face, every fleck of gold in his eyes. Then she wrapped her fingers in his hair and pulled his mouth down to meet hers.

EPILOGUE

PRINCESS Selivia stood atop the battlements as a dazzling parade of soldiers exited the gates far beneath her. The winter sun shimmered on armor and weapons, as if they were made of silver and gold rather than steel. Horses whinnied, and men called to each other, their eager music filling the fresh morning air. The Truren cavalry was going to war.

She and her mother had fled Rallion City for the Far Plains ten days ago. Her grandfather's kingdom was under attack! Selivia could hardly contain her agitation as she drummed her fingers on the ramparts. From the way everyone scurried about, it must be only a matter of time before the Soolen army looked their way. Half of the stronghold's company was riding out to patrol the plains in case the Soolens dared approach them here.

Selivia almost wished she'd been allowed to stay in the capital. It must be terribly exciting to be in the city right now. But the moment the Soolen army left Cindral Forest and crossed the border into Trure, her grandfather had sent her and her mother away.

They had ridden through the endless grasslands to the Far Plains stronghold where her Uncle Valon lived. It was a flat, flat land, full of nothing but grass and the occasional hawk soaring high across the sky. Then the grass had given way to barren sand, and the massive shape of the Rock appeared on the horizon. The natural formation was the tallest thing for miles and miles around. It grew up from the sand like a big stone treasure chest, with a small, lonely building beside it. Selivia hadn't realized just how large the storied Rock was until they drew near enough to see that the tiny building was actually a massive sandstone fortress.

Selivia leaned her elbows on that very sandstone now as the last of the soldiers left through the gates. She wished desperately that she could go with them.

She had hoped she'd at least be able to go riding when they reached the safety of the Far Plains Stronghold, but her mother forbade her from venturing beyond the walls. Her *cousins* were still permitted to go out. A few were old enough to be soldiers, and they rode at the head of the cavalry that would patrol the plains and keep them safe. Selivia was sad to see them go. They were the most interesting of the bunch by far.

Selivia pouted, watching the glittering procession until it faded into the haze. What was the point of staying on the Far Plains if you couldn't go out and enjoy them? It would be spring soon. Rallion City would bloom with a thousand flowers, and the ladies would parade through the streets in a rainbow of sumptuous gowns and dazzling jewels. Well, maybe they wouldn't do that during a war, but still. The Far Plains had to have some nice flowers too. All of Trure was lovely in the spring.

The only place better was Vertigon. Selivia looked to the north. A distant shadow indicated where the glorious mountain range spread across the horizon, drinking in the sun. Vertigon Mountain stood tall at its heart. She missed the beauty and drama of her homeland. And her big sister needed her. Siv was gone too, but Selivia felt confident Dara would bring him back. After her dramatic escape from the palace dungeon, how could she fail? But who would save Sora?

If only Selivia could escape the confines of the Far Plains Stronghold! Not that she'd be foolish enough to return to Vertigon on her own. But maybe if she could talk a few of her younger cousins into escorting her...

She sighed. That would never work. Her cousins were useless, always whispering about the Air and staring off into the distance. Even the boys. Her only true companion here was Zala, her handmaiden. Zala was from these remote lands, and she was only too excited to tell Selivia all about them.

Unfortunately, they couldn't go out and visit any of Zala's old haunts because of this silly house-arrest situation. It was so terribly dreary, especially alone.

"Princess?" Selivia turned at the familiar voice, sweet and low.

"Yes, Fenn?" She supposed her long-time bodyguard counted as a companion too, but Fenn was more like a disapproving aunt than a friend sometimes.

"Your mother wishes to see you."

"Why?"

"A letter from your grandfather."

Selivia abandoned her post atop the ramparts and followed Fenn into the cool darkness of the stronghold. In the summer, the fortress would be a welcome respite from the harsh sun, but in winter, it was positively gloomy. Zala joined her and offered her a damp towel to wipe the dust from her hands. It was always dusty on the plains too.

Her mother waited for them in a private sitting room. It had no windows, but elaborate woven tapestries hinted at the beauties beyond the walls. Her mother lounged on a low couch covered in scratchy linen pillows. Her face was pale and drawn, and she looked as though she'd been spending time in Vertigon rather than in the sunny Truren plains.

"What is it?" Selivia asked, running to clutch her mother's hand.

"Darling," she said, her voice strained and distant. "It is your grandfather. The Soolen army has attempted an assault on the inner walls. Your grandfather is barricaded in his palace, but he is unsure how much longer he can hold the city. He believes someone betrayed him and told the Soolens about his weaknesses."

Selivia gasped. A traitor!

"But the cavalry—"

"They've already been defeated once," her mother said. "We may lose this war."

"Don't say that, Mother," Selivia said, wishing her mother could be the one to comfort *her* for once. "Grandfather has a grand army. And the stronghold will protect us."

"It will not be enough."

Selivia bit her lip, trying desperately not to cry. *Sora* wouldn't cry. *Siv* wouldn't cry. She may be the youngest, but she could be as strong as both of them.

War had come to Trure. Treachery had come to Trure. But Selivia would not dare be afraid.

ACKNOWLEDGMENTS

Writing this series continues to be a wonderful adventure. Thank you to everyone who has emailed to let me know how much you are enjoying this story. I appreciate your enthusiasm and encouragement so much.

I'm grateful for the people who have been with me throughout this journey, including my husband, my family, my writing friends, and the other regulars at my Starbucks/office. The gang at Author's Corner inspires me to set my goals higher with every publication, and the Hong Kong writing community helps me reach them. Thank you all for your feedback, advice, and good company.

Susie and Lynn at Red Adept Editing continue to provide efficient and excellent service. Kitten and Kim at Deranged Doctor Design are a dream come true. Colleen from Write.Dream.Repeat. created my sharp, new Steel and Fire logo. I couldn't wish for a better team to help me turn this story into a finished book.

I'd like to thank my agent, Sarah Hershman, and the team at Tantor Media for your work on the Steel and Fire audiobooks. I especially want to thank narrator Caitlin Kelly for bringing Dara and the others to life.

My favorite authors continue to provide inspiration and escape in equal measures. I'm especially grateful for the works of Lindsay Buroker, Sarah J. Maas, Robert Jordan, Brandon Sanderson, and J. K. Rowling.

Most of all, thank *you* for reading. I can't wait for you to see what happens next!

Jordan Rivet
Hong Kong, 2016

CITY OF WIND EXCERPT

DARA stepped into the murky water. She shivered, wishing they'd waited until summer to try this. She took another step—and her feet slipped out from under her. She landed with a terrific splash, drenching her clothes and dousing her eyes with saltwater. Nearby, Siv doubled over laughing.

"Shut up."

"Dara," he gasped between chuckles. "You're one of the best athletes I've ever met. I don't get why you flail like a greckleflush the minute you encounter water."

"Easy for you to say," Dara said, scrambling to her feet. "Your grandfather rules a city with a giant lake."

"Didn't you ever play in the streams in Vertigon?"

"Those are three feet deep."

"Still." Siv splashed a few feet farther from the shoreline and beckoned for Dara to join him. "I expected more of you. What would Coach Doban say?"

"I'm sure Berg has a healthy respect for open water," Dara mumbled, cheeks heating. Her dueling friends were another story. Kel would find her underdeveloped swimming abilities particularly amusing. Of course, Siv teased her enough for the lot of them.

"Come on, Dara, it's shallow for another twenty paces. You're not even swimming yet."

Dara trudged after him, the cold water quickly rising up her bare legs. She wore her old trousers rolled above the knees. Wyla had given her some clothes in the Pendarkan style to wear when she was out in the city, but she didn't want to get those wet. Firelord knew she owed Wyla enough.

The water of the Black Gulf rippled around her, cloudy with silt and unknown detritus. The volcanic rock that gave the gulf its name was rough on her bare feet. The chilly water was refreshing, though. Pendark grew warmer every day. It would be as hot as a Vertigonian summer soon, and winter had barely come to an end.

Dara and Siv weren't the only pair taking advantage of the sunny afternoon to go for a swim—or wade, as Dara wasn't certain she'd be going out far enough for it to count as a swim today. Children splashed in the shallows, fully clothed, and a few older boys raced each other to the beach from a large black rock sticking out of the gulf. Others lounged at the water's edge or dug in the mud for spiny creatures that always seemed to skitter out of their reach. A handful of adults floated on their backs farther out, allowing the gentle roll of the waves to carry them along. Dara wondered if any of them worked in the Watermight practitioner's manor overlooking this stretch of sand. Orange flags flew from its black stone walls. Siv's pen-fighting friends had assured him the Waterworker, who controlled half of Pendark's port, didn't care if people used his beach. Dara was wary of getting too close to any of them. She had her own Waterworker to worry about.

"Okay." Siv stopped when the water reached their waists. "Let's practice dunking first."

"I'd rather just learn to swim with my head above water," Dara said.

"That's cheating. Besides, you'll never swim really fast like that. You wouldn't want everyone to be able to beat you in a race, would you?"

Dara opened her mouth then closed it again. So she was a bit competitive. It wasn't fair for him to use that against her. Still, if it was the best way ...

She sucked in a breath, squeezed her eyes shut, and dropped into the water. Underneath, a cool rush surrounded her, caressing her skin, blurring sound. She felt weightless and surprisingly calm. Her pendant necklace shifted against her chest, the stone warm compared to the water. This wasn't so bad.

Then something slimy brushed her ankle. She gasped, swallowing a huge mouthful of salty water. She scrambled to her feet, coughing and spluttering.

Siv splashed closer and patted her on the back as she gasped in air.

"Easy there. You're supposed to keep your mouth closed."

"Oh." She coughed. "I didn't know."

Siv chuckled. "You were down there a long time. I was starting to worry you meant to set a record on your first go."

"Maybe on my second," Dara said, still wheezing. The saltwater burned like Fire in her throat. "Something touched me," she said. "Something slimy."

"Probably just seaweed," Siv said. "Although I've heard there are krellfish and the occasional salt adder in these waters."

Dara's eyes bulged, and she felt a sharp kick of panic, but Siv stopped her before she could charge back to the shore. Or leap into his arms.

"I'm kidding. No salt adders." He narrowed his eyes. "Someone's jumpy today."

"Let's get this over with," Dara said. "What's next?"

"Try floating on your back. Once you get used to the feeling, it's really relaxing. Watch me."

Siv flopped backward and drifted on the surface, looking up at the clear blue sky. His bare chest floated high enough out of the water to reveal the thin scars crossing his ribs. White puckered scars from stab wounds dotted his sword arm, and a faint line slashed across his temple. All the blade wounds were old. He had a supply of fresh bruises patterning his body, but Dara was used to those as a duelist. Training could be a rough activity. She was glad to see his more grievous wounds were healed and his strength had returned. If anything, he was more muscular than ever. Kres March kept his pen fighters to a rigorous training schedule, even on the road.

"Liking what you see, eh?" Siv said, and Dara started.

"What? Oh, uh, I was studying your technique."

"Sure you were. My technique." Siv grinned and winked at her.

Water dripped from his short beard and ran over his chest as he stood. Dara cleared her throat. Right. Technique. Swimming.

"Let me get you started." Siv advanced toward her through the water, eyes bright with good humor. "Just take a deep breath and lie back. Try not to move, and let the water do the rest."

He put his hands low on her back and guided her down. She eased back, letting her feet leave the bottom. Siv held her firmly, and she straightened out as much as she could.

"That's it. You're still relying too much on me. Let the water hold you up." He removed one hand, and she balanced on the other, the water lapping her body and filling her ears. She could sense the water buoying her up. She was getting the idea. But she liked the feeling of Siv's hand firm against her back, and she didn't want him to let go just yet.

Something touched her face. She jerked up, imagining toxic salt adders, and flailed out of balance before she realized Siv had just been brushing a strand of hair from her forehead.

"Sorry. Bad timing," Siv said, catching her as she found her feet once more. "You're just so damn pretty. I couldn't resist."

Dara faced him, pressed close against his chest with his arms around her. Her cheeks flushed, and warmth from Siv's body seeped into her, keeping the chill of the water at bay. She still wasn't used to him saying things like this openly. Siv wanted to return to Vertigon, but he no longer seemed to care she wasn't a suitable match for a king in need of alliances. Something huge had changed between them. After everything they had been through, it was clear they wanted to be together no matter what. Wanted each other.

She rested her hands on his chest and looked up, memorizing the lines of his face—many of them new thanks to the scar on his temple and the beard lining his strong jaw. His breath was warm on her face, his arms tight around her, their faces inches apart. The moment was so precious, she felt as if it could shatter at the slightest movement. She'd all but given up on this once. She knew Siv had almost given up on it too. But here in the waters of the Black Gulf on the opposite side of the continent from their home, they were free to hold each other where anyone could see.

They weren't free to be together all the time, though. Dara had struck a bargain with Wyla the Watermight Artist in exchange for her help when Dara and her friends chased Siv to Pendark. Dara had committed to helping Wyla experiment with combining Fire and Watermight. She would stay with Wyla in her manor, her thrall for the next three months. Meanwhile, Siv had taken up residence in the blue house on stilts belonging to the pen fighters who'd adopted him. They had both stolen away from their respective districts for this afternoon swimming lesson.

Dara hadn't seen much of Wyla in the five days since she arrived in the city. The Waterworker had been busy since returning from Fork Town, where they'd met. She'd instructed Dara to practice her Fireworking skills using Fire from a supply of Works she'd had brought in. She wanted Dara in peak condition before they began their research. Dara still wasn't sure what form the research would take.

"You look solemn," Siv said. He brushed a hand through her wet hair, tangling it in the process. "Nervous about your mad Artist friend?"

"I don't know if she's mad," Dara said. "She's dangerous, though."

"Are you sure you can't buy your way out of the bargain?"

"With what money?" Dara didn't have a single coin to her name. For the moment, at least, she was at the Waterworker's mercy in every way.

"I'll make you some," Siv said. "A few rounds in the Steel Pentagon ought to be enough to buy your freedom."

"You're not seriously going through with that, are you?"

"Why not? I'm a decent knife fighter. Kres expects me to contribute to the team if I'm going to stay there for the next few months. I can pick up a few gutter matches too. The coins will roll in."

Dara and Siv's adventures continue in the fourth book in the *Steel and Fire* series, *City of Wind*. Grab a copy to keep reading!

ABOUT THE AUTHOR

Jordan Rivet is an American author of swashbuckling fantasy and post-apocalyptic science fiction. Originally from Arizona, she lives in Hong Kong with her husband. She fenced for many years, and she hasn't decided whether the pen is mightier than the sword.

www.jordanrivet.com
Jordan@jordanrivet.com

ALSO BY JORDAN RIVET

Fantasy

STEEL AND FIRE

Duel of Fire

King of Mist

Dance of Steel

City of Wind

Night of Flame

THE FIRE QUEEN'S APPRENTICE

The Watermight Thief

The Thunderbird Queen

The Dragonfly Oath

EMPIRE OF TALENTS

The Spy in the Silver Palace

An Imposter with a Crown

A Traitor at the Stone Court

ART MAGES OF LURE

Curse Painter

Stone Charmer

Science Fiction

BUNKER SERIES

Wake Me After the Apocalypse

Meet Me at World's End

THE SEABOUND CHRONICLES

Seabound

Seaswept

Seafled

Burnt Sea: A Seabound Prequel